CHASING
Mr. Wright

FATED
HEARTS
SERIES
1

INTERNATIONAL BESTSELLING AUTHOR
AIMEE NICOLE WALKER

*** Chasing Mr. Wright was originally published in 2015. This second edition has been completely re-edited but does not contain new material. ***

Grayson Wright is a man who knows how to do many things but fixing the toxic relationship with his long-time boyfriend isn't one of them. A surprise birthday party to rekindle their old spark sounded like a great idea until Gray is the one who receives the shock of his life.

Chase Rivers is unlucky in love and draws every loser, liar, and cheater like a magnet. After giving up on finding love, a night out with Mr. Right Now will lead him to the doorstep of his very own Mr. Wright. Too bad Chase didn't have homewrecker and party crasher on his dating-disaster bingo card.

If Chase and Gray's first meeting was a fluke, then what were the second and third? Why does every path seem to lead them back to each other? Is it bad luck, a sick joke, or is it fate? Buckle up for a bumpy ride as these two men travel down a broken road of heartache and discovery.

CHASING
Mr. Wright

CHAPTER
One

Chase

I MET DEVON BELLOWS WHILE TENDING BAR AT BOTTOMS UP. HE WAS a mix of sexy and sweet with a healthy dose of flirty. My lonely heart revved up every time he came in. It took him months to talk me into going out with him because I had a nagging suspicion he was already involved in a relationship. It wasn't anything obvious like a tan line on his ring finger; it was more subtle. Take the randomness of his visits to the bar, for example. It was like they coincided with his partner being out of town.

I'd even shared my observations with Devon. He was adamant he wasn't in a relationship and his visits coincided with *his* work travel, not a phantom lover's. And though I wasn't convinced, I agreed to go on a date with him because I was lonely and horny. A recipe for trouble if ever there was one.

A few nights later, I looked across the table at Devon Bellows, my eyes taking in every lovely feature of his face. He truly was a gorgeous man. I didn't normally go for the preppy type, but there was something about Devon that got to me. Beneath the suit and polish was a boyish charm and maybe something a little wicked.

Devon had chosen a swanky, new restaurant called Olivia's for our first date. I was equally impressed he was able to get a reservation and mortified I was underdressed compared to the rest of the patrons. Devon had dismissed my concerns with a lazy wave of his hand. The waitstaff didn't seem bothered by my dark denim jeans and button-down shirt either, so I forced myself to relax and look at the menu. It was one of those places that didn't list the prices beside the food or drinks. *Yikes.*

"Hey," Devon said softly.

I jerked my head up and met his gaze. Pale green eyes shimmered in the candlelight, and his smile was sweet and reassuring. Maybe I'd been wrong about him.

"I work hard to afford the best things in life," Devon said, reaching across the table to take my hand. He swept his thumb over my flesh in tantalizing circles. "I would like to share that with you. Will you let me?"

I took a deep breath to settle my nerves, then nodded.

Devon's smile brightened even more. "Thank—" His phone rang, cutting him off before he could finish, the sound shrilly disrupting the lovely ambiance. He grimaced and quickly fished it from his pocket to silence it. "I thought I turned the volume off. I'm sorry," he said to me and those around us. Some of the diners nodded politely, and others glared at the interruption.

He rose from his chair with his phone in hand. "I'm so sorry, Chase. I need to take this call, but you'll have my full attention afterward. I promise."

What else could I do but nod?

One phone call turned into two and then three. By the time the waiter cleared my dinner plate, Devon had spent the majority of our date outside talking on the phone. I hated the pitying glances I received from the servers and other diners. What happened to the guy who'd pursued me relentlessly for over four months and had never wanted to accept *no* for an answer? I'd finally relented and agreed to go out with him and for what? To be ignored?

When Devon returned after the third interruption, I removed my linen napkin from my lap and set it on the table beside my plate. I took one last sip of the delicious wine he'd chosen before I scooted my chair back and rose to my feet. That got his attention. I reached into my pants pocket and pulled out my wallet. I didn't have a lot of cash, but I wasn't short on dignity.

"What are you doing?" he asked.

"Going home."

"No," he said, reaching across the table to grab my hand. "I'm so sorry about all the interruptions, Chase. I've been terribly neglectful. Please stay."

Devon looked sincere and contrite, but my gut told me to walk out the door and not look back. "Tell me one good reason why I should stay."

"It's my birthday."

"Oh," I said, not expecting his answer. "I didn't know, or I would have bought you a gift."

"*You* are my gift." Devon's voice was low and seductive, and his twinkling, devilish eyes did very funny things to my stomach. "All those interruptions were text messages and Facebook notifications from friends and family wishing me a happy birthday." Devon released my hand to turn off his phone. "I'm all yours now. No more interruptions. Please stay and have some dessert and coffee."

Those eyes. His voice. I caved.

And things got better. We discussed our favorite movies, music, and books. We had a lot in common, and I started to have a really good time. His green eyes darkened, and his voice lowered as the night wore on. He started touching my hand more often as we spoke and rubbed his leg against mine beneath the table. His seductive powers worked to great effect. His simple gestures and undivided attention had me adjusting my dick beneath the table.

"Chase?"

"Hmmmm?"

"I want to take you home now. I want to unwrap the best birthday gift I've ever received."

At that point in my life, I was convinced I was never going to be truly loved for myself. Guys could never see past my looks to the person beneath. They didn't want to keep me for the long haul. Nope, they just wanted to fuck me. Seriously. I attracted every douche nozzle within a hundred-mile radius. I could find perfect mates for my friends but struck out each time I thought I had found *the one* for myself.

I was in the process of helping my best friend, Ava Mitchell, finalize her June wedding to a man I'd introduced her to the previous fall. I'd taken one look at Brandon Willoughby and known he was the one for my best girl. As happy as I was for her, I'd been feeling a little down in the dumps and vulnerable. Devon's soft gaze whispered *maybe I'm the one*.

"Let's get out of here," I told him.

Devon flagged down our waiter, and we were out the door in a flash. He pulled my body close while we waited for the valet to bring his car around. The heat rolling off his body helped to keep me warm on the cool March evening.

"I've wanted you for so long, Chase. I hope I don't embarrass myself once I'm finally inside you." A shiver rippled through his body, turning me on even more. He sank his teeth into my tender earlobe and slid both hands down to cup my ass cheeks. "God, the things I'm going to do to you."

Just then, the valet pulled around, saving me from embarrassing myself. Devon placed his hand at the small of my back and guided me to the car. He opened the door for me like a true gentleman, scoring additional points in my book.

"You have lovely manners," I said, complimenting him as he climbed behind the wheel.

"Unless I'm in the bedroom. Then I leave my chivalry at the fucking door." His vulgar talk fueled my raging lust. It had been so long since I'd been manhandled and fucked. "You've had me hooked since the moment I looked into your chocolate brown eyes. They pulled me in and wouldn't let me go. I haven't been able to get you out of my mind."

Once we pulled into traffic, Devon amped up his sensual assault. He placed his hand between my thighs and rubbed my cock until I was fully erect. The moans and whimpers coming out of his throat had my hips thrusting upward to meet his hand.

"How much farther?" I asked.

"Not much," he replied as he pulled up to a red light. As soon as the car stopped, he leaned over the console and smashed his lips against mine. The kiss should have been too brutal for our first time, but it was just what I wanted, no, needed. Devon's tongue slipped between my lips and dueled fiercely with mine until a car honked behind us, making us jump apart. "You make me forget myself," he teased as he switched his foot from the brake to the gas.

Luckily, there were several other red lights before we got to his townhouse in the historic part of Foggy Bottom. He became more and more aggressive with each stop, testing my restraint.

"We're here," Devon said. He was so eager to get me inside he forgot to put the car in park before getting out. He laughed as he jumped back inside his luxury sedan, put it in park, and killed the engine. "Look what you do to me." Devon leaned forward for another kiss, sliding his hands down my torso to untuck my dress shirt. "I can't wait to get into this hot body." Devon kissed me long and hard, our teeth bumping as we panted into each other's mouths. He abruptly ended our kiss. "Let's go inside."

"Yes," I hissed.

"Stay put."

I waited in my seat and watched as he walked around the front of the vehicle. The streetlamps were bouncing light off his hair almost giving him a halo effect. Devon turned and looked at me just then, and there was nothing angelic about the look in his eyes or the smile stretching across his face. I shivered hard as I waited for him to open my door.

Devon placed his hand on the small of my back, guiding me up the paved walk to the front porch. His hand shifted to cup my ass as I climbed the last few steps, then we were standing at his door.

"I'm going to fuck you so hard, Chase," he said hungrily while fitting his key inside the lock. "You'll be feeling me for days, baby." Devon opened the front door and pushed me inside. His home was pitch black, no lights on anywhere. "But first, I'm going to suck your dick." Devon closed the front door and shoved me back against it. "I've been wondering what you taste like for months."

"Devon." I groaned his name as he nipped and sucked the tender flesh beneath my ear. I was complete putty in his hands.

He slid to his knees in front of me and rubbed his nose along my erection through the denim. My hips jutted out automatically, causing him to laugh wickedly. "Somebody wants me to suck him off just as badly as I want to wrap my lips around his cock." Devon's hands began to unbuckle my belt and made quick work of my button and zipper. I threw my head back against the door, closing my eyes in ecstasy as he placed his lips around the head of my engorged cock. I could feel his hot breath and moist tongue through my cotton briefs.

I tangled my hands in his hair and began to thrust against his mouth, seeking more pressure on the magic spot just below the crown of my dick. I'm pretty sure I chanted "More" over and over.

Even though my eyes were still squeezed shut, I could tell a light had been turned on. It didn't stop me from dry humping Devon's mouth, though. For all I knew his house lights were set on an automatic timer. Someone cleared their throat, and the unexpected sound penetrated my lust-fogged brain.

My eyes flew open. It took a few seconds for reality to really hit me and even longer for my hips to quit thrusting against Devon's face. I locked eyes with the man of my dreams. His eyes were the bluest I'd ever seen and framed by nerdy, black glasses. Angels must have sculpted the guy's face, for no mere mortal could have created a creature so beautiful.

His wide forehead, high cheekbones, and square jaw made him look like a superhero. Add in the thick black hair, and he was a real-life Clark Kent. His luscious, full lips looked like they were made for kissing, and my stomach fluttered thinking about them pressed to mine. But then those sexy lips flattened into a straight line, and his pale eyes narrowed to mere slits when they traveled down my body and saw the man at my feet.

Then I noticed other things, such as the big "Happy Birthday" banner hung from the ceiling. And the dozens of people standing behind Clark wearing a variety of horrified expressions. *Holy fuck!*

"I can taste your arousal through your briefs, baby," Devon said. "You want me so bad."

He was lost in lust and had no idea we had an audience. Clark's pale blue eyes met mine once more, and the fury I witnessed in their depths shamed me. I put my hands squarely on Devon's shoulders and shoved him hard. He sprawled on the floor in front of me, shocked and confused.

"What the fuck, man?" he asked.

"Devon." Clark's voice was deep and beautiful.

Devon leapt to his feet and spun around. His body jerked in shock at the sight before him. "Baby… Oh god…I can explain."

I didn't stick around to hear his excuses. I pushed away from the door, opened it, and left.

CHAPTER
Two

Grayson

I DON'T KNOW WHAT SHOCKED ME MORE. WAS IT FINALLY HAVING THE confirmation that my stagnant relationship with Devon had reached a toxic level? Perhaps it was the jealousy surging through my body because I wasn't the one on my knees about to suck off the beautiful blond with the sultry brown eyes. The raw honesty of the last thought knocked me off-kilter.

"Dude, either go after the blond or deal with Devon, but don't just stand there." I could always count on my best friend, Miller Brexler, to slap me back to reality.

The party guests started leaving in droves to avoid the awkward confrontation they all thought would be coming. Some cast pitying looks my direction. Wouldn't they be shocked to know I felt like a huge burden had been lifted from my shoulders. Others looked relieved to know the end of an era was near.

"Miller, can Gray and I have some privacy?" Devon asked.

"Fuck you," Miller said to him before placing a hand on my shoulder. "I'll head upstairs to the guest bedroom and watch some TV while you toss this fucker out on his ass. Then we'll go out and celebrate your liberation from the mundane life you've been living for five years." He gave my shoulder a squeeze before heading upstairs, leaving me alone with Devon.

"Gray…"

Devon's soft, cajoling voice sliced through the lingering fog. I saw him clearly for the first time in…too long. It was like pulling back tall grass to reveal a hiding serpent.

"How many others were there?" My voice was neither soft nor cajoling.

"None. This was the first time I picked someone up. He's not important to me, Gray. He's just some bartender who kept hitting on me. I've been so lonely with you traveling so much lately, and I…" Devon stepped forward, beseeching me to forgive him with his eyes. "I made a mistake, Gray. I'm sorry."

How many times had I fallen for Devon's shit? He was totally playing me, which meant he was also lying through his fucking teeth. "I want the truth this time, Devon. It's the least you can do after embarrassing us both in front of our family and friends."

"I am telling the truth."

"Devon." My voice took on the tone that meant I wasn't fucking around.

He heaved a defeated sigh. The jig was up, and the asshole knew it. "Four times, not including tonight," he said as casually as if he were discussing a sale on shoes. "I've had sex with four other men in the last year while you were away on the business trips that meant more to you than I ever have."

"Now we're getting somewhere," I told him. My voice was calm and measured when I wanted to scream and rage at him. His behavior disgusted me, and I had to force myself to maintain eye contact. I would not show him how his words had cut me to the quick. "Do you know how many times I've been propositioned by sexy men during our relationship?" I paused to let Devon respond, but he remained silent. "More than I can count, but I never took them up on their offers. I have never been unfaithful to you."

"No," Devon said. "You were just emotionally distant and stopped giving a fuck about anything I wanted or needed out of life. You made me beg and grovel for scraps of your attention and affection, Gray."

My head snapped back as if he'd slapped me. "So this is my fault?"

"When was the last time you initiated sex between us?"

I had to think hard about that. When was the last time we'd even had sex? Had it been months? I'd been making do with my hand for so long that it became the norm. I could rub one out in the shower and relieve the pressure without having to wine, dine, and cajole someone into having sex with me. Devon had started using intimacy as a weapon, and I wasn't interested in playing games.

"See?" Devon said. "It's been so damn long you can't even remember. I never should have cheated on you, Gray, but the truth is, you left me a long time ago. We've been two ships passing in the night for at least three years."

Nothing he said rattled me because I'd had the same thoughts too many times to count. I'd just been too lazy to make the change. It took time and energy I didn't have to meet someone new and date. It had been so much easier to accept the way things were between us. How pathetic was that? It wasn't living at all, and it wasn't fair to either of us.

It took staring into the bottomless brown eyes of Devon's hookup to drive the message home. Preston, my brother and business partner, had been telling me I needed to get a life for the past two years. He was right, but I hadn't wanted to listen. But there was nothing holding me back anymore.

"Devon, I want you to pack your clothes and leave my house tonight. We can make arrangements later this week or next weekend for you to get the rest of your things."

"Where am I supposed to go?"

"That's not my problem," I said. "It should have occurred to you to have a backup plan the minute you started fucking other men. Nothing you can say or do will change my mind. Just pack and go."

Devon glared at me but didn't say anything more before he stomped up the steps to the room we used to share. Miller came down a few minutes later, and we watched college basketball while Devon removed himself from my life. It was all so calm and surreal. Shouldn't I have been more upset? I had no idea what was happening on the television or even upstairs in my own home for that matter. My mind kept wandering back to the blond-haired hottie with the big brown eyes.

"Did you find out blondie's name?" Miller asked, breaking into my thoughts. It didn't surprise me one bit that my best friend knew what I was thinking.

"He's a bartender. That's all I know. Would it be rude of me to ask Devon which bar?"

My question made Miller throw his head back and laugh. The sound was too infectious to ignore, and I found myself joining in, which was how Devon found us when he came downstairs.

He dropped his suitcase by the front door and walked over to where I sat. Devon's face was pinched with anger as he pulled his house keys off the ring and handed them to me. "I bet you're really happy about this, aren't you, Miller? You never liked me anyway."

"You're right on both counts. I've never liked you, and I've never thought you were good enough for Grayson." Miller released a resigned sigh as if he hadn't been waiting to say that since the moment I'd started dating Devon. "You've shown your true colors, and now Gray can find someone who deserves him."

"Someone like you?" Devon asked.

"I've never been in love with Grayson," Miller replied calmly. "I've always wanted the absolute best for him, and that's definitely not me. I don't do hearts, flowers, and happily ever afters."

"You think he does?" Devon asked incredulously.

Miller turned his head and studied me closely before replying. "Yes, I believe he'd do anything for the right guy. I definitely think he's capable of big romantic gestures."

Devon grumbled something beneath his breath as he walked away. "I'll be in touch later to pick up the rest of my stuff." He slammed the front door behind him as he left.

"Ready?" Miller asked and patted my leg. "I'll drive and you can have all the fun your body can handle."

An hour later, I realized I'd made a huge mistake. Men—kids, really—were doing something on the dance floor. I guessed they called it dancing, but it looked more like dry humping. It made me feel old and out of touch.

"Let's get out of here and get something good to eat," I said.

I checked my phone on our way back to Miller's car and saw several missed calls from Preston. Damn, I forgot my brother had probably shown up for the party to find the house dark and no one home. I knew he'd be late due to a prior engagement. I called him back, and he answered on the first ring.

"Did I get the wrong night for the douche bag's surprise birthday party?" My big brother wasn't a fan of Devon either. Come to think of it, no one in my inner circle liked him. They'd simply tolerated him for my sake. It had been a big, flashing warning sign I'd chosen to ignore.

"No, you had the correct night."

"Then where the hell is everyone?" Preston grumbled. "I could have gone straight home to cuddle on the couch with my pregnant wife."

"You won't believe me." I snorted. The inarticulate sound triggered a chuckle, which turned into raucous laughter. Nothing about the evening was funny, yet there I was wiping my eyes like I'd just heard the most hilarious joke ever told. Maybe I was the joke. The thought sobered me up pretty quickly.

"Have you been drinking?"

"A little," I answered, then proceeded to recap the evening for Preston.

"Are you fucking kidding me?" Pres asked when I got to the part where I flipped the lights on and discovered Devon had brought home a friend.

"Huh-uh," I replied. "Blondie shoved Devon on his ass when he realized what was going on. I think he was as surprised as I was."

Preston snorted. "You don't think he knew Devon had a boyfriend?"

I mulled it over for a few seconds. "No. He couldn't fake the horror he felt when he saw me standing there beneath the happy birthday banner."

"Was he hot?" Preston asked. One of my favorite things about my straight brother was his lack of an issue with me being gay. He never got squeamish when gay sex was brought up, and he teased me with sex jokes as much as any brother would. He just changed them up to match my orientation.

"Smoking," I replied.

"You should have gotten his name and phone number. It's obvious Devon wasn't going to be getting to know him better after his stunt, so why not you?"

I ignored his ridiculous question and changed the subject. "We're going to Stanley's to get a bite to eat. You guys want to meet us there? I bet Carly would like a hot fudge sundae."

"Carly would *love* a hot fudge sundae," my sister-in-law said.

My first Saturday night out as a single man in five years and I spent it with three of my favorite people in the world. We laughed over burgers, fries, and hot fudge sundaes. It was the best time I'd had in ages, and I vowed to do it more often.

CHAPTER
Three

Chase

I TACKLED SUNDAY MORNING WITH BLEARY EYES AND A HEAVY HEART. Devon had nearly turned me into the "other man," and my shame felt like a boulder strapped to my back. I'd been relieved when Ava, my best friend and roommate, had slept over at her fiancé's house, but the sound of a key turning in the lock let me know my reprieve had ended.

"Good morning," she said in a cheerful, singsong voice. "I came home early so you could tell me all about your hot date before you head to the bakery."

Forcing a smile, I turned from the coffeepot to face her. "Good morning."

Ava took one look at me and grimaced. "That bad, huh?"

I took a deep breath and said, "I've never been so humiliated in my life."

She crossed the room and wrapped her arms around my waist. I folded her into my embrace and rested my chin on top of her head. "Tell me," she mumbled against my sternum.

And I did, every sordid detail. She jerked her head up in shock when I got to the "Surprise" part and jacked my jaw. She apologized repeatedly while I tried to blink away the tears burning my eyes.

"Damn, girl."

"Sweetie, I'm so sorry. I just couldn't believe the douche lied to you repeatedly and put you in such a horrible position."

"You should have seen the hurt look in Clark's eyes," I said.

"It's not your fault. You didn't know. You can't blame yourself. Also, who's Clark?"

"Sorry. It's the name I gave to Devon's boyfriend. He's the most beautiful man I've ever seen. He looks like a real-life Clark Kent with nerdy black glasses and blue, blue eyes. His hair was longer and shaggier, though. God, I hate that I'm the one who put the hurt in his beautiful eyes."

"But you didn't, honey. Devon did."

"You're right, Ava. I'll get past this. You know I will. My Mr. Right is waiting for me somewhere out there, and I'll find him someday."

"That's the ticket, love." She gave me an extra squeeze. "Exciting things are about to happen for you. I can feel it."

I took a deep breath. "I'm looking forward to starting my new job." It was only an entry-level position as a personal assistant to one of the partners at Wright Creations, an up-and-coming ad agency. I'd recently graduated from Georgetown with my MBA, and I was desperate to get my foot in the door somewhere.

Luckily, Ellie Cruz, the older sister of my childhood friend, Xavier, was the human resources manager for Wright Creations. She had called me the minute the position had become available. I submitted my resume and interviewed with one of the partners the very next day. Preston Wright thought I was overqualified for the position, and I was, but I needed to start somewhere. While I'd interviewed with Preston, I would actually be assisting his brother and business partner. Preston explained his brother was in Chicago looking to land a major account, and he'd been left to interview the candidates.

I had liked Preston Wright immediately. He was intelligent, funny, and seemed pretty easygoing. I was almost disappointed I wasn't interviewing to be his personal assistant, but since his brother had left him in charge of picking a candidate, maybe their personalities were similar.

Ellie had called me yesterday with the news that I had been hired and should report to Wright Creations at eight o'clock on Monday morning. She told me two additional things for my first day: don't be late and bring hazelnut coffee for my new boss to make a good impression. I could easily do both.

I was grateful for the opportunity and was hoping I wouldn't have to keep working my two other jobs for very long. In addition to tending bar at Bottoms Up, I worked at a small bakery called Adam and Steve's on weekend mornings. I'd be losing Ava's monthly rental income once she got married in June, and I either needed to have a roommate lined up or stash enough cash to pay the staggering monthly rent on my own until I could find someone to take Ava's room.

"This thing with Devon is nothing more than one of life's little speed bumps," Ava said. Then she let out a big yawn and stretched.

"You didn't have to rush home at the ass crack of dawn on my account. You could've stayed and cuddled with Brandon."

"Something told me I was needed elsewhere," she said before kissing my cheek.

I rolled my eyes. "Please. You wanted to hear about my date, and you didn't want to wait until I got home later this evening."

"Guilty as charged," Ava said on the way to her bedroom. "I'm going to crash for a bit longer before Brandon picks me up for his nephew's birthday party. I love his family, but there are a lot of them, and they're really loud. I have to mentally prepare. Kiss Gram for me."

"Will do."

Once outside, I unlocked my bike and rode to the bakery. The nippy air helped wake me up more than the shower I'd taken had, and I vowed to have a good day no matter what. I had a five-hour shift to work and then I had to go to dinner with my grandmother.

The first thing I saw when I walked through the back door of the bakery was the owners, Adam and Steve Taylor, locked in a passionate kiss. I smiled at the sight before me, happy I'd introduced them four years ago. Adam was slim and just under six feet tall with shocking red hair and vibrant blue eyes. Steve was a couple of inches taller than me and built like an NFL linebacker. His black hair and dark brown eyes were the complete opposite of his husband.

I cleared my throat and they jumped apart in surprise. They both wore sheepish grins on their happy faces. I just shook my head at them. "Good morning, fellas."

"It's the best morning ever," Steve said dramatically.

Adam nodded. "Tell him why, dumpling."

"No, you tell him."

"He was your friend first, baby," Adam said. "He's the reason we get to experience this moment, so you do the honors."

Steve looked at me with a grin so huge I thought his face might crack in half. "The rabbit died."

"What rabbit?" I asked. "How is that good?"

"Jeez, grandpa. No one says that anymore." Adam slapped Steve playfully on his arm. "What he means is, we're having a baby. Our surrogate confirmed her pregnancy."

"With twins," Steve added. His love-drunk eyes glazed over with unshed tears, and I found myself tearing up too.

"Wow, guys." I pulled them into a group hug. They'd been planning and saving for this day for the last two years. Their dreams of having a family were finally coming true. "I'm so happy for you." I shook my head because the remark was too lame to describe my emotions. "I'm over-the-moon for you guys," I amended.

"We owe it all to you," Adam said. "If you hadn't introduced us…"

"You would have still found one another," I told him. "You're soul mates. You would've found your way to each other eventually. I truly believe that."

"Thank you, Chase Rivers," Steve said as tears streamed down his face.

"You're very welcome." I pulled them both into another quick group hug.

"Oh." Adam jolted and looked up at me. "How was last night?"

I groaned and they offered sympathetic smiles. "It's not worth talking about. I'm chalking it up to another lesson learned and moving on."

"Sweetie, I'm sorry," Steve said, placing a comforting hand on my shoulder. "You're going to find your very own Adam someday. He's probably just as lonely as you are and wondering when you'll appear in his life."

Oddly, an image of Clark with his black-rimmed glasses and sexy, blue eyes popped into my mind. Inside, I laughed at my overactive, wishful imagination. That was one dream I could guarantee would never come true. "I hope you're right," I said, trying to leave my skepticism out of my voice. Judging by the look Steve threw me, I'd failed miserably. "Let's get out there and sell some pastries."

Like always, my Sunday morning shift flew by in a rush of donuts, popovers, streusels, lattes, and cups of coffee. The late morning and early afternoon crowd stopped in for cupcakes and cookies or picked up custom cakes. Adam and Steve's Bakery had become one of Foggy Bottom's most popular hot spots.

I started wiping down the stainless-steel counters, but Steve yanked the rag out of my hand. "Get out of here," he said with a smile. "Is Ava going with you to Gram's for dinner?"

"Not this week," I replied. "She and Brandon have plans with his family, and she couldn't get out of it."

"That's too bad," Adam said. "Hey, good luck with your new job tomorrow. I hope it turns out to be the opportunity you were hoping for because you are way too talented to work for us and tend bar for Jack."

"Thanks, guys. I'm really excited. I'll give you a call tomorrow and let you know what my new boss is like," I told them as I removed my apron and tossed it into the hamper. I gave them both a last hug goodbye, then got back on my bike and headed to Gram's house.

CHAPTER
Four

Gray

I SLEPT IN MUCH LATER THAN I NORMALLY WOULD ON A SUNDAY, AND it felt fantastic. I didn't throw on my workout gear, and I didn't go for a jog. Instead, I made myself some coffee and settled back in bed with the latest Agnes Simmons book I'd recently bought. Some people hide porn from their significant others, but I kept a secret stash of gay romance novels hidden in my closet.

I don't know why I kept my love of gay romance books a secret. Maybe I was afraid I'd get slapped with a stereotype, and maybe I just wanted to avoid the teasing. Reading romance was how I dealt with stress and my own unhappy relationship. I loved the obstacles the fictional characters had to overcome to win their happily ever afters. Instead of living each day to the fullest, I sat on the sidelines and wished my life would imitate the art on the page.

I never really thought myself capable of big romantic gestures, but maybe Miller was right. I wanted a big, happy ending and not the kind you got from a massage parlor. I'm talking real love, dates, laughter, and long, passionate nights. I wanted my lover to be my best friend and confidant. I craved a man who was proud to be on my arm and wouldn't belittle me for working too hard. I wanted a soul mate and future father to our children. I wanted someone who made me want to set work aside and come home. I needed the kind of love where a single text could make my day and the sound of my guy's voice could make me forget my problems. The list of my wants was admittedly long, but just being able to list those things was a huge step in the right direction.

My cellphone rang on the bedside table, startling me out of my daydream. I held my breath and hoped it wasn't Devon calling me so soon. I really wanted to enjoy the rest of my weekend. Luckily, I saw it was Miller. "Aren't you sick of me yet?" I asked in greeting.

"Nope. I expect your ass at flag football today. You have no more excuses, Gray. Plus, you need to get your body fit for all the fun you're about to have now that you're a free man."

I loved to play flag football, but the crew was rough. They were notorious for cheap shots and low blows, but it was a guaranteed good time. "What time do I show up for my ass whipping?"

"Attaboy! That's the spirit, Gray." I knew Miller was mentally shaking his pom-poms. "The ass whipping starts at two."

I glanced over at the clock and saw it was only eleven thirty. "No problem. I'll be stretched out and ready to go."

"Oh, darling," Miller purred. "It sounds like you're looking for a different kind of workout."

"Idiot. You're buying the pizza and beer afterward."

"Deal." Miller said goodbye and hung up.

I went back to reading my book and got lost in the story. The next thing I knew it was one, and I still hadn't taken a shower or limbered up. I reluctantly set my book aside and stretched, loving the feel of my muscles warming up and coming to life. I kept them loose and warm by taking a very hot shower. Water had always made me horny, and thinking of the hot action I'd just read had my dick lengthening. I'd been making do with my own hand for so long it was a wonder my cock hadn't gone on strike.

The damn book lit the spark, but the shower fanned the flame, and I had to take care of business. I couldn't play football with a hard-on. I closed my eyes, tilted my head back, and stroked my shaft while thinking of the intense sex scene I'd just read—two hot and horny guys learning each other's bodies for the first time in the gym shower. Without my permission, my brain replaced the ginger-haired character on his knees with a certain fair-haired man with brown eyes, and I replaced the guy getting his dick sucked. I gasped and tried to force Devon's guy out of my mind. How fucking weird was it that the blond had come to my house to have sex with my boyfriend, but all I could think about was having his mouth on me? A mixture of guilt and disgust twisted my gut, but it wasn't enough to tame the lust spiking through me. Instead of stopping, I gripped my dick harder and sped up my strokes. *Wrong. So wrong.* But it felt so fucking good. What was his name? I'd yell it when I came. *No. Huh-uh.* That guy was off-limits. Didn't stop me from imagining his wet mouth taking me deeper down his throat. I came so hard I had to lean against the tile wall for support.

The disgust I felt prior to climaxing increased tenfold. What the hell was wrong with me? "You just need to get laid." I needed to feel someone else's hands on my body, their breath panting against my ear as I fucked them. "You're going to be okay. Better than okay."

"It's about damn time," Trevor Barnett called out as I walked onto the make-shift football field. "I'll take my twenty now, Benton. I knew he'd show up."

"Asshole," Benton said good-naturedly as he slapped a twenty in Trevor's palm.

"It's good to see you too, Benton." He was one of Miller's friends, and everyone called him by his last name. Come to think of it, I wasn't sure I even knew his first name.

Benton gave me a one-armed hug. "I was calling Trevor an asshole, not you. It's good to see you too. It's been too long since you joined us."

"True." There was no reason to deny it.

"Let's team up," Miller said seriously. I've always been a competitive person, but my best friend took the term to a whole new level. Take no prisoners came to mind. Miller was the worst at doling out the cheapest of the shots and the lowest of the blows when it came to flag football. I hoped like hell he picked me for his team. "Gray," he said when he got his first pick. There was a lot of grumbling from the other players, but I was happy.

At halftime, our team was up by one touchdown, but Benton's team was fighting back. We looked a little winded while they looked like they were just getting started. Miller gave us a serious talking to, and I nodded along as he strategized, but my mind had started to wander because I was ready to go home.

I took a long drink of water and tried not to let everyone see how fucking sore I was after only half a game of flag football. I needed to spend more time in the weight room and less time in the boardroom. I saw a guy riding his bike out of my peripheral vision, but I was still trying to suck precious air into my lungs to pay much attention.

"Oh my god, Gray. Didn't you see him?" Miller asked.

His abrupt switch from rallying the troops caught me off guard. "Who?"

"Blondie! He just rode by on his bike."

My head whipped around to see where Miller was pointing, but the rider was too far away for me to make a positive identification. All I saw for sure was blond hair which looked to be the same color as the mystery man's. My idiot dick was starting to perk up again, and it definitely wasn't the right time. *Read the room, asshole.*

"I can't tell," I said to Miller.

"I saw him with my own eyes. He looked at me for a few seconds. I'd bet your left nut it was him."

My poor left nut tried to tuck up into my gut. "Damn, why didn't you say something sooner? I could've flagged him down."

"I called your name so many times it sounded like we were shooting a porn scene, but you were off in la la land."

"Fuck."

"Hey, are we going to play some fucking flag football or gab all god-damned day," Benton yelled.

I refocused on my team and found them all watching me curiously. "What?"

"Nothing," Jarod said with a shrug. "I've never seen you quite so animated. Must be some guy."

"It's a long story," I said, trying to brush it off.

"Which I'll gladly tell in gory detail over pizza if we kick Benton's ass," Miller added.

The idea of pizza, beer, and hearing my horrible story must have kicked our guys into high gear because we handily won the game by three touchdowns, despite Benton's best efforts and cheap shots. At The Pizza Joint, we scooted as many tables together as possible so everyone could witness my embarrassment. The responses varied from shock and disgust to knee-slapping laughter.

"Here's to freedom," one of the guys said, holding up his beer mug for a toast.

"Freedom," we all said.

I was going to stick with my fictional book boyfriends until my soul mate showed up, but warm, brown eyes popped into my head annoying the hell out of me.

I woke up at five the next morning feeling sore but alive for the first time in ages. I'd had a very restful night's sleep after a few hours of exercise in the fresh air followed by a long soak in the tub with my book. I vowed to open myself up to opportunities. I wanted an epic love like the characters in the novel I was reading, but I'd never have it if I didn't allow myself to first believe in the possibility.

I jumped out of bed, brushed my teeth, put on some workout clothes, and drove myself to the gym for the first time in months. I was surprised my fob still worked when I checked in. Devon would complain when I spent my rare free time working out, always implying I was hoping to meet someone else. I quit going to avoid arguments and worked longer days at the office instead. It should never have taken me so long to end the relationship. Devon had been right about that. I'd checked out a long time ago, which was why I wasn't mourning the loss and was instead basking in the freedom.

"Hey, stranger," Jett, the owner, said as I approached the front desk. "I haven't seen you in ages."

"I've been traveling a lot and got lazy," I replied. "I'm here to fix that now."

"Let me know if there is *anything* I can do to help you get in shape." There was no mistaking his meaning. "You know, like a good cardio workout." Jett really didn't do subtleties.

I looked him over and cocked my head to the side in consideration. "Thanks. I'll keep that in mind." *Possibilities*, I reminded myself.

I alternated between cardio and strengthening machines for ninety minutes, and I was hot and sweaty but not gasping for air like I'd anticipated. My body was still firm and toned, but I wasn't as ripped as I used to be.

"You gave one hell of an effort, Gray," Jett said, walking up to me. I turned around and studied him while I wiped down my neck and face with the towel I'd brought. "You going to hit the showers?" He gave me another once-over, gaze lingering on my crotch, before he offered me a sexy smile.

"Nah, I don't do public showers," I told him before he could offer to wash my back. My blood was rushing through my veins like a racehorse. The result of so much adrenaline would be a raging hard-on, which would require my attention before I went to work. I wasn't into exhibitionism, even if I was willing to risk fungus and bacteria in the gym shower.

"Too bad," he said and sauntered away.

I drove myself home to shower and get myself off. Again, I couldn't keep brown eyes and blond hair out of my mind's eye as I came. Something was going to need to be done about that before it really pissed me off.

I took extra care with my grooming and choice of suits because I wanted to make a good impression on my new personal assistant's first day. I wondered what Chase Rivers was like. I was hoping for organized and punctual. Preston had told me he was overqualified for the position, but he'd seen a lot of potential in his resume and portfolio. The guy had excellent graphic design skills and Preston was hoping to move him to the art department at some point. I had no doubt the guy was talented because Preston had a keen eye and instinct when it came to choosing the best personnel for Wright Creations.

I made a mental note on my way out the door to call my doctor's office for an STD screening. I didn't know if Devon had practiced safe sex, and I didn't trust him not to lie if I asked. He'd obviously been making up for lost sex while we were still together, and it was my turn. I couldn't wait to feel a man's hot mouth working my cock up and down. I forced my mind off sex and back on work to keep my libido under control.

Cranking up a classic rock station on the radio, I sang along all the way to work. It was no surprise to me that I arrived before anyone else. Hell, I was at the office so much I was on a first-name basis with the janitorial staff who came in during third shift to clean the offices. I was usually the last person out the door and the first person back in the next day.

A weird feeling rolled through the pit of my stomach as soon as I walked into the building. It wasn't the kind that made you take the stairs instead of the elevator or refuse to board a plane. This was more a positive feeling like something wonderful was about to happen. *But what?* I wondered. I whistled while I rode the elevator up to our floor and continued whistling on my way to my corner office.

I fired up my laptop and set about organizing my day so I could leave no later than six. If I wanted a fabulous life and a grand love, I needed to go out and find it. It wasn't likely my soul mate would come knocking on my office door.

Preston stopped by my office just before eight. "Have you told Mom and Dad about your breakup?" he asked.

"I figured you told them Saturday night," I replied sarcastically.

"Well, duh. But I still think they'd like to hear it from you so they can make sure you're not pining away in misery."

I gave Preston a doubtful look. "I'm sure they're just fine with the breakup."

"Of course *they're* okay with it. Nobody liked the asshole," Pres said coolly. "They just want to know *you're* okay."

I chuckled at my brother's bluntness. "I'll give them a call tonight," I said, relenting. Truthfully, the last thing I wanted to do was have a dismal postmortem discussion about my relationship with Devon.

"What's on your agenda this week?" Preston asked, and we instantly shifted to discussing work. We went over several things until a knock on the door interrupted us. "Are you ready to meet your new PA?"

"Bring it," I teased. I felt as nervous as I did right before a big presentation, which made absolutely no sense at all. I was only meeting my new PA, not the man of my dreams. *Calm down.*

CHAPTER
Five

Chase

I WAS EXCITED WHEN MONDAY MORNING ROLLED AROUND. I'D HAD A great dinner with Gram, and she'd introduced me to her new boyfriend, Lennie. He looked like an aging mob boss, but Gram was happy, and I was happy for her. She'd also tried to show me a few pages of her newest novel, but I'd respectfully declined.

Most people had grandmothers who knitted blankets or crocheted scarves, but not me. I had a grandmother who'd adopted a pen name— Desiree Amour—and supplemented her income by writing sultry erotic pirate romances full of heaving bosoms, turgid manhoods, and deflowered virgins. She'd recently switched to writing erotic gay romances under a new pen name—Agnes Simmons—and though I'd already vehemently opposed serving as her content area expert, she kept trying to sucker me in to giving her feedback on her characters' sex lives, but there were just some things I refused to talk about with her. There had to be a line somewhere.

Regardless, time with Gram always recharged me—which was why I never missed a Sunday dinner—and I was looking forward to my first day at Wright Creations. I showered, shaved, and put on the clothes Ava had laid out for me. She promised me the charcoal gray suit with a pale blue shirt and striped tie was the perfect ensemble to impress my new boss. She gushed about how the pale blue made my hair look blonder and my eyes a darker shade of brown.

I reminded her I wasn't trying to get a date, but she was undaunted.

"We never know when we'll meet our soul mate. Wouldn't you rather be dressed to kill in a perfect suit?" Point well made.

I drove to Adam and Steve's so I could grab my new boss the best cup of hazelnut coffee in a twenty-mile radius. I decided it wouldn't hurt to throw in a pastry or two. I noticed Adam was sipping tea and nibbling crackers behind the counter when I walked in.

"Upset stomach?"

"Sympathy pains for our surrogate baby mama," Steve said softly. "She's experiencing some pretty nasty morning sickness, and my sweet, sensitive husband is feeling her pain."

"Oh, that's too bad. Well, I hope you both feel better soon," I told Adam.

"Thanks, precious. So, let's talk about how gorgeous you look in that suit this morning. Wow, honey, you sure clean up nice."

I felt a slight blush come on. "Ava picked it out. She said I needed to make a good impression."

"Make a good impression or get bent over his desk?"

Steve admonished Adam for his remark. "Ignore him, Chase. You look very professional and handsome."

"Thanks, guys." I ordered a cup of hazelnut coffee and scoped out the pastries while I waited. I had a hard time deciding what my faceless boss might want, so I just picked a variety of scones, donuts, and muffins.

I thanked the guys for the kind words and drove to my new office. Wright Creations was located on the fourth floor of a very modern-looking building in Dupont Circle. I stopped for a moment to admire the exterior of the building and reflect on the new opportunity. As I approached the door, an older gentleman opened it for me since my hands were full. I thanked him and followed him to the bank of elevators.

I rode the elevator up to the fourth floor and exited into the spacious lobby of Wright Creations. The red-haired receptionist at the front desk looked up at me and then her mouth fell open. Her eyes bugged out of her head, and her lips opened and shut, but no words came out. She looked like some pretty, exotic fish. The helpful man from downstairs had also gotten off the elevator. He looked at the receptionist, whose desk plate read Madelyn. "Get it together, Madelyn." Mr. Manners turned to me and asked if he could help direct me.

"Actually, I've been hired as Grayson Wright's personal assistant." Madelyn squeaked, and Mr. Manners glared in her direction. "I know where his office is, but I need to stop and see Ellie Cruz to pick up some paperwork before beginning my day with Mr. Wright."

"Very well. I'm Jerry Hodson, and I work in accounting. It's nice to meet you…"

"Chase Rivers," I replied. "It's very nice to meet you too."

I headed to Ellie's office, hoping to grab my paperwork and get to Mr. Wright's office before his coffee cooled too much more. I passed several employees who wore various expressions of surprise and astonishment on their faces, and I started to get a complex.

I barely made it to Ellie's office without breaking into a sweat. Her door was open, so I walked inside. "El, is there something wrong with my attire, or is there something on my face or in my hair?"

She squinted and studied me closely. "No. Why?" I explained to her about the odd reaction from the receptionist and several other employees. She waved a dismissive hand in the air. "It's because you are so freaking scrumptious, Chase. I'm sure they were just stunned by the gorgeous new employee."

"I don't think that's it, Ellie." I knew I was an attractive guy, but this was not that kind of reaction. This was more shock or stunned surprise.

"Quit being such a drama queen." She pulled a manila folder off her desk and extended it to me. "You better get up there and meet your new boss."

I took the folder and left her office, heading to the part of the suite where the partners' offices were located. I'd only been there once, but the layout was simple and sensible. I found my desk easily enough and set my folder full of employment paperwork down. I blew out a deep breath and approached the closed door.

I heard faint voices on the other side but not what they were saying. My heart started to pound frantically in my chest, and my mouth went suddenly dry. I gave myself a pep talk and knocked firmly on the door. The voices inside stopped, and I heard footsteps approaching.

The door opened and I looked into the friendly eyes of Preston Wright. "Good morning, Chase." He looked down at my hands and then back to my smiling face. "Did you bring enough for all of us or just my asshole brother?"

"Um…"

"Quit dicking around and get back to your office, Pres. I have real work that requires my attention." The deep, sexy timbre sent shivers down my spine and made my toes curl inside my shoes.

"Fine," Preston said, "but I'm coming back soon, and there better be a treat left for me."

Preston opened the door wider and crossed the threshold, giving me my first look at my new boss. I looked into pretty blue eyes surrounded by black-rimmed glasses. My stomach plummeted to the ground, and I audibly gasped. My new boss was Clark. My Clark—the man of my dreams—was my new boss, Grayson Wright, co-owner of Wright Creations.

"Oh my god," we both said at the same time.

"I don't believe it," Grayson said.

"This can't be happening." I added.

"You two know each other?" Preston inquired.

"No," we both answered.

"I don't get it," Preston said. "What's going on here?" He looked back and forth between us several times before Grayson finally answered him.

"He's the guy from the surprise party. The one Devon brought home."

"Ohhhh," Preston replied. He turned his attention to me and studied me closely. His mouth turned down in a frown, and I saw disappointment in his eyes.

"I had no idea." I pleaded my case to Preston before turning to face Clark—*Grayson*—again. "I truly didn't know, Mr. Wright. I am so very sorry."

Emotions—shock, disappointment, and anger—swirled in Grayson's gorgeous eyes, each one cutting me deeper and deeper.

I looked back at Preston. "Clearly this isn't going to work out. Can we have a second? I feel terrible about what happened, and I've wished all weekend for a chance to explain and apologize."

Preston looked to his brother for guidance. Grayson must have nodded that it was okay because Preston agreed. "Call me if you need anything, Gray." He nodded at me and walked away, leaving us alone for the first time.

I walked into Grayson's office on trembling legs. "I just want to tell you how sorry I am about Saturday." His square jaw was clenched so hard it looked like his teeth were moments from shattering. "I don't expect you to believe me because you don't know me, but I never would have gone out with Devon had I known he was in a relationship with anyone. We never… He and I… We didn't."

Grayson held up a hand. "Stop," he said firmly. "You seem sincere and honest, Mr. Rivers, but I can't work with you. I can't look at you without…"

"I completely understand, Mr. Wright." I walked the rest of the way to his desk and set down the bakery bag and coffee, then stepped back. "Good luck finding a personal assistant."

Our eyes locked and held, and I really couldn't explain the confusing feelings swirling through my body. Of course I was disappointed about the job, but I was more upset about not seeing Grayson again. He was the most attractive man I'd ever laid eyes on. Regret far outweighed disappointment.

I left his office without another word. I grabbed the manila folder off the empty desk and headed to Ellie's office to return it and explain. I passed a few more people who stared openly at me, and I realized they must have recognized me from the party. Still, my humiliation didn't surpass the regret I felt.

Ellie was staring hard at something on her computer screen and didn't notice my approach. I knocked quietly, and she jerked her head up at the interruption. I walked into her office and set the file on her desk. "Done already?"

"I won't be working here after all. I just wanted to stop in and thank you so much for the opportunity."

"What do you mean you won't be working here? Pres thought you'd be a great fit. Did Gray…"

"Ellie," came a breathless, masculine voice from behind me. "Oh. My. God." The man panted like he had sprinted to her office. "Birthday Surprise Guy is here. Did…" I turned to face the newcomer and found a very tall, dark-haired man standing in the doorway. I looked him up and down and he did the same in return. "Oh fuck. You're Birthday Surprise," he said.

"Huh?" a dumfounded Ellie asked. "Ben, have you been sniffing the White Out again?"

Ben's vibrant, green eyes stared at me with censure and disdain. It pissed me off that he'd judged me without knowing a damn thing about me. Of course most would in his situation.

"Chase?"

I turned back to face Ellie, a woman I loved like an older sister. Thankfully, I only saw curiosity in her eyes and not condemnation. "I didn't know, El. You know I'd never hurt someone that way." I rapped my knuckles on her desk. "I just wanted to stop in to say goodbye and thank you again."

She stood from her desk and gave me a big, warm hug. She stood on her tiptoes and kissed me on the cheek. "I love you. Call if you need to talk."

I gave her an extra squeeze, then dropped my arms and stepped back. The dark-haired guy was still standing in the doorway, his eyes narrowed in suspicion. "Excuse me," I said when I reached the door. He stepped aside, and I left.

"How do you know him?" I heard him ask Ellie as I walked down the corridor. I was walking at a brisk pace, hoping to get the fuck out of there without any more confrontations. I rounded the corner and was in the final stretch when I collided with two women.

"So sorry, ladies," I said. I bent over and began picking up the folders I'd knocked out of their arms.

We all stood at the same time, and I held out the papers I'd picked up from the ground. I looked back and forth between them, knowing they must be twin sisters. Their facial features and big brown eyes were identical, and they were the same height and build. The only difference was their hair color. One sister had dark, russet-colored ringlet curls cascading down to her waist, and the other sister's curly hair was two different shades of purple—a light shade of lavender around her face and deep violet everywhere else. She smiled sweetly as she took the stack of folders from my hand.

"Sorry," I said to her again. I looked at her twin to apologize and found her studying me closely. The smile slipped from my face as she narrowed her eyes at me. "Have a good day." I stepped around them and was able to exit the building without any more problems.

Once I was safely outside, I leaned against the building. It would be a perfect time to light a cigarette if I smoked. I felt like I was stuck in some kind of slapstick sitcom. I was more than ready to exit stage right.

I pushed away from the building and drove the four blocks to Ava's office. I hated to drop in unannounced, but I needed to see her. I rode the elevator up to her offices and waited in reception while the new girl, Marcy, called back to Ava's assistant. Minutes later, Nadia came out to retrieve me.

"Hello, gorgeous," she said before leading me into the inner offices of Schwartzmen and Feckman Architects.

"Good morning, beautiful."

We walked into Ava's office, and she shut the door behind us. "Ava will be in a meeting for another few minutes. Do you want to hear about my latest conquest to pass the time?" Nadia asked.

"Hell yes."

But Ava breezed through the door before I could hear the first dirty detail. She put her hands on her hips and cocked her head to the side. "What the hell are you doing in my office when you just started your new job less than an hour ago?"

"About that," I replied, my earlier amusement fading. Ava saw the change in my demeanor and dropped into the chair beside me. I told her everything, including how upset I was about not seeing Grayson anymore.

"Sweetie," she cooed. "I just don't know what to say. I mean…" A look of inspiration crossed her features. "I know exactly what you need right now. JJ."

JJ was a long-time friend and occasional fuck buddy. If Ava was suggesting I call him, she must think this was something I could screw out of my system. She might be right, but… "Jeez, Ava. Maybe he's not even in town. You know how much he travels for his job."

"I saw him zooming through the streets in his sleek Audi this morning. He's here. Call him." She looked at her slender platinum watch. "I have a conference call in two minutes. Get out of here."

I kissed her on the cheek and left her office. I waved goodbye to Nadia as I walked by her desk. I took out my phone on my way to my car and debated texting JJ. Before I started the car, I tapped out a quick message. *Are you available tonight?*

Be at your house at 7:00, was his quick response.

CHAPTER
Six

Gray

"THERE HE WAS, MILLER, STANDING IN MY OFFICE. THE GUY I'D been fantasizing and jacking off over for days. Do you know what I did?" I answered before he could. "Nothing." Miller had met me for a drink after work at one of our favorite watering holes. "I seriously started to tell Chase I couldn't work with him because I would want to kiss him every time I looked at him. Luckily for me, he interrupted before I could make an ass of myself. Fuck me. You should have seen him in a suit."

"You just let the guy leave thinking you were angry with him?"

"I was shocked to see him there, and all these emotions ran through me one right after another. I was disappointed he would be working for me because that would mean sex was off-limits. Then I was angry at fate. I mean, what are the fucking odds?"

"It's pretty spectacular," Miller agreed. "Well, at least you have his name and contact information now. Maybe you can give it some time and call him."

"I don't know," I said. "Sounds like a bad idea. I tell the guy I can't work with him, then call him up later and ask him out? I think I just need to accept we're not meant to be and find someone else."

"There's a good candidate." He nodded toward the bar.

I turned to look and saw a handsome blond guy checking us both out. "Right hair color but wrong eyes."

"Gray?"

"Hmm," I answered turning back to face Miller.

"You're not casting him in a film, and you're not proposing marriage. You're looking to get a bathroom blow job at a bar. Close your eyes and use your imagination." Miller shook his head in disgust, and I threw my head back and laughed. "Go over there and buy the guy a drink. Flirt with him and see where it leads you." Miller cocked his head to the side and pondered. "You do remember how to flirt, right?"

"Yes, jackass."

"Grayson Matthew Wright," he said sternly. "Get over there and charm that cute boy into giving you a blow job. You can always repay him with a hand job, or better yet, demand he stroke himself off while he's blowing you."

A climax was just what I needed to take my mind off Chase Rivers. I took a deep breath and released it slowly. Then I stood up, capturing the cutie's attention. He winked at me, and I nearly sat back down.

"Go," Miller urged. "Fucking amateur."

I kept my head down to make sure I didn't trip over my own two feet on my way to the bathroom. I rolled every kind of pickup line I could imagine through my head during the short walk. I'd recently read a book where an awkward guy used some absolutely adorable ones, but I couldn't remember what they were for the life of me. The blond guy entered the bathroom seconds behind me. Damn, he must've run in here. His eagerness settled my nerves a little until I turned to face him. Up close, I could see his eyes were a pretty shade of green. Seafoam, maybe? Why was I thinking about his eye color when I should be focused on getting his dick out?

"The name's Owen." His voice was soft and sultry, and he batted his eyelashes while closing the distance between us. Owen took two steps forward, and I took three back. We continued this dance until my ass pressed against the porcelain sink.

Owen pressed his body flush against mine and smiled up at me. "Nowhere to go now, except for down." The cutie started to lower himself to his knees. This is what I wanted. Some guy's mouth on my cock. So why didn't said cock so much as twitch in excitement? Why did my lungs seize in my chest?

"Wait," I barked out.

Owen jolted upright and looked at me with a puzzled expression on his face. He took a few steps back, and I felt like I could breathe freely again. "Did I misread the situation?"

"I'm just out of a relationship. I thought I was ready…"

Owen's tense expression softened. "But you're not."

"No."

The guy smiled. "Did your buddy put you up to it?"

I took a deep breath. "He thinks it will help me work past my situation." I smirked. "He's never been in a relationship before, so he doesn't get it."

"I see," Owen said. "Want to hang out here a few minutes to let him think I'm giving you the blow job of your life?"

I laughed at the diabolical expression on his face. "Hell yeah."

"You can't go out there looking like that."

"Like what?" I asked, turning to study my reflection. "I look the same as always."

"And sex should be messy." Owen reached up and messed up my hair and gently shifted my glasses so they hung slightly askance on my nose. "Better but not quite." He yanked my shirt free, unbuttoned the bottom few buttons then purposely put two in the wrong holes so the right side of my dress shirt hung a few inches longer than the left. "Pinch your cheeks. You want to look flushed." I did as he said while Owen set about sucking and biting on his lower lip to make it red and pouty. He slicked them really good, checked his watch, then said, "Okay. We both look thoroughly rumpled, and I think enough time has passed."

Owen led the way out of the bathroom, making a big show of wiping the corner of his mouth.

"Thank you," I said before veering toward the table where Miller stared at me with huge eyes. He didn't think I'd go through with it and for good reason. It was his style, not mine. I flopped down in my chair and took a sip of the beer he'd ordered for me in my absence.

Miller narrowed his eyes suspiciously and studied me. "Liar."

"Where's your proof?"

He leaned forward and inhaled deeply. "I don't smell cum." He slumped back and had a good, long laugh at my expense. "Whose idea was it to stage your clothes, hair, and glasses?"

"Fuck off," I said, rising to my feet. I winked at a smirking Owen on my way to the door.

Miller laughed the entire time he followed me out to our cars. "Grow up, Miller," I yelled at him, which only made him double over.

"You should've seen your face," he said. "You looked so fucking proud of yourself when you strolled out of the bathroom. Christ, Gray." He laughed even harder, apparently finding his comment funnier than I did.

"I'm leaving," I told him. "Thanks for the wonderful night."

I fired up my car and drove home to take a hot shower and curl into bed with a book. I couldn't focus on the words Agnes Simmons had written, which made me even madder. I could always lose myself in her stories, but a certain brown-eyed beauty kept creeping into my thoughts. I regretted letting Chase walk away thinking I was mad at him. I hadn't really given much thought to how he must have felt all weekend. How humiliating it must have been for him to come face to face with me first thing that morning when he'd found out he'd been hired to be my assistant.

What kind of twist of fucking fate were we dealing with? My life was starting to sound a whole lot like one of Agnes's books but without the promise of an epic love and happily ever after. It took me a long time to settle my anxious mind and fall asleep. Unfortunately, Chase Rivers was right there waiting for me as soon as I crossed into dream land.

CHAPTER
Seven

Chase

I PACED THE LIVING ROOM LIKE A NERVOUS SCHOOLBOY GOING ON HIS first date. This was JJ. A guy who knew me better than most. He'd started out as my freshman roommate in college and became my first lover. Our relationship had taken many shapes over the years, and not all of them were pretty. I'd wanted more than JJ could give, but he'd offered me something amazing in return—an unwavering friendship that sometimes included other benefits. Tonight was supposed to be one of those visits.

I'd gone through the motions of getting ready for sex while I showered, but something unpleasant unfurled in my gut. Sex with JJ would be incredible, and I'd feel much more relaxed afterward, so why did the idea leave me feeling cold?

The kitchen timer went off, and I checked the pans on the stove and saw that everything was ready. I don't know why I always felt the need to feed JJ, but I did. Something about him triggered my need to nurture. I drained the pasta and added it to the pan with chicken, parmesan cheese sauce, and broccoli.

I heard a knock on the door at exactly ten minutes before seven. A huge smile split my face as I opened the door to let JJ in. I was nervous as hell about my decision to invite him over but so excited to see my friend. Unfortunately, the dread in the pit of my stomach only got stronger. He pulled me into a hug as soon as the door shut behind him.

"Don't wait so long to call me next time," he admonished. "I've missed you."

I pulled back and looked up at him. "I've missed you too."

JJ's eyebrows knitted together, and he assessed me with a shrewd, dark gaze. Raising his hand, JJ gently traced the skin under my eyes. "Are you sleeping okay?"

"Not really. I've been burning the candle at both ends lately trying to save up for rent." I wasn't ready to talk about the other things that haunted me at night.

"Chase, I could lend—"

"No. The only thing I want from you is your company."

He quirked a brow. "As in we're going to Netflix but not chill?" I was so relieved that I didn't hear disappointment in his voice. The tension I'd been holding on to finally dissipated.

"Well, I did make your favorite dinner."

JJ sniffed the air appreciatively. "It smells delicious."

"I know," I said with false cockiness. "You set the table, and I'll grab the food."

"Are you trying to domesticate me?"

I snorted. "As if. A feral tom cat would be easier to tame."

"True," JJ said. He walked into the kitchen and pulled down the plates and cups. "How's the new job?"

"How'd you know?" I asked, turning to look at him.

"I ran into Ava and Brandon over the weekend. It would've been nice to hear it from you."

"I was afraid to get my hopes up, and it turned out I had good reason."

JJ *thunked* the plates down on the table hard enough to make me cringe. "What's that mean?"

"It's a long story."

JJ crossed his arms over his chest. "And I have all night."

I knew he wasn't going to let it go, so I told him what happened, starting with my date and ending with my confrontation with Grayson.

"Oh fuck."

"Uh-huh."

I'm so sorry. It's terrible you lost the job because of that asshole. You're so damn talented, Chase."

"Thanks," I said with a shrug. "It's probably for the best anyway. I wouldn't have gotten a damn thing accomplished working for Grayson Wright."

"That hot, huh?"

"Yeah," I said on a sigh as I carried the main course to the table.

JJ pulled out my chair and patted the top of it. "Have a seat. I'll grab the salad and drinks." I did as he said. "Well, it's no wonder you called me. Are you sure I can't be of better service to you than a dining companion?"

"Foot rub?" I asked.

"You're on, but I get to pick the movie this time. I am not watching hours of sappy, snot-inducing romance movies."

"Deal."

We ate dinner and settled on an Indiana Jones, though I couldn't say which one since they all ran together. Looking at Harrison Ford for hours while JJ rubbed my feet was no hardship. Unfortunately, it wasn't enough to keep my mind from wandering back to Grayson Wright.

"Hey," JJ said when the credits rolled at the end of the movie. "You haven't said a word this entire time."

I shook myself out of my misery, pulled my feet from his lap, and sat up. "Ice cream will make it better." I retrieved the rocky road from the freezer and grabbed a spoon. I scooped a bite from the container then passed it to him. "I'm sick of talking about my problems. How are things with work? Still lobbying for an institution you hate?"

JJ worked as a lawyer for a lobbyist firm in DC and traveled all over the country trying to get pro-LGBTQ laws passed. His specialties were marriage and adoption initiatives, neither of which were things he ever wanted for himself.

"I don't want to get married or adopt kids, but I want our community to have those opportunities if it's what their hearts desire.

"One of these days some amazing guy is going to come along and sweep you off your feet, J. You're going to have a big gay wedding and adopt a houseful of kids."

He smirked in my direction. "Never going to happen."

"Famous last words."

He rolled his eyes at me, making me laugh. I felt carefree for the first time since my ill-fated date with Devon.

CHAPTER
Eight

Gray

D EVON CALLED ON TUESDAY MORNING. I'D BEEN DREADING THE CALL, but he wanted to come over to pick up the few things he had left— some artwork, dishes, and decorations here and there. He mentioned sharing the photo albums with me and asked if we could look through them and decide who got to keep which pictures. He sounded a little vulnerable and lost, so I gave in and told him he could come over around seven that evening.

My workday was hectic with Preston and me sharing a personal assistant. Preston had already interviewed all the qualified candidates before choosing Chase. He told me none of the others would be a good fit for either of us. It was a lot of work for Rosie to handle both our schedules and put out any fires that popped up. We needed to find another PA before we killed our current one with too much work or she killed us.

My mom called late in the afternoon, and I realized I hadn't called my folks like I'd said I would. It didn't matter that I was thirty-two years old; I was still Alexandria Wright's baby boy. Lord knows I'd heard her say it enough times during my lifetime.

"Hi, Mom," I said with false cheer. If she heard frustration in my voice, she would mistake it for me being upset over my breakup with Devon.

"Hi, yourself. I heard about the incident at the party. And to think I felt guilty for having a prior commitment. Are you doing okay?" My amazing mother's voice was full of love and concern. "I knew things weren't going well between you two, but it's never easy to end a long-term relationship."

My mom knew all about painful breakups. She and my dad had been happily married for twenty years, or so she'd thought until he told her he'd been hiding a secret from her since they'd become a couple. My dad had come out as gay and told her he'd been living a lie. He still loved her and would always love her, but he wasn't *in love* with her.

Most women would have buckled under the crushing blow to their heart, but not my mom. She was angry and heartbroken of course, but she didn't let it define her. She didn't allow her heartache to affect her charity work, and she held her head high when the gossiping biddies talked about her behind her back. She was one hell of a woman, my mom.

Preston and I had been seventeen and fourteen at the time and had differing reactions to the news. Preston had been furious that our dad would hurt our mom and had acted out. I, on the other hand, felt relief that I wasn't alone and that someone would understand what I was going through. I, too, had been living a lie by pretending I was straight. My dad gave me the courage to come out to them.

My mom later told me I was the reason she'd taken my dad's news so well. He'd recognized I was making the same mistakes he had and wanted a better life for me. Dad had been clear he didn't regret his choices because he truly loved and respected my mother and adored his sons. Dad also swore he'd never been unfaithful to my mother in all the years they'd been together, but having no regrets about his choices didn't mean Dad wanted me to choose the same path.

My parents remained a tight-knit unit when it came to Preston and me.

My mother's unwavering support for my dad helped Preston come around and accept we could still be a family, even though we no longer lived together. It took a solid year and a half before things felt natural between us all.

"I'm doing well, Mom. I promise."

"I'm happy to hear you're taking this so well. I know all too well how gossips and busybodies can drive the knife further into your heart. You know you can always talk to me about anything, don't you, Gray?"

"Absolutely," I replied. "You were the one who bought me all those safe sex books when I came out." My face turned red at the memory of my mom sitting on the edge of my bed with the plastic bag from the bookstore.

"I just wanted you to be safe and healthy," she replied with humor in her voice. Mom let out an unladylike snort before she burst into giggles. "You should have seen your face when you pulled the first book out of the bag."

"Are you talking about the book that instructed me on how to find the male G-spot and offered tips on anal douching or the one about the proper way to roll on a condom?"

She laughed louder and snorted again. "Oh my god," she said, gasping for air. I could picture her clutching her stomach. "I forgot about the anal douching tips."

"It was probably the most humiliating thing I've ever been through. Much worse than catching Devon bringing home a hottie to screw."

"Hottie?"

"Of course you picked up on that. Seriously, the guy was the most beautiful man I'd ever seen. I kind of wonder how Devon managed to pick him up." I sighed sadly.

"Did you get his name from Devon?" my mom asked. It was funny how my friends and family all had the same reaction.

"Oh, I know his name," I said dryly. "He showed up here first thing yesterday morning. He was the guy Preston had hired to be my PA while I was out of town. Can you believe it?"

"Sounds like fate to me. What did you do?"

"I let him walk out of my office without a single attempt to stop him." I've regretted nothing more in my life.

"Pride?"

"No," I said honestly. "It was shock more than anything. Believe me when I say there's no way I could have worked with him."

"Well, if it's meant to be, it will be," Mom said wisely. "I won't keep you any longer. I know you've been terribly busy lately."

"Thanks for checking up on me, Mom. I love you."

"Love you more, Grayson."

I sat and pondered what my mom had said about fate for several minutes. I needed to focus on my work, but Chase was still bouncing around in my busy brain, demanding my attention. Before I could dwell on Chase for much longer, Preston burst into my office.

"Holy fuck," he exclaimed loudly. "You won't believe who I just got off the phone with." I waited for him to enlighten me, but he just stood there sucking in air. "The VP of marketing for Heston Luxury Suites," he finally said, panting between each word.

"You're fucking kidding me," I said, sitting up straighter in my chair. "They actually returned my fucking call?"

"They fucking did," Preston said, then burst into a gleeful dance. "You did it, Gray! You did it!"

"Hey, I only got us an appointment. We haven't signed them as a client," I reminded him.

"We will. I can feel it. You've been on fire lately, and I'm telling you, I feel really good about it. Gray, this would be huge for Wright Creations. We could hire and expand our operations."

"I hope you're right, Pres," I told him. I needed something big to focus my attention on instead of Chase Rivers.

"What should I wear?" I asked Miller over the phone later. "I don't want to look like I'm trying to impress him, but I don't want to look sleep rumpled and inviting either."

"Wear bored resignation," came his glib reply. "Who the fuck cares what you're wearing? It only matters how you act and what you say. Just say no, Gray. He wants to take a trip down memory lane via the photo albums to remind you of all the happy times in your past. He's hoping to rekindle the romance or some shit. Screw him. Well, not really. Screw his plans!"

"You really think he's going to try to get me back? How desperate or pathetic does he think I am?"

"Gray, you put up with his pouting bullshit for five years. Why would he think you've changed in a few days? He's hoping you've had time to miss him and be lonely." Miller laughed hard in my ear. "Dumbass has no idea you've already met someone else."

"Nothing happened with the guy at the bar, Miller." *I thought we were never going to speak about it again.*

"I was talking about Chase."

Just hearing his name made my heart beat faster. "There's no path forward with Chase. How could there be? Devon will always be between us."

Miller let out a frustrated sigh. "Not if you don't let him be, Gray."

I started to respond, but the doorbell rang. "Sounds like Devon is here early."

"Stay strong, my friend," Miller said before he disconnected.

I went downstairs and opened the door. Devon was wearing a charcoal gray sweater I'd bought him for his birthday. It was the one I'd said made his eyes look even greener. I stepped aside so he could enter the house. He was wearing the cologne he saved for special occasions. Miller had been right after all. Devon was attempting to patch things between us. I took a minute to really look him over, and I was pleased to discover there wasn't so much as a spark of interest anywhere in my body. I think my dick yawned and went to sleep.

"I started packing things up for you already," I told Devon. I walked to the dining room where a box sat on the table. "I put your dishes, cookbooks, and your grandmother's silverware in here. Is there anything else in the kitchen that belongs to you?"

"In a hurry?" he asked softly. He placed a hand at the small of my back and leaned in. "Can't we talk first?"

I stepped away from his touch and looked into his calculating eyes. I felt a chill all the way to my bones. This was not the life I wanted anymore. No more settling, no more manipulation.

"Devon, we've said all there is to say. I haven't changed my mind. This is the end for us."

"Gray, it can't be the end. I still love..."

"Enough," I said and held up a hand. "If you came here to get me back, then you're wasting your time and mine. You haven't been in love with me for a long time. I want you to take your things and leave."

"What about the pictures?"

"Inside the box," I told him. Sadly, there weren't many pictures of us together. It was something I planned to do differently the next time I fell in love. I would take lots of pictures with the man who owned my heart. After some consideration, I decided to give all the photo albums to Devon since he seemed determined to hold on to the past. I was determined to focus on the future.

Devon didn't stay long after he realized I wouldn't budge. I spent the rest of the night finishing my book. I needed new reading material and planned a trip to the bookstore near my office at lunch tomorrow.

That night, I dreamed of Chase Rivers and his amazing brown eyes. Again.

CHAPTER
Nine

Chase

L UCKILY MY SHIFTS AT THE BAR AND THE BAKERY HADN'T BEEN GIVEN away, so I wouldn't starve this month. It turned out I only had one day off, though, and I decided to pamper myself.

I soaked in a hot bath and exfoliated my skin with the special sea salt rub Gram had bought me for Christmas. It was scented with sandalwood and citrus, and it smelled amazing and left my skin soft and supple.

After my bath, I made French toast and bacon for brunch and settled in to watch my favorite movie, *The Notebook*. I wanted that kind of all-consuming love for myself, and it felt like it was never going to happen for me.

Gram, Ava, and Xavier would tell me to relax and let fate happen to me instead of me trying to force something that wasn't there. I knew they were right. Hell, I was only twenty-five, so what was with my fatalistic attitude?

I called Gram to give her the bad news about my new job once the credits rolled and I'd wiped my moist eyes. She always knew the right thing to say to get my mind off my troubles. Sometimes she shared her pearls of wisdom, and other times she made me laugh until I forgot what ailed me. This conversation fell into the latter category.

"Thanks, Gram. What would I do without you?"

"You won't find out for a very long time, honey. I will be here to support everything you do." I heard a deep voice in the background and realized Gram wasn't alone.

"I didn't know you had company. I should let you go."

"Not so fast. Lennie just asked me if you'd be interested in meeting his grandson, Tomas. He's very handsome, intelligent, and funny."

"Not yet, Gram. I'm not telling you no, but I need a little more time to get over this latest disappointment."

"Okay, sweetheart. I understand. You let me know if and when you're ready."

I worked at both Adam and Steve's and Bottoms Up in the middle of the week, which made the days go by quickly. I checked my voicemail between shifts and was thrilled to find a message from DC Designs, another ad agency, asking me to return their call to set up an interview, which I promptly did for the following Friday afternoon.

Ava's fiancé, Brandon, stopped by to see me at Bottoms Up during happy hour. The gentle giant tilted his head indicating he wanted to have a private word with me away from prying ears and noisy patrons.

"Have you seen those wedding reception videos where the groom performs a dance for his bride?" he asked.

"Sure, I've seen quite a few. What do you have in mind?" Brandon's face turned bright pink, and he looked around to make sure our conversation was still private.

"I want to surprise Ava with a dance," he said sheepishly. "I can't fucking dance, Chase. I need serious help. Can you help me?"

I smiled widely and clapped him on the shoulder. "Of course I can help you. This is so awesome, and she'd never expect it in a million years.

Do you have a song in mind, and will this be just you or do you plan to include your groomsmen?"

"I'm thinking 'Treasure' by Bruno Mars, and my groomsmen are all on board."

"Ava loves that song, and it's so fitting." The love for Ava I saw in his eyes made me so happy they'd found their happily ever after. "I'll come up with some moves, then call you to set up times to meet."

"Thanks, Chase." He looked slightly embarrassed.

I told him not to mention it and said goodbye before I returned to the bar where I served drinks until closing time. I was grateful Devon the Douche didn't make an appearance.

The next day was spent at the bakery working on designs for custom orders. I did the drawings and specs, and Adam and Steve did the decorating. We made a really great team, and the day went by fast.

Later, Xavier called me from San Francisco. "It's so good to hear your voice," I told him. "It's been too long since we've breathed the same air. When will you be home next?"

"Not soon enough." He sounded exhausted, and I was worried.

"Is everything okay?"

"I'm just ready for a break. We have several West Coast gigs over the next few weeks, but then we get a bit of time off. I can't wait to see you, Ellie, and Gram."

Xavier fronted an eighties cover band called Neon Revival. They performed all the top hits from the decade and even performed the numbers by the female powerhouses in full drag. He'd been on tour most of the last few years, and I could hear the strain his schedule was taking on him.

"We can't wait to see you either."

"Speaking of Ellie," he said. "What happened with your job? She told me it didn't work out but wouldn't tell me why when I asked."

I took a deep breath and told him the entire story. He stayed quiet, never once interrupting me.

"I'm sorry, Chase."

"God, you should have seen the hurt in Grayson's pretty eyes."

"Hmmm."

"What?"

"You've mentioned him a lot," Xavier said. "You've said how handsome he is and how much you hated hurting him. You might have mentioned how pretty his eyes are a few times. Oh, and you said you were disappointed you wouldn't be working with him."

"I did?"

"Yep. I think you're more upset about not seeing him again than you are over losing the job." Xavier had me there. "Don't lose hope, babe. The right guy is out there for you."

He'd said "right guy," but I'd heard "Wright guy," immediately adding a *w* and picturing Grayson's gorgeous face. I wondered what he'd look like when he smiled.

"I have to shove off, buddy. We have sound check in ten minutes."

"Sure. Call me when you get a chance. I miss you."

"I miss you too," Xavier said before disconnecting the call.

My interview at DC Designs went smoothly. The people seemed nice, but I didn't get the same warm feeling when I entered their offices as I had at Wright Creations. It seemed like a sterile work environment that would stifle my creativity instead of fostering it. I couldn't get a good feel on how the interview went, so I was surprised when they called me a few hours later and offered me a position at the agency.

My gut instinct told me to think about it over the weekend and to not rush into anything, and for once, I actually listened. Yes, I wanted a grown-up job with the potential for advancement, but I wasn't convinced the job with DC Designs was the right fit for me. They agreed to give me the weekend to make a decision.

I didn't sleep well, tossing and turning until almost two in the morning, which I regretted when I arrived at the bakery the next day. We were balls-to-the-wall busy. There was the normal morning pastry and coffee rush, which was made more difficult because I was training a new employee. He was sweet and kind, and the regulars loved him right away.

Mixed in with the normal clients were the custom design requests Adam asked me to handle, repairing the espresso machine, and the never-ending phone calls. Then there were the patrons that only wanted me to wait on them because I knew their orders better than they did.

A supercharged electrical current rippled through my body in the midst of the chaotic rush. I'd just finished designing a birthday cake for two-year-old twins when I looked up into the pale blue eyes of Grayson Wright. It took me a second to recognize him because he wasn't wearing his black-rimmed glasses. Bummer. His longish black hair was as disheveled as I remembered. We stared mutely at one another for a few seconds before an anxious customer elbowed him. I shifted my attention to the rude person and found myself looking into Preston Wright's smiling eyes.

"Hello again," Preston said in greeting.

"Hi. What can I get you guys this morning?"

"Do you remember what you brought to the office with you on Monday?"

"Ha! He has a photographic memory," Adam said as he walked behind me with a tray of fresh donuts. "He doesn't forget anything."

I picked up a pastry bag and began to fill it. "Would you like some more hazelnut coffee?" I asked Grayson shyly.

"He'd love some, and so would I," Preston answered. "Can you throw in some of those too?" He pointed to the chocolate cherry cheesecake bites. "Mom would love those."

I added several to the bag before handing it to Steve who was running the register. I turned my back on them to pour their coffee, aware of Grayson's eyes on me the whole time.

"Who designed your logo? It's very charming and memorable." The logo was a cartoon of Adam and Steve standing in the Garden of Eden wearing fig leaf undies. They held an apple pie between them instead of an apple. I'd designed the logo as part of a grad school project.

"Chase did," Steve answered. "He's brilliant, and it seems DC Designs agrees since they offered him a position."

I inwardly cringed but kept my face blank as I turned back to them with their coffees. "Anything else?"

"DC Designs," Preston said while Grayson stared at me. "They've been around a long time. Interesting." Preston looked at Grayson and the two appeared to have a silent conversation. Just then a large group of rowdy teenage girls pushed into the bakery and made their way to the counter. "Guess we'll let you get back to work. Good luck with your new job, Chase," Preston said before leaving.

I nodded, then shifted my attention to the young ladies. Still feeling like I was being watched, I looked up and caught Grayson's eyes on me through the bakery's front window while waiting for his brother to unlock the car. His face turned pink, and he offered a half smile before climbing into the vehicle and shutting the door.

That tiny half smile made my heart thump violently in my chest and wrecked my concentration. Finally, after my third failed attempt to fill an order, Steve told me to take a break. I flopped down into a chair in the break room and laid my head on the table.

Why was fate so cruel, taunting me with the man I wanted but could never have?

CHAPTER
Ten

Gray

"I want him back," Preston said as he pulled away from the curb. "Chase has a lot of talent, and we could use him on our team. DC Designs," he grumbled. "Say something," he told me when I sat staring silently out the windshield.

What could I say? I'd been given another chance to talk to him, but I couldn't bring myself to open my mouth in his presence. It was obvious as hell I made him uncomfortable, but could it be for the same reasons he rattled my composure? Did he feel this insane chemistry between us, or was it one-sided?

"I can't work with him, Pres. I just can't."

"Why? Because of shit for brains? Come on. Are you really telling me you're so upset over Devon that you'd pass up on a talent like Chase Rivers?"

"I'm saying I can't work with him because all I can think about is kissing him whenever I see him."

"Oh."

"I shut down like an idiot. I did the same thing when we were alone in my office. Did you see how uncomfortable he is around me?"

"There has to be a way to make this work. We desperately need another PA, Gray. I have a feeling he'd make a good account executive someday. The guy just has it going on. He has the looks, personality, and the creativity needed to succeed in our industry."

"I know," I said lamely. "Let me think about it, okay?"

"Think fast."

We arrived at my mom's house a few minutes later. We heard laughter coming from the kitchen and headed in that direction. My dad leaned against the counter with his arm wrapped around his husband, Jeff. They were laughing at my mom, who was telling a story complete with big arm gestures and hilarious expressions. We came in at the end and had no clue what they were laughing about.

"Where's my wife?" Preston asked.

"She's lying down in my bed, sweetie. My granddaughter will be making her appearance sooner than the doctor says. I can feel it."

"Should I wake her up or let her sleep?" Preston questioned.

"Let her sleep. We'll keep the food warm for her, and she can eat after her nap."

"I'm awake," Carly said, waddling into the room. She'd changed so much since I'd seen her a week ago. "Let's eat."

We gathered around the table and said grace. We passed the platters around and loaded our plates with scrumptious food. As usual, we went around the table talking about our weeks and catching up with each other. I shamefully tuned everyone out, choosing to think about the situation with Chase instead. Preston was right about Chase feeling like a good fit, but how could I look at him every day and keep my hands to myself? I realized the entire room had gone silent. Five sets of eyes stared at me while I sat there with my fork frozen halfway to my mouth.

"You've been sitting like that for five minutes," Carly said. "Are you okay?"

"He has boy problems," Preston said.

"Boy problems? I thought you and Devon broke up?" Dad asked, his faced scrunched in confusion. Thankfully, Dad and Jeff had been out of town and missed the surprise party. Maybe I should've seen my family's lack of attendance or delayed arrival, as in Preston's case, as an omen.

"Wait until you hear this," Preston said and tattled like he had when we were kids.

"Ohhh, I see," Jeff said sympathetically when Preston was done. "What a dilemma."

"Not really," Carly said around a mouthful of food. "You take Rosie as your personal assistant, and Preston can have Chase. Problem solved."

Her proposal made sense, except for one thing. "Won't it hurt his feelings if he thinks I don't want to work with him?"

Carly rolled her eyes like she was dealing with a room full of simpletons, and maybe she wasn't far off the mark with me. "Just tell him I'm jealous. Tell him I think I'm a fat cow, and I don't like Preston working so closely with a gorgeous woman."

Preston nearly choked on his coffee, then kissed his wife on the cheek and told her she was brilliant. "That could work. Lord knows I won't have problems focusing on my work with Chase around. I'm not the one who wants to bend him over my desk."

Carly giggled, and Jeff choked.

"Preston," Dad admonished as he patted his husband's back.

"Preston Michael Wright," Mom chided, but the corner of her mouth was tilted up in mirth. "We don't talk like that at brunch."

Preston smiled at me from across the table, and I couldn't help but return the gesture. My family might be a little unorthodox, but I wouldn't trade them for the world.

Later that afternoon, I lay on the couch and tried to watch college basketball. I couldn't have repeated a single thing that happened. My mind wouldn't move away from Chase Rivers. My instincts told me to set aside my hesitation and hire the guy. Preston was spot on about him, and we needed the help. It wasn't as good a position as what Preston had heard

DC Designs was offering him, but I had a feeling he'd like to work with us at Wright Creations. Preston was also right about Heston's Luxury Suites. If we landed that account, we could promote Chase to the art department, assuming he proved he possessed the talent we needed. My phone rang, interrupting my thoughts.

"How about some darts?" Miller asked. "How long has it been since you've played?"

"A long time. I'd guess about four or five years."

"We have a tournament going on at Sullivan's tonight at seven. You want in?"

My first reaction was to say no and stay home, but I pushed it aside. "I'm in. Meet you there," I said and hung up.

"Okay," I said, looking up at the ceiling and addressing a higher power. "If I lose, I let this thing with Chase go. If I win, I call him tomorrow and offer him the PA job again."

CHAPTER
Eleven

Chase

I'D JUST LOCKED MY BIKE AT GRAM'S VILLA WHEN MY CELLPHONE RANG. I didn't recognize the number and almost let it go to voicemail. It had been a long, draining week, and I just wanted to have a nice dinner with Gram. Curiosity won, though, and I answered my phone right before the call went to voicemail.

"Hello?"

"Hello. Chase?" Warmth coursed through my body when that deep, sexy voice said my name. I'd recognize it anywhere. I'd heard it in my dreams almost every night this week.

"Mr. Wright?"

"Call me Grayson," he said politely. "Otherwise Preston and I won't know which of us you're talking to. Besides, Mr. Wright is my father."

"Um, okay." There was a long, awkward pause where neither of us spoke for several long moments. "What can I do for you?" *Oh, what I'd love to do to him…for him.*

"Yes, the nature of my call." He cleared his throat uncomfortably. "I'll just get right to the point and not take up much of your time."

"Okay."

"Preston and I had a long discussion yesterday after we saw you at Adam and Steve's. We'd really like to offer you the personal assistant position. It hasn't been filled, and we realized yesterday what a tremendous asset you'd be to our company."

"But—"

"You're a really talented and creative guy," Gray continued, speaking over my objections. "You work really well under pressure, and you give multitasking a whole new meaning. Your design for Adam and Steve's Bakery was brilliant."

"Thanks, but—"

"I know DC Designs is offering you a better position with an opportunity to use your creativity, Chase. I understand that accepting the position with us may not be the best career move for you right now. I won't offer you any guarantees on the timeline, but I can promise a promotion as soon as a position on our art staff becomes available."

"But what about us?"

"*Us?*" Gray asked. Why did the word sound so loaded coming from his mouth?

"Won't it be awkward to see each other every day? I don't want to keep reminding you of…that night, Mr. Wright."

"Grayson." His voice was rich like velvet.

"There's no way I could—"

"You won't be working under me," he said quickly, interrupting me again. Gray let out a sexy little growl that made every hair on my body stand at attention. "Christ, I'm really screwing this up. You won't be working directly *for* me. You'll work for Preston, and his assistant, Rosie, will come work for me."

"Oh." Even though I knew it was for the best, a wave of disappointment washed over me. I hoped he hadn't heard it in my voice.

"It's actually a perfect solution," Gray continued. "Had I not been a stubborn ass I'd have thought of it last week. Preston's amazingly perfect wife is pregnant and hormonal. She's convinced she's fat and ugly, which couldn't be further from the truth, and she's afraid Preston will start finding his young, attractive assistant irresistible." Grayson chuckled, and it sent a shiver down my spine. "Rosie would kick him in the balls if he even tried." The chuckling turned to laughing. "Anyway, everyone wins if you come work for us. What do you say? Can you start tomorrow at eight o'clock?"

"Yes," I said without hesitation.

"Really? You're okay with passing up the offer from DC?"

"To be honest, I really didn't like the vibe there. It felt sterile and lacked positive energy between the employees. It's not a team environment. Wright Creations is definitely a team-driven atmosphere. Oh, maybe I'm not the right fit after all."

"Why would you say that?" I hesitated too long to answer. "Chase?"

"Some of your employees recognized me from the birthday party disaster. In fact, they've dubbed me 'Birthday Surprise Guy.' They looked like exaggerated cartoon characters with their bulging eyes and slack jaws when they got a load of me walking through the office with the bag of pastries and coffee. I didn't recognize a single one of them, but they sure as hell recognized me."

Grayson chuckled warmly, and my dick twitched in my pants. "They'll come around. Hey, I have an idea. We can have a staff meeting tomorrow morning, and I'll introduce you to the team. They'll take their cues from me."

"You're sure things will be okay between us? I know I won't be working with you directly, but we'll still see each other a lot. An elevator ride feels like eternity when you're trapped with an unwanted passenger."

"You're wanted, Chase." *If only.* "Besides, you can always win them over with pastries."

It was worth a try. "That sounds like an excellent idea. Thank you, Mr. Wright."

"Grayson."

"Thank you, Grayson. I can't wait to get started."

"See you tomorrow."

"Yes," I said. "See you then."

I disconnected the call and stared at my phone for several moments, not believing my luck. I felt a goofy grin spread across my face, and it stayed there until I reached the dining room at Autumn Years, my grandmother's active senior living community.

Gram hadn't arrived yet, but her fan club of other active seniors had. They waved when I greeted them as I made my way to our usual table. They had their chairs and bodies turned facing the door so they wouldn't miss a second when she walked through it.

Lost in my own thoughts, I didn't realize she'd arrived until I heard the guy next to me choke on his dentures. My head jerked up, and I saw her sauntering toward me wearing a black leather mini skirt, an indecently cut red top, stockings, and stilettos.

My jaw hit the table, but for an entirely different reason. Then I noticed she was walking a little stiffly, and I was irritated she'd put her vanity before her safety and comfort. "I think your heels are too high, Gram."

She cuffed me upside the head. *Ouch.* "My discomfort has nothing to do with my heels," she said snappily. "It's this dental floss thong I put on. Why do women wear this shit? I'm going back to commando as soon as this dinner is over."

Gag. "Boundaries, Gram," I pleaded as my ears began to bleed. She threw her head back and laughed.

"There's no such thing with me, Chase. I'd think you'd know that by now. You've lived with me nearly all your life."

"I wouldn't trade a moment of that time with you for anything." I leaned over and kissed her on her cheek. "You are the most amazing woman I know, undies or not."

"Thanks, honey. You have an amazing glow about you tonight. What's up?"

I told her about the call I'd received from Grayson on my way to meet her. She listened raptly as I repeated the conversation verbatim. She smiled brightly and hugged me tight when I told her I'd reaccepted the job and started tomorrow morning. Then she let out a relieved breath.

"I'm so happy you're in a great mood, Chase. Let's just hope it's also a forgiving one." Gram's cheeks turned pink with a faint blush, something I rarely saw.

"What did you do?"

"Well, you just sounded so down…"

"Gram?"

"I just want you to be happy and settled before I die." *Oh, the guilt trip.* I snorted. "You'll outlive us all. What did you do?"

"I…I…"

"Come on, Gram." My tone told her how frustrated I was. "What? Is this going to be another attempt to get more gay sex details out of me? You want my opinion on rimming this time? Do you want to know if I like to give or receive? I love both, Gram. I love to rim, and I really like to be rimmed. How's that?"

"Evening," said Lennie from behind me. *Ground swallow me up now.* "I hope we're not late."

We? Fuck me!

The reason for Gram's blush became obvious when Lennie walked around the table with a younger version of himself. Tall, dark, and handsome was too tame a description. His inky black hair was on the longer side, giving him a dangerous pirate look. Pale gray eyes met mine and he aimed a wicked smile at me. *And nothing.* Not a speeding pulse or spark of interest in the pit of my gut. I smiled in return hoping it didn't look as forlorn as it felt.

"Chase, this is my grandson Tomas." Lennie said pleasantly, pretending he hadn't heard what I'd said about rimming. "This is the guy I've been telling you about, Tom."

Tomas reached out his hand, and I shook it. Again, no spark. *Damn it.* Was I destined to pine after the one man I could never have?

CHAPTER
Twelve

Gray

"**C**HASE STARTS AS YOUR PA TOMORROW MORNING," I TOLD Preston over the phone.

"I'm relieved to hear it."

"I just hope he shows up looking ugly or something. You've got to help me out and keep him as far away from me as possible." Preston laughed. "I mean it!"

"Fate keeps throwing this guy in your face, and you expect me to somehow circumvent it? I'm glad you think so highly of my abilities, but no thanks. I'm going to sit back and watch nature take its course." The fucker was having way too much fun at my expense. "At least he'll be working for me and out of your way for the most part. There will be staff meetings and the occasional break-room rendezvous, but that can't be avoided. There might be times when he has to travel with you to meet with potential clients. On those occasions, he will be working under you…I mean, under your supervision."

I groaned at the thought of sitting beside Chase on a plane for hours at a time or trying to sleep at night knowing his hotel room bed was probably backed up against the wall behind mine. Then there'd be all the time in between meetings and shared meals. I'd walk around with a perpetual hard-on. *What had I done to deserve this kind of torture? I'd been a good person my whole life.*

"Guess you'll need to exercise a lot and take cold showers to get over your infatuation," Pres said. "Surely this will pass once he's around on a daily basis. I'm sure you can find a flaw to blow out of proportion."

Infatuation. Could Preston be right? Would I get over him once the newness wore off? Could it really be so simple? I had to believe it was, and I'd be back to my normal self in no time. All this single-minded focus on a guy was completely new to me. Sure, I'd dated a little before I'd met Devon, but I was never this obsessed, not even with the first guy I had sex with. I needed to calm down and accept that Chase was now an employee and therefore off-limits.

"I can tell you're giving yourself one of your famous mental pep talks. I can practically hear the gears turning and smell the smoke from here. Gray, relax and let this play out. Seriously, bro. I love your big, beautiful brain, but you tend to overthink things. Let's just take this one day at a time, okay?"

"Okay," I reluctantly agreed.

I did feel marginally better after talking to Preston. I knew offering Chase his job back was the right thing to do for him and Wright Creations. I just needed to act like a mature adult and not a testosterone-driven beast.

I had several hours left before bed and a lot of anxious energy to burn off. I ended up cleaning my house, going for a run, and taking a shower before heading to my favorite bookstore. I hadn't found a chance to stop in earlier in the week like I'd planned.

"Hey, stranger," Sal, the owner, said when I walked in. "You haven't been in for a while. Everything okay with you?"

He had the best people skills I'd ever seen, except for maybe Chase. *Would everything return to him?* Sal had a knack for remembering everyone's favorite authors and genres. His presence was so warm and inviting that you wanted to linger and browse through his store for hours.

"I saved something special for you," he told me with a conspiratorial wink. "You go ahead and look around, and I'll have it for you at the counter when you're ready to check out."

"Thanks, Sal." I wondered what the surprise was. I meandered over to the gay fiction section and started looking through the new releases. I grabbed a few that looked really good and took a step back to move farther down the aisle. I collided with a petite blonde woman with bouncy curls who had several books in her arms. "I'm so sorry," I said to her.

"It's okay," she said softly. "I lose focus and crash into people and things all the time when I'm buying books." She looked at the selection in my hands, and I felt a slight blush coming on. "You have excellent taste in literature," she told me. "This one is amazing and is the first in the series," she said pointing to a book about detectives who become lovers. "It ends with a little bit of a cliffhanger, so you'll probably want the sequel on hand for when you finish it."

"Thanks," I said and added the second book to my stash. "Do you work on commission?"

"No," she said with a giggle. "I just really love to read. My name is Ava, by the way. It's nice to meet you."

"I'm Gray. It's nice to meet you too. Thank you for your suggestions. I appreciate it."

"You're welcome," she called over her shoulder as she disappeared around the corner of the aisle.

I found some Agnes Simmons books I hadn't read and added them to my stash. "Guess I should have grabbed a basket," I told Sal when I unloaded my treasures on the counter. "What's the big surprise you've got for me?"

Sal grinned broadly and pulled a hardback book out from under the counter. It was an autographed copy of Agnes Simmons's very first gay romance. It was hard to find, yet he'd held an autographed version for me.

"Where did you get that?"

"Agnes did a signing last month and donated some of her rarer books to my store. I saved this one for you." Sal slid it across the counter to me.

"How much, Sal?" I touched it reverently.

"Twenty-five dollars. Is that too much?"

"Not enough." I pulled out a fifty and tossed it on the counter. "That's just for the hardcover. I also want to buy all of these as well."

"I appreciate your business, Grayson." His voice went soft with emotion. "It's not easy owning a bookstore in this day and age, but I've managed to prosper thanks to loyal customers like you."

I'd been going to Sal's since I was a kid. Mom used to bring us in for story time, arts and crafts, and other programs. "I'm proud to support your business. Your bookstore was one of my favorite parts of my childhood." I leaned across the counter and lowered my voice. "Does Preston come in here a lot?"

"Oh, once or twice a month. He buys books for himself or his wife."

"What kind of books does he buy? Comics, murder mysteries, BDSM?" Sal cackled at my interrogation. "Come on, Sal. You can tell me." He just shook his head and tried to give me a firm look.

"No. I'd never tell." He looked pointedly down at my stash and back up at me with a raised brow.

"Fair enough." He rang up my purchases and placed them in a recycled brown bag with the store logo on it. I handed him my credit card, then signed the receipt. "See you soon, Sal."

Back at my house, I had a hard time deciding which book to read first. I decided to go with the police detective series Ava had recommended. I clicked on the gas fireplace to take out the chill in the air and curled up in my favorite chair with a blanket and the book. I loved the peace and tranquility I had found in my home. The only thing missing was a cuddly cat.

The next morning found me spending more time than necessary on my appearance. I'd returned to the gym for more torture and was feeling good all over. I felt my body firming up again after just one week of intense training. I still wanted to dress to impress Chase no matter how many lectures I gave myself. My heart and dick ignored my brain completely.

I took one last look in the mirror and wondered if I should wear my contacts instead of my nerdy glasses, but I decided to stick with the glasses. "You've got this, Grayson. Keep your nose to the grindstone and your hands to yourself."

CHAPTER
Thirteen

Chase

I STOPPED AT ADAM AND STEVE'S ON MY WAY TO WORK AND BOUGHT a variety of donuts, pastries, and muffins to go with several pounds of freshly ground coffee beans. I figured if I got to the office early enough, I could brew a few pots of coffee and set out the pastries before the meeting. I wasn't too proud to bribe my new coworkers with sugar and coffee.

I had talked to Ellie on the phone after I got home from dinner with Gram. Ellie promised she'd be in the office early and would give me everything I needed to access the company's network and email. She also told me Rosie had been notified of the switch and would be coming in early to move her desk and help me get set up. She assured me Rosie was fine with the move and promised I'd love her instantly.

It would have been a huge understatement to say I was nervous about the reception I would be receiving. Ellie had agreed with Grayson that all would be fine once they realized the boss had accepted me into their fold. With her assurance, I pushed my nerves aside and focused on making a good impression.

I stopped by Ellie's office first thing and found her hard at work at her desk. I followed her through the quiet offices to the conference room where all staff meetings were held. She stayed and chatted with me while I got the coffee brewing.

"When was the last time you talked to Xavier?" she asked, concern lacing her voice. I turned around to face Ellie, noting her scrunched brow and pinched lips. She was in protective-sister mode.

"Last week," I replied.

"Did he sound exhausted to you?"

"Xavier told me he was tired and looking forward to a break. He didn't say anything was specifically upsetting him, though."

"He sounded depressed to me, and I'm really worried about him."

I pulled her close and gave her a tight hug. She laid her head against my chest. "I'll call him before my shift at Bottoms Up tonight."

"Thanks."

"Um…" A sweet, feminine voice startled me.

Ellie and I pulled away to find a sultry, brown-eyed beauty standing in the doorway with sour-faced Ben. The latter narrowed his eyes at me while the woman smiled sweetly. She walked over with an outstretched hand.

"I'm Rosie," she said. "You must be Chase."

"I am." Her grip was warm and firm. "It's very nice to meet you. Thank you for coming in early to help me get set up. This last-minute switch must be a huge inconvenience." Douche-face Ben grunted, and I'd already had enough of his bullshit attitude. I looked him square in the eyes, not willing to back down. "Burt, isn't it?" His lips curled in a slight sneer, but he didn't say anything.

"Let's get started, shall we," Rosie said. I held my hand out in the classic *after you* gesture, and she exited the conference room. "I think I like you already."

I followed her out the door. "I think I like you too."

Rosie spent the next thirty minutes helping me set up my email and access to company files and showed me how to use the phone system, navigate the electronic records, and update Preston's calendar. She even had me download a company app, which allowed me to access Preston's calendar on my phone so I would always know where he was.

"We'd better head to the conference room," she said after checking her watch. She picked up a huge stack of file folders, and I took the top half to lighten the load. "Thanks," she said gratefully.

I entered the room behind her and braced myself for a negative reaction from everyone already assembled. A quiet pall fell over the room as Rosie and I handed out file folders. Grayson and Preston weren't there yet, so it was extremely awkward. I smiled kindly at everyone as I handed them each their folder. Most smiled back but some just stared.

"Did you bring the donuts?" the lady with purple hair I'd met before asked. There was no censure in her tone.

"I did."

"Thanks," she said, saluting me with her glazed donut before taking a seat.

"You're welcome."

"I smell hazelnut coffee," Grayson said as he breezed into the room. Our eyes locked awkwardly for a brief minute before a genuine smile lit his super sexy face. I nearly swooned into a puddle of goo when I saw his perfect white teeth for the first time. "I'm sure I have you to thank for it, right, Chase?"

I smiled in acknowledgment when he stopped beside me to pour himself a cup of coffee. Unable to resist his proximity, I leaned a little closer. "Someone gave me a great tip on how to win over my coworkers." Grayson poured a cup of coffee and added a bit of creamer before he faced the rest of the staff who sat gawking at us like we were a circus freak show.

"What are you staring at?" he asked the attendees. Everyone wisely kept their mouths shut. "This is Chase Rivers. He is new to our team. He will be working as Preston's personal assistant for the time being, and

Rosie will be moving over to assist me. I want everyone to make Chase feel welcome. Anyone using the phrase 'Birthday Surprise Guy' will answer directly to me, and you will not like the consequences."

He eyed every member of the team as he introduced them to me by name. I detected a slight eye roll from Ben and had to bite back a smile. I didn't know what the fuck that guy's problem was, but I wasn't about to let him ruin things for me. Finally, Gray turned to me and extended his hand. "Welcome to Wright Creations, Chase," he said with a smile as he gripped my hand in a firm shake.

My breath caught in my throat when I felt his skin against mine. Sparks of awareness zigged and zagged up my arm like electrical currents. Grayson's eyes widened slightly, and his nostrils flared. He felt it too. I pulled my hand away from his, eager for relief.

"Okay, then. Let's get started," he said to the team.

I took the empty seat next to Preston and couldn't help noticing the sly smile on his face as he looked from Grayson to me. Grayson narrowed his eyes at his brother from across the table as Ben got up to lead off the meeting.

I listened as Ben talked about the upcoming campaigns they were working on and the various stages the campaigns were in. I couldn't help but be impressed as he talked about Dee Dee's Delightful Catering, Java Joe's, and Heston's Luxury Suites. I was impressed the company had a shot at Heston's campaign. They ran a five-star operation. Wright Creations would be in a great position if they could snag that account.

Gram, Xavier, and I had stayed at many Heston's properties over the years when we'd gone on vacations. The penthouse suites were outfitted with every luxury feature you could imagine, but the décor and layout of the rooms encouraged you to curl up and rest instead of making you worry you might damage the fabric.

I listened to all of Ben's pitches, but none of them struck a chord with me, and I doubted they would resonate with the Heston's execs either. Ben's lackluster campaign ideas had nothing to do with a shortage of talent, but it was apparent he'd never spent any time in their hotels. I accidentally let a deep sigh escape my lips.

"Problem, Mr. Rivers?" Ben sneered at me.

"Hmm? Me? No, I don't have a problem."

"Is there something you wanted to add, Chase?" Preston asked politely after giving Ben a warning glance.

"It really isn't my place."

"We agree on something," Ben said, and his arrogance pushed me to speak out.

"Have you ever stayed in a Heston's suite?" I asked. Ben didn't answer, so I pushed on. "I have stayed there many times, and..."

"You?" He sounded incredulous.

"Yes, me. I've stayed at Heston's many times and in many different cities."

"How?" *Really? What a jerk.*

"My grandmother is a famous author, and she traveled a lot for conventions and speaking engagements over the years. She was my guardian, so I traveled with her when I wasn't in school."

"Who is she?" The question came from Carman, the lady rocking the purple hair.

"She wrote under the pen name Desiree Amour for a few decades but switched to gay fiction a few years back. She now writes as Agnes Simmons."

Gray, who'd been taking a sip of coffee, sputtered and coughed.

"Are you okay?" I asked, pushing back my chair to...what? Pound him on the back? Offer mouth-to-mouth?

Gray cleared his throat and waved off my concern. "Nearly went down the wrong pipe."

"No way," Kayla, Carman's twin sister, said.

"Can you get us an autograph?" Carman asked.

"Sure."

"Can we get back to business?" Ben groused.

"Sorry," Carman, Kayla, and I said contritely. I saw Grayson's lips twitch.

"You were saying, Chase," Preston prompted.

"Heston's hotels offer every conceivable luxury, but it still feels like home. The rooms don't have that generic hotel feel like most chains do, and it's not stiff and sterile like other five-star chains. You're afraid to sit on the furniture in a lot of those places, but that's not the case with Heston's hotels."

"Interesting," Grayson said. He narrowed his beautiful eyes in concentration. *Stop noticing his eyes, moron.* "I like the concept. I've stayed at a few of their hotels, and I agree with you, Chase. All the comforts of home with a luxurious finish." He looked at Ben. "Mock up something along those lines. I think what your team has done is great, but it's not going to be enough to stand out against the competition."

"Yes, sir."

The rest of the meeting went by quickly, and I soon found myself back at my desk, getting it all set up the way I wanted it and working out some details with Rosie, who asked me to join her for lunch at noon. I didn't have plans, so I'd agreed to go with her. I thought it might be a great way to get to know more about my new coworkers.

I received a flower delivery right as we were making plans for where to eat. I'd never received flowers before, especially none as beautiful as the exotic, pale purple orchid. Rosie clapped her hands and danced a happy jig beside me.

"Who is it from?"

"I have no idea," I answered as I plucked the card out of the plastic holder.

Thinking of you this morning. Hoping your first day is going well. I know our grandparents blindsided you yesterday, but I'd like the opportunity to know you better. Join me for lunch at noon? Text me if you're free, and I'll wait for you outside your building.

Tom

He'd scribbled his number at the bottom.

Rosie leaned in to read the card and swayed on her feet, clutching her chest. "So thoughtful. Lunch with me can wait until tomorrow."

"I don't know. Nothing was sparking between us yesterday, and I don't want to give him the wrong impression."

Rosie rolled her eyes. "Maybe it was the environment and not the guy."

"Maybe."

"You won't know unless you give it a try."

"True," I agreed.

"I'm going to head over to my new desk and get to work," Rosie said. "Catch up with me later. I want to hear all about your lunch date."

"Thanks," I said, checking the time.

I pulled out my phone and sent Tom a quick text to thank him for the flowers and accept his lunch invitation. I put my phone away and got to work sorting Preston's emails, answering calls, and scheduling appointments for him to meet with potential clients. It wasn't my dream job, but it was a step in the right direction.

I received a call from an upset client about a scheduling conflict, and I used all my charm to calm her down and find an agreeable solution for both their schedules. By the end of the call, she was laughing and telling me she only wanted to deal with me from then on.

I was so involved in taking notes I wasn't aware I was being watched until I felt a shift in the atmosphere, a crackling that caused the hairs on the back of my neck to stand up. I looked up to find piercing blue eyes watching me work. His black-framed glasses made Grayson's irises look more vibrant.

Grayson kept his eyes locked on mine as he slowly walked toward my desk. I watched as his long, sexy index finger reached out and traced the delicate edge of an orchid petal. I imagined his gentle touch on my body.

Stop it, Chase.

Gray dropped his gaze to the florist card turned over on my desk. When our eyes met again, curiosity and something else sparked in his gaze. Did he want to turn the card over and find out who'd sent the orchid, or was that just wishful thinking on my part? The air felt heavy around us and charged with electricity. I found it hard to breathe. My attraction to Gray was impossible to ignore.

Before I could say anything, he walked past my desk and let himself into Preston's office. I took my first easy breath, but the reprieve didn't last long.

Ben strode toward my desk, not bothering to glance in my direction. "Pres and Gray are expecting me." His voice was as chilly as it had been during the staff meeting. Ben moved past me before giving me the chance to announce his arrival, closing the door with a solid *thunk* in his wake.

The pleaser part of me wanted to understand his animosity toward me and fix the rift. That part had already gone to lunch, however, so Ben was stuck with the version of me that held up his middle finger.

CHAPTER
Fourteen

Gray

I looked up as Ben crashed through the door like a thunder-cloud. I didn't understand his negativity toward Chase, but I was putting an end to it.

"Ben, I won't tolerate you treating Chase that way again. You were downright hostile during the meeting, and now you're slamming the door like a petulant child. It's unacceptable. This is not a conversation you want to have with me again. Am I clear?"

"Yes, sir," Ben said.

Fuck, I was pissed and not just at Ben. I was pissed at myself for pining after Chase like a fucking lovesick fool. Who was the orchid from and why did I care? He wasn't for me.

Preston could tell I was mad and distracted, so he pretty much took over the meeting between the three of us. I made comments here and there but mainly let him do all the talking. All my focus was on Chase. His grandmother was my favorite author. Was the world really that small? Had he felt a fraction of the heat between us? What about the electricity when our hands touched?

Preston cleared his throat. "Anything else you'd like to add, Gray?"

"Uh, no," I said after completely losing track of the conversation. "That's all for now."

Ben got up and exited Preston's office without another word. I knew he was unhappy about my admonishment, but I couldn't allow him to treat Chase so rudely. At least I'd done it in the privacy of Pres's office and not in front of the entire design team. Ben's tone and facial expressions when he asked Chase how he knew about Heston's suites had really made me angry. If I was offended, then Chase must've been really hurt.

"You okay?" Preston asked. Before I could respond, he spoke again. "Was hiring Chase a mistake?"

"No," I answered quickly. "My distraction isn't his fault."

"I didn't say it was. The situation is no one's fault. But if Chase working here is bad for both of you, then maybe it was a mistake."

"Stop saying that, Pres." I blew out a frustrated breath. I stood up and began to pace his office. "I've told myself over and over that nothing can happen between Chase and me. I'm a partner and co-owner of this business, and he's an employee. There is still a part of me wondering why he keeps getting thrown in my face if he's not meant to be mine. Am I being punished for something? Do you have any idea how it feels to want someone so badly but know you'll never have him?"

"No, I don't," Preston said sympathetically. "I'm one of the lucky ones."

"You are, Pres. You have an amazing wife and a baby girl on the way. I want that happiness for myself."

"Gray, you'll have that life someday. You'll meet the right guy. So, you've had some odd run-ins with Chase, and he pops up everywhere you least expect him, but it doesn't mean he's the one for you. He may not be your destiny."

Preston's words hurt far worse than they should have. My brain said Preston was speaking the truth, but my heart said he needed to shut the fuck up. "I'm going to be out of town for the rest of the week. That should help him settle in and give me a chance to get my shit together."

"Are you sure, Gray?"

"Positive. Chase is as sharp as we thought, and his ideas are fresh."

"I want you to be happy, Gray. I want you to find a love like I have just as badly as you do. No one deserves it more than you. You've made a lot of sacrifices to make sure our company gets off the ground. It's time for you to find the same level of success in your personal life too." He pointed to his office door. "If he is the key to your happiness, we'll find a way to make this work." A wry smile stretched across my brother's face. "So you're a fan of his grandmother's books, huh?"

"What makes you say that?"

Preston snorted. "Do you think I missed how you choked on your coffee?" He shook his head. "Wrong pipe."

Shrugging, I said, "I might have heard of her books."

"Uh-huh," Preston said, clearly not buying my glib response. "It really does make you wonder."

"About what?"

"All these similarities between you and Chase. It makes you want to connect the dots to see what picture forms."

"You're not helping," I practically growled at him.

"I bet you're hoping for something really dirty, aren't you?"

"Still not helping, Preston."

Pres threw back his head and laughed at my misery. I glared at him, which only made him laugh harder. "Let's go to lunch. Maybe a good meal will make you look less constipated."

"Asshole." I waited until he turned his back to crack a smile.

CHAPTER
Fifteen

Chase

B EN EXITED PRESTON'S OFFICE LIKE A SCALDED CAT WITHOUT SO much as acknowledging my existence. I didn't let his petulant behavior drag me down since I was working furiously through my list of tasks, determined to make a big dent before lunch.

Preston's door opened again just as I was about to push away from my desk and head for the elevator.

"Join us for lunch," Preston said cheerfully when he exited his office. "It will be my treat since it's your first day."

I turned to smile at him as I slipped on my suit jacket. "Thanks, but I already have lunch plans. Rain check?"

"Sure."

"See you in a bit." I beat a hasty retreat away from the awkwardness, fully aware of Gray's icy blue eyes on me the entire time.

Tom was parked at the curb as promised, and I waved as I made my way over. We smiled at each other when I dropped into the passenger seat.

"Thank you again for the orchid and lunch invitation. Both are welcome distractions for a hectic day."

"My pleasure." Tom moved forward like maybe he wanted to kiss me but stopped suddenly. A wry smile tugged at the corner of his mouth, and he shook his head. "I'd hoped I was wrong."

"About?"

"Me having a chance with you."

I winced. "It's not you. It's—"

Tom cut me off with a wave. "No need to finish. I don't mind the friend zone."

"I'm kind of hung up on someone," I admitted. "Ridiculous though it may be."

Tom patted my knee. "You can tell me all about it at lunch."

"Where are you taking me?"

"Roma's Italian Eatery," Tom said as he pulled away from the curb and merged into traffic. "It's my absolute favorite."

Once inside the restaurant, we were shown to a table in a private alcove near a rustic fireplace. I loved the atmosphere and wondered why I'd never heard of it or tried it before now. Our waitress greeted Tom by name, dropped off the menus, and took our drink order.

"I'm in the mood for chicken parmesan, and Roma's makes the best," Tom said.

"I love it too, but I made some recently. I think I'll go with the baked rigatoni."

Tom nodded approvingly. "You like to cook?"

"Love it. How about you?"

Tom smiled sheepishly. "I like to cook, but I'm not very good at it. I'm better at baking."

"How about we collaborate one night this week?" I suggested. Tom quirked a brow and my body tensed in response. "Friends have dinner, right? I'll cook, and you can bring dessert?"

Tom smiled. "We can compare stories about our grandparents."

The tension in my shoulders eased. "Perfect."

"What night works best for you?" Tom asked.

"Wednesday," I answered after checking my phone. "Does that work for you?"

"Yes," Tom said just as our waitress returned with our drinks. She took our order, complimented us on our choices, then left us alone once more. Tom lifted his glass. "To the friend zone."

Grinning, I lifted mine too. "The friend zone."

I didn't run into Gray for the rest of the day, which helped me relax and accomplish everything on my to-do list. I hummed happily as I headed to the men's bathroom at the end of my workday to swap out my suit for my Bottoms Up T-shirt, jeans, boots, and a leather jacket. A sharp whistle grabbed my attention as I walked to the elevator. I looked up to find Carman and Kayla waiting in the lobby.

"You look really hot in casual clothes," Carman said. "Are you heading out for a night on the town?"

"No, not me. I'm off to tend bar for a few hours," I replied.

"Is that the name of the bar?" Kayla asked, gesturing to my black T-shirt.

"Yeah. Bottoms Up. You should check it out sometime. We have great food and drink specials. There's always some kind of sport playing on the big screens and pool games going on in the back. Saturday night is karaoke night, which is always popular."

"We'll definitely have to check it out," Carman said.

"How many jobs do you have?" Kayla asked.

"Three right now, but I'm hoping to cut it down to two soon."

"Wow," Carman said. "Why so many?" I told them about Ava and my roommate situation. "I'd be willing to move in and split the expenses if you promise to clean the apartment in your underwear." She let out a squeak and covered her mouth with both hands. She stared at Chase with wide, horrified eyes. Lowering her hands, she said, "I can't believe I said that."

"Me either," said a deep voice from behind us. *Shit.*

All three of us turned around quickly. Grayson and Preston stood behind us. Preston was fighting off a grin while his brother scowled. Gray raked his eyes over my attire before turning his full attention to Carman.

"Do I need to remind you about our personal conduct policy?" Gray asked. "The comment you just made to Mr. Rivers could be construed as sexual harassment."

I wanted to interfere, even opened my mouth to do so until Gray snapped his angry gaze back to me. Beside him, Preston gave a sudden shake of his head, urging me to stay out of it. I bit my lip and did as he suggested, even though I wanted to reach out and hug Carman.

"I apologize, sir." She turned to face me, and her face was as red as mine. "I'm sorry, Chase. I didn't mean to be inappropriate or embarrass you." Her chin wobbled, and it nearly broke my heart.

"It's okay, Carman. I knew you were just teasing, and I didn't feel violated or threatened by your comment." I gave her a quick hug, rules be damned. "I think I'll take the stairs," I said to the group. "Have a nice night, everyone." I felt their eyes on me as I walked away.

CHAPTER
Sixteen

Gray

I HAD A SERIOUS DECISION TO MAKE BECAUSE I COULDN'T CONTINUE on like this. I'd turned into a pissed-off thundercloud, obsessing over Chase's lunch plans and raining my irritation down on those all around me. I had never been that kind of employer, and I hated myself for it when I saw the looks of misery on the faces of my staff.

Christ, I couldn't get the image of Chase dancing around in his underwear out of my mind. I didn't even know what kind he wore, but that didn't slow down my imagination. I must have made a strangled noise in my throat because Preston looked at me worriedly. Damn, I was making a mess of everything.

I regretted the harsh way I spoke to Carman and the embarrassment I saw on Chase's face. "Carman, I'm sorry I snapped at you. It was truly uncalled for, and I apologize."

"Thanks," she said softly.

It was an awkward ride down to the ground floor. Carman and Kayla made a beeline for their vehicles, leaving Preston and me to walk at a more leisurely pace. I could tell Preston had something he wanted to say and was just searching for the right words.

"You're a fucking idiot," Preston said as we made our way to our cars. There was the older brother I loved so much. He stopped and put his hand on my arm. He looked around to see if anyone was in earshot. "Get your shit together, man. Think long and hard about what you want while you're in Colorado with Ben. Make up your mind and act on it for all our sakes. Chase deserves better, our employees deserve better, and you certainly deserve better."

"I know," I said quietly. It was mortifying that my brother had to have this conversation with me. "I'll sort it out, Pres. I promise."

Preston pulled me into a hug. "I know you will, Gray." He pulled back and looked into my eyes. "

I nodded. "Thanks for always having my back."

"Always. Call me if you need to talk. It might prevent you from making an ass of yourself."

"Thanks." I slapped him on the shoulder, and he walked away. He was right. I needed to sort myself out. I thought I could stifle my attraction to Chase at work, but I'd been delusional. Only one option remained: I'd have to win him over for myself.

Peace settled over me as I walked toward my car. There was more between Chase and me than just lust. I could feel it in my bones. I wouldn't say he was my soul mate or happily ever after, but my need for him was a tangible thing.

There was always a chance my decision would blow up in my face, but I had to risk it. I'd been willing to sink every penny I had ever saved into Wright Creations without blinking an eye. I had to trust those same instincts when it came to pursuing Chase. All my life, I'd been capable of stepping back and looking at the big picture. I had always analyzed the situation to figure out what the worst outcome would be and whether or not I could live with it. The worst that could happen was rejection or that we'd try and it wouldn't work out. I could live with either outcome as long as I gave it my all. Chase and I were adults and could act accordingly at work, not that I'd set a sterling example for him so far.

I felt lighter than air when I got home. I turned up the music and danced while making a quick dinner. My good mood lasted while I packed my bags for my trip and got ready for bed.

I dreamed about Chase, and the images were so vivid and real it was like I could feel his skin, taste him on my lips, and hear the sounds he made when I entered his body. I woke up expecting him to be beside me in bed. I was up an hour before my alarm clock was set to go off and more than a little aroused. Instead of lazily stroking my cock to fantasies of what could be, I threw back the covers to start my day.

I went through my morning workout routine, grateful Jett wasn't around. My brain and heart were on a mission, and I didn't want to be sidetracked by his aggressiveness. It was getting to the point where I was thinking about switching gyms. I mean, there's flirty and then there's obnoxious.

I was due to pick up Ben at his house at ten. Since I was still ahead of schedule, I swung by Adam and Steve's to get coffee and a pastry. I didn't feel the need to apologize to Ben for reprimanding him as I'd done with Carman. Ben had treated Chase poorly, and I would've admonished him the same regardless of how I personally felt about Chase. More importantly, I needed to find out why Ben was acting so hostile toward the man. Was he feeling insecure about his job, or was it more personal? It didn't take me long to find out.

"I bought us some preflight goodies," I said to Ben when he slid into my car. "I figured we could use a little sugar. At least I can. I hate flying, but it's a necessary evil for this job."

"How can you stand to work with *him*?" I knew by his snide tone who Ben was referring to.

"Why would I have a problem working with Chase?"

"I fucking hate cheaters," Ben said with contempt. "How can you look at him every day knowing what he almost did to you?"

Clearly Ben had serious issues with infidelity. I didn't want to dismiss his feelings on the subject, but I needed to explain why *I* didn't have an issue with Chase. "Because Devon was the cheater. Chase was just another victim of Devon's manipulation. He's the fucking master."

"You're willing to take him at his word?" Ben asked incredulously.

"No, I didn't just take his word for it. Even if Devon hadn't admitted the truth, I would've seen it with my own eyes. Chase's horror and outrage weren't contrived or fake. I don't want you treating him unfairly because of what *almost* happened that night. It's not fair to judge him without knowing the truth. You need to give him a chance."

Ben sat quietly for a few minutes before he replied. "I'll try."

"That's all I ask." I held out my fist toward him, and he bumped it. "Now let's go to Colorado and sign The Lodge as Wright Creation's newest client."

I whistled as I walked to my office early on Friday morning. I decided to go in before anyone else and get a head start on the work that had probably piled up in my absence. Ben and I had had a very successful trip out west, and we'd signed The Lodge as our client. I was also very happy because it was the day I would begin wooing Chase. *Wooing.* I needed to stop reading so many historical novels.

I dropped my briefcase on my desk and headed to the break room for another jolt of caffeine. I jerked to a stop in the doorway when my eyes landed on the sexiest thing I'd ever seen. *Holy shit.*

Chase was in the break room with his earbuds in, dancing to a song while he filled the coffeepots. Even though my eyes and dick were on sensory overload from watching his denim-clad ass sway left and right, my nose still detected hazelnut coffee. Chase was lost in the music and hadn't sensed my presence.

I walked farther into the room, my eyes taking in every inch of his tall, lean frame. I had never been so thankful for casual Fridays as I was right then. Chase Rivers in a suit was a beautiful sight to behold, but Chase in a button-down shirt and a pair of ass-hugging jeans was seriously sexy. It was all I could do not to move up behind him and join in. How long had it been since I'd danced with a sexy man? *Too damn long.* Chase turned to the side and rolled his hips seductively. His eyes were closed, and his lips were moving as he silently sang along. He opened his eyes and did a little spin, and that's when our gazes collided.

He let out an adorable squeak and yanked the earbuds from his ears. "Oh, fuck me." *Gladly.* Realizing he just dropped the F-bomb he slapped his hand over his mouth and turned the brightest shade of red I'd ever seen on a person. "I'm so sorry," he mumbled behind his hand.

I couldn't hold back. I threw my head back and laughed like I hadn't in too long to remember. By the time I regained my composure, Chase's color had returned to normal, and he was looking at me with a crooked grin on his face. I wanted to kiss his mouth more than I wanted my next breath. I took a step toward him to do just that.

"What's going on in here?" My brother's voice had the same effect as getting doused with a bucket of ice water. The smile on Chase's face spread until his pearly white teeth gleamed beneath the overhead lights. I suddenly found it hard to breathe.

"I'm laughing at him laughing at me," Chase replied.

"I'm laughing at both of you idiots," Preston said in good humor. "So what are you two kids up to in here?" Did I detect a bit of suggestiveness in his voice?

"Gray caught me dancing while firing up the coffeepots." Chase had used my nickname, and I liked it. A lot. In fact, my devious, sex-starved brain wanted to hear him chant it over and over but in a completely different setting.

"He has some great moves," I said.

"Oh yeah?" Pres asked. "You preparing for a special event?" My brother casually strolled to the coffeepots and poured himself a cup.

"My best friend, Ava, is getting married in a few months. Her fiancé asked me to come up with a dance for him and the groomsmen to perform for her at the reception. They're all these big, lumbering football-player types, and I'm not sure how well they can dance."

"That's really sweet," I said. *Damn, another thing to admire about him.*

"When's the big day?" I walked to the coffeepot and poured myself a large cup of hazelnut coffee. I held the cup to my lips, closed my eyes, and breathed in the delicious aroma. A slight moan may have slipped out after I took my first sip. I licked my lips to catch the little drops of heaven clinging to them. When I reopened my eyes, I found Chase staring at me. I heard Preston chuckle as he left the break room.

"Um, they're getting married in June."

Chase blinked rapidly, but his gaze kept returning to my lips, so I licked them. This time it was slow and deliberate. Somewhere in the back of my mind a voice screamed, *What are you doing, moron? You're at work*! I tuned the fucker out and focused on my prey.

"Do you have lunch plans today?" *Where the fuck had that come from?* Chase spun around, looking as surprised as I was. His mouth opened, but no words came out. "I mean, I heard Preston say he wants to take you to lunch to welcome you to our team."

"I can't."

"Can't or won't? Do you already have plans?" I was badgering him like a witness under cross examination. I needed to back off.

"I have plans with my grandmother and Ava."

Agnes Simmons was coming to my office! I could barely contain my excitement. "I'd love to meet them. What time are they coming by?"

"Just before noon so they can meet everyone and take a look around the office."

"Great," I told him as I started to back away toward the door. "I'll catch you then."

"Okay." Chase smiled shyly at me, and it made me happier than if I'd won the lottery.

I hummed all the way back to my office, knowing I was grinning like a fool. I didn't care because there was a glimmer of hope that Chase Rivers wanted me as badly as I wanted him. If he gave me an inch, I'd take a hundred miles.

CHAPTER
Seventeen

Chase

I WAS SO FUCKING EMBARRASSED GRAY HAD CAUGHT ME DANCING. Could I have been any more ridiculous? At least I'd toned it down and hadn't looked like I was working a pole.

There was something really different in the way Gray had looked at me this morning. Gone were the anger and distrust, and it looked a whole lot like desire and need had replaced them. Nope, I wasn't going to let my mind wander down that path. Only hurt and heartbreak lay that way.

I met with Preston in his office thirty minutes later to go over his schedule for the upcoming week. He and Gray would be meeting with executives from Heston's in Los Angeles. Preston seemed confident they would nail the pitch and land the account. Preston also gave me a list of things he wanted me to mock up in his absence because Ben would also be in the field. He told me to make sure all the details for the Heston's account were on the shared drive so we could have access in an emergency.

I took notes while he talked, but I couldn't help but notice an extra gleam in his eyes. I wasn't sure what he was up to, but I was certain it was no good. I looked back up at him after he finished talking and saw he was aiming a lopsided grin my way. He opened his mouth to speak, but his office door opened suddenly. His face went from amused to love-drunk in less than a second.

"There's my lady."

I turned in my chair and saw a stunning woman enter the office and walk to him. Walk might have been a slight exaggeration because she looked like she was due to have a baby at any moment. Her cheeks were flushed pink, giving her a healthy glow. Her shoulder-length curls bounced as she made her way to her husband, who had come around the desk to meet her halfway.

"What did the doctor say?" Preston caressed her wild curls away from her face. "Are my princesses doing okay?"

"Princesses?" I didn't realize I'd spoken out loud until they both turned to look at me. They looked like they had forgotten I was in the room.

"Chase, I'd like you to meet my wife, Carly." I stood up to shake her hand. "Sweetie, this is the guy I've been telling you about."

"It's so nice to finally meet you, Chase. I meant to bake you a pie to welcome you to the Wright Creations family, but I've been a little off my game lately." She shook my hand warmly before leaning against her husband.

"Are you having twins? Preston said princesses."

Carly giggled sweetly. "I'm princess number one and this"—she caressed her belly—"is princess number two."

"Ahhh. When are you due?"

"Four weeks if you go by my original due date, but—"

"Original due date?" Pres interrupted. "What does that mean?"

"Well, the doctor said I'm measuring farther along, and he thinks our baby will arrive next week."

"*Next week*," Preston repeated, his voice barely above a whisper. He looked poleaxed, and I suddenly felt like an intruder.

"I'm just gonna…" I pointed to the door, but neither noticed.

I returned to my desk and got busy making travel arrangements for

Preston and Gray. I fielded calls and put out fires, then went to find Kayla and Carman to pick up the presentation materials they were putting together for the Heston's campaign. Even though most campaign pitches were done via PowerPoint, major accounts like these also got glossy prints.

Gram and Ava were standing next to my desk talking to Gray when I returned. Both were sizing Gray up, and I knew I needed to get in there before they did something to embarrass me.

"You do look like a sexy Clark Kent," Ava said just as I reached them. *Too late.* Gray looked at me and quirked a brow, earning a shrug. "I should have known who you were when we bumped into each other at the bookstore." *What? When?*

"I loved your recommendations by the way. It was hard to put those books down." Gray turned to Gram and held out his hand to her. "I'm Grayson Wright. And you are still my favorite author."

Gram giggled sweetly as he shook her hand. "Wow, I'm flattered." She narrowed her eyes in contemplation, and I could almost hear her wheels turning. *Oh no.* I had to get them out of here before things went sideways. "You kind of look like that guy who plays the vampire in Chase's favorite show."

Too late once again. "Ready for lunch?" They ignored me.

"Wow. Clark Kent and a sexy vampire," Gray said.

"No one said the vampire was sexy," I pointed out.

"Hmmm, maybe I should write a gay vampire series," Gram said absently. She stared into space, retreating to her own little world where she went to plot her stories.

"I don't want to hold anyone up," Gray said. "I asked Chase to lunch today, but he told me he already had plans with you."

"You asked Chase to lunch?" Gram asked, popping back into reality. She pinned me with a disbelieving look. "You should have canceled with us, honey. We could have had dinner or something. It isn't every day a handsome man asks you out."

"It was just a business lunch," I told her. "Besides, I need your final approval on your latest book cover and to make some party plans with Ava."

"Book cover?" Gray asked.

"Chase designs all the covers for my books."

"Join us for lunch," Ava interjected.

Gray held up both hands and waved them, slowly backing away. "I couldn't possibly."

"We insist," Gram told him.

"Chase?" Ava asked.

"They insist," was the only thing I could think to say.

Gray searched my eyes for a few seconds before relenting. "Where are you eating? I'll meet you there. I need to have a quick word with my brother, then I'll head over."

"Landry's," Gram answered sweetly, too sweetly, which meant she was up to something. Thank god we were driving separately so Gram and Ava could get their orneriness out of their systems. As soon as we were in Ava's car, they started in.

"Oh my god, how do you work near him?" Ava questioned. "Those fuck-me eyes and lips. He's every hero Gram has ever written."

"Did you see his body? Whew," Gram said, fanning herself with her hand. "Beneath the tailored suit is a bitching gym bod. If you don't climb him like a tree, then you can't be my grandson."

I shook my head. "Never going to happen, Gram."

"Never say never," Ava and Gram said in unison.

Once we arrived at the restaurant and placed our drink orders, the conversation turned more serious. "Ellie mentioned there's something wrong with Xavier. What do you know?" Gram asked.

"I honestly don't know anything. Ellie expressed the same concern to me, and I've called him a few times. He says he's just tired, but I think something else is going on. He seemed withdrawn, and there are times he doesn't return my calls or messages. When I do talk to him, he sounds anxious to get off the phone. Whatever is going on with him is a recent thing. He was fine a few weeks ago."

"Would it help if I called him?" Gram asked, unable to keep the worry from her voice.

"I don't think so, Gram. If he wanted to talk, he'd talk to me before anyone else." Our waitress returned with our drinks, and I took a quick sip of soda. "On the bright side, he'll be home in a few weeks, and then we can get a better handle on what's going on with him."

"Okay," Gram said, resigning herself to be patient. "Honey, are you okay? Lennie said Tom is moving to New York. If I would've known, then…"

"I'm fine, Gram. Tom told me about the move when we had dinner last week. He couldn't pass up his dream job for a guy he just met, and we were better as friends anyway. We're going to keep in touch."

"You can always call Jagger to make you feel better," Gram said. I narrowed my eyes at Ava, hating that my Gram knew I occasionally hooked up with JJ.

Ava smirked. "We already thought of that." She giggled and leaned closer to Gram. "His heart wasn't in it. I think they ended up eating ice cream and cuddling."

I dropped my head into my hands. "I did get a foot rub out of it."

"It's for the best," Gram said. "I love JJ, but the two of you want very different things out of life."

"JJ and I will only ever be friends with occasional benefits. I love him, but I'm not *in love* with him. That ship sailed and sank when I was nineteen," I said, digging the heels of my palms into my eyes. "Sadly, I'll never have the guy I really want."

When my declaration was met with silence, I snapped my head up to find Gray standing behind Gram's chair. His smoldering blue eyes incinerated me on the spot.

"Never say never," my three lunch companions said simultaneously.

CHAPTER
Eighteen

Gray

I SAT IN THE EMPTY CHAIR BESIDE CHASE. I SMILED POLITELY AT THE ladies sitting across from me, who looked a little apprehensive about what I'd just overheard. I wished I hadn't heard it, but maybe it was the push I needed. Two major points stuck out in my mind.

First, Chase had a fuck buddy. I heard the word *occasional* come out of his mouth, but how infrequent? Once a week? Once a month? Once a year? I needed to know what I was up against because I didn't believe he could fuck the same person repeatedly and not form an emotional attachment.

Second, who was the guy he wanted but thought he couldn't have? Chase's wide eyes and pink cheeks had made me think he meant me. Or was that just more wishful thinking? Did he want me as badly as I wanted him? Did I star in his fantasies like he did in mine? What would I do if he was talking about me? How could I let him know I was ready and willing? Or should I do nothing at all?

Our knees bumped under the table, and just like that, I abandoned any thoughts of ignoring the possibility of a relationship with Chase. The simple, brief touch set me on fire. I looked over at Chase and saw the same shock in his soulful brown eyes.

The lips I'd dreamed about kissing were slightly parted, and a soft sigh escaped from them. I found myself unable to look away, wondering if his lips were as soft as they looked. My hands twitched in my lap with the need to touch them, my mouth watered at the idea of tasting them, and my dick lengthened. I saw his lips move, and I think they said my name, but my mind was still in the gutter. God, he made me want to live again.

"Gray." This time his voice penetrated my lust haze.

"Hmmm?"

"The waitress wants to know what you'd like to eat," he said.

"Oh, yeah." I looked away from Chase and gave the amused waitress my order. I looked across the table at Agnes and Ava and found them smiling at me. Great, I'd just made an ass of myself in front of Chase's grandmother and best friend. I needed to think fast to keep my mind from mentally undressing her grandson. "So, Agnes, how did you get started writing books?" That was all it took.

The four of us had an amazing lunch. It felt like I'd known the trio for a long time, and their love for one another was evident in every word or gesture.

Chase excused himself to use the restroom before we headed back to the office. As soon as he was out of earshot, Agnes leaned toward me.

"Do you have staying power?"

Unfortunately, I'd just taken a drink and nearly choked to death on it.

"Jesus, Aggie," Ava admonished. "You're asking about the man's stamina? That's bold, even for you."

She waved a hand at Ava and pinned me to my seat. "I don't mean that. Sexual prowess practically oozes from his pores." Chase's grandmother plowed full steam ahead. "I see the way you two look at each other, and I need to be sure Chase isn't going to get hurt again by another person who decides not to stick around."

"Agnes—"

"Call me Gram."

"Gram," I said, "I'm not sure Chase would appreciate me having this conversation with you before I talk to him."

"You're right. He wouldn't. I was out of line, and I apologize."

I leaned over so only she could hear. "Everything I hold dear is in DC. I'm not going anywhere." I leaned back in my chair and shot her a wink.

"Let's go, Ava." Gram stood quickly. "I just remembered I have a hair appointment." I rose from my chair as she came around the table and hugged me. "Chase can ride back to the office with you, right?" I failed to keep the smile from my face as I agreed to play along with her scheme. "Please tell my sweet boy I had to leave." She reached into her purse and started to pull out her wallet.

"I don't think so, Gram." I snatched the bill off the table before she could grab it. "It was so nice meeting you," I said, then dropped a kiss on her up-turned cheek. I turned to Ava and repeated the gesture. "It was lovely running into you again. I'd love to chat books with you some more."

"Absolutely," she said, squeezing my arm.

The two women linked arms and strolled across the restaurant—heads ducked together in deep conversation.

"Where'd Gram and Ava go?" Chase asked when he returned to the table a few moments later.

"Gram had a hair appointment, so Ava had to get her back." Chase narrowed his eyes. "No worries, though. I promised to give you a ride." I might have put extra emphasis on the last word because Chase blushed furiously. "Let's get out of here. The company I work for is run by a bunch of ballbusters."

I settled our bill before leading Chase to my car. The urge to open his door for him was overwhelming, but I refrained. This wasn't a date, and I needed to be very careful how I proceeded. Office romances were never a good idea, and the intensity of our attraction only made it harder. I knew without touching or tasting him that one night with Chase would never be enough for me. So before I did anything physical with him, I needed to know something deeper could develop between us.

"You think I look like Clark Kent, huh?" I glanced over and saw his face turn a pretty shade of pink.

"God, Gram and Ava are so embarrassing. I didn't know your name, and there might be a slight resemblance in the right light," he said dismissively. "Did Gram say anything to humiliate me while I was gone? I hadn't realized the stupidity of leaving you alone with her until it was too late. I'm so used to her antics I forget others might not be prepared to handle her."

"She was perfectly charming." He scoffed at my reply, making me smile. "Chase, can we talk about Devon?" He didn't say anything right away, so I glanced at him. He was watching me closely. "I want to clear the air so there are no more misunderstandings."

"Okay," he said softly, and I got a glimpse at the wounds his grandmother had mentioned. I wanted so badly to reach across the console and take his hand in mine.

"I don't blame you for what happened between Devon and me. You were an innocent victim. I'm sorry if I ever gave you the impression I was angry with you."

"How could you *not* be angry? I've been down that road, and all I felt was fury for a long time. Were you together long?"

"Five years."

Chase sucked in a sharp breath. "Oh my god."

"Hey." This time I did reach over and grab his hand. I ignored the zing vibrating up my arm and focused on easing his worry. "Chase, my relationship with Devon should have ended a long time ago. We stayed together for all the wrong reasons. If it hadn't been you, it would have been someone else. In fact, there were others before you." I released his hand so I could turn into the parking garage.

"Are you just saying that to make me feel better?"

"No, I'm not. I was furious he brought a man back to our house, but Devon's actions made it crystal clear we needed to cut ties and move on. I feel better than I have in a very long time." I looked over at him after I put the car in park. He was looking straight ahead, and I needed to see his eyes. I reached over and put my hand beneath his chin, turning his face in my direction. "Tell me what you're thinking."

"If you weren't angry at me, then why were you so hostile?"

I blew out a breath because I really needed to be careful what I said to him. I had to walk a fine line, but his eyes melted my resolve. I didn't lean into him like I wanted, but I let myself speak from my heart. "I was furious Devon found you first." A soft gasp escaped Chase's sweet lips, and his eyes widened. He shook his head slightly as if he didn't believe me. *Keep it clean.* "It's true. I got so lost in your eyes that it took me a minute to realize what Devon was doing. All weekend long I kicked myself for not chasing after you."

"But the following Monday you said you couldn't be around me."

"I know, and I realized my mistake as soon as you walked out my office door, but I was too much of a coward to do anything about it. I knew I had to make it right when I saw you at the bakery the following Saturday."

Chase blew out a frustrated breath, but before he could say anything, I continued. "Then I got…jealous."

"Jealous?" He sounded incredulous. "Of who?"

"The person who sent you the orchid and took you to lunch." A snarl might have darkened my voice, and Chase's face turned bright red. "Then I saw you in those fucking jeans and that damn leather jacket. I had to listen to Kayla or Carman, I don't remember which, go on and on about wanting to see you in your underwear. God, this is so not an appropriate conversation, Chase. You work for my company." I laid my head in my hands and let out a frustrated growl.

"Gray, I really like working here, and I need this job. I passed up a good opportunity at DC Designs to work for Wright Creations. I won't let myself be your rebound."

"You're not giving yourself enough credit, Chase."

"Regardless, I won't put myself in that situation. I'd like to think I'm learning from my mistakes."

A mistake. The verbal jab landed as solidly as a physical blow, and I rubbed my aching chest.

"I'm sorry," Chase said before exiting the car.

I sat with my feelings a little longer, trying to figure out my next step. Maybe Chase was right, and I should forget about my attraction. But it wasn't just *my attraction*. He was right there with me, and I knew it. I thought back to what Gram had said at lunch. She didn't want him to fall for another guy who wouldn't stick around.

Chase hadn't rejected me because he didn't want this too; he rejected me out of self-preservation. I glanced over in time to catch a glimpse of his face before the elevator closed. With his head down, I couldn't see his expression, but his body language screamed dejection.

Hell if I was giving up so easily.

100

CHAPTER
Nineteen

Chase

G RAY STOPPED BY MY DESK A FEW HOURS LATER, AND I LOOKED UP at him. I hoped my features were as neutral as his, but I somehow doubted it.

Gray smiled. It was small, but it helped ease the tension holding my body in its grip. "Preston wants to see us."

"Both of us?"

"Yes, but I don't know why."

"Um, would you like a cup of coffee first?"

"You know me so well already." The timid smile grew into one worthy of a toothpaste commercial. We could do this—work together and ignore the attraction. It would fade over time, and this would all be a distant memory. "I'd graciously accept your offer, but it sounded urgent."

"Oh," I said, grabbing my tablet and following Gray into his brother's office. The normally jovial and dapper Preston Wright had been replaced by a man who looked like he had stuck his finger in a light socket. His hair was sticking up all over, and his face was pinched with stress.

"Sit," Preston said and gestured to the chair next to Gray. I immediately dropped into the seat. "I'm not going to LA with you next week to pitch our final campaign to Heston's. Carly's due date has been moved up, and I'm not leaving her. I'm sending Chase in my place."

"Chase?"

"Me?"

Gray and I exchanged surprised looks before we refocused on Preston.

"Yes, Chase," Preston said to Gray. "Ben will be in Chicago, so Chase will need to go with you." Preston focused his attention on me. "You won't have to do a lot. Gray will do most of the presentation, but he'll need someone to assist him. This is your chance to prove yourself, Chase. If we can land the Heston's account, it would mean a promotion for you."

"I won't let you down," I promised him.

"I know you won't. Calls to your extension will be routed to Rosie." He turned to look at his brother. "She's going to pull double duty until you leave so you can prepare Chase for the meeting. I don't want either of you interrupted for the rest of the day. If you need to prep on Monday before you leave for the airport, then so be it. Are we all clear on what needs to be done?"

"Yes," Gray and I both said.

"Great. Get out of here and get to work."

I stood slowly and went back to my desk to grab the things I might need. Gray breezed by. "I'll be waiting in my office." My gaze got snagged on his fine ass, and I wondered how I was going to survive this challenge.

Rosie greeted me with a big hug once I got to Gray's office. "Congrats on the opportunity," she said sweetly. "Gray said for you to go straight in when you arrived."

"Thanks."

We reviewed the campaign for two and a half hours before calling it quits for the night. I wished Gray a good weekend and headed to my desk so I could retrieve my backpack and get changed for my shift at Bottoms

Up. By the time I finished, the same people from last time were waiting for the elevator.

As if he sensed I was near, Gray's head turned in my direction. He gave me another once-over, but this time his eyes returned to my chest and stayed there, widening when he saw the outline of my nipple ring through my snug shirt. Once I reached the group, Gray shifted his eyes up to meet mine. The lust I saw there sent me up in flames.

Kayla and Carman were talking, but I couldn't hear what they were saying over the pounding of my heart. Gray's lips started to move, and I snapped myself back to the present.

"No, I don't have plans," he said. What do you ladies have in mind?"

"We're checking out Bottoms Up tonight. You want to come with us?"

Say no. Say no.

"Sounds great," Gray said still looking at me.

I was so fucked. Friday nights were packed, and I couldn't allow myself to be distracted or my tips would suffer. The elevator arrived, and we all filed in. I remained quiet while the rest of them made plans to meet at the bar.

I arrived at Bottoms Up about thirty minutes later. Alex was behind the bar, but I didn't see Jack anywhere. I really needed to tell him about my business trip so he could make arrangements to cover my shifts.

"Hi, kid," Alex said. He was only a few years older than me, but he still called me kid.

"Hey, Alex."

"Jack is in the office interviewing a potential bartender. He wanted you to come see him as soon as you arrived."

"Okay." I headed straight back to Jack's office and rapped on the door a few times before opening it. "You wanted to see me?"

"Yep, come on in," came his gruff reply.

Jack Murphy looked up from his desk when I entered, and the slender guy with chestnut hair sitting in front of Jack's desk turned to face me. He smiled shyly, looking a little shell-shocked, but Jack had that impact on people.

I couldn't be positive of Jack's age, but I thought he was in his early to midthirties. He was bald by choice, which was a contrast to his dark eyebrows and light green eyes. He had the longest eyelashes I'd ever seen on a man, but I wisely refrained from comment.

Jack had spent a long time in the military, and I'd overheard some customers mention his tattoos looked like he'd served in the Special Forces. He never spoke about his service, except to say he'd known when it was time to get out.

"This is Liam. He's going to be working with us," Jack said. "I want you to show him the ropes tonight, okay?"

"Sure," I agreed, extending my hand to Liam. "It's nice to meet you," I said when he took it. "I need to talk to you about a scheduling conflict if you have the time," I said to Jack.

"Of course," he agreed. "Alex will get you started while you wait for Chase," Jack said to Liam.

"Okay." Liam rose. "Thanks for the opportunity." Jack only nodded in return. Liam turned to leave, and I got to see him from the front for the first time. He was really cute. Not my type but beautiful was beautiful. He was on the short side, maybe five foot seven, and lean. He wore his chestnut hair in a faux hawk, and his eyes were a pretty shade of hazel. He smiled shyly at me, and two adorable dimples popped out.

"I'll be right out," I told him, then turned back to Jack once the door shut behind Liam. The bar owner appeared to have forgotten I was in the room with him. He kept staring at the closed door for several long moments. "Jack?"

He looked at me as if I hadn't just caught him staring after his new hire. "Yeah?"

I told him about my unplanned work trip, and he didn't seem fazed by the change in schedule. "Don't worry about it. We'll cover for you. I hope this is the opportunity you've been waiting for, Chase." It was as touchy-feely as Jack got.

"Thanks, boss."

I went back out to the bar and got busy showing Liam around. He picked things up quickly, and I was confident he would be a great addition to the team. I was having such a fun time with Liam that I'd momentarily forgotten my Wright Creations coworkers would be popping by until I saw Carman waving at me from the opposite end of the bar. It didn't take me long to spot the rest of the gang. I saw Gray bent over the pool table lining up his shot, and I nearly dropped the pint glass I was pouring.

He broke perfectly and laughed while Ben groaned. Seeing Ben relaxed and having a good time was a surprise. I wondered if he was playing with one of our pool cues or the stick he kept shoved up his ass. I told myself to play nice and got busy serving drinks.

Carman and Kayla ogled Jack when he came out of the office to assist us because the bar had gotten too busy for Alex, Liam, and I to handle. Ben and Gray sat at the bar next to Carman and Kayla. I caught Ben sizing up the new bartender every time Liam checked to see if Ben wanted another beer. When Gray and the twins moved on to darts, Ben remained at the bar. *Wonderful.*

Next thing I knew, Ben was waving me over to him. "What do you know about him?" Ben asked. "Is he seeing anyone?"

I cocked my head to the side. "Now you want to be friends?"

Ben had the good grace to grimace. "Okay, maybe I've acted like an asshole."

"Maybe?"

Ben took a deep breath. "I shouldn't have judged you without knowing the full situation. I'm sorry." He extended his hand. "Truce?"

I smiled as we shook. "Truce." I turned to glance at Liam and noticed Ben wasn't the only one watching him. Several other patrons were vying for his attention, and Jack had his eagle eyes trained on him. I decided I wasn't playing matchmaker in this scenario.

"I don't really know much about him. He just started today," I answered honestly. "He seems like a really sweet guy, though."

"Mmm, I bet," Ben nearly purred.

I don't know where the thought came from, but I had the sudden urge to introduce Ben to Xavier if they hadn't already met through Ellie. Xavier was similar to Liam in looks and demeanor.

"Looks like I'm not the only one who likes what he sees," Ben said, nodding his head to where Jack was intercepting a rowdy patron. "He's been keeping a close eye on Liam all night, and I'm not sure I can compete with all that hotness," Ben joked. I smiled and patted him on the shoulder before walking away.

I felt Gray's eyes on me as I waited on patrons for the next hour, but every time I looked in his direction, he was busy talking to someone. Maybe it was just wishful thinking on my part. And why? Gray had put himself out there, and I had shut him down without really giving him a chance. Had I been wrong? Should I have stayed?

"Is that him?" a familiar voice asked.

I turned and smiled at JJ. "I'm so happy to see you."

"Are you avoiding my question?"

"No, counselor."

JJ cocked his head to the side. "No, you're not avoiding my question? Or, no, super nerd isn't the guy you're jonesing for?"

"Jonesing?"

"Hey, I was giving you my best moves the other night, and you didn't know I was there."

"Best moves?" I asked. "You rubbed my feet."

"Yeah, but I dug my thumb into your arches. That usually makes you moan and melt. I didn't get so much as a whimper out of you."

"Yeah, I was a little distracted."

"Because of him?"

I looked over at Gray and found him watching me through narrowed eyes. I refocused my attention on JJ. "Yeah."

"He wants you just as bad, so don't you dare give in to your fear."

"I'm afraid." I could admit it to JJ because he wrestled with his own demons.

"I know." He crooked his finger, and I leaned closer. JJ pressed his mouth to my ear. "Not everyone leaves."

I pulled back and stared into his eyes. He gave me an encouraging wink before leaving the bar.

CHAPTER
Twenty

Chase

GRAY WAS THE LAST PERSON I EXPECTED TO SEE WHEN I STEPPED OFF the elevator in my apartment building the next night. My heart raced faster walking down the corridor than it had when I'd been running on the treadmill.

"I come in peace," Gray said, throwing up his hands. "Can we talk?"

He wanted to talk? About work? About us? Though I knew I shouldn't hang my hat on the latter since I'd shot him down after he'd made himself vulnerable for me. JJ's encouragement echoed in my head and the seed of hope in my gut sprouted and unfurled.

"Please." Gray's voice cracked slightly, and I broke. I couldn't form words, so I simply nodded and led him to my apartment. "Thank you, Chase." The relief was evident in his voice.

I felt the heat radiating off his body when he stood behind me as I unlocked my door. I cleared my throat when I let us inside my apartment. "Would you like anything to drink?" I asked.

"No thank you."

"Okay. I'm just going to take a quick shower." Lust flared in his eyes, and my body responded in turn, which was a bad idea since all I was wearing was a thin pair of running shorts.

"Your tattoo is beautiful," Gray said softly. "There must be a story there."

"There is," I answered vaguely. "Remote is on the coffee table. Make yourself comfortable. I won't be long."

I didn't wait for a response, choosing to escape to the privacy of my bathroom. I showered quickly, trying not to think about Gray being in my apartment. My dirty mind conjured up a fantasy of him joining me in the shower. I forced away the images of him pressing me against the wall and ravishing my mouth. I refused to jerk off to fantasies of Gray while he sat in my living room.

I dressed in my favorite distressed jeans and a Baltimore Ravens T-shirt. I found Gray sitting on my couch, staring at a blank TV. His bouncing knees were the only part of him moving. If not for them, it would look like he was in a trance. I sat down beside him, and he looked over at me. His beautiful baby blues looked so solemn and remorseful. My heart rate tripled as I contemplated what he was going to say. He didn't make me wait long.

"I want to respect your wishes and ignore the connection I feel with you, but I..."

"You can't," I said.

Gray tilted his head. "Can you?"

I closed my eyes to block out the look of hopefulness on his face. I took a deep breath to settle my nerves, then met his gaze once more. "No."

Gray twisted his fingers together, and it was a few moments before he spoke again. "I saw you with your fuck buddy last night and kind of lost my shit. I—"

"How'd you know I was talking to JJ?"

Gray grinned crookedly. "It was the way he looked at you and the way your body responded to him. I've never been so jealous or wanted to hit someone so badly."

I felt my face shift into a scowl. "Gray, JJ—"

"No. It's okay. It gave me the incentive I needed to come over here," Gray said. "To tell you…I learned something recently."

"What?"

"I don't laugh enough, I work too hard, and I've been locked up inside myself for too long. Do you know who helped me realize those things?" I shook my head. "You."

"Me?"

"Since the moment I saw you, you've made me want to live again, to take chances, and most of all, you've made me want to laugh. I'm going to do my very best to earn you."

"Gray," I said on a sigh. "Working as close as we do will make navigating a relationship so much harder. How will we manage things if we break up?"

"There's no pressure to tell anyone at work what we're doing. We'll take the time to get to know each other and see where this leads," he told me. "I know you have a lot of responsibilities, but I'm hoping you'll spend some of your free time with me."

For once in my life, my heart, brain, and gut were all on the same page. All of me wanted to take a chance on Grayson Wright, but he was right about taking things slowly. "We'll need to have rules."

Gray perked up, his eyes turning vibrant with hope. "What kind of rules?"

"We remain professional at work at all times. No one in the office needs to know our business." I used my serious voice to make sure he was listening. His lips twitched, and I thought maybe I was being a little over the top. "I'm serious, Gray. No bathroom blow jobs, no grab-your-ankles nooners, and no conference room hand jobs. I mean it."

He swallowed hard, probably visualizing all the things I'd just mentioned. God knew I was. "Is that a permanent rule or just until we get to know each other better? I mean, my desk is really sturdy. And the things I could do to you on the table in the corner…"

"Gray," I warned.

"Okay, fine. Agreed. What else?" he asked.

"This can't be just about sex. I need to know I'm more to you than a quick fuck." Gray narrowed his eyes but didn't interrupt me. "No hooking up with anyone else."

"No fuck buddies either," Gray fired back at me.

"It's already over," I replied. "I won't be calling him for sex again, but he's still one of my closest friends." I pointed my finger at Gray. "You need to accept that."

"Wait a minute. How would you feel if Devon and I started hanging out again?" My stomach churned with nausea at the thought. "I see you wouldn't be a fan," he added after seeing my reaction.

"It's not the same thing. JJ and I dated for like five minutes when we were freshmen in college. Since then we've been friends more than anything else. You're picturing a weekly fuckfest, but in reality, I've gone years without having sex with him. You and Devon dated for five years and lived together, so that's hardly a fair comparison." Gray's skepticism was plain to see, but I held my ground. "I am all JJ has, and I will not turn my back on him. He stays, or we can't do this."

Gray's nostrils flared like a bull's, and I wasn't sure if it was from anger or lust. "And you've fucked on and off for six years or longer. It's going to take me some time to accept." His eyes softened and his voice lowered seductively. "But for you, I'll try."

"Thank you." Before I could talk myself out of it, I leaned forward and pressed my lips to his. They were firm and warm and everything I imagined them to be. My flesh tingled where it touched his and delicious heat unfurled in my core, spreading throughout my body. Gray didn't try to deepen the kiss or push for more, but his mouth parted and his breath ghosted over my lips, teasing and tempting me. I didn't want to pull back from his lips, but I did. I was serious when I said I needed to be more to him. He groaned when I pulled away, and he kept his eyes closed for a few heartbeats.

"We covered office behavior, hookups, and fuck buddies. Is there anything else you want to hash out? Maybe you want to tell me what I can and can't do? Do we need to go on a certain number of dates before I can really kiss you? And how long before you'll let me tug on your nipple ring with my teeth?"

I was about to combust right there on my sofa, but I needed to stay focused and not launch myself onto his lap and rip my shirt off over my head. "I haven't given it much thought. It's not like I was planning to have this conversation today or any day, really. Can I have time to think about it?"

"Sure," he readily agreed. "Can I begin wooing you tonight or do you have to work?"

"Wooing? Have you been reading one of Gram's historical novels?"

Gray blushed. He was so fucking adorable. "Maybe." He cleared his throat. "About tonight…"

"I'm free. What did you have in mind?"

"I want you to pick," Gray told me. "I'm up for anything."

"Bowling and burgers." It was the first thing that popped into my mind. "If you beat me, you'll get a real kiss. With tongue." I batted my eyelashes playfully and smiled like the cat who ate the canary.

"You're on."

CHAPTER
Twenty-One

Gray

"QUIT FONDLING THE BALLS AND GET OVER HERE. I'M READY TO play," Chase said.

I turned around to find him looking over his shoulder at me. His ornery grin and innuendo made it obvious the night was going to be a test of my will power. I decided to play along. "I'm looking for the right size hole. I have a really big…thumb." Chase's eyes widened slightly before they traveled down my body to study my package. *If he wanted proof…* I cut myself off before I finished the thought.

I sorted through the balls until I found one that fit my fingers comfortably. I turned to go back to our lane, lucky number seven, but my feet froze, and I nearly swallowed my tongue. Chase was swaying to an upbeat song I'd never heard before while he programmed our names into the computer. His moves were simple and not meant to seduce, but fuck if I wasn't ensnared by the motion. He had such natural grace, moving his hips slowly to the beat.

I walked over and *thunked* my ball down on the ball return. I came up behind him and wrapped my arms around his waist. "New rule," I whispered in his ear. I placed a chaste kiss on the back of his neck, and I felt his body tremble against mine. "No dancing if you expect me to behave." I kissed his neck one last time and slowly stepped away. I looked up at the monitor, saw he'd typed in the names Clark Kent and Jimmy Olsen as the players, and burst into laughter.

"What?" he asked incredulously. "You expected me to be Lois Lane?"

He only made me laugh harder and soon he was laughing too. "You really are good for me, Chase," I told him when we both settled down. I caressed his cheek, and he melted me with the warmth in his brown eyes. I had to tell myself to behave over and over. "Looks like I'm up first," I said, putting some distance between us.

I retrieved my ball and pushed the button on the computer monitor to start the game. I stepped up onto the platform and got into position to throw the ball. Just as I was about to move, the children's bumpers popped up along the gutters. Chase started laughing behind me. I pivoted and found him snapping a picture of me with his phone.

"If you want to kiss me so badly, then do it, Chase." His smile showed off his adorable dimples. "There's no need for subterfuge."

"You're going to need all the help you can get, blue eyes."

"Really?" I loved a good challenge, but they brought out both the best and worst in me. "Okay." I took position in the center of the lane, went through my wind up, and let the ball sail down the lane. I walked backward and watched as the ball knocked down all ten pins with a resounding crash. "Yesssss," I said, pumping my fist in the air. "You're up, brown eyes."

Chase smiled mischievously as he walked by to pick up his bowling ball. I tried not to drool as I stared at his long legs and taut ass. I heard the pins fall, but I didn't look to see how many were down because it would've required me to look away from his perfect body. But the victory shimmy Chase performed told me all I needed to know. His bright smile almost had me lunging for him—consequences be damned.

I'd traveled all over the world with my friends and later with Devon.

I'd been to the most romantic places, eaten the most delicious foods, but I knew all those things would pale in comparison to bowling and burgers with Chase. I had to win so I could taste his mouth. I hoped it would be enough to tide me over until the next time. And there would be a next time.

Chase was an excellent bowler, and it came down to the final frame of the last game to determine the winner. We had decided on best out of five games because we were having so much fun. I had never tried so hard to win something in my life, but I did it. If I were being honest, it seemed like Chase might have let me win, but I wasn't about to cry foul. Hell no. I was going to claim my victory kiss. I pulled him beside me and took a selfie of us together. I was grinning like an idiot because I knew I was getting my kiss.

I'd learned a lot about Chase as we'd played, and I'd rediscovered just as much about myself. We both loved to read. We had similar taste in music, although his taste was a lot more eclectic than mine. Chase preferred TV series over movies because he said you got to know the characters better whereas the time was limited in a movie. I preferred movies because I didn't like a story to be drawn out episode after episode versus resolved in two hours.

"Are you ready to eat?" I asked him after we'd returned our shoes.

"Famished. You really need to feed me, or I might not last long enough for you to kiss me at the end of the night."

I held open the door for him, and we exited into the cool night air. "I could kiss you right now to make sure I get my victory kiss."

"Nope, feed me first." Chase reached over and took my hand as we walked to my car. I loved the feel of his flesh pressing against mine and was shocked such a simple gesture from him could make my heart race. I wasn't one to snuggle, cuddle, or engage in PDA, but he made me want those things. I was in danger of making a complete fool of myself over him.

"I was thinking Louie's Diner. Is that okay with you?"

"Mmmm," Chase moaned. "It's my favorite place to eat. I love the '50s retro feel."

"The food is great." I opened his door for him, and he kissed me on the cheek before climbing inside. How in the hell was he still single? I didn't skip around to my side of the car, but I was embarrassingly close. "Can I ask you about your tattoo, or is its significance too personal?" I had seen heartbeat tattoos before, but his was different because of the cursive script beneath it. He didn't say anything until I'd pulled out of the parking lot, and I was afraid I'd ruined our date.

"It's in memory of my mom," he said softly. I reached across the console and held his hand. "I was really little when she died of cancer. She wrote a bunch of letters and poems so Gram could give them to me. Toward the end of her life, she wrote me a poem titled *Through You, I Will Live.* My favorite line said 'Though my heart will soon stop beating, I fear not, my darling boy. Through you, I will live.' Those lines got me through some of the hardest times of my life, so I had it tattooed on my body before leaving for college. The tattoo artist photocopied the line from the poem and transferred it onto my chest so it looks like my mom wrote it across my heart."

Chase rendered me completely speechless. Tears burned the back of my eyes, and I blinked rapidly to keep them from falling. "Wow," I finally said around the lump in my throat. I cleared my throat and blew out an emotional breath. "That's the most beautiful thing I've ever heard. I can't imagine how she felt when she wrote those words to you." I squeezed his hand, then lifted it to my mouth for a kiss. "It's no wonder you're so special."

"I'm not," Chase said shyly. He tried to pull his hand away, but I wouldn't give it up.

"I'm going to make sure you see what everyone else sees when they look at you."

A frustrated sigh escaped his lips. "They see my face but not who I am."

I pulled into a parking spot at Louie's and put my car into park. I turned in my seat slightly so I could see him better. I needed him to see me and really hear what I wanted to say. "Look at me, Chase." My voice was firm but not mean. He looked surprised by my tone, but it got his attention. "You're a beautiful man, brown eyes. When you smile at me, it takes my breath away." Chase's jaw tensed, telling me the compliment hadn't landed well. Someday I would find out why. "There's so much more to you than your gorgeous face and pretty smile, though. You radiate kindness, Chase. You love with everything you have, and it's a beautiful gift." I didn't tell him how I'd hoped to be on the receiving end of his devoted affection one day.

"Gray, you…"

"Shh," I said and covered his mouth with my hand. "Don't tell me how to feel or what to think about you. You'll believe me someday, and I'm willing to wait patiently." I felt a small smile beneath my hand. "Now let's go eat. Beating your ass at bowling really worked up my appetite."

"Beat my ass? You won by five pins," he said as he climbed from the car.

I walked around the car and stood in front of him. The lights from the diner lit up his beautiful face, and his eyes were alive with playfulness. "How often do you lose?"

He cocked his head to the side as if he had to think about it long and hard. I had something long and hard he could ponder. "Actually, I don't think I've lost since my junior year of high school when I lost in the state finals."

"State finals?"

"Yep, I was on my high school bowling team. I won the state championship my senior year. I'm sure Gram still has the trophy somewhere." Chase reached for my hand once more as we made our way across the parking lot.

"Did you let me win?" I asked suspiciously. I dropped his hand to open the door for him. "If you wanted to kiss me so badly, you could've just done it."

We approached the hostess, and he scoffed. I placed my hand at the small of his back and felt a shiver roll through him. "I'd never blow a game for just a kiss," he said over his shoulder.

I leaned forward until my mouth was against his ear. "Just a kiss? You think that's all there is at stake here? Just a kiss?" He turned his head to the side so my lips pressed against his cheek.

"What else is at stake?"

"Hi, guys," the teenage hostess said, breaking our connection. She was wearing the retro, pastel sweater set and poodle skirt all Louie's female employees wore. "Just two of you tonight?" Chase confirmed it would just be us. "Follow me," she said and pivoted on her shiny saddle shoes. Her ponytail bounced and swayed as she led us to a booth in the corner. "Liam will be your server tonight. Enjoy." She gave us a bright smile before returning to her station.

Chase looked pointedly at me. "You were saying…"

"Hey, Chase."

I looked up at the interruption and found Liam, the new bartender from Bottoms Up, standing at our table. He was wearing the male version of the retro uniform, which was black pants rolled up at the bottom, a white T-shirt, and a white-and-red letterman's sweater. There was something oddly familiar about him, but I couldn't put my finger on it.

"Hi, Liam. How's it going?" Liam looked back and forth between Chase and me. "Oh, this is my friend, Grayson," Chase told him.

"Call me Gray," I told Liam, and he smiled shyly. "Busy night?"

"It's been crazy," he answered. "It's finally slowed down a bit. I'd rather be earning tips at Bottoms Up, but for now I have to work both jobs. I hope it doesn't cause too many problems for Jack."

"He's used to juggling schedules," Chase told him. "He works around my three jobs, so he's used to it. Just give him as much notice as you can if you need to make a change. There's usually someone willing to step in and pick up an extra shift."

"Good to know," Liam said, nodding. "Three jobs, though? That's brutal."

"My roommate is getting married in a few months, so I'm saving up in case I can't find a new one right away. I don't want to settle for just anyone."

"Makes sense. Do you guys know what you want to order, or do you need a minute?" Liam asked.

"I know what I want," I said, looking into Chase's eyes. He narrowed his eyes at me in admonishment, but his crooked smile ruined the effect. "Do you know what you want, Chase?"

"Yes, actually." He looked up and smiled innocently at Liam. "I'll have a bacon cheeseburger with no onions, fries, and a strawberry milkshake."

"I'll have the same, except I'd like a chocolate milkshake."

"Great," Liam said as he took our menus. "I'll put your order in right now. It should be ready soon."

"This won't be just a kiss, Chase," I told him as soon as Liam left our table. "It will set the tone for us."

"Set the tone?" Chase snickered for a second. "Wait a minute. Are you being serious right now?"

"As a heart attack." It had been five years since my last *first kiss*, and I didn't want to screw it up. "What if I give you too much tongue and gross you out?" Chase started laughing at me, and I would have been offended if it wasn't so damn cute. "Would you stop laughing at me?"

"I'm laughing near you, not at you," he clarified. "If you only knew..."

"Here's some water while you wait." Liam had horrible timing. He placed the glasses on the table, but neither of us acknowledged him. My attention was focused solely on the man sitting across from me, and Chase was focused just as intently on me. "Your food should be right out," he said before leaving.

"Knew what?" I asked. "And answer quickly before someone interrupts us again."

Chase aimed his sexy, crooked smile my way and leaned over the table. I met him in the middle, and he pressed his lips against my ear. The feel of his breath on my flesh sent shivers down my spine. "How often I thought about kissing your lips. Among other things."

"Chase." I dropped my gaze to his lips. Right then, I forgot where we were and our agreement to take things slow. I was going to get my victory kiss, and I was going to get it now. I cupped my hand around the back of his neck and inched my mouth closer to his until I felt his breath on my lips. I licked mine to moisten them, then...

"Here you go, guys," Liam said. "Hot off the grill." Chase and I jerked away from each other, and Liam set our food on the table in front of us. Once again, we continued to gaze into each other's eyes instead of acknowledging the waiter. Liam chuckled. "Enjoy. I'll check back later."

Neither of us made a move to eat our food. Our eyes remained locked on one another, both of us thinking about the kiss we'd almost shared. I needed to get my head in the game, the one on my shoulders, not the one between my legs.

"We should eat while it's still hot," I said. "I hate cold fries."

"Me too." But neither of us reached for our food. "I haven't eaten since this morning, and I'm starving."

"Dig in," I said, breaking eye contact to look down at my plate. Hearing how hungry he was gave me the kick in the ass I needed to focus on his needs and ignore my own. "I want you alert when I plant one on you." I looked up to smile at him, but my gaze got stuck on his pretty lips wrapped around his straw. His cheeks hollowed out as he sucked hard. I nearly broke out in a sweat. His lips released it with a pop, and his pink tongue darted out to lick his lips. I knew he'd been vamping it up for me when I saw those sexy lips spread into a cocky grin. "Damn tease," I mumbled.

He chuckled at my misery for a minute. "Tell me about your family. I've told you almost everything, but I hardly know anything about you."

"Fair enough," I agreed. In between bites of delicious food I told him all about my family dynamics.

"Wow, your mom must be an incredible woman."

"She's the best. It wasn't easy for her, and there was a lot of tension for a long time, especially after Dad and Jeff got serious," I said.

"Understandable. How'd you and Preston take the news?"

"Pres took it hard at first because no kid wants to be singled out for that kind of thing. My reaction was different." I took a deep breath. "I know a lot of people look at him and judge him harshly, accusing him of ruining my mom's life, but Dad's my hero. He paved the path for me. Until he openly started dating Jeff, I thought I was the only gay person in my family—hell in my entire inner circle. I wanted to be normal like everyone else. I didn't want to be gay."

"Normal," Chase said with derision. "I hate when people apply that word to someone's sexuality."

"I know better now, but at the time, I was a confused teenager. I did what other *normal* boys did and fought to date the hottest girl in school. When I won her affection, I didn't know what the fuck to do with her. Kissing and touching her felt all wrong, but so did admitting out loud that I was gay. She thought I hung the moon and was a real gentleman, but the truth was I really wanted her older brother. I never went past second base with her. My dad recognized what I was going through, and he said it was the reason he came out to my mom. He wanted to set a better example for me." My voice broke slightly, and I cleared my throat. "God, can you imagine how hard that was for him? It was a horrible time for both my parents, but I'd never been so proud of my dad. He saved me from a life of misery, Chase."

"Wow," he said softly. "I always knew I was lucky to have Gram, but it's sometimes really easy to forget everyone doesn't live with that kind of openness."

"Do you want to tell me about it?"

"Not tonight. It's too heavy, and I feel like I've ruined our fun." His brow was furrowed in worry.

"Hey, you haven't ruined anything, and I feel so much better now that I told you. You weren't a dick to me at all. I'm really sorry I brought up painful memories for you in the process of airing my dirty laundry. If anyone ruined our date, it was me."

"Gray, you didn't ruin—"

"You guys all finished?" Overeager Liam was getting on my last nerve.

"Uh, yeah," I said and leaned back so he could clear our plates away. He placed our bill on the table before he started to gather our dirty dishes. "Have a nice night. Sounds like I won't be seeing you until Friday," Liam said to Chase. His disappointment was obvious, and I narrowed my eyes and assessed the level of threat.

"Yep," Chase said casually. "Gray and I are going to LA for a few days." I liked that he hadn't clarified the travel was for business.

"Great. Well, you guys have fun." There was no sincerity in his voice, which puzzled me a bit. He left without another word, and I raised my eyebrow at Chase in question. He just shrugged.

"Have you known him long?" I asked as we made our way to the cashier. Chase tried to take the bill from me, but I slapped his hand away.

"I just met him last night," Chase told me. "He seems like a really sweet guy. He looks a little lost sometimes, and there's sadness in his eyes and smile at times like he's seen a lot more than a person his age should."

I swiped my card through the machine and added a tip for Liam before signing my name. The tip I wanted to give was verbal, but I left it alone. It was obvious Chase didn't have any romantic feelings for the kid, so I wouldn't get my undies in a twist.

"Are you going to write our date off as a business expense?" Chase teased once we were in the parking lot. I reached over and pinched his ass hard. "Ouch," he hissed out between his teeth. "Okay, those jokes are off-limits too."

"Damn straight," I said as I opened his door for him. He turned to look at me over the door instead of getting in the car.

"I'm a sucker for impeccable manners. They make me all gooey inside."

"Good to know," I said casually while my heart thumped out of control. Neither of us said much on the trip back to Chase's apartment. I was too focused on the coming kiss, and I figured Chase was too. I wasn't as nervous as I'd been before, but I still had concerns. Too much tongue, wrong angle, bumping noses, my glasses getting in the way, or scraping teeth. I wanted an epic movie kiss. "I'm going to walk you to your door and kiss you good-night like a proper gentleman," I said after I pulled up in front of his building.

"You're not coming in?" he asked, a slight pout pulling at his lips. I took his disappointment as a good sign. I needed Chase to want me as badly as I wanted him.

"Not tonight." He nodded.

I rode with him up to his floor, my pulse hammering in my veins the entire time. Anticipation replaced my nerves with every step I took toward his apartment door. I crowded Chase against it when we arrived. "I won fair and square, and I'm claiming my kiss." I pressed my body against his until there was no space between us. He sucked in a shaky breath when he felt how badly I wanted him. I wasn't embarrassed. In fact, I wanted him to know what he did to me. "Kiss me right here. If not, I'll still be in your bed when the sun comes up tomorrow morning."

"Gray," he whispered huskily while staring at my lips. "Kiss me." I cupped his head in my hands and angled his head slightly to the side. "Please."

I pressed my lips firmly against his, giving us what we had both wanted since the first time we'd seen each other. His breath came out raggedly through his nose as I gave him several chaste kisses before sliding my tongue along his lips. He parted for me instantly, and I slid my tongue into his hot, wet mouth.

My fingers clutched his hair tighter when I slid my tongue teasingly over his several times before curling it around his and kissing him with everything I had. I didn't just caress him with my lips and tongue; I put my entire heart and soul into it. His hands slid into my hair, and he pressed his lips harder against mine, his tongue challenging mine for dominance. Chase sucked on my tongue and my hips bucked forward. Holy fuck, I was in big trouble. I returned the favor, and he thrust his erection against mine.

"Get ya some," a woman said and followed it up with a catcall as she walked down the hallway.

Chase and I jerked apart, both shocked our kiss had gotten that intense so quickly. "Come inside," he whispered huskily. The naked need in his eyes was almost enough to have me going back on my word. *Almost.*

"I can't wait to hear you say those words to me when you're spread and pinned beneath me with my dick buried balls-deep inside you, Chase."

"Fuck, Gray."

"We'll get there, brown eyes, but not tonight." I gave him one last peck on his lips before I stepped back, removing myself from temptation. "Can I call you tomorrow night?"

"Please."

"Dream of me," I told him as I started to back away.

"That's a given," he replied, adjusting himself.

"Go inside right now, Chase. I promised to be good, and you have to do your part."

"Spoilsport," he said, but he did as I asked.

I waited until he was out of sight before I began walking away again. My unsatisfied dick ached, and my body vibrated with need, but I couldn't remember ever feeling this happy. I whistled to myself as I made my way to my car. My phone rang, and I pulled it out of my pocket.

"Hey, bro."

"It's time," he said frantically into the phone. "Carly's water broke, and we're on our way to the hospital right now."

"Yes!" I shouted into the night air. "What can I do, Pres?"

"Get your ass to the hospital because the contractions are close and getting closer. I need my brother."

"I'm heading there right now. I can't wait to meet our new princess. Love you, Pres."

"Love you too."

Could my night get any better?

CHAPTER
Twenty-Two

Chase

T HE SEXUAL TENSION IN FIRST CLASS SEATS 10A AND 10B WAS through the fucking roof. I had to keep reminding myself we were going on a business trip and not a romantic getaway, but Gray made behaving so damn difficult. One little smile, small touch, or even the sound of his voice made me want to throw him down and risk it all.

He was the kind of man I'd been waiting for my whole life. I loved his quick wit, his keen intelligence, and the mix of gentleness and aggression I'd seen in him. He'd been hell-bent on beating me at bowling, and I'd been hell-bent on making him work harder for our first kiss. I'd found his competitiveness sexy, and it had distracted me enough that he'd won the final game. My god, could the man kiss. If he could affect me so much with just his lips, what would it be like when I finally had him inside me?

"Are you ready?" his deep voice said in my ear. *God, yes!*

"For what, the mile high club?" Yeah, I went there.

"Don't play with me, Chase. It's all I can do to keep my hands to myself."

"Sorry." *Not sorry.*

"I hate flying," Gray confessed. "Fucking you in the bathroom would be a great diversion. Since the option isn't available, I need you to talk to me and keep me distracted."

Our hands rested on the armrests between us. I wanted to hold his hand, but I wasn't sure he'd appreciate the gesture. Instead, I lightly rubbed my pinky over the back of his hand. The fire zipping through my veins was completely ridiculous and also frightening. "Show me pictures of Grace," I told him.

"My princess," he said wistfully. Gray pulled out his cellphone and showed me at least two dozen pictures of his brand-new niece. He was completely in love with her, and it gave me insight into the kind of father he would be someday.

"That's my favorite so far," I told him, and he stopped thumbing through them. It was the most beautiful thing I'd ever seen. Gray was balancing Grace in his strong hands in front of him while he kissed her forehead. "Stunning." My heart was stuck in my throat because the picture made me want things with him, and it scared me. It was too soon. Gray leaned over and kissed me softly on the cheek before he started showing me more pictures. "Oh, that one," I said. It was a similar pose, but this time he was kissing her dainty little fist.

"She has the tiniest feet and hands I've ever seen. God, you should see all her hair. They wouldn't let me take pictures without her hat on because she'd get too cold."

"You are so smitten, and it's so adorable," I told him. "I'm so glad you called and shared your excitement with me."

"I'm sorry for waking you up in the middle of the night. I just had to tell you all about her." Gray let out a big yawn.

"Why don't you close your eyes and try to sleep. You must be exhausted."

"I can't sleep on these death traps," he said right as a flight attendant walked by. She gave him a comforting pat as she went. "Talk to me, Chase.

Tell me about Sunday dinner with Gram and Ava. That should keep me entertained for the entire flight."

I couldn't help but laugh at how well Gray had Ava and Gram pegged already. I was willing to tell him some of the things we'd discussed but not all. "Gram finally picked the book cover she wanted for her new series, *Brothers in Blue*. It's a cop spin-off series from…"

"I can't wait to read it. I think I might know who the main characters are already."

"If you're a really good boy, I bet Gram would give you an advanced copy. She'd probably even sign it for you." He clapped his hands happily and it was just one more thing I found endearing about him. "Ava and I finalized her prewedding events down to the tiniest details. I feel so much better about everything now."

What I didn't tell Gray was that Gram had told me to pounce on Gray and ride him like a horse. Hand to god, I'd nearly choked to death on a potato. I also left out the part where she told me to pack plenty of condoms and lube, which I told her wouldn't be necessary. I told Gram we were going on a business trip not a fuckfest getaway. Gram and Ava had both laughed hysterically.

"If only you could see the way that boy looks at you," Gram had said.

"And how you look at him in return," Ava added.

"I think Gram is in love with Lennie," I said to Gray. "I'd noticed Gram had toned down her outfits lately and commented on it. She confessed Lennie had been getting in altercations lately defending her honor and she felt bad. That's a very big deal," I told Gray.

"How do you feel about it?"

"I think Lennie is really good for her, and she seems happier than I've seen her since my grandpa passed away. She's the most amazing woman I know, and I want her to be this happy all the time."

We talked back and forth for the rest of the flight. It was so odd because I never ran out of things to talk to Gray about, and I can honestly say that's only happened with a few people. It seemed like only a few minutes had passed when our plane touched down at LAX. We gathered our luggage and met our car service out front. Checking in at Heston's was always a pleasant experience. Their well-trained, friendly staff was the best benefit of staying at their hotels. When I'd booked the reservation, Gray and Preston were going to be making the trip, so I'd booked them a large suite with two bedrooms, which seemed appropriate. I was feeling uncertain about us sharing a hotel suite, regardless of how large it was or how many bedrooms there were.

"Relax," Gray said quietly once we were in the elevator. "It's going to be okay." I forgot all about my nerves when I saw the most amazing view of the Pacific Ocean. I heard Gray talking to the bellhop and thanking him for his assistance, but all my attention was on the water. "Let's go outside and check it out," Gray said in my ear. I hadn't realized he'd approached me until he spoke. He put his hand on the small of my back and ushered me to the oversized sliding doors.

"It's so beautiful," I said, then tilted my head back to enjoy the sun and breeze on my face.

"Mmm, I agree." I turned to look at him, but he wasn't looking at the ocean. Gray was looking at me. He broke his gaze after several moments and looked around. "A private hot tub," he said, turning back to look at me. He waggled his eyebrows, and I laughed.

"Business trip," I said in a singsong voice.

"Business starts tomorrow," he reminded me. "Tonight is for us." I swallowed hard because the look in his eyes did funny things to my insides. Was I ready for that step? "Will you go on a date with me tonight?" I nodded. "It's my turn to pick." He winked, then checked his watch. "Can you be ready in an hour?" Gray started backing away from me, a devilish look on his face. My ability to speak seemed to vanish, so I nodded again. "I'm going to take a shower and wash away the airplane germs. I'll take the bedroom on the right."

"Okay." My voice sounded thick and untried. I cleared my throat. "I'll be ready." Gray turned away and headed inside. I didn't follow right away because I wanted to take in the view a little longer.

"Don't jack off," Gray demanded from somewhere inside the suite.

Holy shit. I hadn't thought about jacking off until Gray forbade it. I pictured him wet and naked in the shower in the next room over, and my dick lengthened in response. I thought about ignoring his demand and told myself he wouldn't know, but in the end, I just took a cold shower.

Gray didn't tell me where he was taking me, but I figured it would be casual. I chose comfort over style and put on my favorite pair of khaki cargo shorts and a Georgetown T-shirt. I smiled when I returned to the living room and found Gray dressed just as casually. He wore faded jeans that hugged his body like a glove, a National's tee, and a pair of flip flops. Even his feet were sexy.

"Do you like seafood?" he asked as he approached.

"Love it."

"Great." Gray took my hand as we left our suite. I tried not to act like a smitten schoolboy when he kept holding my hand as we walked through the lobby. "Does this make you uncomfortable?"

"Not at all. I like it." I bumped his shoulder with mine. "Where are we going?"

"A seafood restaurant down the street. They serve the freshest fish I've ever had. I thought we could go to the amusement park on the boardwalk afterward."

"That sounds perfect." We walked down the street to a restaurant called Alexander's. The aromas wafting from the place had my mouth watering when we were still a block away. "Mmmm."

"Please don't make that sound, Chase. You're making me hungry for you instead of dinner."

"I'll try harder to behave." Gray's wry smile called my bluff.

The hostess greeted us and showed us to an open table on the veranda. It was early for dinner by California standards, but Gray and I were still on East Coast time. We looked over the menu and decided to get an order of smoked oysters and fried clams for an appetizer. Neither of us said much, choosing to sit in comfortable silence and look at the amazing view instead. I heard the sounds of the amusement park farther down the beach.

"Here are your beers and appetizers," our waitress, Cami, said. "Are you ready to order your entrees yet?"

"I'm ready. Are you ready, Gray?"

"I'm absolutely ready," he replied. I didn't miss the wicked gleam in his eyes. Cami was oblivious to the sexual tension radiating between us, or she was choosing to ignore it. "I'll have the lobster trio with butter. Lots of butter."

"And for you, sir?" she asked turning to me.

"I'd like the seared halibut, steamed veggies, and rice."

"Wonderful choice. I'll get your orders in. Enjoy your appetizers." She threw an extra smile my direction.

"I think Cami likes you," Gray teased.

"Stop it. Eat your food." There were six small white bowls with glass domes on top to hold in the smoke. I scooted a bowl to me, lifted the dome, and inhaled the smoke from inside. I tipped back the little bowl and swallowed the oyster down. "Oh god. So good." The smoky, salty flavor lingered on my tongue.

"You make everything sound sexual." Gray was staring at me and ignoring his food. "You've made me so hard I could go out there and spear a fish." The absurdity of his statement made me laugh. "I'm not kidding." His tone only made me laugh harder.

"Gray, you must be sexually repressed if a little 'Mmm, so good' gives you a hard-on."

"Honestly, it's been a pretty long dry spell." I found that hard to believe. He had been in a relationship, one he admitted had gone bad a long time ago, but weren't they still having sex? I wasn't about to ask something so personal, and I wasn't sure I really wanted to know. "I told you things had been really bad for a while, and I wasn't exaggerating."

"I'm really sorry, Gray. You deserve better."

"Devon did too. We were wrong for each other, and we were either too lazy or too stubborn to make a change. I haven't decided which, and it really doesn't matter now."

"You're handling your breakup far better than I've dealt with any of my own."

"Are you ready to talk about it?"

I was but not when we were sitting by the ocean on a dream date. "When we get back to DC. I don't want to tarnish our time here."

"When you're ready," Gray said softly. I wanted to lean across the table and kiss him so badly, but I held back. I must have given away my longing because he reached over and traced my lips with his thumb. "Soon, Chase." I nipped his thumb softly, and he sucked in a shaky breath. "Damn you." The smile on his face took the sting out of his words.

"I'm not as nice as you think I am," I teased. He swallowed hard and fidgeted in his chair, so I took pity on him…for a second. "Eat, Gray." I pointed to his plate with my fork. "You might need your strength."

"Yeah?" His voiced lowered sexily.

"Ohhh yeah," I lowered my voice to match his and leaned across the table. "I've always wanted a boy to win me a stuffed animal from one of those carnival games. I'll let you pick the game."

"You're on." He dug into his food with gusto.

"Can you just roll me down to the boardwalk?" I asked forty minutes later. "I ate way too much."

"You didn't save room for cotton candy or ice cream? We can't go to the amusement park and skip those things. It's tradition."

"I could force myself to share ice cream with you," I told him. The image of Gray's tongue swirling around the tip of an ice cream cone came to mind. Everything he did seemed sexual. Which reminded me, "I don't want you talking anymore about the noises I make when I eat. The way you licked the butter from your fingers was nearly pornographic."

Gray snickered and squeezed my hand harder. "Liked that, did you?"

"You damn well know I did. You're going to pay for that later."

"Promises, promises," he said as we approached the ticket booth. I shoved him out of the way when he went for his wallet.

"I got the tickets. You need to save your cash in case it takes you a long time to win my stuffed animal. I'll even buy the ice cream." I could tell he didn't want me to pay, but he put his wallet back in his pants and waited until I handed him his ticket.

"Thank you," he said and gave me a quick kiss. "What do you want to do first?"

"No rides yet. I'm too full, and I want to ride the Ferris wheel around sunset."

"That's really romantic," Gray told me. "Being raised by a romance writer must have rubbed off on you."

"I have my moments." The wind picked up, and my senses were overwhelmed with the smell of peanuts, popcorn, cotton candy, and saltwater taffy. "Show me everything," I told him.

Gray took me to all his favorite attractions, including the photo booth where we spent most of our time kissing. We tore the picture strip in half so each of us got three pictures. We rode all the rides, saving the Ferris wheel for last. He timed it perfectly because the sun was just setting over the Pacific as we crested the top. Our car stopped at the top and swayed in the ocean breeze as people got off the ride below.

"Gray."

"Hmm?" He turned to look at me, and I could tell he was enjoying this moment as much as I was.

"Thank you for tonight. It's been the best date I've ever had." I leaned over and kissed him gently on the lips. A pitiful whimper escaped when we pulled apart.

"Our night is just getting started, brown eyes." One last peck on my lips and he looked back at the sunset.

What did he mean by that? Was there more excitement to come at the amusement park? Was he referring to things getting more intimate between us when we got back to the hotel, and if so, how did I feel about that?

"You're thinking so hard I can hear it," Gray said as our car came to a stop at the very bottom. He bumped shoulders with me playfully while the park employee unlocked our door. "We're taking this at your pace, Chase. You're in the driver's seat, okay? I will wait as long as you want."

"God, you make it sound like I'm some frightened virgin, Gray."

"Hey," he grabbed my hand and pulled me to him. "That's not my intention at all. I'm trying to show you the respect you deserve while earning your trust." Gray placed his hand firmly beneath my chin and held tight while he kissed me. "Now let's go win you a big stuffed teddy bear or something." Gray led us to the baseball pitching booth. There was a pyramid of heavy milk bottles stacked behind the counter. He had to knock all the bottles down with one throw or no prize. "Start picking out the animal you want." He handed a five to the guy and received three baseballs in return.

"This could get pricey," I whispered in his ear.

"Just step aside and watch the master." Gray laid two of the balls down and took several steps back. The employee watched him with a skeptical eye, and I'm sure I looked the same. Gray got into position like he was taking the mound at a baseball game. He bounced the ball with the fingers of his right hand. He nodded at the milk bottles like they were his catcher giving him a signal. He wound up, slid his left leg forward, and let the ball fly. The jugs fell to the ground with a loud crash.

"Holy shit," I said as I stared at him in awe.

"Which one did you pick, Chase?"

I pointed to a big brown monkey, and the attendant got it down for us. Grayson looked damned pleased with himself as he handed me my prize. I threw my arms around his neck and hugged him gleefully. "That was so fucking hot," I told him.

"I've had a lot of practice. Played baseball from the age of seven all the way through college." He stretched and rotated his arm loosening the muscles.

"You must look amazing in baseball pants," I told him as I looked him up and down. "Got any at home?"

"It just so happens I still play in a summer league. Maybe you can come watch a game sometime."

"I'm there." I probably looked ridiculous carrying the giant monkey around, but I didn't care. "I owe you an ice cream cone."

Sharing an ice cream cone with him was erotic as fuck. Watching his tongue dart out of his mouth and swirl around the cone drove me insane. I practically dragged him back to our hotel room. I wasn't quite sure what I was going to do to him, but I knew it was going to end in a mutual orgasm.

Gray was on me as soon as he shut the door to our suite. He ripped the monkey out of my arms and tossed him on the couch. Later I'd talk to him about his callous treatment of my prized possession, but for now, I just wanted his lips on me, anywhere and everywhere.

Our mouths crashed together, and our tongues circled in a frenzy. We both gasped for air as we grappled for some sort of self-control. He nipped my tongue with his sharp teeth, and I nearly threw him down to the floor. We broke apart long enough to whip our shirts off over our heads and toss them aside. I chuckled at Gray's glasses sitting askew on top of his nose and reached out to straighten them.

"I gotta…" I knew mentally what he was about to do, but physically I wasn't prepared for the sensation. Gray tugged on my nipple ring, and I nearly shouted with ecstasy. "I can't wait to pull this with my teeth."

Gray dropped his mouth to my neck and nibbled a path to my ear while tugging at my nipple. My neck was the most erogenous zone on my body besides my cock and prostate, and I loved neck kisses. "Gray," I begged. "I'm going to embarrass myself if you don't slow down."

"Sorry," he said but didn't stop. I slid my hands down the back of his jeans and cupped his ass through his tight briefs. He ripped his mouth away and looked at me. His fuck-me eyes were the lightest shade of blue I'd ever seen. "I don't have condoms. I didn't want to be presumptuous."

"I didn't bring any either," I admitted.

"I want to make you come," he said in a near growl. "Can I?" I couldn't form words, so I nodded. "I'm going to grab a few beers, you go out to the hot tub, and we'll slow things down a bit." I unlocked the sliding door and went out onto the spacious balcony. I started to unbutton my shorts. "Oh, no," Gray said, stilling my hands. "I want to unwrap you."

Gray set the beers down on the hot tub ledge and walked over to me. He dropped into a chair next to me and turned me so I was facing him. He placed both his hands on my upper chest and slowly lowered them down my torso until he reached the button of my cargos. He looked up at me and maintained eye contact until he had me unbuttoned and unzipped. I stepped out of my shoes while Gray slid my shorts down my legs.

He rested his forehead against my stomach while his hands rubbed up and down the backs of my thighs. Gray turned his head and rubbed his cheek along the erection straining against my boxer briefs. I almost cried when he ran his nose along my hard length. Gray rose to his feet, and I must have looked confused. "It will be all over once I strip you bare. I want this to last, so keep them on for now."

It was my turn to take off his jeans, and I copied his moves. My eyes widened when I unveiled Gray's bright blue bikini briefs. His bulge was so hard and so big it pulled his briefs away from his body, giving me a little peep show. I couldn't resist the temptation of licking the exposed flesh just beneath the elastic on his thighs. Gray tangled his hands in my hair, but he didn't pull me off. I breathed his scent in deep. "You smell so good, Gray, and I can't wait to taste you."

"Hot tub. Now."

He stepped away from my searching tongue and pulled me to my feet. Gray lowered himself into the water first. I knew he expected me to sit beside him, but I had other ideas. I stepped down into the water but straddled his lap instead of sitting next to him.

"Chase," his moan was half-prayer and half-curse. He grabbed my ass and rocked his hips upward at the same time, grinding our erections together. "You're making it too hard to be good."

"Mmm, I feel how hard it is," I whispered in his ear, then nipped his earlobe. "Being good is overrated." I captured his mouth with a hard kiss while I rocked up and down against his length. "God, I can't wait to feel this monster inside me." I ran my hands up and down his chest, loving the feel of crisp hair beneath my palms. "Perfect."

Gray captured my hand and held it over his heart. "Feel what you do to me, Chase." His sexy eyes and sensual voice held me in his spell.

"Oh, I feel it, Gray." I squeezed my legs tighter around his waist.

"No," he tapped the hand resting over his heart. "Feel what you do to me here. I need you to feel it and know this is more than just a physical reaction." I felt his heart thundering beneath my palm, and it was all just for me. "Kiss me like you mean it."

I slowly lowered my mouth to his and licked his full bottom lip before I tugged it between my teeth. His excited breath hissed out between his parted lips. I licked the tender flesh to soothe the sting. Gray sucked my tongue inside his mouth, working it in and out, simulating what I wanted him to do to my cock.

I called out his name when he slipped his hand beneath my boxers and grabbed my ass. I put my heart and soul into the kiss, slowly tangling my tongue around his. His blunt fingertip circled my hole, teasing and driving me crazy. Gray tapped the puckered rim with the pad of his finger. I broke our kiss and gasped for air. "Gray, please."

"You beg so prettily," he teased as he kissed his way down my throat. I tipped my head back farther granting him more access. He nipped, sucked, and licked all the way down until he reached my chest. I knew where he was going, and my body quivered all over in anticipation. He felt my reaction and chuckled darkly. "Your body begs so prettily too."

Gray licked one swipe across my sensitive nipple before sucking the ring into his mouth, tugging it gently. I felt the sensation clear to my balls. I felt them tighten and draw up tight against my body. Gray increased his suction on my nipple and started sucking rhythmically to match my thrusts against his cock. "Gray, I'm so close." He didn't stop or slow down. "I'm going to come in my shorts. I don't want to come yet."

Gray pulled off my nipple with one last lick. "I won't last either. Take off your underwear and let's come together." I rose off his lap, peeled my underwear off, and threw them onto the balcony. Gray raised his hips up off the seat so he could remove his briefs and sent them sailing behind him. He eyed my cock hungrily. "Fuck me, you're beautiful," he said huskily. "Come back here and let me feel you."

I wasted no time straddling his hips again. I pinned our cocks between our stomachs and ground myself against him. The flesh-on-flesh connection had us groaning and seeking out each other's mouths. "So good," I told him. "Don't stop." I leaned back and took his hard dick in my hand and began to jack him slowly. "I have a foreskin obsession," I told him when I felt the extra skin at the top of his dick. "I love to suck it, pull it, and nibble it." Gray's eyes nearly rolled back in his head.

Gray fisted my erection in his hand and matched my tempo. We stroked slowly up and down from root to tip. "So big and hard for me," Gray growled against my mouth. "So beautiful," he said when he looked down at us beneath the water. The underwater lighting illuminated us perfectly.

"Gray…I need…" He leaned forward and sucked my nipple hard into his mouth, and that was all it took. "Fuck," I roared as my orgasm ripped through me. Gray kept sucking and pumping until the last tremor left my body. I drowsily opened my eyes and found him smiling wickedly at me. "Your turn," I told him. "Stand up," I said scooting off his lap. "I want to suck this monster cock."

"Oh god," he whimpered. "I might not survive." Goose bumps popped out all over his body as he rose out of the water like some beautiful mythical creature. I wanted to admire him, but I was too far gone. I opened wide and lowered my mouth until I felt his neatly trimmed pubic hair tickle my nose. "Oh fuck," Gray cried. I felt his legs trembling, and I knew he wouldn't last long, but I wanted this to be amazing for him.

I cupped his firm balls in my hand and slowly raised my mouth up his cock until just the head remained in my mouth. I tightened my lips, capturing his foreskin, and pulled off his cock until I stretched the skin over his crown. "Baby," he whimpered. I looked up at him and found his startling blue eyes watching my every move. I'd never liked making eye contact while giving head, but with Gray it was different. I wanted to see him vulnerable for me. "So good," he whispered.

I repeated my slow torture of swallowing his cock on my downward thrusts and stretching his foreskin on my way up. "Going to come," he told me, but I already knew. I could feel it in the way his entire body shook and how hard his balls got. If he expected me to pull back, he was in for a surprise. "Chase," he said my name as I buried him in my throat. I swallowed around the head of his dick and felt him begin to release. I raised my head up and let the final spurt land on my mouth and chin. I made a big show of licking him off my lips. Gray wiped his cum off my chin with his thumb, held it up to my lips, and I sucked it clean. "Damn, baby, that little cum catcher on your chin is adorable," he said in reference to my dimple.

Gray lowered himself back into the water, and I climbed back onto his lap, taking his face in my hands. "Thank you for the most fabulous night I've ever had." I kissed him hesitantly, not sure how he felt about the taste of his cum on my lips. I was pleasantly surprised when he kissed me back passionately. After several minutes, Gray pulled back from our kiss.

"The night isn't over yet."

CHAPTER
Twenty-Three

Gray

I CHECKED OUT MY APPEARANCE IN THE BATHROOM MIRROR WHILE straightening my tie. I saw a brightness and alertness in my eyes I'd not seen in a while…if ever. It wasn't because I'd gotten a lot of sleep either. I'd actually stayed up way too late the night before such an important meeting. I had no regrets aside from sleeping alone when we finally parted. Chase didn't have to sleep alone; he got to sleep with the stuffed monkey. My irrational jealousy over a stuffed animal had me smiling at my reflection.

I was falling fast and hard, but was it too fast and too hard? Only time would tell.

Normally, I'd be a fucking train wreck the morning before a big campaign pitch, and none had ever been as important as this one. So why was I feeling so damn confident and calm? I checked my appearance again and went in search of Chase.

I found him sipping coffee on the balcony while reviewing the marketing materials. Room service had just delivered our breakfast before I stepped outside. Once I was seated, we dug into our food and discussed the meeting one last time. I found myself struggling to focus on the conversation. Instead, I remembered every sound of pleasure Chase had made the night before and into the wee hours. How long before I could make him do it again? Lack of focus had never been an issue for me, in fact the opposite had always been true. Normally, I'd be so focused on the campaign I wouldn't even know Chase was present. There were times I'd been a downright dick to those around me, especially Devon.

My phone chimed with an incoming text. I laughed when I saw it was from Preston asking me how I was feeling and if I had puked yet. I fired back that I'd never felt better or more confident. Then I demanded new pictures of my princess.

"What's so funny?" Chase asked me.

"Pres wants to know if I've puked yet this morning." I looked up and saw confusion on his face. "Usually I'm a nervous wreck before these meetings and it usually results in vomiting."

"What's different this time?"

"You're here."

"Gray, you're making it really hard to be good," Chase said in a sinfully seductive voice.

I reached out and cupped his jaw in my hand. "Someone recently told me that being good was overrated." I checked my watch and saw it was time to head downstairs to the executive wing of the hotel. "Kiss me for good luck," I demanded when we reached the door to our suite.

I expected him to remind me about blurred lines, but instead, he placed his hands on either side of my neck and pressed his mouth to mine. I closed my eyes and sighed against his lips. He pecked my lips several times, then pulled away. "Let's go get 'em, blue eyes," he told me.

We were shown into the conference room almost immediately. The room was packed with VPs who showed no reaction as Chase and I made our presentation. Damn, we made an awesome team. We were completely in sync for every part as if we'd been working together for years instead of days. At no point did I feel nervous or uncertain.

"Thank you, Mr. Wright and Mr. Rivers," said one of the executives. "We will share this presentation with Mr. Heston, and we'll be in touch."

"Thank you for your time," I told them and ushered Chase out of the conference room. He looked anxious, and I could tell he wanted to ask me a lot of questions. "Let's talk about it in our suite."

"How do you think it went?" Chase asked as soon as we were back in our room.

"I think we were great," I assured him. "You were awesome today, and I never would've known it was your first presentation." I hugged him tight.

"What's next?"

"If Mitchell Heston isn't interested in our ad campaign, then someone from today's meeting will call us and let us know they've decided to go with another company. We won't get any face time with him at all."

"That's disappointing," Chase said.

"It's just how it goes. You don't get to the top dog until you've jumped through all the hoops." I kissed him softly because he looked so damn cute when he was worried. "We've got this, Chase. I can feel it in my bones."

"I hope you're right."

"I know I am." I walked by him and swatted him on his ass. "Did you pack your swimsuit like I told you to? I want to spend the day at the beach with you even though the water might still be too cold."

"Yes, dear," he said mockingly in a falsetto voice. He headed for his own room for what I hoped would be the last time.

"I'm going to check in with the office really quick to see if there are any concerns I need to address. And I'm going to find out why my dick-head brother hasn't sent me new pictures of baby Grace like I asked him to this morning."

"You're so damn adorable," Chase told me. He was grinning from ear to ear.

"I bet she's changed a bunch in just two days," I whined. Fuck, I sounded pretty pathetic. My phone calls were brief, and there were no urgent emails or crises needing my attention. I was free to enjoy the rest of the day with a beautiful man, one I hoped to call mine very soon. Chase was waiting for me on the balcony when I finished getting dressed. "Where are your swim shorts?" I asked when I saw he was wearing a pair of faded jeans, flip flops, and a T-shirt.

"Under my jeans." *Gulp*. His swim shorts must be awfully small to fit under his jeans. I looked down at my boring black and white board shorts. "Ready?" he asked. He sounded extra cheerful, and I wondered what he was up to.

We picked up beach towels from the lobby and headed down to the surf. I rented an umbrella and chairs in case we wanted some shade later in the afternoon. The beach wasn't too crowded late on a Tuesday morning in March. The locals were at work or school, but I expected it would get busier later. I sat on my chair, took off my flip-flops and T-shirt, and stashed them under my chair. I looked up just as Chase discarded his shirt. My eyes locked on the piercing that drove me insane. My body immediately responded to the stimulation. He dropped his jeans, and I got my first look at his swimwear.

"Oh god," I mumbled. "What the hell are you wearing?"

"These old things?" He turned around in a slow circle so I could see his glorious body from all angles. "They're swim shorts. A little shorter and tighter than I'm used to wearing, but I thought I'd try something new on my West Coast adventure."

"Those are almost indecent." I could see his bulge in almost perfect detail. I checked to see who else might be looking. I had this insane urge to cover him back up so no one else could see him in those skimpy shorts. "Fuck me." His legs looked long, lean, and endless. I wanted to feel them wrapped around my waist. Right now. He turned to look out over the water, and I couldn't help but stare at his round, tight ass.

"Are we going in?"

"Huh?" He laughed, and I looked up and found him looking at me. "What?"

"You're staring at my ass like it's a juicy steak you can't wait to sink your teeth into."

"Pretty much," I told him, resisting the urge to pin him to the chair and claim his sassy mouth. Instead, I rose to my feet and held out my hand for him to take. I wanted everyone to know he was with me and unavailable. This whole chest-thumping attitude was new to me.

We frolicked in the ocean off and on for hours, keeping it relatively clean since we were in public. The lack of sleep from the previous night and battling the waves wore us out, and we both fell asleep beneath the umbrella. Chase woke with a start, jerking me out of my sleep abruptly.

"What's wrong?" I asked, sitting up slowly.

"I panicked that I slept too late, and we missed the show."

"Show?"

"I got us tickets to see Cruz's band perform tonight. I called him on Sunday, and he has tickets waiting for us."

"Seriously? I've never seen him perform, but I've heard he's a wonderful entertainer."

"He's amazing." Chase sounded worshipful, and I wondered if I should be jealous of their connection. Who wouldn't love Chase? Damn, my new-found insecurity was getting on my nerves. The only thing I could do was meet Cruz and see how they interacted.

"Thank you for the surprise." I leaned over and kissed him softly on his lips. "You ready to head back to our room and get cleaned up before dinner?"

"Depends."

"On?"

"Are we getting cleaned up together or separately?"

I had a vision of a wet, soapy Chase in my shower. "Together," I replied without hesitation.

"Good answer. Your shower or mine?"

"Mine is closer."

We gathered our stuff quickly and headed back to our room. I was so thankful when Chase voluntarily covered his luscious ass with his jeans so I didn't have to beg, plead, or throw a goddamned fit. I was really starting to hate myself. We walked casually and calmly through the hotel lobby when what we really wanted to do was run to our room. My body shook during the elevator ride. I looked over at him and saw the same emotion in his eyes, and I was thankful I wasn't in this alone.

Ding. The sound had become my new favorite because it signaled we had arrived, and I was close to touching and tasting him again. Chase growled and launched himself at me once we were inside our suite. He attacked my mouth like a starving beast, and I reciprocated, knowing our lips would be swollen and red but not giving a damn. I wrapped my arms around his waist and spun us, pinning Chase to the wall. I went to work unfastening his jeans but didn't remove them right away. Instead, I reached inside and fondled him through the tight fabric of his swim shorts. I broke our kiss so I could look at his face while I teased him. I alternated between lightly tracing my finger along his erection and gripping hard and stroking.

"Gray," he hissed between his teeth. "Shower. Now."

"Mmm, I like when you're bossy." I pulled him behind me to my bathroom. I flipped on the shower, and we finished undressing each other while the water warmed up. I laid my glasses on the vanity and pulled him into my arms. "God, I woke up hard and aching for you this morning. I didn't take care of it myself because I wanted it to be your hands and mouth making me come."

"We really need condoms," Chase said when we stepped under the steaming water. He grabbed hold of my cock and stroked it up and down. "I need this inside me tonight. No more waiting, Gray."

"If you're sure…"

"Never been more certain about anything." He released my aching dick, picked up my shampoo, and squirted some into his hands. "May I?"

I nodded. No one had washed my hair for me since I was a kid, but the idea of Chase running his fingers through my hair and massaging my scalp appealed to me on an animalistic level. I closed my eyes and let myself feel his strong fingers working the lather through my hair. It was so arousing. He stepped closer to me, and his cock brushed against mine. Chase tipped my head back and pecked at my lips while he rinsed the shampoo from my hair.

"My turn," I said when he finished. I spun us around and returned the favor. His face looked as blissful as I'd felt when he was washing mine. "Feel good?"

"God yes, Gray. You have amazing hands."

"That's not all," I teased as I tipped his head back to rinse the suds away. I grabbed my body wash next and tried not to acknowledge how happy it made me that he was about to smell like me. Maybe that would soothe the new beast residing inside me.

I ran my soapy hands all over his impressive chest and abdomen, loving how his muscles jumped and twitched beneath my fingers. I thought he was going to cry when I soaped up his cock and balls, making sure to linger and tease. I dropped to my knees and washed his legs and feet. I leaned to the side for a minute so the spray washed the soap away from the front of his body. "I'm not done," I told him when he reached for the body wash.

I stayed on my knees and let the hot water beat on my back. I placed my hand around his left calf, lifted his leg, and propped it up on the edge of the bathtub. "Gray." I loved the sound of my name on his lips. My heart raced in my chest, but I ignored my urge to devour when I'd rather savor. I poured a little more body wash into my hands and lathered them. I placed my soapy hands on his firm ass at the same time I kissed the tender skin where his inner thigh met his groin. I swapped body wash for conditioner then eased a finger along his smooth crack, slowly up and down. I nipped his sensitive flesh while Chase fisted both hands in my hair.

Feeling the man I'd been fantasizing about for weeks trembling beneath my touch was the biggest aphrodisiac. I needed to be the best he'd ever had. I swirled my middle finger around his pucker a few times before I eased it inside him. I sucked hard on his tender flesh, hoping like hell I'd marked his body. I crooked my finger, hitting the magic spot just right.

"Fuck," he cried out. "Gray...so good." He began rocking back on my finger, causing his cock to rub against the side of my face. "I need you." I released his tender flesh, smiling at the angry red mark I'd left. I turned my face and stuck out my tongue so the bottom of his cock rubbed over it with every thrust of his hips. "Oh, please..." I knew what he was begging for, but I wasn't ready to give it yet. I enjoyed working him up too much to ease off.

I tasted his salty essence every time the head of his cock rubbed against my tongue. Chase unclenched his fists from my hair to grab the sides of my head. He turned my face and lined his cock up with my mouth. "Suck me. Now."

I looked up into Chase's smoldering brown eyes and couldn't resist pleasing him a second longer. I opened my mouth wide to accommodate his girth, pressed my lips firmly around his rigid flesh, and let him fuck my mouth while I slid my finger in and out of his tight channel. Chase gave in to his body's demands, driving hard for his release. The sexy sounds he made nearly had me reaching for my own cock so we could come together, but I reached for his balls instead.

"Oh, fuck me," Chase cried out. I added a second finger inside him, twisting up to drive him wild. "Gray…harder." I gave him everything harder—my lips on his cock, my fingers in his ass, and my hand gripping his sac. "Baby…so good." I tasted the first splash of his cum on my tongue before he pulled out of my mouth and came on my chest. I watched as he painted my chest, marking me in the most primal way. I rubbed his essence into my skin while he leaned heavily against the tiled shower wall. "So sexy," he panted.

I rose to my feet and wrapped my arms around him. "You're the sexy one. The way you took what you wanted was so hot." I rubbed my erection against his hard stomach.

"Your turn," he said. Chase soaped up his hands and washed me just as thoroughly as I had washed him, but this time he rinsed my back before turning me to face the spray and dropping to his knees behind me. I thought I knew where he was going, but I'd never experienced this particular sex act. I wasn't sure how I felt about it until I felt him spread my ass cheeks apart and glide his tongue from the top of my crack down to my taint.

"Chase." His name rolled off my tongue like a prayer. Chase applied pressure on my anus until the tip of his tongue breached the tight ring. "I've never… Feels…so damn good." One hand reached between my legs to cup my sac while the other reached around and began stroking my cock. The sensations were too much, and I was already overly stimulated from pleasing him. I knew I was going to embarrass myself with the fastest orgasm on record. I gritted my teeth and tightened every muscle in my body to hold it off, but Chase pulled on my foreskin just how I liked it, and I lost all control. My orgasm started in my core and rippled through my body. Chase stayed with me the entire time, stroking my cock and teasing my ass, until the power of my orgasm drove me to the shower floor in front of him. Never had I experienced anything like it in my life.

"Feel good?" he asked. I collapsed back against Chase's chest. My only answer was a pathetic whimper. "I'll take that as a yes." He chuckled in my ear and nuzzled his nose against my temple.

"Chase, I've never felt…"

"Me either." I was content just to rest against him on the tile floor of the hotel shower while the water cascaded down on us. "It's kind of scary, isn't it?" he asked.

"Terrifying."

Hearing Chase say he was scared made me feel better. If he was scared, it meant he cared, which also meant there was hope for a future with him. It was shocking just how badly I wanted that chance.

"You ready to get out?" he whispered in my ear. "I could really use some food before we go to the show."

"Yes, but I'm probably going to need some help." Chase stood and helped me to my feet, then pulled me back into his arms. He kissed me so passionately that I didn't care where his tongue had just been.

Ninety minutes later, our bellies were full of delicious Mexican food, and we were headed inside a club to watch his childhood friend perform. "Let's grab a table up front," Chase said and led me by the hand to a table meeting his requirements. He was so excited to be in the same zip code with Cruz, and his joy was contagious. "You don't want to miss anything," he told me seriously. "People will get up and dance and block your view."

"So how does this work?"

"They have wardrobe changes in between songs. For example, Cruz will come out as Tina Turner and take the lead for a song and do Joan Jett a few songs later. They switch things up between the two guitar players. The drummer even gets in on the act and Cruz or Pax will go back and play drums so Stix gets a turn at singing. They've really fine-tuned their performance over the years. It's amazing."

We sipped a few beers and made small talk while we waited for the band to come on. I was looking forward to the show, but I was more excited about finding a pharmacy and a box of condoms. It wouldn't be much longer, and Chase was more than worth the wait. I'd only caught a small glimpse of the passionate animal living inside him, and I was ready to see what else he kept hidden behind his mild exterior. I knew for certain our sex life would be physical, often dirty, and always mind-blowing.

It didn't take long for the club to fill up with noisy, fun-seeking fans. Like with Chase, their excitement was catching, and I found myself cheering along with them when the club lights dimmed, the stage lights came on, and the emcee announced Neon Revival.

Cruz's first performance was beside his bandmate, Pax. They performed as Ann and Nancy Wilson and belted out some of Heart's best rock hits. He put so much heart and soul into "Magic Man," and it was breathtaking. They switched things up like Chase said they would and performed cover songs from the most popular rock bands and pop princesses of the eighties.

My favorite performance by far was when Cruz took center stage by himself with nothing but his guitar and a stool. The only light on in the place was a spotlight aimed down on him. He sang Poison's "Every Rose Has Its Thorn" and held us all spellbound from the first strum of his guitar to the last. The song was raw with emotion, making my eyes tear up. I wasn't sure what was going on in his life, but it was obvious he'd really connected with the lyrics.

"Thanks for bringing me to the show," I told Chase after it was over. Most of the crowd had left, but a few fans lingered in hopes of meeting up with the band. "They were amazing, especially Cruz."

"Should I be jealous?" he asked coyly.

"Not in a million years." I pulled him close and kissed him passionately as an exclamation to my statement.

A throat cleared from behind us. "Chase, you need to come with me.

Cruz needs you." The brawny guy was dressed all in black and looked like a bodyguard or bouncer. "Come quick," he said urgently.

"Deacon, what's wrong?" Chase said, tugging on his arm as we followed him.

"You need to get him out of here before it's too late." Deacon was walking so fast Chase and I had to jog to keep up with him.

"Deacon, you're scaring the fuck out of me. What's wrong with Cruz?" Deacon didn't say anything else. He led us outside and around the corner of the building where Cruz was curled into himself as he leaned against the brick wall. "Xavier," Chase cried out and ran to him. Cruz collapsed against his chest and sobbed brokenly.

"I can't do this anymore, Chase. Please take me home." Cruz cried against Chase's chest. "Please help me." He made the most pitiful sounds I'd ever heard. My throat squeezed tight, and tears formed and fell from my eyes as my heart broke for someone I didn't even know. I looked at Chase and saw tears rolling down his beautiful face. Every protective instinct I had, even ones I didn't know existed, rose to the surface, and I went into action.

"We'll help you, Cruz," I said as I carefully approached him. I pulled out my phone to call a cab, but Deacon stopped me and pointed down the alleyway to where a yellow cab had pulled to a stop.

"The cab is for you. Get him the fuck away from here and don't let him come back." I did as Deacon told me and guided Cruz and Chase to the waiting cab. Chase slid into the backseat first, pulling Cruz in behind him, and I climbed in last.

Cruz curled into Chase the minute he got in the cab. Chase smoothed his black hair away from his face and tried to get a good look at his friend, but Cruz kept his face against his chest. "Xavier, please tell me what's wrong. I'm freaking out."

"Please," Cruz panted and sobbed. "I…can't right…now."

"Okay, Xavier, but try to calm down," Chase murmured to him soothingly. "I got you."

I didn't know what to say or do, but I wanted to help in some way. I reached over and patted his knee. "We won't let anyone hurt you, Cruz."

Cruz stiffened against Chase as if he just realized my presence. It surprised him enough to temporarily take his mind off his misery. He sat up straight and turned to look at me. "You're Clark," he said to me. He turned back to Chase. "Your boyfriend probably wears a cape and flies around saving damsels in distress. Oh my god, I'm the damsel." His rambling made me smile. "You're fucking beautiful," he said to me, and I'm pretty sure I blushed. "Chase, he's as gorgeous as you said on the phone and in your texts. Wow, you finally have a boyfriend as pretty as you."

"We haven't really put a label on our relationship," Chase said. It was his turn to blush. "This is all really new, and we..."

"We are dating, but I haven't earned the title of boyfriend. Yet." I smiled at Chase's dumbfounded expression. "Soon, I hope."

Cruz looked back and forth between us. "I'd say you're about there."

The rest of the cab ride to our hotel was spent in silence. Cruz seemed to compose himself and calm down a bit, but I heard the gears grinding as they turned in Chase's brain. Nothing was said until we reached the privacy of our suite.

"Can I take a shower?" Cruz asked Chase.

"Of course," he replied as he turned to me. "I'm going to get him something to wear and make sure he's okay, and I'll be right back out."

"Take your time, Chase. He's your best friend, and he needs you now."

"Thank you for understanding. I know this isn't how you wanted—"

"Shh," I said, placing my fingers over his lips. "There's no need for that." His look seared me to my soul. Something truly special was brewing between us. Chase gave me a soft lingering kiss, then left to get Cruz into the shower.

I spotted a gift basket wrapped in shiny onyx wrapping paper with a red bow sitting on the coffee table. They weren't Heston's colors, but who else would have sent us a gift? Having nothing else to do, I decided to unwrap it. Inside was an array of lube, a variety of condoms, fuzzy handcuffs, a blindfold, and flavored massage oil. This was definitely *not* a gift from Heston's. I finally found a card nestled between the bottles of lube and flavored condoms.

Pace yourselves, boys. Life is a marathon, not a sprint. Love, Gram

"What's all that?" Chase snuck up behind me and wrapped his arms around my waist. I handed him the card, and he read it out loud.

"We won't need to stop at a pharmacy anytime soon," I joked.

Chase groaned when he saw the gifts she'd sent us. "That crazy, wonderful woman," he said, laughing softly. He sobered and looked at me. "Gray, I'm so sorry..."

"Don't say it. We'll have plenty of opportunities. This changes nothing between us."

"He's going to bunk with me," he told me. "There's never been anything sexual between us. He's been raised as my brother, which is exactly how I feel about him."

"I know." Chase leaned in and gave me a slow, sensual kiss that lingered for a long time. He pulled back slowly, and I watched his beautiful face as his eyes slowly opened. Yeah, he was feeling it too. "Maybe you could let me borrow the monkey to help guard against loneliness tonight."

"You got it, Clark."

CHAPTER
Twenty-Four

Chase

"**T**ALK TO ME, XAVIER," I WHISPERED IN HIS EAR. HE WAS WOUND around me like a vine, his arms and legs tangled in mine. I ran my hand up and down his back in a comforting gesture, and it seemed to help calm him.

"Not yet," he said pitifully. "Deacon is going to try to meet me with my stuff sometime tomorrow but only if he can get away without anyone noticing. The minute you told me you were coming to LA, I started making plans to run." He raised his head from my chest and looked into my eyes. His eyes were swollen and red from crying so much. "You're my guardian angel, Chase. You always have been."

"What am I guarding you from, though? Are you in trouble with the law? What's with all this cloak and dagger stuff?"

Cruz laughed dryly and laid his head back on my chest. "I'm just in a really bad spot. One of my own making. I knew better, Chase. I really did."

"Are you having problems with one of your bandmates?"

"Close but not quite." He snuggled closer if that was even possible. "I've done something so damn stupid. I put my whole career in jeopardy."

"How?"

"I started dating our band manager, Damien Diamond. I resisted him for a long time because I knew it was a bad career move, but he wore me down. Damn, it started out so good, so sweet." He swallowed audibly and shivered in my arms. "Then he became jealous and controlling."

"Did he abuse you?" My stomach pitched and rolled at the idea of someone hurting Xavier again.

"The things he said and did hurt me so much more than a black eye or busted lip." Hot tears splashed against my shirt, and my heart shattered into a million pieces while my mind raced with various scenarios. "I can't talk anymore tonight, Chase. Can we please talk about this after I've had some sleep?"

"Sure, X."

I kept rubbing his back until he fell asleep, but it took me a lot longer. I thought of what he'd said about destroying his career by getting involved with Damien, and I was potentially doing the same with Gray. I had no concerns Gray would abuse me, physically or otherwise, but getting involved with him was a bad career move. The thing was, I felt powerless to stop the train from reaching the station. To be honest, I didn't want to. I had to take the risk and hope it didn't backfire in my face.

I looked over at the alarm clock and saw it was nearly three in the morning. I closed my eyes and willed myself to fall asleep. Oddly enough, the thought of Gray cuddling with my monkey brought me enough inner peace to help me fall asleep.

The next thing I knew, I was waking up to the smell of freshly brewed coffee. I unwrapped Xavier from around me and headed to my bathroom to make myself presentable. The mirror showed I looked a little tired, but it wasn't too bad. I brushed my teeth and splashed cold water on my face and went in search of Gray.

"This is Grayson Wright," I heard his sexy voice say. He was sitting on the balcony with his back to me. "We'll be happy to meet with Mr. Heston today at ten. Yes, that is correct. We will be heading back to DC tomorrow morning. Will that be a problem? Okay, we'll see you at ten."

I was about to make my presence known to him, but he dialed another number right away. I listened in stunned silence as he called the airline and purchased an extra ticket for our flight back to DC tomorrow. "I'd prefer another first-class seat if one is available, but it's short notice, and I understand if you are unable to accommodate the request. Yes, I understand. That will work just fine. Thank you for your help." Oh fuck, I was falling hard in spite of what Xavier was going through.

Gray hung up his phone, and I pounced. I climbed onto his lap, cupped his face in my hands, and kissed him with every fiber of my being. I lingered for a long time, never wanting to end our kiss until the need for oxygen won out.

"I missed you too," Gray said between pants. "You probably shouldn't kiss me like that until we're prepared to do something about this," he said, gesturing to the erection straining his lounge pants.

I scooted up farther until my eager dick pressed against his, rocking myself against him. Gray dug his hands into my hips to stop me from rocking. "We have supplies," I reminded him with an exaggerated eyebrow wiggle.

"I want to lay you down and fill you up more than I've ever wanted anything in my life, Chase, but not when we only have an hour and a guest. I'm going to need some privacy and a lot more time once I finally get inside you."

"Fuck." The visuals accompanying his hot words were insane. I could so clearly see him spreading my legs wide and penetrating me. The need and ache arcing through my body curled my toes.

"I will when we get home, and that's a promise." He pecked me softly on my lips a few times.

"I heard you buying a plane ticket for Xavier." I looked into his eyes, needing him to see how much his kindness meant to me. "I can't believe how nice you're being to a virtual stranger, Gray."

"He's important to you, which makes him important to me. Besides, anyone with half a heart would want to help him." Gray cocked his head to the side. "Any clue about what's going on with him?"

I didn't want to betray Xavier's confidence, but I was falling hard for Gray, and I didn't want there to be any secrets between us. So I told him what little I knew. Gray tensed when I got to the part about Damien being his band manager and Xavier's concern that it had ruined his career.

"That's not going to be us," Gray said, sensing my fears right away. "We won't let it."

"You can't make that guarantee."

He cupped my face, and I stared into his beautiful eyes, noticing for the first time just how long his eyelashes were. They were thick and dark and nearly touched the lenses of his glasses. "There are very few guarantees in life, Chase. Life is fleeting, fragile, and often cruel. I can fucking well guarantee I will never hurt you, physically or otherwise, and should you choose to end our relationship, I will treat you with the professional courtesy you deserve."

After all his beautiful words, the ones I chose to focus on were the ones about me being the one to end our relationship. It sounded like he was sure about me, about us. "I haven't changed my mind about us if that's what you're thinking. I admit it made me think about our situation, but the truth is…I couldn't stop this if I wanted to, and I *don't* want to."

"Good. I don't want us to end because of Xavier's terrible situation. We"—he pointed back and forth between us—"are the ones in this rela-tionship. No one else." He lifted his face and kissed me again, careful to keep it light.

"I want to sleep with you tonight," I whispered in his ear. "I don't want to cuddle a stuffed monkey or Xavier all night. I want to cuddle you."

"There's no way I can have you in my bed and be good."

"Being good is overrated," I reminded him with a wink. "I can be re-ally, really good if you want me to be." I started to rock my hips against his, and I could tell he was about to give in and take me to his bedroom, but the sound of someone clearing his throat jolted us back to reality.

"I'm really sorry," Xavier said. "I just got a call from Deacon, and he was able to get some of my clothes and Bess. He wants to meet me this afternoon as long as he's not being followed. Are you free to go with me, Chase?"

I looked at Gray, who nodded slightly. "We have a meeting with a client at ten, but we'll probably be available mid to late afternoon."

"We?" Xavier raised an eyebrow questioningly.

Gray sat up in his chair and turned to look at him. "We're all going together," he said. "I don't want you guys walking into a dangerous situation by yourselves. This Damien guy sounds like a real douche. If Deacon thinks he's going to be followed, then he sounds like a dangerous douche too. Who is Bess? Your dog?"

"She's my guitar and most prized possession. She belonged to Chase's grandfather, and Gram gave her to me when I was about eight and wanted to learn how to play."

"Dangerous douche?" I asked Gray. "Not the eloquence I'm used to hearing from you." Gray shrugged and Xavier burst into laughter. It was the first real laugh I'd heard from him in a long time. I was so thankful for Gray, and I leaned forward to kiss him. "I really do adore you," I told him. He smiled brightly at me and kissed me back. "I better hit the shower and get ready for the meeting," I said as I slid from his lap. "Meet you back here in a bit." I dropped one last kiss on his mouth and headed inside. Xavier gave me a once-over and spotted my semi-erection and grinned wickedly. "Shut the fuck up, Xavier."

"I didn't say a word."

"Keep it that way, and don't perv on Clark either. I. Do. Not. Share." I heard them both laugh as I entered my bedroom, and it made me smile.

"Are you nervous?" I asked Gray as we waited to meet with Mitchell Heston.

"Surprisingly, I'm not nervous at all." The look in his eyes when he turned to look at me took my breath away. "You're very good for me, Chase." Mr. Heston's personal assistant returned before I had a chance to reply. It was probably a good thing, or I might have made a fool of myself.

Gray and I followed behind her as she led us to a huge office fit for the

CEO of a luxury hotel chain. The furnishings were all antique and elegant, but what impressed me the most was the man who stood up to greet us. When I'd pictured Mr. Heston in my mind, I'd imagined a sixty-five-year-old man with graying hair and a body that had gone a little soft around the middle.

"Wow," I heard myself whisper. Gray looked at me sharply. He was not at all pleased with my reaction, but I couldn't help it. Mitchell Heston was so beautiful it was shocking. He wore his black hair short and immaculately groomed. His bespoke suit framed a large, muscular body, but what got me the most were his shrewd, black-as-night eyes. His gaze locked on me and didn't look away for several long moments. I felt myself blush.

"Mr. Heston," Gray said, pulling his attention to him. "Thank you for meeting with us today. It's an honor for Wright Creations to be on the short list of ad agencies you're considering."

Mr. Heston nodded at Gray and looked back at me, which prompted Gray to introduce us. Mitchell Heston shook my hand, then he shook Gray's.

"Let's get down to business, shall we?" Mr. Heston gestured to a table and chairs in the far corner of the room. Our slicks and the marketing materials we'd presented to his teams were already laid out on the table.

I took a seat, and Gray sat to my right. I had hoped Mr. Heston would sit across from us so I could discreetly squeeze Gray's hand reassuringly beneath the table. My hopes were not realized because Mitchell Heston dropped into the seat next to mine.

"Tell me about your campaign and why you feel you can best represent Heston's Luxury Suites." I turned to look at Gray, prepared for him to take the lead. "I want to hear your thoughts, Chase." My head whipped around to look at him.

"Sir, I just came on board at Wright Creations. Grayson best represents his company and the direction they'd like to take on your campaign."

"That's all well and good, but I still want to hear *you* tell me why Heston's should be the number one destination for someone looking for a luxury vacation."

"Well, as our campaign states…"

"Don't pitch me, Chase. Speak from your heart. You've stayed two nights in my hotel, so tell me why you'd recommend it to others." Too much was riding on this meeting, and I refused to blow it.

"Actually, I've stayed at many Heston's Luxury Suites locations all over the world," I said. "My grandmother is an international best-selling author, and we stayed at one of your hotels almost every time we traveled for book tours or speaking engagements. It was the part I looked forward to the most."

"Why?"

"As luxurious and beautiful as your suites are, they are also comfortable and inviting. I was never afraid to touch anything when I was an awkward, clumsy teenager."

"That's a unique perspective."

"And your staff."

"What about them?" He sat up straighter like he was prepared to get defensive.

"They're your absolute best asset. I don't know what kind of screening process you have in place, but the customer service you provide is second to none."

"Do you want a job here?" He looked at me appraisingly, and it made me nervous.

"Thank you, but no. I love my job."

"Well," Mitchell Heston said as he rose to his feet. Gray and I stood also. "I'd like to discuss this further over lunch. Are you available, Chase?" He made it clear the offer was extended only to me, and it was a massive understatement to say it made me uneasy.

"Uh...I'm sorry, but I already have plans." I had clothes and an antique guitar to rescue.

"Dinner, then? I happen to know you aren't leaving until tomorrow morning." I looked at Gray, who outwardly appeared calm and collected, but I knew better. "Surely you can spare your employee for dinner, can't you, Mr. Wright?" It was the first time he'd acknowledged Gray since the meeting had begun. I wanted to shout that our connection ran much deeper than boss and employee, but it would've been a sure-fire way to fuck up a potential deal.

Gray plastered on a fake smile. Surely an intelligent man, such as Mitchell Heston, could see right through it. "Of course he can have dinner with you."

"Great," Mitchell said and rubbed his hands together. "Leave your number with my receptionist, and I will call you with the time."

"I'm sorry, Mr. Heston, but that is against our company policy. Our employees do not give out their personal phone numbers to our clients. Surely you can see where that could become a problem." Gray's voice was firm but friendly. Mitchell didn't like it, but he didn't argue. "Your assistant can leave a message for him at concierge or on our suite phone." Mitchell narrowed his eyes.

"I'll be in touch, Chase. You both have a pleasant afternoon." We were dismissed just like that.

"What the fuck was that?" I almost shouted when we were alone in the elevator.

"He was impressed with you," Gray responded.

"Gray, please don't…"

"No," he interrupted, "he was impressed with you physically, but *I'm* referring to your sales pitch. I should have listened closer when you talked about it on your first day, but I honestly couldn't focus beyond how much I wanted you."

"Gray," I groaned.

"Hey, I've come a long way since then." We stepped off the elevator and made our way to our door.

"I don't want to go to dinner with him. You know that, right?" I grabbed his arm and stopped him from swiping our room card.

"I don't know," he said in a singsong voice. "I heard that little *wow* when you first laid eyes on him."

I pushed him against the door, pressing my body hard against his, much like he'd done to me after our bowling date. "I only want you, Gray." I took his lips in a passionate kiss, not caring who might walk by and see us. This was the kind of moment that called for bold action. I gloried in his pants and groans as I made my feelings for him clear.

"Chase," he whispered when I finally tore my mouth away from his lips so I could kiss his neck beneath his ear, having learned it was a spot that drove him crazy. "I—" The suite door opened from within, and we both tumbled through the door with Gray landing on his back and me on top of him.

I looked up at Xavier through narrowed eyes. "What the fuck was that for?"

"You two were about to fuck like animals in the hallway of a five-star resort. One that you're trying to land as a client. I thought you might need a little ice water thrown on you to bring you back to reality."

I climbed off Gray, who was still struggling to pull air into his lungs. Xavier and I both held out a hand to help him off the ground.

"Guess who has a hot date with the young CEO of Heston's Luxury Suites?" Gray wiggled his eyebrows playfully, but I felt his worry. Xavier must have seen through the playfulness too because he looked at me with a puzzled expression on his face.

"The guy wouldn't take no for an answer," I said defensively. "I tried to get out of it."

"How young and how hot?" I knew better than to answer that question. Xavier smiled wickedly when I remained quiet. "That hot, huh?" He slapped Gray's shoulder in commiseration. "You don't have a thing to worry about."

"I know," Gray said, his voice resolute and certain. "What time can we pick up your stuff? We'll need time for Chase to get ready for his date, and we all need a good night's sleep because our plane leaves at seven tomorrow morning."

"Plane?"

"Oh, right," Gray said casually. "You're booked on our flight home."

Xavier got really quiet, and his eyes filled. "You did that for me?" He looked back and forth between us, and I pointed at Gray. "Thank you, Gray. You don't know how...um." His voice cracked. "I'm just going to go give Deacon a call." He walked swiftly to my bedroom.

"God, you're such a good man." I wrapped my arms around Gray and held him tight. I breathed in his smell and let the peacefulness of the moment calm my rioting soul.

"I'm quickly learning there isn't much I wouldn't do for you," he whispered in my ear. "Except share you. I don't give a fuck about the deal if I find out Heston has crossed the line with you. I trust you, Chase, but I don't know him. He was completely unprofessional in front of me, so I can't imagine what he'll be like when he gets you alone."

"I'll get up and walk out of there if he does anything inappropriate," I promised. I pulled Gray close and kissed him softly until he started to yield to me. Then I increased the pressure against his lips, sliding my tongue into his mouth.

"Gross," Xavier said dramatically. As much as I loved him, I was ready to kill him. "Deacon is going to meet us near Rosita's on the pier in one hour. We can grab lunch if you have time."

"Sure," I said.

"Great, then we can come back here and help you pick out the perfect outfit. You'll probably even have time to manscape."

"You little…" I looked hurriedly for something to throw at him, but Gray blocked me.

"We can't afford to break anything. I'm afraid to find out how Mr. Heston would want to be compensated for the damage," Gray said. I heard Xavier laughing hysterically from the other room where he'd run to hide from me.

"Fuck you both," I said.

CHAPTER
Twenty-Five

Gray

GOING WITH THE GUYS TO RETRIEVE CRUZ'S BELONGINGS GAVE ME greater insight into their relationship. Although I'd met Cruz while he was under duress, I could tell he had a lively and quick-witted personality. I could also tell Cruz and Chase genuinely loved one another but not in a sexual way.

We looked ridiculous as we walked down the street wearing baseball hats and sunglasses like we were movie stars trying to go unrecognized in public. Cruz explained he'd always dressed that way because he was well known to the locals. The goal was to meet Deacon for lunch, grab Cruz's belongings, and get him back to our hotel suite with Damien the Douche being none the wiser.

Things started off well, and Deacon arrived just a few minutes after us. He'd decided to leave Cruz's things in the car while we ate instead of dragging his suitcase and guitar case into the crowded cantina. The big man dwarfed Cruz when he'd pulled him close for a hug. Cruz fought back tears, but Deacon said nothing about the situation. We shared some chips and salsa while we waited for our entrees and focused our conversation on the weather, tourist hot spots, and other safe topics. It was awkward and tense because Chase and I had no clue what was going on. Occasionally, I'd see a soft expression wash over Deacon's face when he looked at Cruz. *Interesting.* We ate our food and drank our beers in strained silence. The fun didn't start until we left the cantina and headed toward Deacon's car.

"Where the fuck is my car?" Deacon yelled. He spun around in a small circle, looking up and down both sides of the street. "It was right fucking here."

"You mean in the no parking zone?" Cruz asked, pointing to a sign.

"Damn," Deacon said, running his hands through his hair. "I'm so damn sorry, Cruz. I was so worried about you that I didn't pay attention."

"The phone number for the towing company and impound lot are on the sign. Let's just call them to see when we can pick up your car." Chase was the voice of reason while the other two looked like they were going to break down. In the grand scheme of things, this wasn't the worst thing that could happen. What happened next was though.

"Cruz! What fucking game are you playing?" yelled an irate man. We all pivoted to see a handsome but unhinged-looking guy barreling toward us. I could tell by Cruz's gasp that this had to be Damien the Douche.

Chase and Deacon both moved in front of Cruz to shield his smaller frame while I turned and squared my body to prepare for a fight. "Move on, man," I told Damien as he advanced on us.

"Get out of my way," he snarled at me. "Who the fuck do you think you are?" He tried to move around me, but I blocked his path. "Come on, baby," he said to Cruz in a pleading tone. "We can work this out like we always do. I love you, and you love me." The loser softened his voice and cooed, which made my skin crawl. "Don't involve other people in our business, Cruz." This time his words and voice held a hint of a warning or threat.

I held my hand up to block another move to get around me. "It's over, and you need to move on before I call the police."

"Your band needs you, Cruz. You're going to bail on your bandmates over a little lover's spat? Are you really that selfish? I worked my ass off to build your career and reputation, and I can just as easily destroy you. Get in my fucking car."

"No," Cruz said boldly as he stepped around Deacon. "We're through, Damien. The only way I'm going back to the band is if you resign as our manager and leave."

Damien threw back his head and laughed. "Yeah, right. Quit dicking around and get in my fucking car." He lunged for Cruz, but Deacon intercepted him. "Did he finally let you have a piece of his tight ass, Deacon? Is that why you're so eager to ruin your career over him? I bet it was the sweetest and tightest you've ever had."

Deacon answered by plowing his fist into Damien's gut. All the air left the douche's lungs in a rush as he doubled over. Deacon fisted Damien's shirt and jerked him upward until the coward met his gaze. "Listen to me very carefully, you little piece of shit. I've never had the privilege to know Cruz as anything other than my friend. He says he's through with you, and that's final. You either leave the band or he does, so what's it going to be?"

"You're both fired," Damien said between gasps. Deacon gave him a small push when he released his shirt, and Damien stumbled away. "You haven't heard the last of me, Cruz." We watched as Damien made his way to his car and sped off.

"I didn't drink enough beer for this shit," Chase said, breaking the silence. He pulled out his phone and dialed the number of the towing company listed on the no parking sign. He got the address and an approximate time Deacon's car could be picked up. "Two-hundred-dollar fine?" he said loudly into the phone. "That's outrageous."

"It's okay," Deacon said softly. "It's worth it." He rubbed his giant paw of a hand up and down Cruz's back. "You're going to be okay." I wondered again if something more could have or would have developed between them if the situation had been different.

"Thanks, Deacon."

"Let's get another beer and eat some more chips, then we can call a cab to take us to the impound lot," I suggested. No one disagreed, so we headed back inside the cantina to pass the time.

Two and a half hours later, Deacon had his car, Cruz had his stuff, and I had a buzz. Chase and I went inside after saying goodbye to Deacon when he dropped us off at Heston's, giving Cruz and Deacon a private moment to say goodbye. I wanted to eavesdrop, but Chase pulled me away.

I was buzzed enough that I started coming on to him once we got inside our suite. I didn't notice the flashing light on the telephone, but Chase did. I followed him to the end table where the phone sat. I rubbed my crotch against his fine ass and nibbled his neck while he played back the message. I listened as Heston's assistant told Chase what time he needed to arrive at the penthouse suite for dinner. She advised him there would be an access card left at the concierge desk for him. Finally, she told him to dress casually. My ardor cooled with every fucking word she said. I needed to put a little distance between us so I could get my head on straight. I walked away and was standing on the balcony by the time the call ended.

"I need you to tell me right now if you have a problem with this, Gray." I didn't turn to face him because it would be impossible for me to keep my emotions hidden. It wasn't Chase's fault I was feeling jealous and unbalanced. He walked up behind me and wrapped his arms around my waist and pressed his forehead against the back of my head. "I'd hate it too. Don't shut me out, okay?"

"I'm upset with myself and my insane need to pound my chest like an angry gorilla."

"I'm flattered."

"You say that until I try to piss on your leg."

Chase's giggle broke my sour mood. I turned around and started making gorilla noises and pounding my chest, which only made him laugh harder. He turned and fled, leaving me to chase after him while doing my best gorilla impersonation. I nearly had him when Cruz came through the door. Chase and I instantly froze but not before he'd seen us. His eyes were red, and I could tell he'd been crying, but my ridiculous antics made him smile.

"Please don't tell me that's your mating call or that blondie likes it."

"How embarrassing," Chase muttered.

"I'm sorry about cramping your style," Cruz said sadly. "I called Ellie and told her I was coming home. I'll be staying with her instead of crashing with you, Chase.

"You're not cramping our style, and you're more than welcome to stay with me."

"Ellie's really worried about me, and I want her to know I'm okay. Well, I will be."

"All right, if that is what you want to do," Chase said.

"It is. Hey, isn't it about time for someone to get ready for their big date?"

"Not funny, Xavier." Chase looked at me, and I gave him a reassuring wink.

Cruz and I played a few rounds of poker while Chase got ready for his dinner with Heston. I was studying my hand and trying to figure out if the little shit across from me was bluffing again when I heard Cruz let out a soft whistle.

"Shut up," Chase said from behind me.

I turned around and raked my eyes over Chase from top to bottom and back up again. I loved how he looked in the dark denim jeans that hugged his perfect body and made his legs look a mile long. I would be wrapping those legs around my waist tomorrow night come hell or high water. His crisp, white button-down shirt looked flawless against his tan skin. He'd thrown on a dark blue jacket but wore Converse on his feet. I preferred the outfit over everything I'd seen him in so far, except for when he'd been naked.

"Chase, you look smokin' hot." I meant every word. "Let me walk you out." I followed him to the door. "I'll be waiting when you get back. I'm going to take you to my room, take off all your sexy clothes, and hold you in my arms all night."

"But you said…"

"Don't listen to me. I'm an idiot." I kissed him softly and stepped back so he could open the door. "I'll see you soon."

"Bye." I noticed the reluctance in his eyes, so I assured him with a smile.

After he left, I flopped onto the sofa and looked over at Cruz, who was studying me closely. "Are you going to pump me for information?" Cruz asked.

"Tempting but no."

"Why not?"

"I want to learn everything there is to know about Chase Rivers, but I want it to come from him." Cruz narrowed his eyes, trying to gauge my sincerity.

"I like you," he finally announced. "You've revealed your true character several times, probably without meaning to, and I like what I see. But you and Chase work together, and that's usually not a good idea, even if one of you isn't an abusive douche nozzle. Can I offer you some advice as Chase's oldest friend?"

"Sure."

"I can tell he has very strong feelings for you." My heart pounded with his words. "It seems like they get stronger every day, and a sure-fire way to kill those feelings would be to treat him as anything other than a coworker while you're at the office or in front of his peers. Do not give him special treatment or be too hard on him to compensate for what you perceive as an unfair advantage."

"Thanks, Cruz. He's already made that one of his rules, and I promised I would keep things separate and professional while at work. I will keep that promise."

"Saying it and doing it are two different things. Just keep that in the forefront of your mind every workday. I want to see my best friend happy for the first time in his life, and it's obvious you're important to him. Chase's smile reaches his eyes now. So don't blow it."

I could barely swallow around the lump in my throat. "I won't blow it. I can't." I meant it with all my heart. I'd only known Chase for a short while, but I already knew I would regret it for the rest of my life if I screwed up my shot with him."

"Let's get something to eat and have some fun while we wait for Chase to get back."

We ordered Chinese and had it delivered to our suite. We played more poker, watched a movie, and still Chase wasn't back. Cruz took Bess out of her case along with a battered notebook and a chewed-up pencil. He'd strum a few chords, jot down some words, and repeat. He was lost in his thoughts and his music, and it made me feel like a voyeur to watch him during such an intimate moment.

I went to my bedroom and lay on the bed to read one of Agnes's novels I'd found in the airport bookstore. The book worked as a distraction at first, but the main characters matched Chase's and Heston's descriptions, and I started to replace their images with the characters', which stirred up those crazy jealous feelings again. I was just about to call him when I heard the door to our suite open. Chase strolled into my bedroom carrying his jacket over his arm and a brown paper bag with handles.

"Hi, beautiful," he said.

"I believe that's my line. So, how'd it go?"

"It was really strange at first. Tense, I guess." He shrugged dismissively and tossed his jacket on an empty chair. He came over to the bed and set the brown bag on the bedside table. "I mean, he came to the door wearing nothing but a pair of jeans. I wasn't planning for the night to be *that* casual."

"Surely you're winding me up?"

Chase grinned wickedly as he looked down at me. "I am winding you up, but it was awkward at first." He crooked his finger at me, and I sat up. "Weren't you saying something earlier about undressing me?"

"Indeed." I set the book aside and scooted so I was sitting on the edge of the bed. I unbuckled his belt while urging myself to go slow. I wanted to prove to him, and to myself, I could control myself and not act like a wild animal every time I caught his scent. I had to show Chase I valued him beyond the physical, or we'd be doomed to fail. "Did Heston behave himself?" Chase chuckled and ran his hands through my hair. The tender feeling the simple action garnered was indescribable.

"He was very polite, but I set him straight right away. I wasn't there to play games or lead him on." The relief washing over me was ridiculous. "He knows about us, Gray. He's a very perceptive guy and easily picked up on our unease over the dinner invitation." I stopped working to open his pants and looked up at him. "I couldn't deny us. I wouldn't." His brown eyes were shining with emotions I easily read. Did they always look like melted chocolate when he looked at me?

"I'm glad you told him the truth about us, but I'm sorry if it made you feel uncomfortable. I guess there will be awkward moments like these when we work so closely together." My heart pounded in my chest because I knew what I needed to ask, even though I was terrified of his answer. "Are you having second thoughts?"

"None." His answer was firm and resolute. He slid his hands out of my hair and cupped my face. "I brought home some dessert. I thought I could climb into your bed and feed you." He looked over and saw the book lying on the bed. "I love the way the cover turned out for that one. Any good?"

"I'm just getting to the good parts," I confessed while I started unbuttoning his shirt. I placed my mouth against his stomach and smiled when I felt Chase's abdominal muscles quiver at the slight touch. I kissed a path up his chest with each inch of skin I revealed. I had to rise to my feet to unbutton and kiss the last few inches. "God, I love the way you taste and smell." I slipped his shirt off his shoulders and tossed it onto the chair with his jacket.

"I want to undress you too." I raised my arms over my head and Chase pulled my shirt off. "How about you read the book out loud while I feed us dessert. Naked." He untied my pajama pants, making sure to rub the back of his hand against my bulge before sliding them over my hips and down my legs. "I love your sexy underwear," Chase whispered hotly in my ear. He made to remove them, but I stopped him.

"We better leave them on," I told him. "I want our first time to be special. One more night, Chase."

"It seems too far away," he said with a pout.

"I know, but I promise you won't regret waiting until we can be completely alone. Oh, the things I will do to you." I reached for his jeans again and set about removing them from his body. He stepped out of his shoes, and I slid the denim down to his ankles. I might have detoured slightly, rubbing my nose along his cloth-covered cock. Chase growled at me as he kicked his jeans aside. He looked like he was about to pounce, so I threw my hands up in surrender. "I'm sorry," I said quickly. "I'll behave."

Chase pointed to the bed, and I climbed in, pulling the covers up to my waist. He picked up the paper bag and crawled over me to get into bed instead of walking around to the other side, but I wasn't complaining. He started unloading different containers and plastic cutlery from the bag. I picked up the book and opened it up to where I'd left off.

"This really is a beautiful cover, by the way." It depicted a weathered pirate ship in the background while in the foreground a young baron was wrapped in a passionate embrace with his pirate. The colors and font were spectacular.

"Thank you," Chase said humbly. "It's one of my favorites." I looked over at his mini picnic and smiled. "I wasn't sure what you'd like. There are chocolate-covered strawberries, key lime pie with a huge helping of whipped cream, and brownies."

"Would it be glutinous to say I want a little bit of everything?"

"If so, we are both gluttons. Which do you want first?"

"Key lime. It's my absolute favorite."

"Good choice," he said.

Chase cut off a bite for me and held the fork up to my lips. I tried to be seductive when I wrapped my mouth around the fork's tines. The sweet, tangy flavor of the pie burst on my tongue. The appreciative moan that escaped my lips was not an attempt to be sexy, but it had the same effect on Chase.

"You can't make those noises if you expect me to stay over here and be good."

"Sorry," I said around a mouthful of pie. I wasn't. The smoldering look in his eyes was worth it. He slid a bite of pie between his pouty lips and closed his eyes in bliss. "Good, right?" Chase pointed to the book with his fork, and I took it as my cue to read.

I did my best imitation of a British accent, and Chase choked on his pie. I reached over and pounded on his back. "Are you okay?" I asked when he finally settled down.

"Water," he said in a raspy voice. I got a bottle of water from the mini fridge and brought it back to bed with me. He drank half of the bottle and spent several seconds clearing his throat afterward. "Graham cracker crust went down the wrong pipe."

"Uh-huh. Shall I continue reading?"

"Yes, but have a strawberry first." He brought the berry to my lips, and I gently bit into the luscious fruit. "You have a little…" he said, gesturing to the corner of my lip. I stuck my tongue out and licked the excess juice from my lip.

"Better?" He was still staring at my mouth. "Chase?"

"Huh? Yeah, go ahead."

I continued reading about a cock-hungry pirate teasing and taunting the horny duke held captive on his ship. Sexual tension filled the page and the air Chase and I breathed.

"Jesus, Gram," Chase said after I'd read for a while.

"She's fucking awesome," I countered. Chase held up a decadent brownie for me, and I leaned over to take a bite. A small chunk fell onto my chest. I was going to pick it up, but Chase lowered his mouth and ate it off my body. I felt his tongue dart out to lick my skin beneath the morsel. "Chase," I said on a whisper. Between Chase and the book, my dick was hard enough to use as a weapon. I turned back to the book and read a little more.

"Enough," Chase said pleadingly. "My Gram wrote those words, and I'm sitting here with a raging boner. It's making me nauseous."

I closed the book and set it on the bedside table. I'd finish it when I got home. "Let's eat the rest of our dessert and turn in. We have to head to the airport before sunrise." I grabbed the second fork from his stash of goodies, and we fed each other every bite of dessert he'd brought. I should have felt guilty about eating so much junk, but all I felt was turned on. I'd probably not get any sleep knowing Chase was so close.

"I've got a problem," Chase said, interrupting my thoughts.

"Yeah?"

He grabbed my hand, pushed it beneath the covers, and placed it over his erection. "I need to come, Gray. I won't fall asleep feeling like this, and I don't want to rub one out in the shower. Make me come."

In a lightning-fast move, I rolled and pulled him beneath me. I attacked his mouth with mine at the same time I reached down and yanked his boxers down to midthigh. I broke our kiss long enough to strip the underwear from both our bodies. Chase spread his legs wide, and I made a home there. We both cried out when I lowered my body so our dicks touched.

Chase wrapped his legs around my waist, and I slowly rocked my body against his. The slide of our cocks was aided by our leaking precum. "Kiss me," he pleaded. I eagerly gave in to his demands and kissed him slowly as I loved him. We panted and groaned into each other's mouths. Chase's hands touched me everywhere—my arms, my hair, my back, then finally grabbed ahold of my ass. "More, Gray. Please."

I reached between our straining bodies and wrapped my hand around both our cocks to grip them tight. "Harder?" He shook his head. The muscles in my ass and thighs bunched as I thrust harder and faster against him. "Like that?"

"Yes. God, Gray, don't stop. I'm almost there." His voice had turned breathy and raspy with lust. "Come with me, Gray." That wasn't going to be a problem. I was right there, and the slightest sensation would put me over the edge. "I can't wait to feel you driving deep inside me." And there it was. All systems go as my balls tucked in tight against my body, signaling that blastoff was near. "Oh, Gray…" He tilted his head farther back into his pillow and bit his lip to keep from crying out as the first stream of creamy white cum burst from his cock.

"Chase…" I groaned and moaned loudly as my orgasm ripped through me almost violently. I kept thrusting until we had no more to give. I looked down to find our cum mixed together over his stomach and my hands. It was so fucking sexy, and I could only stare at it for several moments while my heart rate tried to return to normal. "I'll go get us a warm washcloth to clean up with if you let go of me." His legs were still gripping my waist, and his hands were still grabbing two big handfuls of my ass.

"Oh, sorry." He loosened his legs and hands from my body.

"Don't be. I loved it." I dropped a quick kiss on his nose before climbing off the bed. "I'll be right back." I flipped on the light for the bathroom and nearly gasped when I saw my reflection. My hair was sticking up in every direction, my glasses were hanging crooked on my nose, and I was wearing the happiest expression I'd ever seen on my face. I grinned at my disheveled appearance and quickly wet a cloth under the hot water.

"Here you go," I said when I returned from the bathroom. Chase was almost asleep, so I made quick work of cleaning us both off. I returned the dirty cloth to the bathroom and crawled into the bed beside him. He turned to his side facing away from me, and I moved in behind him. Chase released a blissful sigh when I pressed my chest to his back and wrapped my arms around his waist. *My god, I could get used to this.* I kissed the back of his neck. "Night, babe."

"Night," he said barely above a whisper.

I closed my eyes and listened as his breathing evened out and he fell asleep in my arms. I wanted to stay awake for a little longer to enjoy the rightness of the moment, but the combination of his warmth and my sated body quickly pulled me under.

"Less than twenty-four hours before I really make you mine," I whispered to him right before I drifted off.

CHAPTER
Twenty-Six

Chase

"I can't believe you're taking that thing home," Gray said as we stood in line to check our luggage at the airport.

"I love him."

"You've fulfilled one of his teenage dreams," Xavier added. "He's never going to give up that monkey. I bet it already has a name."

"Spunky Monkey," Gray tossed out.

"Nope."

"George," Xavier said, and I smiled. "*Curious George* was his favorite book. He probably still has a copy."

"Guilty," I admitted. "Gram said my mom read those books to me every night. I like knowing she used to hold them in her hands."

"George is a great name for your monkey," Gray said to me. He leaned over and gave me a lingering kiss. "I'm glad I got to fulfill one of your teenage fantasies by winning him for you."

"I have a few others I'd let you fulfill for me."

"Yeah? I want to hear all about them."

"Gross, not me. You two are making me sick," Xavier said, but I could tell he was teasing. I noticed the closer we got to leaving LA, the more like his old self he became.

"Awww, does someone need to cuddle with George to feel better?" I asked mockingly.

"Dick."

"Bitch."

"Douche."

"Sluuuuuuut."

We burst into laughter at how easily we'd fallen back into our old game of tossing insults at one another. We could go back and forth forever.

"Children, we're next in line," Gray said in mock exaggeration.

Xavier was first up to the counter, followed by Gray. When it was my turn, I got motioned over to the side so they could search my bag. Congratulations, I was the lucky random search winner, or in my case, loser. The TSA agent opened my bag and took everything out, making sure to hold up the sex toys, condoms, and lube Gram had sent so everyone could get a good look.

My face was so red I could have fried an egg on my forehead. I heard Gray and Xavier laughing off to the side as they waited for me. Dicks. The monkey was too big to carry on, so I had to check him in at the counter and pay an extra fee. I wasn't giving up my George no matter what.

"Cruz, you can have my first-class ticket so you can sit with Chase if you want."

"The honeymoon is over already?" I asked Gray and added a few sniffles.

"Baby, we've not even started the honeymoon yet."

"Thanks, Gray, but you guys go ahead and sit together. It was a really nice thought, and I appreciate it, but it's not necessary."

We didn't have to wait too long before boarding the plane. It seemed like we were in the air and on our way home in no time at all. I just wished we didn't have such a long layover in Chicago.

"Can we make plans for tonight?" Gray asked when the plane leveled off. He had a death grip on my hand.

"Absolutely. What do you have in mind?"

"Takeout and hours of uninterrupted sex. Does that tempt you at all?"

I pretended to think it over when in reality I was already semi-hard just from hearing the word *sex* roll off his tongue. "Mmm, I guess it depends on the quality of the takeout you bring to my apartment."

"I'll bring you steak and lobster if that's what it takes to get to spend the night in your bed with your arms and legs wrapped around me. I'm not going to play games and pretend I don't want you."

"Then I won't bother playing hard to get either," I said, leaning closer until my lips were pressed against Gray's ear. "I dreamed about us last night." He turned his head and looked at me, heat flaring in his beautiful blue eyes. He squirmed a little in his seat. "It was so intense and real that I woke up panting, sweaty, and hard as a rock. My ass was quivering and begging to be filled by you. It was all I could do to let you sleep."

"Chase," Gray whispered hoarsely.

"I'm not playing either. I want you just as badly as you want me. I've wanted you since the second our eyes first met. In fact, it feels like I've waited my whole life for the moment I get to take you into my body."

"No pressure." Gray suddenly looked nervous.

"You're going to be amazing. I have no doubt." I kissed him softly. "At least I made you forget about your fear of flying for a few minutes."

"Maybe the next time we travel we can join the mile high club." He placed his hand on my leg and slowly moved it up my thigh, stopping just before he got to my crotch. My breathing hitched in my throat as the image of Gray screwing me fast and furious in a tiny airplane bathroom popped into my mind. His pinky finger grazed over my bulge, and my dick jerked to life. I swallowed hard.

"Tease."

"It's a promise," Gray said with a wicked gleam in his eye.

We behaved for the rest of the trip home. I worked on my iPad while he read more of his book. Every once in a while, he'd dog-ear a page. I finally asked why he was doing that, and he said he was marking sexual positions he wanted to try with me. Hmm.

It was three thirty in the afternoon when we finally pulled up in front of Ellie's house. I got out of the car and walked Xavier to the front door, needing a private moment with him. I set Bess down on the front porch.

"Call me anytime you want to talk or if you just want to hang out. I'm here for you whenever you need me, okay?"

Xavier threw his arms around me and hugged me tight. "Thank you for everything, Chase. You're still my hero." His voice still held a trace of sadness.

"I will slay any dragon, any place, any time for you." One more hug and I jogged back to Gray's car that was idling at the curb.

"Everything okay?" he asked when I climbed inside.

"It will be now that he's home and surrounded by the people who love him most." Gray pulled away from the curb and aimed his car in the direction of my apartment. "What time do you want to come over tonight?"

"Does six work for you? I want to drop by and smooch my princess, get cleaned up, and pick up our dinner."

"Are we *really* going to eat the dinner you bring over? I would settle for frozen pizza after—" Gray silenced me with a kiss hot enough to fog up his glasses.

"I have something to prove," Gray said once he'd broken our kiss.

"You already have," I told him, loving the boyish smile that spread across his handsome face. "You're so fucking cute."

"Cute?" He pouted prettily at me. "I don't think I want to be called cute. Hot or sexy maybe. But not cute. You make me sound like a fuzzy kitten."

"I think you're hot and sexy all the fucking time," I told him honestly. "You push all my buttons, but then there are times you say the cutest, sweetest things. *Wooing* happens to be cute, sweet, and funny." He seemed pleased with my explanation. "See you in a few hours, Gray." He started to get out of the car to help me, but I stopped him. "If you come up now, you won't leave. Go see your princess."

I kissed him quickly on the lips and pulled back. Gray popped the trunk, and I retrieved my suitcase and George. I didn't look back as I walked into my apartment building because if I did, I'd beg him to stay, and it would ruin his plans for wooing me. He wanted to do this right, and I'd be a fool not to let him. There was nothing wrong with wanting to be treated like I was special.

I called Gram as soon as I got done sorting out my clothes and the new novelty items. She answered on the first ring as if she'd been waiting for my call all day.

"Soooo, did you boys get your care package in LA?"

"Gram, I'd have another talk about boundaries if I thought it would help. Clearly it goes in one ear and out the other."

"Bah," she said dismissively. "Just thank me for my thoughtfulness. I sure hope you boys were able to enjoy the goodies."

"Thank you for your thoughtfulness, although no man wants his grandmother buying him sex toys and condoms. We didn't get a chance to use them. In fact, the only person who got any pleasure from them was the TSA agent who humiliated me when she pulled them out of my bag for everyone to see."

"That's horrible," Gram said. "You guys were there for three nights and didn't screw like rabbits?" Of course that was the part she'd think was horrible.

"Xavier had an emergency and needed me. He ended up staying in our suite."

"What happened to my boy?" Concern for him made her voice rise several octaves.

"I really don't know what happened. Xavier was very tight-lipped about it. I only know that he's left his band and come home. Gray and I dropped him off at Ellie's after our plane landed."

"I need to call him right now," Gram said. "Are you free for dinner tonight?"

"I have plans with Gray, but thanks for the invite."

"So tonight's the night?"

"Gram." My voice held a warning that had her backing down.

"Okay, honey. Call me when you get a chance, and I'll see you on Sunday. Invite Gray to join us."

"I will, Gram."

"Great. I love you."

"I love you too."

I sent Ava a text as soon as I finished talking to Gram. She hadn't been home in weeks, but I figured with the way things had been going lately, I'd better let her know I was planning on entertaining company. All night.

Attaboy, was her immediate reply.

I looked at my watch and saw that I had about an hour to get ready. I spent a lot of time showering, manscaping, and making sure every part of me looked its best. Every muscle in my body tensed with the realization that Gray would have me very soon. I stood in my closet for a ridiculous amount of time trying to figure out what to wear. In the end, I decided on a snug T-shirt and faded jeans. I checked my reflection in the mirror and liked the way the jeans clung to my ass and made my legs look really long. The shirt clung to my chest and arms without being tacky. I noticed my nipple ring stood out and wondered how that would affect Gray. Would he stare at it throughout dinner, or would it turn him on enough that he'd want to set dinner aside and take me to bed first? I was fine with either scenario and had myself worked up to semi-hard by the time the doorbell rang.

I opened my door fast, not bothering to pretend I wasn't over-the-moon happy about him being there. I noticed Gray carried a large takeout bag in one hand and his overnight bag in the other. I took the bag of food from him and headed to the kitchen. "This smells great."

"Italian," Gray answered as he followed behind me. "I wasn't sure what you liked, so I ordered a few different things."

I placed the bag on the table and turned to him. "You didn't have to go to so much trouble. I like just about anything." I wrapped my arms around his neck and pressed my body to his. "I'm so glad you're here, Gray." He gave me a one-armed hug since he still held his overnight bag in his other hand. "Here, let me take your jacket and bag."

I hung his jacket up in the coat closet by the door, then retreated to my bedroom. Chills of anticipation rippled through me when I set his bag on my dresser. We were really going to spend the night together. Gray was standing in the exact spot where I'd left him. I took in his casual attire and noticed we were dressed identically, the only difference being that he wore a long-sleeved T-shirt.

Gray's eyes landed on my chest, and I knew the instant his eyes locked onto my nipple ring. I felt my nipples hardening just from his smoldering look. At that point, I wondered if I'd combust before he even got inside me.

"Did you wear that shirt to test me, Chase?" His voice was sinful. "Are you testing my limits? I have to tell you that I'm at my limit and about to snap."

"Would it help you at all if I said that you've charmed me more than you can imagine? Both before and during LA." Gray silently took a step closer to me, but we were still separated by a foot or more. "Winning George for me scored high marks." His eyes returned to my nipple, and he licked his lips. Almost there. "Rushing to help my best friend during his darkest hour sent you off the charts." He needed a little prodding, so I reached up and caressed my nipple with a finger, lightly tugging the ring and gasping in pleasure. His resistance broke like a dam, and he was on me in a flash.

"I warned you, Chase." I was shoved up against the kitchen wall so hard the air whooshed out of my lungs. He crashed his lips hard against mine, taking what he wanted, and I loved every second of it. He drove me wild and brought out a side of me I hadn't known existed. "Take me to your bedroom," he whispered hungrily in my ear after he was done ravaging my lips. I did exactly what he demanded.

Once inside, we didn't even bother to close the door; we just began tearing each other's clothes off. We were desperate for that skin-on-skin contact, to touch, taste, and fuck each other senseless. No interruptions and no obligations.

We came together in a tangled heap in the middle of my bed, rolling, kissing, and rutting like animals. Had I ever been so turned on in my life? The honest answer was no. "I need you inside me, Gray."

"Not yet."

Gray pinned my hands over my head and rocked his dick against mine. The pleasure was so intense I could have come right then. I needed him to stop or slow down. I dug my knees into either side of his waist and rolled him so I was on top. I had his cock in my mouth before he had a chance to catch up with what was happening.

Gray fisted both hands in my hair but must have been at war with himself. One minute he was pulling me down farther on his cock and the next he was trying to push me off. "This how you want to play, baby?" He wrapped his strong arms around my head, wrapped his legs around my upper torso and rolled me so he straddled my head with his cock still in my mouth. "Fuck. That's hot."

Gray fucked my mouth, alternating between fast bursts and slow glides against my tongue. He dominated me, and it was the sexiest thing I'd ever seen in my life. His eyes were the purest blue when his lustful, inner beast took over. Gray's hands were still tangled in my hair, and he kept growling my name over and over.

I grabbed his firm ass cheeks with both hands and spread them wide, exposing his hole. I felt his muscles tense and bunch beneath my hands. I circled his tight hole with my middle finger several times, driving him out of his mind. He dropped his hands to the bed above my head and snapped his hips harder, fucking my mouth deeper.

Gray was leaking heavily on my tongue, signaling he was about to come. I gripped his ass harder, wanting him to finish in my mouth, but he had other ideas. He lifted off my body, rolled off the bed, and walked to his overnight bag. Gray pulled out a large box of condoms and a bottle of lube and brandished them in the air.

"We already have supplies," I teased.

"Those cute novelty condoms probably won't hold up to my raging desire to have you, Chase." I watched as he tore open a condom wrapper with his teeth and quickly rolled it on his dick. I never knew watching a man put on a condom could be so fucking hot. "It would be like someone trying to plug a leak in the Hoover Dam with a Band-Aid. And I'm not going to trust your comfort to a brand of lube I've never heard of."

He prowled back over to the bed—no other word could describe his predatory gait. His body was drawn tight with need, and I started to feel apprehensive about having all that intensity aimed at me. I'd never been on the receiving end of anyone like him. My ass quivered in fear and excitement.

Gray climbed onto the bed, then caressed my face until my apprehension faded. Yes, this man wanted me so bad I could smell it, but he'd never hurt me. "I'm going to slow things down a bit," he told me as he placed kisses on my face. "The ferocious need that's clawing at me is scaring me a little bit."

Gray cupped my face in both hands and made love to my mouth with his lips and tongue. I felt like I'd been turned inside out with every part of me on display for him to see. I felt restless and peaceful at the same time.

"Gray, I need more. I need you inside me." I'd never been so unafraid to voice my wants and needs. "I don't want to wait any more."

"I like you pleading for my cock, Chase." He reached over and grabbed the lube from where he'd dropped it on the bed. The snick of the cap was the sexiest thing I'd ever heard. I unashamedly spread my legs when Gray moved into position between them. "Why do I feel like I've waited my whole life to be with you?" He poured a generous amount of lube on his fingers.

His words moved me like nothing else could because they were genuine and spoken from his heart. He literally had me where he wanted me so there was no need for false flattery to get me into bed. "You can dial it back. You've already won me over."

"I meant every word."

Gray leaned forward and braced his elbow over my shoulder, lowering himself until his lips touched mine. He deepened the kiss, his tongue licking and stroking mine, while below, he smeared the lube around the rim of my nerve-laden ring. The hot kiss and cool, tingly lube were a beautiful attack on my senses, and I couldn't get enough. I fisted his hair to hold him in place while arching my body into his touch, silently begging for more.

A devilish chuckle rumbled through him as he slid one finger deep inside me. *Stingy bastard*. It wasn't enough. Gray crooked his finger to peg my prostate and stars exploded behind my closed eyelids. He slowly withdrew his digit and teased my puckered rim before pushing back inside me and pegging me once more. Gray repeated the pattern until I became a shaking, snarling mess beneath him.

He added a second finger on his next penetration and that's when I lost all control of myself. The crazed need to have Gray inside me took over, blocking out any thought or reason. I yanked his head back to break our kiss. Gray's lips formed a feral smile when he saw the crazed look in my eyes.

"Fuck me now," I demanded.

"You want to feel my dick inside you?" His words were gruff and spoken barely above a gravelly whisper. I nodded my head, too caught up in his eyes to speak. "Take it, Chase. Take what you need from me. Show me how badly you want me inside you." Gray withdrew his fingers from my tight channel and slicked up his condom-covered dick with lube from the bottle. "It's right here and ready for you," he said, stroking his dick for my viewing pleasure. He released his cock and leaned over me, placing both hands on the bed beside my head.

I reached between our bodies and wrapped my hand around his dick. It was iron hard and pulsed in my hand as I lined it up with my puckered hole. This was it, the moment I'd wanted since I'd first seen him. I kept my eyes locked on his, not wanting to miss a single expression on his beautiful face when he breached me for the first time.

I wrapped my legs around the back of his muscular thighs and raised my hips up off the mattress at the same time I fed the swollen head of his dick into my ass. The coolness of the lube helped offset the burn of being stretched to accept his size. Gray was by far the largest man I'd been with. I thrust my hips up in short jabs until he was buried balls deep inside me.

Gray's beautiful eyes looked wild. "You're burning me alive," he whispered hungrily. His muscles bunched beneath my hands as he prepared to pull back.

"Don't move yet," I told him, wrapping my arms around his neck. "I need a minute." He grinned wickedly, the primal beast inside him pounding its hairy chest over the fact that I needed extra time to adjust to his size. His sexy arrogance only turned me on more, which helped my body relax around him. Gray moved as soon as he felt the tension leave my body.

With breath hissing through his lips, Gray carefully pulled his hips back. I felt every ridge, every vein rasp across my nerve endings; the intensity had me whimpering in his arms.

"Feel good, baby?" His voice was sinfully dark, and I wanted to hear it in my ears every day going forward.

"So good, Gray." He drove back in, making sure to graze over my prostate as he got as far inside me as humanly possible. My eyes rolled back in my head, and I slid my hands down to grab his firm ass. "Please don't stop."

"Hadn't planned on it." Gray ran his fingers through my hair so gently it brought tears to my eyes. The look in his eyes was one I'd never seen aimed at me, and any doubt that might have remained vanished into thin air. He lowered his lips and made love to my mouth while he made love to my body.

I gripped his ass harder, gouging my fingers into his firm flesh, trying to get closer to him. He resisted my efforts and kept his strokes slow and steady, his lips never leaving mine. It seemed like he relished every moan, sigh, and whimper I breathed into his mouth.

An unfamiliar urge to rut and fuck began to build inside me and got stronger every time he ignored my silent pleas for more. I tore my mouth from his and looked into his bedroom eyes. "I want more, and I will take it." Without warning, I wrapped my arms tighter around him, rose up suddenly, and caught him off guard. I used my momentum to push him to his back and mount him. I wrapped my hands around the rail of the headboard as leverage and rode up and down his hard dick.

"Fuck me," he said in shock.

"That's what I'm doing. Perhaps I'm not doing it right." I released the bed, arched my back and placed my hands on his tense thighs. I threw my head back in ecstasy as I rode him with everything I had.

"Chase." It was his turn to do the begging. He put his hands on my waist and pulled me down harder on his cock. "You feel so fucking good, so tight it feels like you're strangling my dick."

I sat up straight and placed my hands over his on my waist. I looked down at his gorgeous face and loved what I saw. His head was tilted back, his eyes were closed, and he was biting his bottom lip. I could have come right then without touching my cock, which was something that had never happened to me. I slowed my motion to a slow roll of my hips, ratcheting up the lust another notch.

"Jesus, Chase," he said, looking up into my face. Gray's lips were slightly parted as he panted for breath, but it was the look of wonder and reverence in his eyes that grabbed me and wouldn't let go.

"I know, Gray." I laid my chest against his and pressed our lips together, hoping to show him how I felt as words failed me. We clung to each other, both our mouths and bodies, as we rode out the waves of desire that threatened to pull us under.

Gray wrapped his arms around me tightly and rolled us over so he was once again on top. He placed his arms beneath my knees and pushed them toward my chest. I started to think about taking a yoga class to improve my flexibility, but Gray snapped his hips forward and all was forgotten.

I grabbed his biceps and held on for dear life while he fucked in and out of me like a jackhammer. Never in my life had anything felt so good. I don't know what I said at that point or if I said anything at all. I just drifted off into some alternate universe of pleasure while my orgasm built and built until the need to come physically hurt me.

"I love how you curl your toes, Chase. It tells me how well I'm fucking you."

"Yesss."

"You're squeezing my cock so hard. Your orgasm is right fucking there." The broad head of his dick jabbed my prostate, and blinding pleasure ripped through my body. I felt my body tighten one last painful time before I came long and hard; the pleasure singeing me from head to toe. My release splashed all over my chest and abdomen. Gray growled deep in his throat and kept hitting that spot inside me until my body quit shaking and he'd wrung every drop from me.

"God, you're beautiful," Gray said from above me, bringing me back down to earth.

I opened my eyes and focused on his face as he continued to drive deep inside me in long, hard strokes. Eyes locked on mine, Gray looked like a savage man who was desperate to come. He pumped into me a few more times before he pulled out suddenly and yanked off the condom. I watched in awe as he began jerking his dick in short rapid motions.

"Chase." His mouth fell open, and his face contorted into a mask of masculine beauty as Gray's orgasm tore through him. He painted my chest with his seed while he jerked above me, calling out my name.

I knew it then, even if I wasn't ready to admit it out loud, that our souls had connected.

Gray lay down on top of me, not caring that he was covering himself in our mixed spunk, and kissed me while our breathing and rapidly beating hearts returned to normal. Eventually he rolled beside me, and I rolled onto my side so I could look at him. We both wore the same look of shock and awe like *what the fuck had just happened here?*

Acknowledging how I really felt about him, even if only to myself, had my nerves feeling frayed. I wanted to hide behind a flippant remark, but I couldn't. This moment meant too much to me to casually blow it off. Maybe Gray sensed how I was feeling, and maybe he felt it too because he ran the backs of his fingers over my cheek. His tenderness brought tears to my eyes.

"I feel it too," Gray whispered. "I know it's scary, but one step at a time, remember?"

Gray pressed his lips to mine and kissed me so thoroughly and sweetly that I forgot to be afraid. Instead, I chose to live in the moment and enjoy the beautiful man in my bed. I'd worry about the tomorrows when they arrived.

CHAPTER
Twenty-Seven

Gray

O KAY, SO IT WAS GOING TO BE HARDER THAN I THOUGHT TO PRETEND I hadn't just spent the best night of my life with the guy beside me on the elevator. That morning had been even more amazing than the night before. I found myself in a tangled knot with Chase, our legs and feet interwoven, as I clung to him as if he were a life raft. I used Chase's body wash, and it made me almost giddy to smell like him. I just wished we could have driven to work together instead of arriving separately, but I understood why he declined.

I couldn't resist looking at him out of the corner of my eye and caught him doing the same. It was going to be hard to keep our blossoming feelings to ourselves. I didn't know what I'd do if Chase looked at me in the boardroom like he had the previous night when he'd realized just how deep our connection went. He'd worn the same expression that morning when he finished sucking me off in the shower. He'd risen to his feet and looked into my eyes.

"Can we be boyfriends now?" he'd asked me.

My answer had been a resounding yes followed by me dropping to my knees to thank him properly for the gift he'd given me. The memory was still so fresh in my mind that I easily recalled every sound, touch, and taste from our joint shower. I could definitely get used to waking up to him every morning. I knew it was too soon, but... My phone ringing in my pocket interrupted my train of thought, which was probably a good thing. I looked at the number on the display and smiled broadly. I looked over at Chase and found him watching me. I gave him a thumbs up and answered the call.

"Good morning, Mr. Heston," I said into the phone.

"Mr. Wright." His voice was clipped but professional. "I trust you had a good flight home."

"I did, thank you. What can I do for you this morning?"

"We've decided to go with your ad campaign. I'd like you to send over the contracts within the next hour so my legal team can look them over. I want to have this finalized by the end of the day so we can proceed."

"That's great news, Mr. Heston. I really appreciate the opportunity, and I'm positive you won't regret it. My personal assistant will be in touch within the hour."

"I'm looking forward to it. Please give my best to Chase." *Bastard.*

"Of course." I refused to let his parting remark ruin the best morning I'd ever had. Chase and I signing our agency's biggest client was a pretty big deal too.

"Oh my god," Chase said and began to dance excitedly just as the elevator opened on our floor. "We did it. He agreed to sign with us, didn't he?" His brown eyes were alight with happiness and pride, and I was glad I hadn't let my jealous beast make a mockery of our accomplishment by sounding off to Heston on the phone.

"We sure did," I answered, matching his happy dance moves. We danced our way into the lobby, not caring who saw us. Luckily, not many people had arrived as early as we had. "I'm going to send an email to everyone telling them that we are having an impromptu meeting at ten."

We stood looking at each other with matching goofy expressions. I wanted to kiss him so fucking bad to celebrate our success and because he looked so damn beautiful. I settled for a fist bump before we reluctantly went our separate ways.

I sent out the email to all employees, except my brother who was still out on paternity leave. I called him instead.

"This better be fucking good," Preston growled into my ear. "Do you know that we've only had three hours of sleep?"

"Sorry, bro. I'll call you back in a few hours to tell you we got the Heston's account. Go back to sleep." I worked hard to keep the laughter out of my voice.

"Wait," he said into the phone. "Are you serious right now? You and Chase reeled them in?"

"Chase, mostly," I admitted. "He was amazing. Mitchell took a shine to him, but he remained professional and really sold him on our campaign."

"You know what this means, right?"

"Um, I'm the greatest brother in all the land?"

"Well, there is that, but I was referring to promoting Chase to the art department. I know he's destined for even greater things, but the position would gain him much needed experience. Even without the added revenue the campaign will provide, Chase deserves a bump in pay for putting up with you for three nights and four days." Four nights. And with any luck I'd get to share many more.

"You're absolutely right. I'll have Ellie put the package together and present it to him this afternoon."

"You don't want to do it yourself?" I could tell by his tone of voice he found that odd.

"It would be best for everyone involved if I recused myself from Chase's performance reviews, promotions, or even reprimands."

"It's like that, huh?" Preston could barely contain his gloating. "I want to be present when you make the announcement to the team. What do you have planned?"

"I just sent an email to all employees to be in the conference room at ten for a special announcement."

"I'll pick up some celebratory donuts and pastries from Adam and Steve's Bakery and be there in time for the meeting. Afterward, I will personally meet with Chase and offer him the promotion."

"Thanks, Pres. It means a lot to me." *He means a lot to me.*

"I'm really proud of you, Gray. It has never escaped my notice how hard you work so I can spend more time with my wife. I want you to know I'll be committed to doing the same for you when the time comes."

I was pretty sure the time had arrived, but it was too soon to think about it, let alone say it out loud. If I was ready to say it, I sure as hell wouldn't say it to Preston first. "Thanks, bro. I'm going to email Ellie and ask her to have the benefits and salary details ready for you to present to Chase. Give my love to the ladies," I said before we ended our call.

I typed out a quick email to Ellie. She was always one of the first employees to arrive, so I knew she'd get the email and put the offer and benefits package together right away. I ended my email by asking how Cruz was. My desk phone rang immediately.

"Wow, one business trip with you and Chase gets promoted," she said jokingly. I cringed because this was Chase's biggest fear. I had to bite back the first remark that came to mind. I couldn't have thin skin and lash out every time someone made a comment I didn't like.

"He earned it, El." My calm tone made me proud. "Chase is tremendously talented and handled Heston like a champ. I promised him a better position as soon as one became available, and one just did."

"You won't regret giving him a chance, Gray. And thank you for bringing my brother home to me. He said you refused to accept any money for his ticket, but—"

"I won't take your money either. How's he doing?"

"Xavier is going out of his way to cover up his broken heart. He keeps telling me he wants to put it behind him and move on. He did get choked up when he talked about how much he'll miss his bandmates. I don't know how to help him, Gray."

"All you can do is continue to be there for him."

"Thank you. You're a great guy, you know that?"

"El…"

"I mean it. You are a wonderful employer, friend, brother, son, and the list goes on and on. Someday some lucky guy is going to come along and snatch you up and never let go." I prayed my lucky guy had already found me.

"Thank you, Ellie. That means a lot." It was obvious Cruz hadn't told his sister about Chase and me. Shockingly, asking Cruz to keep our secret hadn't even occurred to me. Would she be so proud of me if she knew I was engaging in a sexual relationship with an employee, one she thought of like a little brother? Would she still think I was a good employer then? I forced those thoughts out of my head and cleared my throat. "Will you be able to get the salary and benefits ready for Preston by ten?"

"Absolutely. I wish I could be there to see the look on Chase's face." So did I, but I knew that wasn't a good idea.

"Thank you, El. See you in the conference room."

I hung up and started a detailed email to Rosie. I needed her to get the contracts to Heston's assistant right away so we could get the deal signed, sealed, and delivered this afternoon. Once Heston signed the contract, he'd be expected to wire half our consulting fee within twenty-four hours. God, this was a big deal, and I needed it to all go perfectly. Anxiety started to set in when I thought about how much needed to be done and how many things could go wrong. I started to feel nauseous and opened my desk drawer to look for antacids. There was a quick knock on my door before it opened. I looked up and saw Chase peeking around the door. Just the sight of him calmed me.

"Hi, come in." Chase entered my office and closed the door behind him. "Do you miss me already?"

"Maybe or maybe I just wanted to bring you some coffee." He smiled mischievously at me. "This is going to be harder than we thought, isn't it?"

He handed me a steaming cup of hazelnut coffee and sat down in a chair in front of my desk.

"Yes, it's going to be very difficult to keep my hands and lips off you. You don't know how badly I wanted to kiss you in that elevator." Chase's eyes darkened with desire. "But we're grown men who can and will control ourselves. I made a promise to you, Chase, and I plan on keeping it." The desire in his eyes changed to something softer, almost like… *Nope.* I couldn't allow myself to get my hopes up.

"I also stopped by to ask if you wanted to go with me to Gram's for dinner on Sunday. I wasn't sure when I'd get another chance to ask you."

Chase shifted his gaze away and began fiddling with the buttons on the front of his shirt. What was the reason for his sudden nervousness? Did he think I didn't want to see him this weekend? Where was his head? I rose from my chair and walked around to sit on the edge of my desk, planting myself directly in front of him. He looked up at me curiously.

"I was hoping you'd go to brunch at my mom's house tomorrow to meet my family." His eyes widened in surprise. "In fact, I was hoping to spend the entire weekend with you." I laid it all out there for him. I wanted to be with him, and I wasn't about to pretend any differently.

"I…um," he began. "I have to work a few hours at Bottoms Up tonight, but I'm free the rest of the weekend."

"Do you want to spend the weekend with me, Chase?"

He swallowed nervously. "Yes, I really do."

I was about to break my promise to him already. I started to lean toward him with the intent of giving him a reassuring kiss. His soulful eyes stared at my lips as they inched closer. My office door flew open suddenly, and I jerked myself upright. Chase's eyes were wide as saucers, and my heart pounded in my chest. Damn, that was close.

"Oh, I didn't realize you were in a meeting with Chase. I'm so sorry." Rosie began to back out the door.

"Rosie, stay." My voice was firmer than I had intended. "You're not interrupting anything. We were just going over a few things before our big announcement in"—I looked at my watch—"ninety minutes." I aimed for casual but wasn't sure I'd achieved it because the blood rushing through my ears dulled my hearing.

"I was just about to leave," Chase said as he rose to his feet. "Are you free for lunch?" he asked Rosie.

"Sure, I can't wait to catch up and hear all about your trip." Rosie patted his arm as he walked by.

My mind immediately catalogued every wonderful moment I'd shared with him. I could hear the seagulls and smell the cotton candy as we made our way down the boardwalk. I heard the sounds he made when we made out in the hot tub. My ass cheeks tightened at the thought of the rim job he'd given me. The final night where he fed me dessert while I read. I could almost feel the silkiness of his hair as it sifted through my fingers and see his sleepy, early-morning smile.

"Sounds great," Chase said to Rosie, but his eyes were locked on mine. A faint blush spread across his cheeks and he bit his bottom lip, making me think he was reliving special moments too. Luckily, Rosie had her back toward Chase, or the jig would be up. No way she'd misread the dreamy look in Chase's beautiful eyes. "See you both in the conference room."

"Okay," I said, returning to my desk chair as Chase left my office. "The first thing we need to do…"

"Gray," Rosie said softly. "You two will need to do a better job if you don't want us to know you're dating."

"What?"

"I've known you for five years. I was one of your first employees." She paused for a second and studied me with narrowed eyes. "I've never seen you look at anyone or anything the way you just looked at Chase Rivers. You should've seen your face when I told him I wanted to hear all about his trip. Your eyes were burning so brightly I expected laser beams to shoot out of them." I gave her my best death glare, but it only made her giggle. "I didn't need to turn around to know Chase was wearing some similar sappy expression on his face because I could feel it radiating off him." She slapped her slim hand on my desk. "Then there was the kiss you were about to plant on his lips when I walked in." She *tsk*ed at me and rolled her eyes. "Work harder, Gray, or he's going to have a very difficult time working here."

"Rosie, please…"

She held up her tiny hand to stop me. "I adore him, Gray. I would never do anything to hurt him or you. I mean it." And I knew she did.

"You can't say anything to him, Rosie. If you do, he might break things off, and I…" I couldn't finish the sentence. "I will do better."

"Okay," Rosie nodded. "Now, let's go over the Heston contracts once more before I send them. God, this is huge, Gray," she said, then squealed. "I'm so happy for our agency."

I spent the next thirty minutes giving her step-by-step instructions. I knew I could count on Rosie, and that helped my anxiety tremendously. After she returned to her desk to start working, I returned calls and emails that had come in while I was away. They were minor enough that they could wait for my return, but I didn't want them hanging over my head until Monday. I couldn't ignore all my clients in favor of Mitchell Heston.

Rosie copied me on the email she sent to Heston's assistant, Miss Rollins, with the contracts. She did everything exactly like I'd asked her to, and I was very proud of her professionalism. Preston and I had surrounded ourselves with quality employees at every level, which was the true reason behind our early success.

My brother showed up a half hour before our meeting. He took the time to visit with everyone and show them pictures of my Gracie. I missed her already and couldn't wait to hold her again. I couldn't wait for Chase to meet her too. *Chase.* I remembered what Rosie said about doing a better job of hiding my feelings for him. I closed my eyes and took several calming breaths. I focused my thoughts and energy on the presentation and behaving professionally for both our benefits. I could do this. I would do this. For us.

At ten o'clock sharp, all eyes shifted to me when I entered the conference room. Judging by their grins, our staff had all guessed what the big announcement was going to be. I stood in front of the room and took in the happy faces of the Wright Creations employees. Every person in the room had played a part in signing the Heston's account, so this was their victory too. I decided to talk to Preston about issuing performance bonuses to everyone with the payout based on their level of involvement.

"I received a verbal commitment from Mitchell Heston this morning that we have been awarded the Heston's Luxury Suites account." The room erupted into cheers and congratulations all around. I waited for everyone to quiet down before I spoke again. "Preston and I want to thank each and every one of you for your dedication to this project. I think this is the beginning of new and exciting things for our company."

Preston added a few words before we shared some pastries and coffee. I thanked everyone again as they came up and congratulated me. I saw Preston approach Chase right before the celebration ended, and I wished again that I could join them. I squelched the ridiculous urge to follow them as they left the conference room. I was certain I'd hear from Chase soon after the meeting.

Thirty minutes later, I received a text from him. He asked if I had a few minutes to spare for him, and of course I said yes. My pulse hummed loudly in my ears while I waited for him to arrive. Did he think he was getting the promotion because of our relationship? Luckily, he didn't keep me waiting long.

"Hey," he said shyly. It wasn't the reaction I'd expected.

"Hey, yourself. What's up?"

"I need to ask you two questions about my promotion."

"Okay." *Fuck, here we go.*

"Was this your idea?"

"No, it was all Preston. He reminded me that we promised you a promotion when a position became available. You've proved yourself and earned it all on your own, Chase. I had nothing to do with this promotion except to agree with Preston when he brought it up."

"Is the salary package being offered standard for the position, Gray? It seems like one hell of a pay increase to doodle and come up with slogans all day. I feel so fucking stupid asking you these questions, but I have to, or it will fester."

I picked up the phone and dialed Rosie's extension. "I don't want to be disturbed unless Jesus walks in or Mitchell Heston or his assistant calls."

"Got it," she said perkily.

I hung up the phone and walked around to sit in the chair beside my boyfriend. A thrill vibrated through my body just thinking the words to myself. I angled my body toward him, and he did the same. I reached over and took his hands in mine.

"Chase, I honestly don't know what your new salary is, and I don't need to know. Preston reminded me of our promise to you when I called him this morning. He asked me to email Ellie and have the package details put together so he could present it to you this morning, and I did. That was my only involvement." He took a deep breath, then his expression softened.

"I was afraid you padded the offer so I would quit my other jobs and spend more time with you." He looked slightly embarrassed, but he shouldn't.

"I do want to spend more time with you—last night and this morning felt…right—but I want your creative talent working in the art department too."

"It really did," he said wistfully. He closed his eyes and let out a soft sigh.

Fuck, this man could unravel me with the simplest of gestures. "Chase?"

"Hmmm," his dreamy eyes popped open, and he looked at me.

"You need to leave my office before I do something really irresponsible."

"Like what?" he whispered sexily.

I released one of his hands so I could knock on my desk with a fist. "This is a really solid desk, Chase."

His mouth popped open in a silent "Oh."

"Run for your life, baby." A promise was a promise, so I returned to my chair behind my desk. "Is it okay with you if I come by Bottoms Up tonight? I'd like to bring my best friend by to meet my boyfriend."

"Mmm, I love the way that sounds." He licked his lips naughtily, and his eyes screamed at me to take him right then and there. Chase grinned wickedly as he rose from the chair. I did the only thing I could think of to save us from each other.

"Out," I said firmly while pointing to the door.

CHAPTER
Twenty-Eight

Chase

I KNOCKED ON JACK'S OFFICE DOOR AND WAITED FOR HIS ACKNOWL-
edgment before I entered. Jack's dog, Charlie, came around the desk to
greet me, so I squatted down to pet him. The German shepherd held up
his paw, and I shook it. I didn't know much about Jack Murphy, no one really
did, but I knew he was having a hard time if Charlie was in the bar with him.

Charlie was a service dog who'd been trained to assist veterans suffering from PTSD. That wasn't something Jack had divulged. Charlie wore
special tags and sometimes a vest that allowed him to go places other dogs
couldn't. I had googled the initials I'd seen on Charlie's tag and learned about
his training and the things he could do to assist Jack.

"What's up," Jack asked in his gruff voice. "Did you have a nice trip?"

"It was awesome," I said. Jack raised an eyebrow, and I must have let
the dreaminess of my new relationship seep into my voice. "We signed the
client, and I got a promotion."

"Congratulations, Chase. Does that mean you're leaving us?" Jack gave nothing away in his voice or body language. I was pretty sure he liked having me as an employee, but it was hard to tell.

"Not if it leaves you shorthanded. Liam is new, and Dave hasn't been here very long. You've always been really good to me, Jack, and I've enjoyed working for you. I'll stay as long as you—" Jack held up his hand to cut me off.

"Chase, I appreciate your offer to stay on, but we'll be just fine. Tonight can be your last night. I had a feeling you'd be leaving soon." He smiled crookedly. "I hope everything works out for you the way you want it to, but if not, my door is always open, okay?" *Wow*.

"That means a lot to me, Jack. Thank you." An awkward silence fell between us, so I decided to say goodbye and get back to work behind the bar.

Gray came in with his best friend an hour or so later. It was the first time I'd seen Gray since he'd thrown me out of his office before lunch. Poor guy. I'd made rules for him to follow, then tempted him to break every single one of them. Gray's eyes met mine, and his face lit up like the Christmas tree at Rockefeller Center. God, would I ever look at him and not want to kiss his lips off?

Gray walked up to the bar, and I did what came naturally to me. I leaned over and he met me halfway for a kiss. The feel of his warm mouth against mine felt like coming home. A happy sigh escaped my lips when we pulled apart. We stared at each other for countless minutes, grinning like two idiots. Miller finally waved his hand between us to break our connection.

"Hi, I'm Miller Brexler." He shoved his hand toward me, and I shook it. He narrowed his eyes and studied me closely. It made me uneasy and nervous because I wanted Miller to like me. He had been there the night of the surprise party and probably didn't have a very good first impression of me. "It's great to meet you, Chase." He was the kind of jovial guy whose eyes glittered with good humor.

"It's great to meet you too. First round is on me, boys, so pick your poison?" Miller ordered a beer, and Gray ordered a rum and Coke.

"Thanks, babe," Gray said to me when I handed him the drink. "We're going to go shoot pool for a bit." Miller offered a small wave before moving over to the pool tables.

"It's about to get crazy in here. I get off at midnight if you want to come over." Gray's eyes took on that stormy quality that let me know exactly what he thought about spending the night with me. He looked down at his watch and back up at me.

"Do you mind if I just wait here for you, and we can leave together? Miller and I can play darts and pool and get caught up." I must have looked skeptical because he started to explain. "I'm not trying to keep an eye on you or anything, and I'll leave if you're uncomfortable."

"I don't mind if you stay. I just don't want you to get bored."

"Fat chance." Gray winked before following Miller.

"I see things are going well for you two," said a soft voice behind me. I turned and found Liam standing behind me. His eyes were tracking Gray as he made his way to the pool tables. Liam's hazel eyes shifted back to me. "Isn't he your boss?"

Damn it. "Technically, I work for his brother, but since he's part owner of the company, yes, he is."

"Wow." I was prepared to get defensive if need be, but there was no censure in his voice. "Jack said this is your last night working with us." He slapped me on the arm. "It's been really fun getting to know you. I hope you won't be a stranger." He sauntered down to his side of the bar and began taking orders.

"There's something familiar about that kid," came a voice I'd know anywhere. I turned and found JJ practically lying across the bar so he could get a look at Liam's ass. I flicked his forehead, and he sat back in his stool.

"What's up with you?" I asked, aiming for casual. He'd appeared out of the blue twice, both times when Gray was at the bar. JJ didn't just show up anywhere. There was a rhyme and reason to everything he did.

"Just thought I'd pop by to see if you're busy later."

"He's going to be very, very busy later." I was so shocked by JJ's appearance I hadn't noticed Gray had returned to the bar. *Oh fuck, this wasn't going to be pretty.* "You must be JJ," Gray said to him and held out a hand.

"I am, and you must be Clark," JJ responded as he shook my boyfriend's hand. Gray smiled a little at the nickname I'd given him before we'd been formally introduced. They squeezed each other's hands until their knuckles were white. The demonstration of machismo was a little funny but mostly lame. I was with Gray, and nothing JJ did or said would change my mind.

"Grayson Wright," Gray corrected as he released JJ's hand. They continued to stare each other down for a few awkward seconds before Gray turned his baby blues on me. "Could I get another rum and Coke, babe?"

"Sure," I said to him, then turned to JJ. "Behave."

J placed his hand on his chest and mouthed, "Who, me?"

I moved off quickly to make Gray's drink and get back before too much could be said in my absence. Liam was using the premium rum I wanted for Gray's drink, so I had to wait. I kept an eye on the two of them, wishing I could hear what they were saying. Then again, maybe not.

"Is that your old boyfriend getting acquainted with your new boyfriend?" Liam asked.

"Sort of."

"Is your ex seeing anyone? He's fine," Liam said. He looked back in JJ's direction and licked his bottom lip. I saw that JJ caught the small gesture and returned Liam's interest.

"Liam, I'm not sure that's a good idea. JJ is not boyfriend material. He believes in fucking and nothing more."

"A hard fuck is all I can handle right now anyway."

"Is this the proverbial water cooler?" Jack said as he joined us. We turned and found him scowling. Then I realized all his ire was aimed at Liam, who shrank beneath Jack's penetrating green-eyed stare. "We have customers waiting, fellas."

"Sorry," Liam and I said in unison.

I mixed Gray's drink, then faced my past and present. "Here you go," I said, handing the drink to Gray.

"Is that cute new bartender single?" JJ asked, gesturing toward Liam, who happened to look over and smile shyly. I didn't know the newcomer very well, but I was pretty sure he deserved better than a one-off from JJ, regardless of how good he was in bed. Now that I knew the difference, I wanted everyone to feel what I did with Gray.

"He's not for you, JJ."

"Why? Jealous?" Was he always a pompous jerk?

"No, I'm not jealous." I felt anger rolling off Gray in waves and knew I needed to diffuse the situation ASAP. "Jack has a rule about bartenders dating our customers. He said it's bad for business."

JJ looked between Gray and me. "So, you don't have to adhere to that rule, but Liam does?"

"This is my last night working here, so it hardly matters, J."

"You found a roommate?"

"No, I got a promotion, and I don't need to work three jobs anymore." JJ burst into laughter after my announcement.

"Oh. My. Fucking. God," he said when he finally stopped laughing. I looked at Gray, whose jaw was clenched so tight I was afraid he was going to break a few of his beautiful teeth. "That's hilarious. You've worked there for a few weeks, started screwing your boss, and got a promotion. Wow, I didn't know you had it in you, kid. Congratulations."

Tears of hurt and betrayal stung my eyes, and I stepped back from the bar. I saw Jack making his way down to us because he had a sixth sense that told him when a fight was about to break out.

"You fucking bastard," Gray yelled at him. "Don't you dare project your lowlife behavior onto Chase."

It happened so fast, yet it was like seeing it in slow motion, and I did nothing but stand there gaping like an idiot. Gray pulled back his fist and drove it into JJ's mouth, JJ's head flew backward, and blood gushed from a cut on his lip. Gray lowered his head like a bull and rammed his head into JJ's chest knocking him off the stool. JJ landed on his back with Gray on top of him. Gray reared back to strike again, but JJ was quicker. He jabbed Gray's face and sent his glasses soaring.

"Son of a bitch," JJ yelled and pushed Gray off him.

Gray lunged for him, but Miller wrapped his arms around his friend's chest and pulled him back. JJ was scrambling to his knees and lunged for Gray, but Jack grabbed him by the neck of his shirt and pulled him to his feet.

"Get the fuck out of my bar, Jackson, and don't ever come back."

"Me? What about him?" JJ said, gesturing at Gray, who was struggling to get away from Miller so he could have another go at JJ.

"You had no fucking right to say that to him," Gray shouted. His face was strained and beet red. Miller was doing his best to calm his friend down, but he wasn't having any of it.

"Enough," Jack shouted so loud the room practically vibrated. "I didn't hear what you said to Chase, but I saw the look on his face afterward, so I'm going to guess you had that punch coming. Regardless," he said as he turned to look at Gray, "I do not tolerate this bullshit in my bar. I'm going to warn you one time and one time only."

Gray ceased struggling and nodded respectfully at Jack. "I'm sorry. It won't happen again." Miller dropped his arms from around Gray's chest and took a step back. *Crunch.* I cringed when I realized Miller had just stepped on Gray's sexy-as-fuck glasses.

"Damn, Gray. I'm so sorry," Miller said, but Gray waved him off. His attention was focused on me and assessing how badly he might have screwed up.

"Can I have five minutes?" I asked Jack.

"Sure, you can borrow my office," he replied. "Maybe Charlie can help calm your boyfriend down."

I nodded for Gray to follow me to the end of the bar, and he did. I heard JJ call my name, but I kept walking. I'd deal with him later. I knew the asshole hadn't truly wanted to crush my soul. Walking out from behind the bar, I reached for Gray's hand and led him down the private hallway to Jack's office. My heart was pounding so hard in my chest I had to remind myself to breathe. I opened the door to the office and closed it as soon as Gray entered behind me.

"Babe, I—"

Gray didn't get to finish his sentence because I shoved him against the door and smashed my lips against his. Fisting his hair, I yanked his head back so I could ravage his luscious mouth. Gray initially froze but responded quickly by tangling his tongue with mine and reaching down to grab my ass with both hands. We basically dry humped each other until we had to break apart to catch our breaths.

"Gray," I said when I had enough air in my lungs to speak. "You can't go around hitting people every time they insult me or hurt my feelings. I'm grateful you care so much, and fuck it was hot, but fighting isn't the answer." Gray reached up and ran his thumbs over my cheekbones.

"I know, Chase. I'm sorry I hit your friend. If that's what you want to call him." Gray looked pissed all over again as he began to think about JJ's words. "He's someone you obviously care about, and it cut me open to see him hurt you like that." He rubbed a spot over his heart as if he were trying to alleviate the pain. "I'll try harder."

"It's not going to work," I said to him. I immediately realized my mistake when I saw devastation wash over his handsome face. "I wasn't talking about us, Gray." He sagged against the door in relief. "I was talking about keeping us a secret. Hell, I practically begged you to fuck me today in your office, and you went all caveman out there when JJ insulted me."

"What are you saying?" Gray looked hopeful, and I knew what we had to do for us.

"We have to own it, Gray. Neither of us deserves to be kept a dirty secret. We are consenting adults who just happen to work together." I sounded braver and more confident than I really felt. "We aren't breaking company policy by dating, and it's really no one's business what we're doing."

"Chase, are you sure? You said—" I cut him off by placing my finger over his lips.

"I know what I said, and at the time, I felt it was the right thing for us. We hadn't even gone on a single date then. I only knew that we were really attracted to one another, and I didn't know if it would go beyond the physical attraction. It's gone way beyond that, though, at least for me."

"For me too," Gray admitted. "It's like nothing I've ever felt before." He pulled me tight against his body, wrapped his strong arms around me, and held me tightly. "We're going to be scrutinized and judged, especially you. I am one of the owners, so the employees aren't likely to give me a hard time. They'll take all their frustration and judgment out on you. Can we survive that?"

I thought of each employee I'd interacted with since I'd started working for Gray and Preston. There were only one or two who I thought would actually be bothered by it and only one who might make trouble for me. Ben. I doubted the tenuous truce I'd formed with the ad exec would hold up once word got around. Was I going to allow him to ruin the beautiful thing Gray and I were building together? Fuck no.

"We can handle it, Gray. There's no other alternative. I'm not able to keep my feelings for you a secret." He raised a brow at me. "That doesn't mean I'll seek you out for office blow jobs because we still need to remain professional, but I can't keep my feelings for you out of my eyes."

"Me either," he said. "I don't want to deny who you are to me." Wow, those words packed a wallop. I wanted to stay cocooned in Jack's office for the rest of my shift, but that wasn't possible.

I heaved a deep sigh. "I need to get back out to the bar and finish my night. Then I will be all yours for the weekend."

"God, I love the sound of that."

A soft whimpering sound came from the opposite corner of the room, and I turned to find Charlie standing behind us. His ears were perked up, and his head was cocked to the side as he watched us closely.

"Did we wake you up from your nap, Charlie?" He stood up and stretched. "This is Jack's dog, Charlie," I told Gray.

"You are a beautiful boy, Charlie."

And he was gorgeous. I longed to stroke his ears to see if they were as soft as they looked, but his service dog vest instructed people not to pet him. I gave Gray one last quick peck on his lips before I dove back into the Friday night madness.

Four hours later, the bar was still packed, but my shift was over. I never closed because I usually had to work the next day. I wiped the bar down for the final time and said goodbye to my fellow bartenders and Charlie.

"Don't be a stranger, kid," Jack said gruffly. It almost seemed like he was sad to see me go.

"I'll be back," I promised him. "No one serves better chicken finger baskets than you."

Gray and Miller had behaved themselves for the rest of the night. They didn't play much pool or darts after Gray's glasses got broken. Instead, they sat and drank, so it didn't surprise me when I discovered Gray was tipsy when I approached their table at the end of my shift.

"Hey, baby," Gray said sweetly. "I've missed you."

"What do we have here?" I asked in reference to his almost intoxicated state. Gray just kept grinning like a sappy fool. I looked at Miller for some answers.

"He doesn't do so well when he mixes alcohol," Miller said with a cringe. "He had two rum and Cokes followed by two beers. I tried talking him out of it. Luckily, he stopped at the tipsy phase and didn't continue on to the violently-ill phase."

"I hear you, Miller," Gray said leaning toward his friend. "I'm just feeling really good. So good I can't wait to get my boyfriend home and naked."

Jesus. "It's time to go now, Gray. Let's tell Miller goodnight." I helped Gray to his feet and watched for signs he was drunker than I thought. He stood upright and didn't waver. "It was nice to meet you, Miller. I'm looking forward to getting to know you better. How about dinner soon?"

"Sounds great, but don't ask me to cook. I'm horrible at it, and he's not much better," Miller said, jerking his thumb in Gray's direction. He leaned in until his mouth was close to my ear. "You should know alcohol for Gray is like truth serum. If you have any information you want to pry out of him, now's the time to do it." Miller shot me a wink, hugged Gray goodbye, and left the bar.

Gray wrapped his arm around my waist as we walked to my car. He leaned into me a little, but I got the feeling it was because he needed the connection, not because he was unsteady on his feet. I opened the door for him, and he kissed me long and soft before lowering himself into the seat.

"I'm glad it wasn't awkward meeting Miller tonight," I said once I pulled out of the parking lot and headed toward my apartment. "I'm lucky he's giving me another chance."

Gray placed his hand on my thigh and gave a light squeeze. "He's my best friend, and he wants me to be happy. You make me very happy, Chase." Wow, truth serum indeed.

"You make me happy too."

"It's not just the sex either. Nope. Everything about you brings me joy. I love that you are honest and open with me. I never have to guess what you're feeling or thinking. Do you know how refreshing that is?" I found it hard to talk with a huge lump in my throat, so I shook my head. "Well, it's fucking amazing." He moved his hand higher up my thigh until he cupped my package. "Your cock is also amazing, Chase." He stroked me through my jeans, and I immediately started to harden. I was thankful the drive home was short and traffic was relatively light. "I like to suck it and stroke it," he said in a singsong voice. "I love when you come in my mouth."

"I bet you're going to regret saying these things to me in the morning. If you can remember saying them," I amended wryly.

"I'm not drunk, baby. I'm just really, really happy." I glanced over to see him smiling wide. "Okay, I might be a little embarrassed when I remember what I said, but I won't regret it."

"Fair enough, but you might want to quit rubbing my dick so I don't crash into a tree." Gray laughed darkly and amped up his attack. I could have squeezed my legs together to try to make it difficult for him, but instead I spread them wider.

"I'm going to have your ass again tonight." Thank fuck he waited to say that until I'd pulled into my assigned parking spot. Gray behaved himself as we walked through the lobby of my building but was on me as soon as the elevator doors closed. "Too bad there aren't more floors in this building, or I'd drop to my knees and blow you right here." My entire body shook with lust from just his words.

"I need a shower first," I said as we stumbled through my apartment door tangled up in one another. I had no clue if Ava was home, but it was highly unlikely. I pulled him behind me to my bedroom and locked us inside. "Do you want to shower with me or wait for me in bed?"

"I'm not passing up the opportunity to run my hands over your wet body," Gray replied with a devilish smile. He walked over to the bedside table and pulled out a condom and the bottle of lube, then turned to me. "I'm warning you now that it won't be easy tonight. My need for you has been building every minute I spent in the bar. This will be more like a claiming than a fucking. You said you're going to let the world know you belong to me, and I want to consummate that by possessing every inch of your gorgeous body."

If he thought he was warning me away, he was grossly mistaken. His words made me so hot I expected my clothes to start smoking. "Alrighty then. Let's get to the claiming."

I started removing my clothes before I even made it to the bathroom. I opened the shower door and turned it on so the water could heat up. Gray shoved me up against the glass shower wall. I gasped at the sensation of cool glass against my feverish skin. Gray claimed my mouth—there was no other word for it—like he wanted to own my body. The only thing I could do was hold on for dear life. We were so lost in each other that we temporarily forgot about the shower. Gray pulled back when steam started to fill the bathroom. He grabbed the lube and condom off the vanity, then followed me into the shower.

"I would give everything I have to fuck you with nothing between us," Gray said hungrily as he set the supplies on the shelf. "I got tested after the Devon debacle, but I'd gladly take another test for you."

His words conjured up images and feelings I'd never entertained before. I'd never wanted a lover bare inside me, but I wanted that deeper connection with Gray. "I've never, Gray. It's not something I wanted…"

"Shh," Gray said, misunderstanding what I was trying to say. "We don't have to, Chase."

"I do want that with you," I declared. "I was trying to tell you that I never wanted it *before* you. I'll go to the clinic this week."

Gray kissed me hungrily under the hot shower spray while our hands roamed all over each other's wet, hard bodies. He wrapped his strong hand around my shaft and started stroking it up and down. I wasn't going to last long if he kept up that pace.

"Fuck me now," I pleaded, not caring how needy I sounded. I turned and faced the tile wall, put my palms on the wall above my head, spread my legs, and pushed my ass out a little to make things easier for him. Gray sure took his time massaging my ass and teasing my hole for a man who was frantic to fuck me just a minute ago. "Quit teasing me," I said when he began to roll my balls in his hand.

Gray pulled away, and I instantly missed the feel of his body against mine. My ass clenched in excitement when he tore the condom wrapper open with his teeth. I looked over my shoulder so I could watch him roll the condom down his hard length. His cock looked huge and angry as if it'd been denied for too long. Gray wasted no time lubing his dick and stretching my ass.

"Ready?" he asked when he lined the head of his dick up with my hole. I nodded and he began to push inside me, slow and steady, until he was as deep as he could go. "I'd climb inside you if I could," he whispered hungrily in my ear. "I can never get as close to you as I want." His voice was raw with vulnerable emotion.

"I feel the same, Gray."

"Thank god," he said as he pulled out of me completely. I whimpered pitifully at the empty feeling he left behind, but in the next second my whimper was replaced by a shout of sheer ecstasy when Gray gripped my hips and buried his dick deep inside me in one hard thrust. He stopped, and I felt my walls clenching and squeezing him. "Are you okay?"

"Unh."

"More?" I answered with a nod. "You feel so fucking good, so tight and hot for me." He repeated his slow withdrawal but this time left the head of his dick inside me. I squeezed him as hard as I could. "I could come from just that alone. I have no control tonight."

"Give me all you've got, Gray"

"Fuck," Gray yelled, thrusting so hard into me that he drove me up on to my tiptoes. He reached around and started jacking my dick in the same rhythm his dick was plowing my ass. "I want to see you come all over these pretty navy tiles," he growled in my ear. Gray pulled my hips out a little farther, and I nearly fainted from pleasure as he hit my gland with every hard thrust home. "So close now, baby. I need you to come for me, Chase. Come for me now."

I relaxed my body and let the pleasure burst inside me. I cried out his name as he rode me like a stallion through my orgasm. "So beautiful," he said as I painted the shower wall with my release. Two more strokes and Gray wrapped both his arms around my chest and came deep inside me. The sounds he made while he spilled inside the condom made me resent the barrier between us. "Someday I'll be spilling inside you."

We dried each other off and collapsed onto my bed. It had been a long day, and I was thankful I would no longer have to work two or three jobs. I could spend more time lying in my boyfriend's arms. Gray spooned up behind me and nuzzled his nose in my hair and along the back of my neck. My eyes closed as a feeling of true contentment settled over me. I was just drifting off when Gray pressed his lips against my ear.

"I'm falling for you so hard, Chase."

"I think I'm already there."

CHAPTER
Twenty-Nine

Gray

I WOKE UP TO SOFT KISSES ON MY FACE. I SMELLED MINT, WHICH MEANT Chase had already been up and brushed his teeth. He delicately touched the tender skin beneath my eye before kissing it.

"You have a bit of a shiner this morning." My eyes flew open.

"Really? Do I look like a total badass?" I sat up suddenly, knocking Chase back onto his side of the bed.

"Total badass, baby." Chase's smile was huge and endearing. "Although, this wasn't the reaction I was expecting."

"I got a black eye while defending my man's honor, so I will wear it proudly." I threw back the covers and went into the bathroom to inspect the damage. I was disappointed to see it was just a tiny bruise. Chase entered the bathroom behind me. He pressed his chest against my back, wrapped his arms around my waist, and propped his chin on my shoulder. "You should see the other guy," I said with a little swagger.

"I bet his lip is really swollen this morning," Chase agreed with a soft chuckle.

His voice held a hint of sadness, and I wished again that his so-called friend hadn't hurt his feelings. That was the only thing I regretted about the previous evening. Our gazes connected in the mirror, and our sappy smiles made it obvious we were both remembering our declarations to one another and our commitment to getting tested so we could skip the condoms. Our eyes darkened at the same time, and I felt his dick hardening against my ass. Chase lowered his right hand and began stroking my dick as he rubbed his erection against me.

"Was I too rough with you last night?" I needed to know because I'd barely taken the time to prep him properly. If I'd hurt him…

"You were amazing, and I loved every second of it."

I saw the sincerity in his eyes and let my worry fade so I could enjoy the feel of him jacking me while he pleasured himself against me. I laid my head on his shoulder, exposing my neck to him. Chase nipped and sucked his way from the base of my neck to my ear while he increased the pressure and speed of his strokes. I knew I wasn't going to last much longer when he sucked my earlobe into his hot mouth.

"That's it," he whispered hungrily. "Let go and come for me, Gray. I want to watch you."

I couldn't tear my eyes off our reflections. I loved watching his hand work my cock and the look in his eyes while he chased his own orgasm. I reached behind me to tangle my hands in his hair. I'd kill to have a picture of that for my own viewing pleasure. I loved the feel of his dick sliding along my ass crack. I'd never bottomed for anyone, but I would for him.

"I'm so damn close already," he growled. I came apart in his arms with his voice in my ears. "You are so fucking beautiful, Gray." He stroked me through my orgasm, then placed his hands on my waist, gripping me hard and grinding his dick against me. Chase called out my name seconds before he came against my back. "I made a horrible mess." Chase laughed and smacked my ass before reaching inside the shower to turn it on. "Now I'll have to clean you up."

Thirty minutes later, Chase was driving us to my house. He had a death grip on the steering wheel, and I could tell he was uncomfortable about returning to the "scene of the crime" as he put it. I needed to grab my backup glasses so I could see clearly and watch the interactions between Chase and my family. I couldn't wait for them to meet him.

"I bought my house independent of Devon," I told him patiently. I understood his discomfort about going to my place, but I wanted him to see it as my space. Devon had only lived at my house for a year. It was mine before him, and it was mine after him.

"I know this in theory," Chase replied. "It's just going to take some time for me to feel comfortable here." He let go of the steering wheel with his right hand and reached across the console to hold mine. "I'm sure you'd feel similarly if the situation were reversed."

"I know," I said excitedly. "How about we stop by the clinic and you help me shop for a new bed after brunch. You can help me pick it out, and we will break it in together."

"I like that idea," Chase said with a big grin. "We can break it in properly after we get our results."

"Keep talking like that and we're going to be late." He glanced over at me, and I could tell by his smile that his discomfort had lessened. Still I felt it necessary to ask if he preferred to wait in the car while I ran in and got my extra pair of glasses. He waved off the suggestion, and a few minutes later, we were standing on the front steps of my house.

"It hasn't changed much since the last time you were here," I said casually. I was rambling, but he said nothing. I spun around and saw him standing in the doorway. He was looking around at my house with a bemused expression on his face. Finally, he turned his beautiful eyes on me.

"Honestly, Gray, I only saw you that night, and you're all I've seen since."

His honesty touched my soul. The sincerity in his eyes as they locked unwaveringly with mine nearly brought me to my knees. Where had he been all my life? "Damn, we're going to be late." I moved so quickly he didn't have time to react. "You're all I see too." The feel of his lips on mine went beyond a kiss; it was more of a promise or a blending of souls. I felt the electricity of our connection in every fiber of my being. I'd known him for such a short time, but I felt closer to him than I had to any other person, including my family. My heart knew he was the one, even if my brain urged caution. I broke the kiss after a few minutes. "I'm just going to run upstairs and grab my glasses. I'll be right back."

When I returned to the living room, Chase was looking at the family photos I kept on my mantle. I loved the way he looked in my house. I could actually visualize Chase standing in front of a roaring fire while he hung Christmas stockings over the fireplace. I imagined classic Christmas tunes playing in the background. Would we drink wine or hot chocolate? Chase must have heard me come into the room because he turned to look at me.

"What?" he asked with a puzzled expression on his face.

"Huh?"

Chase laughed at my response. "You had this dazed look on your face like you were in a trance. Is it okay that I was looking at your family photos?" His unease snapped me back to reality.

"I love that you're curious about my things. Feel free to go through every room, every drawer, and every closet. I have no skeletons or secrets to hide from you."

Narrowing his eyes, Chase said, "What was going through your mind just now?"

"Do you really want to know?" I asked, making my voice as sinister as possible. "It might scare you a little."

"Does it involve a bloody dungeon and tools of torture?"

I smiled and shook my head.

"Then I want to know."

"I saw you standing at the fireplace when I came down the stairs and had a daydream or something."

"Was I naked?" Chase waggled his eyebrows suggestively and made me laugh.

"No, you weren't naked, but I have no doubt it was heading in that direction." I walked to him and wrapped my arms around him, pulling him in close. "You were hanging Christmas stockings on the mantle and there was Christmas music playing in the background."

"I could totally see myself doing that," he said, his head cocked to the side. He looked off into space over my shoulder. "I've never had a fireplace before, and it sounds lovely." He straightened up and looked at me seriously. "How many stockings was I hanging?"

"Excuse me?"

"Was I just hanging stockings for each of us, or were there more?" My breath caught in my throat. Did he mean..."Do I finally get my cat?" It was stupid how disappointed I felt. "Or was I hanging up a stocking for little Grayson?" He leaned in and rubbed his nose against mine. I closed my eyes, hoping to hide the raw emotion I was feeling. I didn't want to appear desperate. "It's a beautiful vision, Gray. Thank you for sharing it with me."

My phone vibrated in my pocket. It was a text from Preston reminding me to stop and get pastries from Adam and Steve's on the way to brunch. It was the jolt I needed to bring me back to reality. "We need to get pastries on the way," I told Chase.

I locked my front door, and we were on our way. I couldn't help but check out my sexy boyfriend as he navigated to the bakery. I placed my left hand on the back of his neck and ran my fingers through his hair. I'm pretty sure Chase purred beneath my touch. He parked in front of the bakery, and we walked inside holding hands, which did not go unnoticed by Adam or Steve.

"Well, well, well," Adam said teasingly.

"What do we have here?" Steve asked. He turned to his husband and grinned like a fool. "You owe me twenty bucks."

"You were right about them," Adam told him as he pulled cash out of his pocket and handed it over. I laughed and looked over at Chase who just grinned and shook his head. "What will it be, boys?"

I picked out the same pastries I'd been buying each Saturday since I'd met Chase. Steve handed me a piping hot cup of hazelnut coffee with a knowing wink. We thanked them both and left.

"I can't wait for you to meet my family," I said.

"I'm excited too. I thought I'd be really nervous, but I'm not."

"They're going to love you." *Just like I do.*

"I hope."

"I know," I assured him.

My mom came out to the driveway to meet us when we pulled up. She threw her arms around my neck. "He's beautiful," she whispered in my ear.

"Inside and out," I whispered back, which caused her to squeeze me tighter. "Mom, this is Chase Rivers. Chase, this is my mother, Alexandria Wright."

"You could pass for brother and sister," Chase said in awe. He wasn't wrong. My mom looked twenty years younger than her true age. I had inherited my jet-black hair and light blue eyes from her as well. Everyone thought she was my slightly older sister.

"You are welcome here *anytime.*" Mom gave Chase a tight hug. I saw his eyes close as he soaked in the moment. My heart broke for him all over again, knowing he wished he could hug his own mother. I had already told my mom about Chase's circumstances after our first date. I think it was the reason she held on to him a little longer. She finally pulled back and cupped his face in both her hands. "Thank you for making my son so happy, Chase. I have never, ever seen him like this."

Chase looked over at me disbelievingly. I confirmed my mom's statement with a nod because it was true. I couldn't remember feeling this happy or content at any other time in my life. Chase might not believe it yet, but he was the reason.

"Thank you," he said looking back at my mom. "Your sons are amazing men. You must be so proud of them."

"I'm extremely honored to call them mine," she replied. Mom grabbed Chase's hand and led him up to the front door. I followed behind them like a pleased puppy. "But I didn't always think they'd turn out so good." I cringed as we entered my childhood home.

"Do tell."

"Well, when Grayson was about five years old he—"

"Is this him?" My dad picked the perfect time to intercept us in the hallway.

"Who else would it be, Darren?" my mom asked good-naturedly.

"Darren Wright," my dad said as Chase shook his hand. "I'm this lunk-head's father or so *she* tells me," Dad said while pointing at my mom with his thumb. It was a common joke between my parents because I looked nothing like my dad. Preston, on the other hand, was his clone. "Come meet my husband, Chase." Dad clapped Chase on the back and kept his hand on his shoulder as we walked into the kitchen where Jeff had just stood up from removing a casserole dish from the oven.

"Wow, you are a beauty," Jeff said as he shook Chase's hand. My boyfriend's face blushed a cute shade of pink from all the attention aimed at him. Jeff sensed his discomfort and looked at my mom. "Alex, this breakfast casserole looks and smells amazing."

"Thanks, honey. Cecily Winters served a similar dish earlier this week when we were at her house finalizing the Cherry Blossom Ball details. I'll give you the recipe if you want it. I remember how much this one"—she pointed at my father—"likes sausage." My mother's awesomeness never, ever ceased to amaze me. Her willingness to not only accept Jeff but to offer her friendship was nothing less than a saintly act. "Well, I guess I didn't realize just how into *sausage* he was until eighteen years ago," she said. Jeff nearly cried laughing at her joke.

"Jesus, Alexandria," my dad said sternly, which he totally ruined when he started to laugh too.

"What? It's true," Mom said.

I looked away from the parental trio to make sure my boyfriend hadn't run for the nearest exit. He stood there grinning as he took in the three of them.

"Oh god," Jeff kept saying as he tried to catch his breath. "It hurts. It hurts," he said, holding his stomach.

"What's going on in here?" Preston said as he came in from the dining room. He looked at each of us, trying to figure out what was so funny. "Why does his stomach hurt?"

"Where's my angel?" I asked my brother.

"He's right here looking at our parents like they've lost their damn minds. I think he might be right." Preston's censure only made the three of them laugh harder. "*My* angel is in her bassinette sleeping." I grabbed Chase's hand and playfully shoved Preston out of the way as we walked by him. "Don't wake her up, Gray."

"I won't." I totally did. I dropped a kiss on Carly's gorgeous head as I walked by the couch to get to the bassinette. I pulled Chase with me so we could both look down on the slumbering beauty. "Isn't she amazing?" I ran the fingers of my free hand over her soft, downy cheeks. "I have to hold her." I released Chase's hand and picked her up the way Carly had shown me. She stirred slightly when I put her up on my shoulder.

"She's perfect," Chase said in awe. He gently stroked her tiny back.

Carly glared at me. "You have to feed her if she wakes up, Gray."

"I don't have the right equipment for that."

"Au contraire," Carly said. "I pumped a few bottles this morning so I wouldn't hog all her attention."

"Yes," I said a little too loud. Grace's little arms jerked up like she was signaling a touchdown. *Uh oh.* She whimpered softly and began to cry. I did what felt natural and bounced a little while I rubbed her back and made soothing noises.

"You've got the touch," Carly said when Grace settled right back down. "See if you can lay her back down without waking her so we can eat." I pouted, which made Carly smile widely. "You can feed her when she wakes up." I reluctantly laid Grace back down, and we joined everyone else in the dining room.

We passed the dishes around the table so we could serve ourselves. We talked about our weeks like we always did, which included a lot of ribbing and laughing. I squeezed Chase's hand beneath the table and leaned over to kiss his cheek. He answered my kiss with one of his own, right on the lips. I realized no one was talking, moving, or possibly breathing. I tore my attention away from Chase and glanced around the table. My family wore various looks of amusement and surprise.

"What?" I asked. Everyone went back to eating and talking like normal. I shrugged and also turned back to my plate.

"So, Alexandria, earlier you were about to tell me why you were surprised Grayson and Preston turned out so well. You didn't get to finish your story, and I'd love to hear it."

"When Preston was five and Grayson was two…"

"Your family is amazing," Chase said a few hours later as we pulled up to the furniture store. "Thank you so much for introducing them to me." He put his car in park and turned in his seat to look at me. "I promise to never tease you about your obsession with your niece again." His eyes had that dreamy quality I loved so much. "I've never seen such a beautiful baby."

I'd never seen a more beautiful sight than when Chase cradled Grace against him and talked sweetly to her. At one point, he looked up at me and our eyes connected and held. It scared me how much I wanted that to be our future.

"They loved you so much," I told him honestly. Mom, Dad, and Jeff each caught me alone to tell me how much they liked Chase and how happy they were for us. It seemed like our future was a foregone conclusion to all of them. I leaned in for a kiss, and he met me halfway. What started out as a slow peck quickly turned into a heated exchange. "Maybe they'll let us put those mattresses to the test before I buy a set."

"Somehow I don't think that would go over very well."

"It was worth a shot."

We spent the next forty-five minutes looking at every bed until I found the one I could picture making love to Chase in. It was a massive, four-poster in a cherry finish. Oh yeah, I could see us rolling around in that big sucker just as easily as I could see us spending lazy Sunday mornings in it while we sipped coffee and read the paper.

"Do you think you could give us a minute to talk?" I asked the overzealous salesman.

"Sure. I'll just be up front if you need me."

"Can you picture us in this bed?" I asked Chase as soon as the salesman was out of earshot, not that I gave a damn if he overheard me. I moved closer to him, invading his personal space. His eyes lit up with mischief, and I wondered if I'd miscalculated again. "Can you envision yourself lying beneath me on this bed as I make love to you?"

Chase grabbed hold of one of the posts and gave it a hard tug. "Seems really sturdy," he replied with a wicked gleam in his eyes. I watched as he trailed his fingers over the intricate carvings in the post and along the footboard. "It's stunning, and I can definitely see you lying beneath me as I sit astride you, taking your cock deep inside my body."

"Sold," I told him. "Let's find a new mattress." I grabbed his hand and pulled him over to the mattress displays where we tested out a few until we found the one we both liked. "Let's go find our salesman, then I want to go to the department store so you can help me pick out new bedding."

It was early evening before we returned to Chase's apartment. We agreed to a light dinner after eating such a hearty brunch at my mom's house. I helped him put together leafy green salads with sliced chicken breast, avocado, tomatoes, and peppers. My amazing boyfriend taught me how to make homemade vinaigrette dressing, and it was delicious.

Afterward, we decided to watch a marathon of classic black-and-white horror films. We either jumped from fright or laughed over the cheesiness. Chase fell asleep against my chest midway through the third movie. I ran my fingers through his hair and enjoyed the sweet sighs that escaped his beautiful lips. As much as I loved the sexy times we shared, that tender moment eclipsed them. I sat there for two hours with numb arms just so he could rest peacefully.

I led him to his bedroom after he woke and undressed us both before we climbed into bed. I pulled Chase into my arms as soon as we settled beneath the blankets and let sleep pull us both under. I'm positive I fell asleep with the sappiest grin on my face.

CHAPTER
Thirty

Chase

I BLINKED AND IT WAS MIDWEEK. I SETTLED INTO MY NEW POSITION ON the art staff easily enough. Everyone had been warm and welcoming, and I loved working closely with Carman and Kayla every day. The truce I'd made with Ben held, but I could tell he still had his guard up around me. My new job allowed me to witness him interacting with the other artists, and I saw his generosity and kindness firsthand. I could only hope that one day I'd be on the receiving end of one of his smiles.

Gray and I decided that keeping our relationship a secret was both impractical and insulting to those around us. We agreed on some ground rules to ensure we didn't make anyone feel uncomfortable. There'd be no hand holding, kissing, or inappropriate workplace behavior. I also insisted we spend some nights apart, which did not go over well with Gray at all. I held my ground because I believed it would be healthier for our relationship.

We tried it out Monday night, and it was fucking horrible. Neither one of us slept worth a damn, then we had to behave all day at work the next day with no touching or kissing. There wasn't enough coffee in the world to get me through Tuesday.

When six o'clock rolled around, Gray appeared in the art room. I knew it was him without looking because I felt the charge in the air. Everyone else had left at five, but I was bound and determined to wow Ben. He'd needed a few different mock-ups for a campaign pitch. I wanted to think the assignment was further proof that our truce was working, but an ornery glint in Ben's eye tipped me off that he was up to something.

Backing down or refusing wasn't an option, so I forced a smile and agreed to help. That's when Ben divulged the potential client was a cat litter manufacturer, and his smirk said, "Good luck making that imagery appealing."

I struggled for a bit when I was focused on the visuals of the product, but then I had an epiphany and switched the graphics to feature people who benefited from the cat litter. Rather than pull up stock photos, I drew my own, using Gray's fireplace fantasy to fuel my idea. Instead of hanging stockings, I had two dads sitting on the couch with their children between them and a large tabby cat stretched out on the back of the sofa. I wasn't completely satisfied with the graphics but felt it was a good start.

Gray stopped behind my chair and leaned over to see what I was working on. "That's adorable," he said, "but it's time to go, Chase." I'd never heard his voice sound so husky.

"I'm not done working, Gray. My boss is a total dickhead, and I need to get my first mock-ups ready. Ben expects me to fall flat on my face. Not gonna happen."

"Shut that computer down and leave with me right now, or I won't be responsible for what I do in the next thirty seconds." Holy hot fuck. That was a side of Gray I'd never seen before but hoped to see often. His blue eyes went stormy, and my pulse began to race. He reached up and began to loosen his tie, and I knew he wasn't kidding around. Gray was a man who was desperate to be inside me.

I saved my work and shut my computer down without further hesitation.

We'd parked next to each other that morning, which was as close as we'd been all day. I looked over at him as I started my car. The look he gave me told me I was in for a very rough ride, and I couldn't wait.

We began tearing our clothes off as soon as we cleared my apartment door. I shouted Ava's name to see if she was home and was relieved when she didn't holler back. Regardless, I wasn't going to let Gray fuck me in the living room. I pulled Gray into my room where I submitted my body to his every whim.

I had expected things to be fast and hard, and they were, but not until he worshiped every part of me. He made me feel like a rare and precious gem, which was a foreign feeling for me. Sex had always been about the physical but not with Grayson. With him, our bodies came together like a flawlessly executed dance between two partners who were completely in tune with each other. He was all I ever wanted but never dreamed I'd have. I lay in the circle of his arms that night and knew there was no place I'd rather be. Ever.

The next morning was so much better for both of us and not just because I'd obliged Gray when he'd insisted on morning blow jobs before breakfast. It was about the balance and sense of rightness I felt when we brushed our teeth at the same time or when Gray borrowed my lucky tie because he forgot to pack one in his overnight bag. It was those everyday little things that made me feel like dancing as I made my way into the office.

Gray and Preston had a meeting with their banker first thing that morning, so I went into the office early to get a jump start on my mock-ups that were due later in the day.

I stopped down the hall from Ben's office to straighten my tie and adjust my posture after spending too many hours hunkering over my workspace. I knew my idea was solid and my artwork was impeccable, but that didn't mean Ben would give me a fair shake after our tumultuous start. I took a fortifying breath, then forced my feet to move.

Ben was staring intently at his computer when I arrived, so I rapped my knuckles on the doorframe to get his attention.

"May I?" I asked, gesturing to the chair in front of his desk.

"Of course. I'm excited to see what you've come up with." Ben's mouth twitched as if he wanted to smile but thought better of it. The ass had literally given me a crap job, but Ben would soon find out no job was too shitty for Chase Rivers.

I handed the campaign material to Ben and watched him closely to gauge his reaction. The ad exec met my gaze after examining each piece, but his expression never betrayed his thoughts. I was both impressed and a little worried.

Ben set the final graphic down, then folded his hands on top of his desk. He sighed and said, "This is good work. Excellent work, actually."

"You sound surprised."

Ben smiled. "More relieved than surprised. I thought maybe a certain someone was more impressed by your looks than your—"

"I didn't fuck my way to a promotion." I could feel my blood pressure rising to an alarming level. "You have some goddamned nerve, Ben." I began pacing in front of his desk, trying to calm down and find a way to phrase this without sounding callous. *Fuck it.* "My relationship with Grayson is none of your business. Furthermore, I..."

"Grayson?" Ben asked in shock. "I was talking about Mitchell Heston. I heard he was quite smitten with you."

"I..."

"You and Gray are..." A sly grin spread across his face. *Shit.* This wasn't how I wanted people to find out. "No wonder you're a little sensitive," Ben said in contemplation and then started to laugh. "Oh fuck, this is hilarious. Devon drags you home to fuck, thinking Gray is out of town. You turn up here the following Monday as his new personal assistant. You quit on the spot, but he tracks you down and hires you back. We all sat and watched the chemistry pop and sizzle between you, but we thought it was repressed anger over your almost-affair with Devon. None of us could figure out why he insisted on hiring you, no matter how nice you seemed to be. Now I know." Tears were rolling down his cheeks at this point, and I was finding it hard to stay irritated. "Talk about a twist of fate."

"I'm glad you're enjoying yourself at my expense, Ben." I tried for scolding, but my twitching lip gave me away.

"How long?"

"None of your business." He threw up his hands in surrender. "I would appreciate it if you didn't say anything. We're not keeping our relationship a secret, but we're not exactly broadcasting it either. I don't want to make people uncomfortable around me."

"I won't say anything," he said, crossing his heart. "I'd like to take you to lunch to make up for our shitty start."

I held up my hand. "Not necessary.

"I don't agree, and I must insist," Ben said. "I have lunch plans with Ellie today, but I'm sure she wouldn't mind if you joined us, seeing that you're like family."

"That works for me. Maybe Xavier can join us too. Have you met him?" Ben shook his head, and I decided to text Xavier and insist he meet us for lunch. "You'll like him." I recalled how drawn to Liam Ben had been, and I had the feeling Xavier would really send him reeling.

"Sounds good," Ben agreed. "I better get back to work on my presentation for the meeting. This is exceptional work, Chase."

"Thank you."

I had extra pep in my step when I stopped by the break room to make myself a cup of coffee.

"Is that mine?" Gray asked from behind me. I slowly turned to find him leaning in the doorway.

"All yours," I replied in a voice that made it obvious I wasn't talking about the java. I set my mug aside and started to make him a cup.

"Damn, you don't play fair." Gray walked over and accepted the proffered mug. "No kissing, no touching, no flirting, and definitely no fucking," he said, mimicking me. I couldn't keep the grin off my face as he scowled at me. "Then you go and break your own rules. Again."

"Sorry." I wasn't really. "I'll try to behave better."

"Don't," Gray said, leaning into my space. "I like when you're bad." He straightened back up and finished adding cream and sugar to his coffee and took a sip. "Do you have lunch plans?"

"I'm having lunch with Ben and Ellie. I've decided Xavier is coming too, whether he likes it or not."

"Ben?"

"What can I say? He liked my shitty kitty pitch." It was more complex than that but it wasn't necessary to rehash our conversation. Well, except for one part. "And he knows about us."

Gray arched a brow but didn't look concerned. "How did that go over?"

"He laughed hysterically," I replied, then repeated Ben's twist-of-fate theory. I ran my finger down the front of my lucky tie, which looked much better on Gray. I dropped my hand from him before I did something stupid like pull him to me for a kiss.

"I think he has a point. I think our hearts were fated to be together, Chase." He reached up to caress my face but jerked his hand back when someone came into the break room.

"Well, hello, boys," Rosie said cheerfully. "You might want to use a little more discretion if you two are trying to keep this a secret."

"We're not," Gray replied.

"Fair enough, but maybe dial it down a little. I don't want Chase to be treated unfairly by coworkers who will think he's getting preferential treatment," Rosie said kindly.

"You're right again, Rosie," Gray affirmed. He grabbed his coffee and patted me on the shoulder before he left the room.

"I'm sorry if you think I overstepped, Chase," she said sweetly.

"Not at all." I gave her a quick hug. "See you in a bit, Rosie."

I went back to my desk and sent Xavier a text about lunch. I left out the fact Ben would be there too and told him to find out from Ellie where to meet us. I was surprised when I received his reply almost immediately. I was even more surprised he'd agreed without a fuss.

My first production meeting went really well, and I earned high praise from Ben for the artwork he presented at the meeting. Gray got up at the end to address all of us and make suggestions on our campaigns. I looked up at one point and caught Carman and Kayla looking back and forth between Gray and me. I hadn't interacted with Gray, and I couldn't imagine what they were seeing, but their wicked smiles indicated they'd seen something.

Gray ran his hand over the tie he borrowed from me this morning and I realized what had given us away to Carman and Kayla. They'd both complimented me on the tie the first time I'd worn it to work. Well, I guess it was a good thing we weren't trying to keep it a secret any longer.

The rest of the meeting flew by. I tried not to stare at my beautiful boyfriend or make eye contact with Carman or Kayla, who continued to stare at me until they were called upon to answer questions about the progress of various ad prints and art projects they were working on.

I made a beeline out of the conference room once the meeting ended, hoping to avoid Carman and Kayla's probing questions, but it wasn't meant to be. They were swarming my desk within minutes.

"You shouldn't be sharing clothes if you're trying to keep your relationship a secret," Carman advised.

"We're not," I told her.

"It would be pointless," Kayla said. "It was only a matter of time before you guys got together. It was obvious from the start."

"It's not going to be easy, honey," Carman said sweetly.

"Nothing worth having is ever easy."

"So true," Kayla said. "Are you free for lunch?"

"I'm having lunch with Ben, Ellie, and her brother, Xavier. How about tomorrow?"

"Sure," Kayla said. "We'll let you get back to work."

I blew out a deep breath. I loved my new job, but I was already looking forward to getting home where I didn't have to guard my every action. Ben popped in just before noon.

"Ready?" he asked.

"Yes, I'm starved to death. I regret not eating breakfast this morning."

"I'm famished myself," Gray said as he joined us by the elevator. "Thanks for inviting me to join you for lunch, Ben. It was so considerate of you. I was hoping my boyfriend would've thought of it, but I think he's ashamed of me."

"Am not," I said defensively. Grayson gave me a playful smile, and I was thankful that Ben invited him to join us. "I'm just trying to figure out how we should handle these things."

"We both need to eat lunch, Chase," he said casually. "Besides, I just had to schedule a trip to Pittsburgh to meet with a potential client. I have to go home and pack tonight so I'll be ready to go to the airport at five in the morning." I must have looked as crestfallen as I felt. "I'll be back in time for dinner tomorrow night," Gray assured me.

"Okay."

"You guys are kind of cute together," Ben teased. "Ellie's waiting for me in the parking lot. I'll ride with her to the restaurant so you guys can have some private time."

Our alone time consisted of us holding hands as Gray navigated traffic. I expected him to pull away when we walked into the restaurant, but he didn't. He only let go long enough to open the door for me to enter before him. Ellie and Ben were waiting inside for us. Ellie saw our joined hands but refrained from commenting. I was sure I'd get a call from her later.

"Xavier will be here any minute," Ellie told us. "Let's go ahead and grab a table. I can order for him so we don't have to wait." She turned to the hostess. "There will be five in our party. My brother will be joining us in just a few minutes."

We were led to a table in the back of the room, but we still had a clear view of the hostess station so we could see when Xavier arrived. I wanted to make sure I could gauge Ben's reaction when they were introduced.

The waiter came and took our orders. I saw Xavier approach the hostess as soon as our waiter left, and I held up my arm so he could see me. I stood as he arrived and gave him a big hug. I was so glad to see him looking rested and healthy. I pulled back, and we both took a seat at the table. I kept my eyes on Ben as Ellie made the introductions, and just as I'd expected, Ben was immediately taken with Xavier. You could almost see the hearts in his eyes.

Ben and Xavier did most of the talking while the rest of us ate and watched them. Ellie smiled sweetly as she watched her baby brother open up and talk happily with her friend. Gray reached beneath the table and squeezed my hand affectionately.

"It's good to be back home," Xavier said. "I will miss singing and performing on stage but not the constant traveling. It gets old in a hurry."

"You can always sing at open mic night at Bottoms Up," I interjected.

"I'll think about it," Xavier replied with a shoulder shrug. I thought it was a good suggestion until I saw the strain around his eyes and mouth.

"Are you two going to the Cherry Blossom Ball together?" Ben asked. It took me a minute to realize he was addressing me.

"Is that the event your mom was talking about at brunch on Saturday?"

"Wow, you've met his parents already," Ben teased, but I ignored him.

"Yes, she's on the planning committee. All the proceeds benefit the children's hospital, and it's a really big deal to her. Wright Creations donates the marketing and advertising for the event, so the employees and their plus-ones are given tickets."

"It sounds lovely."

"It is lovely, and it raises a lot of money for the hospital." That was all he said about the event, and he didn't comment on us going as a couple. Gray glanced at his watch and grimaced. "I really need to get back to the office. Are you ready to go, Chase?" He suddenly seemed awkward and nervous.

"Yeah, sure." I reached for my wallet to pay for my lunch, but Gray stopped me by lightly grabbing my wrist.

"This is on me," Gray said. He tossed several bills on the table to cover the check and leave a generous tip for the waiter. "It was great seeing you again, Xavier. We all need to get together for dinner soon."

"Sounds great," Xavier said.

"See you two back at the office," Gray told Ellie and Ben, who exchanged a brief glance before nodding.

Gray took my hand and led me out of the restaurant to his car. He kept the pace leisurely, but there was a tension in him that made me wary. He opened the car door for me like he always did and even kissed me lightly before shutting it and walking around to his side. I sat in silence while I waited for him to say something about his odd behavior. I wondered if I should just call him on it. Then I noticed we weren't heading in the direction of the office. I looked over at him.

"Gray, where are we going?"

"I just need a private moment with you before we go back, especially since we won't see each other until tomorrow night." I was relieved he wasn't angry, but his behavior still puzzled me.

After a few minutes of driving, Gray pulled into a picturesque park. We quietly watched some young kids and toddlers feed chunks of bread to the geese. My mind kept whirling with all the possibilities of why talking about the ball had upset him. It seemed like an eternity before he spoke.

"As a Wright Creations employee, you will be given two tickets to the Cherry Blossom Ball." He unclipped his seatbelt and turned to face me, and I did the same. "However, I'd really like it if you went as my plus-one. You can give your tickets to whomever you choose."

"Oh."

"I'm so embarrassed I didn't ask you before now. It totally slipped my mind, even when my mom mentioned it on Saturday. God, I feel like a fucking idiot." He looked so upset that I couldn't resist giving him a slow, sweet kiss to make him feel better.

"I'd love to go to the ball with you, but you have to promise not to call me Cinderfella."

"Deal, now let's seal it with another kiss."

Gray treated me to a languid kiss in the park before he drove us back to the office. We reluctantly parted ways when we stepped off the elevator. I noticed several pairs of eyes watching our every move. News about our relationship status was quickly making its way through the building. I just smiled at everyone like normal and went to my desk.

Ben was there waiting for my return. He apologized profusely about the awkwardness he caused by bringing up the ball. I told him it wasn't a big deal and explained Gray felt horrible it had been brought up before he'd asked me. Ben seemed relieved when he went back to his office.

I sat at my desk for a few worthless minutes trying to come up with plans to occupy my mind so I wouldn't miss Gray so badly while he was in

Pittsburgh. Who was I fooling? Gray was going to be on my mind no matter what I did.

I sent a text to Brandon to arrange a time when I could get together with him and his groomsmen to start working on the surprise dance for Ava. I followed that with a text to my best friend to invite her to dinner. We hadn't spent much quality time together since the first night I'd met Gray. We were long overdue. She quickly replied that she missed me too and would love to have a night with just the two of us. She was going to bring home takeout, and we were going to have a romantic movie marathon. It sounded like a perfect distraction to keep me from missing Gray so badly.

Yeah, right. Who was I trying to kid?

CHAPTER
Thirty-One

Gray

THE NEXT THREE DAYS WERE THE LONGEST OF MY LIFE. MY SHORT trip to Pittsburgh ended up being one day there plus two days in Cincinnati. I was thrilled to have the opportunity to sign more clients to our agency, but I really missed Chase.

I hated the disappointment in his voice when I called him to say I wouldn't be home like I had planned. Preston still had two weeks left of paternity leave, so I just needed to suck it up and keep working until he got back. Even then, I'd take on the lion's share of traveling so he could be home with Carly and Grace.

I stood under the scalding hot shower and hoped it worked some of the tension out of my body. My angry dick stood at attention, begging me to take some action to alleviate the pressure that had been building in my balls since Tuesday night when I'd last had Chase beneath me. My dick loved all the sexy action it had been getting and was pissed when it stopped as suddenly as it had started. I ignored him and went about getting ready for our date. I did mentally remind my dick that tonight we'd get to have Chase with nothing between us.

We had finally gotten our test results, and luckily, my new bed had been delivered while I was out of town. Preston was nice enough to let the delivery men in so they could set up the new bed and haul the old one away. I'd made my bed with the new linens Chase and I had picked out the previous week. I found the shades of pale blue and gray romantic and soothing.

I quickly finished my shower and got dressed so I could get my ass to Chase's house and pick him up for our date. More than sex, I needed to feel him in my arms, hear his voice in person, smell his body wash on his skin, and taste his sweet lips. I practically skipped my way down the stairs. I found myself whistling as I grabbed my keys off the entry table and opened the door. My good mood turned sour in a heartbeat when I saw who stood on my front porch. Maybe I should sell this house after all.

"What are you doing here, Devon?"

"You haven't answered my calls or returned the messages I've left for you, so I decided to stop by."

"There's a reason I haven't answered your calls or returned your messages. I don't have anything to say to you. We've said all there is to say."

"I miss you. I miss us. Can you just let me in for five minutes?" he pleaded. He looked crestfallen, and a few months ago, it would have worked on me. Not anymore.

"No, I have plans, and I am not going to be late just so you can beat a dead horse."

"Plans? As in a date?" he asked. There was a lot of hurt in his voice, but it was hard to tell if his emotion was genuine. Devon had mastered the art of manipulation.

"Yes, a date. I've moved on, and you should too." I didn't want to hurt him, but I needed him to know there was absolutely no way he was going to worm his way back into my life.

"Is it serious?" Devon asked.

"Very."

"Wow," he said weakly. "I guess I wasn't ready for us to really be over. We were together for five years and even though you said we were over, there was a part of me that thought, or hoped, we'd find our way back to one another."

It was all I could do to not roll my eyes at his poetic prose. Not a single word he spoke rang true to me. He wasn't in love with me and hadn't been for a very long time. He either wanted me back because I was comfortable or he had ulterior motives. Either way it wasn't going to work.

"It's not going to happen," I said firmly. Let there be no doubt. "If you'll excuse me, I need to be on my way to pick up my boyfriend." I pulled the door firmly shut behind me and maneuvered around him. I didn't look at him as I walked to my car, got in, and drove off. It may have been rude as fuck, but I couldn't find it in me to care.

I cranked up the music in my car and sang along with The Rolling Stones as I drove to Chase's home. It was a special night for us, and I needed to shake off my irritation at finding Devon on my doorstep. I must have failed miserably because Chase took one look at my face and knew something was wrong.

"What's wrong?" He pulled me into his apartment and looked me over from head to toe. "Are you sick? We don't have to go anywhere tonight. I'd be happy to snuggle with you on the couch."

I didn't want to ruin our night, but I had to tell him the truth. He'd be pissed and hurt if he happened to find out any other way. "Devon has been calling and leaving me messages the last few days. I haven't returned any of them because I had nothing to say to him. I thought we'd hashed it all out the night Devon came to pick up his stuff."

"So what has you upset tonight?"

"The idiot was on my front porch when I opened the door to leave. He gave me some sad song and dance, which I didn't believe for a second, and it just pissed me off."

"Are you upset because you still care about him?"

"Not at all. I told him about us. I said that I'd moved on and was involved in a serious relationship. I excused myself, locked my front door, and left."

"That was it?"

"Yep." I pulled Chase into my arms and held him tight. I did all the things I'd missed so much the past few days. I felt his solid strength in my arms, smelled his body wash on his skin. I already heard his masculine voice so all that was left was to taste his lips. "I really need to feel your lips against mine."

Chase pulled back slowly and looked into my eyes. His smile spread slowly across his face. He closed his eyes and pressed our lips together. Our kiss started out slow but quickly changed to a passionate exchange that left us panting for air. I had missed the feel of his tongue wrestling with mine.

"We better get going, or we won't ever leave," Chase told me after he ended our kiss.

"I'm fine with staying in. A few minutes ago you said you were fine with it too."

"That was when I thought you were sick," he argued. "I expect our promised date now that I know you're just irritated with your ex."

"Fine," I grumbled as I adjusted my package. "What did you plan for us tonight?" Chase had insisted on planning our date.

"We're going roller skating and eating the world's best pizza."

"Roller skating?"

"Yes, roller skating," Chase affirmed.

"I don't know," I said looking down at my hard-on. "If I fall, I might break something vital, then I won't be able to use it tonight." I leaned in and lowered my voice a few octaves. "My new bed arrived and is set up with the new linens we picked out. You know what that means, right?"

Chase's eyes darkened with need. "I get to feel all of you without any barriers," he replied. I seriously whimpered out loud at that point. I was in jeopardy of spontaneous combustion. "I won't let you fall, baby."

I should've told him I'd already fallen. For him. I waited too long and missed my chance unless I wanted to blurt it out in the hallway or the elevator with other people. I could've told him in the car, but it didn't feel like the right time. What did I really know about love and when I should declare it? I'd said it to Devon for five years, and I realized I had just been going through the motions. I had felt many things for Devon—lust, admiration, friendship, and puppy love, but none of those feelings were like anything I felt for Chase. I just questioned the timing and delivery of my declaration.

"I'm going to love skating with you, Chase."

"Don't forget about the greasy, delicious pizza," he reminded me.

"That too."

This was Chase's date, so he decided he was driving. He walked me to his car and held open the passenger door for me. I'd done this for men many times over the years, but this was the first time someone had done it for me. I liked it. I also liked it when he put his hand at my lower back and guided me into the skating rink.

It wasn't my idea of a romantic date, but I couldn't help but smile as people of various ages circled around the rink. Chase led me to the skate rental booth after paying the entrance fee, and a kid behind the counter retrieved skates for us.

"Are you as good at skating as you are bowling?" Chase asked.

"I'm definitely better at bowling, but I was a decent skater. It's been a while, though." I looked at the rink in time to watch a guy my age roll toward us. Well, it wasn't really a roll, it was some awkward attempt to roll that turned into a stumble on wheels. He flailed his arms like giant pinwheels as he tried to gain his balance, which only delayed the inevitable. I grimaced as he landed hard on his ass right in front of me and Chase. "I'm better than that guy. Maybe."

We laced up our skates, and I practiced a few minutes on the carpeted area before we made our way onto the wooden rink. Chase held my hand and smoothly skated while it took me a few minutes to get my balance and relax. I had forgotten just how much I used to like coming here when I was a kid.

Soft-colored lights and a disco ball lit up the floor playfully. We skated and laughed for a long time. I took several selfies of us in various poses as had become our habit. I loved thumbing through all the pictures of us on my phone.

"Send me that one," Chase said pointing to my phone. I happily obliged him, then we skated to a sappy slow song. "Are you hungry?" Chase asked me after the slow song ended and a Lady Gaga song came on.

"Starving," I said in a low, sexy voice. I had cast an ornery grin and an exaggerated wink at Chase, which made him smile. Fuck, I loved that smile.

Chase bought us the greasiest, cheesiest, and most delicious pizza I'd ever eaten. It was a vast improvement from the crap they used to serve. In between bites, we discussed our weeks. Mine had been boring as hell, but Chase had stayed busy and made the best of his alone time. It oddly made me feel better that he adapted to my absence instead of being lonely, which would lead to resentment. I'd been there and done that, and I wasn't willing to make a return trip.

"It's really hard, though," Chase said, referring to the secret he was keeping from Ava. "We tell each other everything. Even though this secret is a surprise for her, it's still hard. I've kept the dance routine really simple, and they're catching on pretty quickly, so hopefully we'll be done this upcoming week. They can all practice in their free time. We'll get together one last time before the wedding to make sure it looks good."

"You're remarkable," I told him.

"I am not."

"Don't scoff at me when I'm paying you a compliment. You are a remarkable friend, Chase. You'd do anything to make the people you love happy, and that is so rare these days." I wanted to be counted among his beloveds. The look in Chase's eyes told me I was in that elite group of people or at least really close to gaining entrance.

"I doubt it's rare," he argued. "I do love to see my friends and family happy, though. I guess it just comes naturally to me." He looked embarrassed at my compliment.

"It's an amazing gift." I tossed my napkin on my empty plate and patted my belly. "We better go work off some of those calories."

We skated for a few more hours, laughing and ribbing each other the entire time. We took part in the chicken dance and all the other challenges the DJ threw out. My favorite, by far, was the couple skate. They dimmed the lights even more and played Ellie Goulding's "Love Me Like You Do." Chase turned and skated backward while holding my hands and staring into my eyes. The lyrics perfectly expressed how Chase made me feel, and

I willed my brain to tuck the memory someplace safe. I'd rather forget my own name than the romantic skate with him.

"Are you ready to go back to your house?" he asked when the song ended. I answered with a kiss that left no doubt I was ready to be alone with him.

The drive to my house was pretty quiet, and it seemed we were both doing a little reflecting. Our hands remained connected, only parting when we had to exit the car in my driveway. I even fumbled one-handed to unlock the front door.

"At last," I said after tossing my keys onto the table. I pulled Chase to me for a kiss. We began to peel off and discard one another's clothes in a trail as we made our way to my bedroom. "I should light some candles or something," I said when we were finally standing beside my bed. I'd hit the dimmer toggle as we came through the door to mute the light, but it didn't seem right to me.

"I don't need candles, Gray. I just need you."

"You have me."

Chase pulled the duvet and top sheet down to the end of the bed before he climbed in. I followed behind him and we met in the middle. We were pressed together from head to toe, and it felt incredible. I wasted no time kissing his delectable lips. I'd gone too many days without feeling them on my body.

Our mouths mingled slowly, savoring the kiss, neither of us wanting to rush the moment. There would be plenty of times that we'd want to come together in a frenzy, our mouths ravaging one another, but that night wasn't one of them.

"Thank you for a perfect evening," I told him.

"It was skating and pizza."

"It was the best date I've ever had." I meant it, and I could tell he knew. "Besides, it's not where I went and what I did that counts but who I did it with. You've ruined me for anyone else, Chase."

"Gray," he whispered. I loved hearing my name spoken so tenderly

236

from his lips. His eyes watered, and he swallowed hard. He didn't need to say anything else because everything he was feeling was shining in his eyes.

I pressed my lips to his and rolled Chase until he was on his back and I was on top of him. He parted his legs, and I slid between them. Our bodies fit perfectly together like they were made for each other, and for the first time in my life, I started to believe in fate and destiny. I didn't need logic or reason when it came to Chase. I accepted that my heart was fated to beat for him and him alone.

I made love to him with my mouth until he began to squirm beneath me seeking some friction. I pinned his hands above his head when they began to roam all over my body. I needed him to be good so I could make it last. The last thing I wanted was to spill all over him before I had the chance to worship him properly.

"Be good," I warned.

"No foreplay right now. I just want to feel you inside me. I've been thinking of nothing else for days."

"Good things come to those who wait," I whispered in his ear. "Have you been a good boy, Chase, or have you eased the ache while I was out of town?"

"I've saved it all for you." He groaned as I bit down sharply on his ear. That was just what I wanted to hear, so I rewarded him by grinding my cock against his. "Fuck," he hissed between his lips.

"I saved it all for you too. I feel like I could go off like a powder keg, but I refuse to give in and rush this. It means too much to me." I kissed across his neck until I reached his other ear. I licked the outer shell and sucked the lobe into my mouth. "Are you going to take me bare tonight?"

"Please, Gray." He sounded just as desperate as I was. I couldn't deny him anything, especially something we both wanted.

I released his hands long enough to reach for the lube. I grabbed his hand and poured a small amount into his palm, then wrapped it around my cock. The breath hissed out of me when he began to slowly work the lube up and down my hard length. I poured lube on my fingers and began working his tight hole open for me with one finger then two. Chase started pleading again when my fingers repeatedly grazed his gland. He got even by milking my cock harder.

"Playtime is over," I told him when I removed his hand from my cock. I wrapped my hand around my dick and lined it up with his entrance. Chase wrapped his legs tightly around my waist. I pressed in slowly until the head of my cock penetrated the tight ring of muscle. We both groaned in blissful ecstasy as I entered him gently. His tight heat was like nothing I'd ever felt, and it was all I ever wanted.

I slid my fingers between his and pinned his hands to his pillow. I began rocking in and out until I was buried to the hilt inside his heat. Chase's fingers gripped mine so hard it was almost painful. Our eyes stayed locked while I slowly worked in and out of him. I fought the urge to drive into him fast and hard. I couldn't get close enough, even though every part of his skin was touching mine.

Sweat broke out all over both our bodies helping me slide against him. I felt the stickiness of his precum where his cock rubbed against my abs. Chase tilted his hips up, altering the angle of my penetration. His beautiful brown eyes glazed over as I jabbed his prostate with every forward snap of my hips. I could tell he was close from the way his body shook and his tight ass strangled my cock.

"Does that feel good?" He'd never had sex bare before, and I wanted to make it the best experience he ever had.

"Fucking incredible." His lips trembled and the words came out in a stutter. "Feels so primal. Like a claiming. I love it." His word struck a chord inside me, giving me the strength to resist the urge to come. I concentrated every forward thrust to hit his gland at the same time my tight stomach rubbed hard against his cock. "Ah, Gray. So close."

"Not yet." His lust-dazed eyes searched mine and seemed to calm at whatever he saw in them. I rolled my body so Chase sat astride my hips with my cock still buried inside him. "Ride me. Slow."

Chase placed his hands on my pecs for balance and began to rock his hips back and forth, taking me in and out of his hot body. He relaxed, letting his body take over as he worked my cock. I could do nothing but watch him in awe. He lifted his hands and tangled them in his hair, lost in the pleasure of us. He arched his neck and threw his head back in ecstasy. The words that came from his lips were indecipherable like he was speaking an ancient language.

I was so fucking close to spilling inside him, but I didn't want it to end. I gripped the sheets beneath me and fought off my orgasm so he could ride me until his heart was content. My breaking point nearly came when he leaned back and placed his hands on my thighs. Chase arched his back and spread his legs wide, allowing me to see my cock slipping in and out of his beautiful body.

"Gray," he begged. I knew what he needed from me, and I wasn't going to deny him. I wrapped my fist around his erection and pumped it up and down, matching the pace he rode my cock. The faster he rode me, the harder I stroked him. "Gray, baby."

"Look at me when you come." I needed to see the pleasure in his eyes when he unraveled around me. Chase's sexy eyes opened and locked on mine. "There they are. I love your eyes, and only I get to see them like this, Chase."

"Yes, just you." His body bowed like a rubber band stretched beyond its limit. He dug his fingers painfully into my thighs. "Baby... Oh my... god. Gray," he cried my name as his eyes lost focus right before his orgasm ripped through him.

"Give it all to me," I demanded when the first ribbon of his cum landed on my upper chest. I kept pumping him hard until there was nothing left to give, and he collapsed on top of me. "Kiss me."

My dick throbbed inside him, begging to come, but I ignored it as I made love to his mouth until I couldn't ignore my body's needs any longer. I gripped his hips hard and raised my ass off the bed, slamming my dick hard inside his body. I was afraid it was too much, but his moans said differently. He kissed me passionately as I pounded inside him, harder and faster until I came with a shout.

I held him tight against my chest while we came down from our orgasmic high. I felt his heart hammering against me and his warm breath against my neck. I reached up and ran my hand through his hair and wished I wasn't so afraid to speak the words in my heart. Why was I being such a coward? It was because it meant more than any other time. I lay there wishing I could take back the times I'd told Devon that I loved him so Chase would be the only man to hear those words from my lips, but that wasn't life. It wouldn't be fair to Devon and the relationship we once shared.

Chase's breath evened out, and I realized he had fallen asleep on top of me with my cock still buried inside him. I hated to have to wake him, but I didn't want him to be sore, and we both needed to wash up before we went to bed. "Hey, beautiful," I whispered into his ear. Chase slowly woke up and rose up enough to look down at me. The sated look in his eyes and his sappy smile made me chuckle. "We need to take a quick shower, then we can sleep."

"Too tired." He traced my lips with a finger.

"We'll be quick," I countered. "We're going to be stuck together once your cum dries." He grumbled but gently pulled himself off my cock. He slid off the bed and got to his feet, but his legs must not have been ready to support him yet because he fell against the edge of the bed.

"Oh my god," he mumbled into the sheets where he buried his head in embarrassment. He popped back up to his feet a minute later and threw his arms up in the air like a gymnast. "How about that dismount?" I cracked up, laughing at his recovery. He turned and faced away and pretended to pose for the judges. "Is that the sexiest thing you've ever seen?"

"Damn straight," I said as I rose off the bed. I grabbed his hand and dragged him to the shower so we could get cleaned up before bed, although I doubted we'd sleep much.

CHAPTER
Thirty-Two

Chase

GRAY TRAVELED A FEW TIMES OVER THE NEXT TWO WEEKS, SO I SPENT my free time with my friends or Gram. I finished teaching Brandon and the boys the dance routine to Bruno Mars's "Treasure," and I even let Gram talk me into making ebook covers for a few of her writer friends. Even though I missed Gray like crazy when he was gone, I felt fulfilled and content in ways I'd never known before. I did give serious thought to getting a cat to keep me company. I would love the sound of a purring cat to break up the silence at home.

My feelings for Gray got stronger and stronger each and every day. There were days I thought I would explode from the happiness building inside me. I wanted to tell him. In fact, I almost had a few times, but it never seemed like the ideal moment. I didn't want to tell him over the phone while he was away or blurt it out in the conference room at work or in the middle of an orgasm. I wanted something as beautiful as Gray was to me.

The moment came on a bright, unseasonably warm day in April when Gray took me to the tidal basin to see the cherry blossom trees in full bloom. We strolled hand-in-hand while taking in the magnificent sight. Afterward, Gray surprised me with a paddle boat excursion and a picnic.

I sat across from him, taking in his flushed cheeks, tussled hair, and boyish smile and knew. *This is it. Tell him.* I set my sandwich down and took a calming breath.

"I've been meaning to tell you something," Gray stated at the same time I said, "I need to say something." We broke into laughter, and Gray leaned over and kissed my lips.

"You go first," he said. "You sound really serious."

"So do you. Maybe you should go first."

"How about we count to three and both say whatever it is at the same time," he offered.

I cocked my head to the side and contemplated what he'd suggested. It could work, or it could blow up in my face. I could tell him that I loved him, and he could tell me he was excited about the Cherry Blossom Ball later that night. I studied the intense look in is blue eyes and knew he wasn't talking about the dance. I also saw the wickedness lurking there. "Okay, I'll play along," I agreed. "Start counting."

"One. Two. Three." We both took a breath and blurted…

"I used to eat glue," Gray said at the same time I said, "Blue is my favorite color."

We laughed so hard we fell over on the blanket. We lay there facing each other, and I could see the mirth in his twinkling eyes. I ran my hand over his cheek and kissed him softly on the lips. Gray wrapped his hand around my neck and pulled me into a deeper kiss.

"You ate glue?" I asked when our mouths finally parted.

"No, I was just throwing something out there. The best you could come up with is your favorite color?"

"It used to be green until I met you and fell into those blue, blue eyes of yours." His gaze darkened with a deeper emotion I wanted to hear him confess. "You were so a glue eater. No way that was a random thought."

"Believe what you want," he scoffed with an arrogant upturn of his chin.

"Let's try this again," I told him. Gray turned his head toward me, and the intensity was back. I hoped he saw the same when he looked into my eyes. This time I counted us down, my voice pitched low with emotion. "One. Two. Three…"

"I love you, Chase," he confessed as I said, "I love you, Gray."

We both expelled a happy sigh before our lips met. I wanted to roll him onto his back and lie on top of him, but I remembered we were in a public place. I made do with sweet kisses which became salty from my tears.

"Baby, don't cry," Gray whispered against my lips. "I know it probably seems too soon, but I'm crazy in love with you. I've never been this happy in my life."

"Happy tears, Gray." I caressed his face. "I've stopped worrying about how long we've known each other. It doesn't matter if it's one day, one month, or one year. Our hearts know what they want, and that's all that matters."

"Fated hearts."

"I finally found my Mr. Right."

"With a *W*," Gray clarified.

We smooched a little longer before we had to pack up and head back to his house to get ready for the ball.

"I have one more surprise for you, but I'm not sure it's the right time." Gray looked nervous, and I couldn't imagine what kind of surprise would worry him like that. He was practically chewing off his lip.

"Well, I'm curious as hell now. You have to give it to me, or I'll be thinking about it all night long."

"Okay," he said reluctantly and walked into his closet. He came back with a box that was beautifully wrapped in shiny blue paper and topped with a white ribbon. He was really going to town on his lip as he handed me the box.

"Thank you," I told him. I would love whatever he'd given me because it had come from him. I set the box on the bed and tugged on the white satin ribbon until it unfurled. I slowly lifted the lid and parted the tissue paper. Inside was a knitted blanket. I could tell it had writing on it, but I couldn't tell what it said because it was folded. I pulled it out of the box and held it in front of me so I could see the whole thing. My heart literally stuttered in my chest for a few seconds when I saw what he'd done for me. "Oh my god," I said, unable to fight back the tears. "How did you do this? Those are my mother's words, and it looks just like her handwriting."

"Gram helped me," he said softly as he came to stand by me. "It turned out so much better than I dreamed." He tried to wipe my tears away, but it was futile because they kept coming fast and hard. "I wanted you to be able to wrap her words around you like a warm hug." Gray's voice broke at the end. "Gram told me some of her favorite things and gave me a copy of the poem. Do you really like it?"

"I love it." I raked my gaze over the fine details of the blanket. I saw the hummingbirds and butterflies my mom had loved so much. I couldn't believe how lifelike the tiger lilies looked. Then I read the words my mother had written to me on those final days of her young life.

Through You, I will live…

Though my heart may soon stop beating, I fear not, my darling boy
Through you, I will live
My eyes may soon close forever, but I do not fear the darkness
Through you, I will see
I may soon take my final breath, but no sorrow shall accompany it
Through you, I will breathe

You will feel me in the sun that warms your skin, the wind that blows through your hair, and the beating of your heart. I will be with you every step that you take, every dance that you dance, and every tear that you cry. Through you, I will live.

Love with everything you have, my son, never hold back. A life without love has no meaning or purpose. Don't be afraid to take chances because you can't have rewards without first taking risks.

I didn't want to leave you; I did everything I could to stay. Though I will leave this earth in body, my spirit will remain. And through you, I will live.

Love always,

Mom

I gently folded the blanket and placed it back in the box. I turned and wrapped my arms around Gray's neck. He folded his arms around me and held me tight, rocking us back and forth. I had never received such a thoughtful gift from anyone. I pulled back, and we wiped each other's faces and exchanged watery smiles.

"I love it, and I love you, Gray. Your thoughtfulness means the world to me. Thank you."

"You're welcome." He kissed my lips. "I love you too."

I wiped my face and stepped back. Gray's eyes were red and puffy from crying, and I knew I looked the same or worse. "We look kind of scary."

"Good thing we have plenty of time to get ready for the ball, Cinder— Ouch," Gray yelped when I tweaked his nipple hard to keep him from finishing his sentence. "I'm going to get you for that," he said as he lunged for me. I evaded him on his first attempt as I ran for the bathroom, but he successfully captured me as soon as I cleared the door. "Got ya," he whispered in my ear.

And, boy, did he ever.

"How long do we have to stay?" Gray asked in a whiny voice as soon as we entered the ballroom. It was an event he was forced to attend every year, but it was the first time I'd been to anything so grand. I was excited, and he was decidedly not.

"Knock it off," I said looking around the grand ballroom. "It's amazing." The artificial cherry trees lining the walls of the room looked so real I would have sworn I could smell them. "They look so real."

"They are real," Gray told me, then explained they would be planted in honor of a child who lost their battle with cancer the previous year.

"There are so many." My heart broke seeing so many trees waiting to be planted in memoriam. "How sad."

Gray raised my hand and kissed it tenderly. "It's tragic, but at least we are doing something to try to make a difference."

"You're absolutely right." I smooched him quickly and looked around the room some more. "Shall we mingle?"

"We shall."

The ballroom was packed with people by the time all the attendees arrived. Other than a professional sporting event, I'd never been in one place with so many people. It seemed like Gray knew most of them.

"I certainly hope there won't be a pop quiz later," I teased.

"Yes, there will be, and you'll get a swat on your fine ass for every name you get wrong," Gray growled in my ear.

"Oh." It was all I could say. He made me forget the hundreds of people milling around us with just a few words. I was ready to drag him off to the nearest broom closet and have my wicked way with him.

"I know exactly what you're thinking," he said.

"You've become clairvoyant?"

"No, I know what you're thinking because I'm thinking it too."

"Great minds." I started looking for an exit. "How do you want to do this?" Gray didn't answer me, so I looked at him, but he wasn't paying attention. He was glowering over my shoulder. I turned to see what had upset him and found JJ walking toward me. I'd been ignoring my friend's texts and calls ever since the night of the bar fight. It seemed he wasn't willing to be put off any longer.

"Not here," Gray said angrily when JJ came to a stop in front of me.

"I can't apologize if you won't talk to me," JJ said to me, completely ignoring Gray's request. "Chase, can we go somewhere to talk for a few minutes?"

I looked into his dark brown eyes and saw the sincerity in his words. JJ was not a man who apologized to anyone, but he valued our friendship, and he knew he'd hurt me badly with his callous remark.

"Sure." I turned to look at Gray. I leaned forward and kissed his lips. "I'll be right back."

"I'll be waiting." He gave JJ a warning glare.

I followed JJ out of the ballroom and down a hallway until the noise faded. He stopped suddenly and turned to face me. "I've really missed you," he said, shocking me with his confession.

"We sometimes go months without speaking to each other, and it's only been a few weeks."

"It's been a month," JJ corrected, "and this was different."

"How so?"

"You weren't mad at me those other times, and I knew you had my back no matter what happened to me out in the shitty world." He ran his hands through his hair and paced a little. "I've always taken that for granted, but I won't anymore. I will be a better friend to you if you'll have me."

"JJ," I said softly. "You'll always have my friendship. I don't know what made you say what you did, but I know you didn't mean to hurt me."

"I was afraid of losing you." His words astonished me. "I saw the way you and Gray were together, and I knew he was going to be the one to take you away from me for good. I'm sorry I hurt your feelings. I didn't mean it."

"You will never lose my friendship, JJ." I put my arms around his waist and hugged him. "You're right about Gray and me, but I'm not leaving you behind." I stepped back and gave him a reassuring smile. "Gray knows about our history, and it makes him uncomfortable, but I told him that giving up your friendship was a sacrifice I wasn't willing to make."

JJ briefly closed his eyes and took a deep breath. Once he gathered himself, he met my gaze again and smiled. "Let's get you back before he comes looking for us with guns blazing."

I felt lighter inside since JJ and I had made peace. It was true what I'd said about us going months without talking, but he was also right. We'd always had each other's backs, and no matter how happy I'd been these past weeks, something had been missing, and now I knew what. When we walked back into the ballroom, Gray was standing right where I'd left him, but he wasn't alone. Devon stood in front of him, much too close for my comfort.

"Who's that?" JJ asked when I came to an abrupt stop.

"His ex who wants him back." As soon as the words left my mouth, Devon placed his hand on Gray's shoulder and slid it down to his bicep. Thankfully, Gray took hold of Devon's hand and removed it from his body. That simple gesture gave me the confidence I needed to approach them with my head held high.

Gray's eyes connected with mine as I approached them. Devon noticed his distraction and turned to see the cause. He ran his eyes up and down my body like I was a snack. He finally looked at my face, and his mouth opened in shock when he recognized me.

"I'm back," I told Gray. I wanted to lean in and kiss him, but his body language was tight with tension and frosty. Gray told me that Devon knew about us the night we went skating. I vividly remembered it because it had made me feel more secure in our relationship.

"Hi," Gray said neutrally.

"Wait, you two know each other now?" Devon asked as he looked back and forth between us.

I looked to Gray for guidance. I was confused, and I knew he could see it in my eyes. "Chase works in the art department at Wright Creations."

Devon laughed as if that was the funniest thing he'd ever heard. "You're serious?" Gray didn't try to say anything else, and that's when I realized the joke was on me. Or was I the joke? I felt my heart splinter, crack, and shatter in a matter of a few seconds. Gray's expression gave nothing away, and that somehow made it all worse. My lungs burned, and my vision dimmed. I realized I'd been holding my breath, hoping and praying Gray would tell Devon the truth about us.

I sucked precious air into my lungs, although why I wanted to live through the devastation was beyond me. I'd been so hesitant in the past to give my heart away, but Gray was different. I willingly threw caution aside to have the chance to be with him. Fuck, he'd fooled me good. I'd trusted him, believed in him, and fallen head over heels in love with him. For a short time, I had experienced joyful heights I'd never known existed. And now I was plummeting to earth without a parachute. How had I been so wrong about him?

I wouldn't let Gray see how badly his betrayal hurt me, though. We'd have a conversation later, but this wasn't the time or place. I had about five minutes before I lost control and cried like my world was ending because that was how it felt. I felt JJ move closer to me, which gave me the strength I needed. I stood straight and looked Gray squarely in the eyes. I saw a trace of unreadable emotion there. Was it regret or sorrow? I couldn't be sure.

"I do work for Wright Creations," I said, looking back at Devon. "I started the Monday after your birthday surprise. It's been…interesting."

"I bet." Devon wasn't an idiot. He sensed the undercurrent between Gray and me, but he'd never guess that we are…*were* lovers.

"I just wanted to stop by and thank you again for the tickets to the ball, Mr. Wright." Gray narrowed his eyes slightly when I reached for JJ's hand. I forced a smile when I looked up at my friend. "Are you ready, J?"

"Baby, I was born ready."

"Goodnight," I said as I turned away. I kept a death grip on JJ's hand until we got to his car.

"Keep it together for just a few more minutes, Chase," JJ whispered in my ear. He knew I wouldn't want anyone to witness what was about to happen. I bit my lip to keep from sobbing and squeezed my eyes shut to try to hold the tears back until we pulled away from the event. "Okay. Let it out."

I broke. "He said…said that…he loved me. I thought Gray would be the one who stayed." JJ held my hand tightly while I sobbed brokenly. "He told me…he said Devon…knew about us." Who the fuck said letting it all out would make a person feel better? There was nothing about my torrent of tears, broken words, and snotty nose that made me feel better. "Why would he lie to me? Was I just a game to him, J?"

"It didn't look like a game to me, Chase. You weren't the only one he fooled." JJ let out a soft sigh. "Maybe you should try to talk to him…"

"No."

"Chase, I know you're really hurt right now, but is there any way we could have misread the situation?"

"No. He looked me in the eye and referred to me as his employee when just a few hours ago he was declaring his love for me. I would understand him being uncomfortable if he hadn't told me Devon knew about us. That's the part I just don't understand. It doesn't matter because we're over."

"Chase, just…"

"I can't talk about this anymore. Please just take me home."

"Okay."

CHAPTER
Thirty-Three

Gray

I KNEW I FUCKED UP THE MINUTE THE WORDS LEFT MY MOUTH. I WAS so irritated with Devon's pleading for another chance. He was needling me about my new boyfriend and wondering why he hadn't attended the ball with me. He must've just arrived because I'd been holding Chase's hand all night. The final straw was when he put his hand on me and tried to caress my arm. I firmly, even rudely, told him there was no chance for us again. Ever.

I sensed Chase was near before I even laid eyes on him. I glanced over and saw him walking toward us. Chase's eyes narrowed when he saw Devon standing so close to me. My guy didn't like anyone touching what belonged to him. I found his possessiveness very sexy.

"Mmm, mmm, mmm," Devon said softly as he eye-fucked my boyfriend. "Damn, I'd like to… Oh," he said when he finally looked at Chase's face. His words were like a dagger to my heart because he had been minutes away from fucking Chase in my home; a fact I'd avoided thinking about at all costs. But Devon drooling over my boyfriend—the man I loved—broke the lock on Pandora's box.

A red haze blurred my vision as fury burned through my body. I knew I was overreacting to the situation, but I couldn't seem to control myself. I needed Devon to get the fuck away from us. I had already told him I'd moved on a few weeks ago and again tonight. There was nothing else he needed to know, including who I was seeing. It wasn't his business. I certainly didn't want to hear the snide remarks he'd make if he knew I was dating Chase. Sure, he'd find out someday and make trouble, but it didn't have to be the day Chase and I finally admitted our feelings for each other.

I fucked up royally. Chase tried so hard to keep the hurt out of his eyes and voice, but I saw what my words had done to him. Then I watched as he took JJ's hand and let his friend lead him from the ballroom. It would have hurt less if he had stabbed me in the heart or bashed me over the head with a blunt object.

"What a hot piece of ass he is," Devon said. "It's a damn shame that—"

"Don't fucking finish that thought, asshole." Devon whipped his head in my direction. He had to see the possessiveness in my eyes and hear it in my voice. "And you stay the hell away from him." A wicked gleam lit Devon's eyes, and I realized my ex thought my possessiveness was over him.

"Don't want to see me happy too? Maybe you're not over me after all. If you can have a little fun, why can't I? Maybe we could find a playmate we'd both enjoy. You think Chase would be up for a threesome?"

"Shut your disgusting mouth, Devon. No fucking way. I'd never share him with you or anyone."

"Share him? Chase is your boyfriend? Are you so pathetic you can only score with my castoffs? My sloppy seconds."

"Except you never had him, did you, Devon? Fate intervened and gave me the love of my life." Devon looked shocked to hear me talk so openly about my feelings. "Chase was always destined to be mine. You were just a steppingstone on his path to get to me. Do not ever contact me or Chase ever again."

I walked away without a backward glance. I wouldn't give that fucker another second of my time. I had to find Chase. I searched the hotel lobby but didn't see him or JJ anywhere. I called his phone, but it went straight to voice mail. Fuck! He'd turned it off. I practically ran to the valet station. I showed the three attendants the picture I'd taken of us this afternoon and asked if any of them had seen him leave.

"I saw him leave with a different guy," the blond attendant said. "He didn't look nearly as happy as he did in that picture. He looked like his whole world was coming to an end."

"Good luck, dude," added a brunet kid.

"I think you're gonna need it," the ginger-haired valet chimed in.

I handed the blond kid my ticket and paced while he retrieved my car. It felt like all the blood had been drained from my body. I was chilled to the bone, and I felt hollow inside like my heart had been cut out. I slapped a tip in the kid's hand as I climbed into my car and sped off into the night.

I caught a red light at every intersection. My mind played all kinds of horrible tricks on me while I waited, but I shoved them aside. JJ taking him home didn't have a hidden meaning. Chase wouldn't betray me, no matter how upset he was. *You betrayed him by not being truthful.*

When I arrived at Chase's apartment complex, I nearly put the car in park before it came to a complete stop. I pleaded and prayed that he'd forgive my stupidity as I rode the elevator up to his floor. My hand shook as I knocked on the door. Chase didn't answer, so I knocked again, but still nothing. I tried the knob and found the door unlocked. Even though I shouldn't have, I let myself into his apartment.

The sounds of Chase crying gutted me, and tears filled my eyes. I found them in the living room, JJ holding Chase in a tight embrace. I hated seeing the love of my life accepting comfort from him. I wanted to be the one to ease all his hurts, especially when I was the source.

"He said he loved me, J," Chase said pitifully into JJ's broad chest.

"I do love you," I said.

They both turned to look at me at the same time. It would have been funny in a different set of circumstances. One pair of brown eyes looked at me skeptically as if he wanted to believe me but wasn't quite sure. I couldn't blame him for his wariness. The other set of brown eyes, the most beautiful I'd ever seen, looked at me in utter devastation. All the air rushed out of my lungs when I saw the extent of the pain I'd caused Chase. He was beyond hurt. He was destroyed.

"Chase, I'm going to go and let you guys talk," JJ said and tried to step away. Chase was still gripping his arms and didn't let go. JJ had always been his safety net, and Chase was clinging to him with all his might.

"I don't want *you* to go. *He* can go." I had been reduced to *he.*

"Please, just let me explain, babe."

"Do. Not. Call. Me. That."

"Okay, Chase." I held up my hands. "I'd like the opportunity to apologize for my hurtful behavior. I'd appreciate if we could do this without an audience."

"You sure as fuck didn't mind breaking my heart in front of an audience. Why the need for privacy now?"

JJ looked pained that he was caught in the middle. He cupped Chase's face tenderly and turned his head to face him. "I'm going to leave and let you talk. Call me later if you need me, okay?" Chase nodded and released his friend. JJ dropped a tender kiss on Chase's forehead before he turned to leave but not before leveling a warning glare in my direction.

"Do you want to sit?" I asked after JJ left. Chase was looking down and avoiding eye contact.

"I want you to leave so I can start putting the pieces of me back together again."

"This doesn't have to be the end for us, Chase. Please talk to me."

He lifted his head and finally looked at me. "Are you ashamed of me?"

"No, never. What I said was a knee-jerk reaction to Devon sizing you up like he still wanted to try you on for size. And I didn't want to hear his snide remarks when he found out about us."

"You lied to me, Gray." Hurt replaced his anger. I was so mesmerized by how beautiful he looked when angry that it took me a few seconds to catch on to what he said.

"When did I lie to you?"

"The afternoon of our skating date," Chase told me. "You stood in this room and said you had told Devon about us when he showed up to win you back."

"I did?"

"You did. Why would you lie about something like that? You obviously didn't tell him about us."

"I did tell him about us, but I didn't tell him your name. I told him I'd met someone, and it was very serious. I almost told him I was in love with you, but I couldn't tell him before I told you." I saw his anger soften for a brief instant, and I took a small step forward, which was a mistake. Chase's walls went right back up. "I didn't owe Devon a damn thing, Chase. I only told him about us, meaning I'd fallen in love with someone else, and encouraged him to move on."

"You don't love me."

"Stop saying I don't love you just because I screwed up. I made one goddamned mistake, and you're ready to throw in the towel. You are my everything. Please don't give up on me."

"You lied to me, and you denied what I meant to you, Gray. That's more than just one mistake. You make it sound like I'm breaking up with you because you left the toilet seat up."

"I didn't lie," I argued.

"Fine, you misled me. That doesn't explain or excuse you telling Devon I was your employee. I'm breaking up with you because I don't trust you. Trust is everything to me."

"Chase, please don't do this." It was my turn to break, and I did. Tears ran down my cheeks as I walked to him. "Please just give me another chance. Please don't…" I couldn't finish my sentence until I regained my composure. I turned my back and walked a few steps away. Fuck! I blew out a breath and walked back to him, but this time I didn't stop until we were almost touching. He stepped back, and I followed. He placed his hand on my chest to stop me, and I placed my hand on top of it, holding it over my heart. "This heart belongs to you, Chase." I placed my free hand over his chest. "Your heart belongs to me." He closed his eyes to avoid looking at me. "We belong together. I understand if you need time to think, but don't do anything drastic. Listen to what your heart is telling you, and don't end us." He was shaking all over but still hadn't opened his eyes. I pressed my lips softly to his, begging him to feel our connection. "I'm not giving you up, Chase."

I dropped my hands and stepped back. He still hadn't opened his eyes, and I wanted to believe it was because he couldn't bear to watch me leave. I turned and let myself out of his apartment, even though my heart screamed for me to stay.

I'm sure I looked like a death row inmate making his final walk when I made my way through the building and out to my car in the parking lot. I was so lost in thought I didn't realize I wasn't alone until JJ's voice broke through my misery.

"Don't let him give up," he said. "Give him time to think but not too much, or he'll convince himself what he felt wasn't real."

"I'm surprised you're not trying to take advantage of the situation and get him back for yourself."

"You're the one he loves. He never felt about me the way he does you, Gray. Don't you fucking blow this." His voice cracked, showing a vulnerability I would have never guessed existed. "I need Chase to get his happily ever after."

"Because you couldn't give it to him," I finished his unspoken thought. "You love him."

"I will never be what he needs, and I would only cause him more hurt, but you can give him the world. It hurts like hell to see another man making him happy, but I love him enough to let him go. Don't fuck this up, asshole." I watched JJ walk away, a solitary man in the night.

I sat in my car for several long minutes thinking over what JJ had said. I needed a strategy, so I called the best strategist I knew.

"Why the fuck do you insist on waking me up?" Preston growled into the phone.

"I need your help, Preston. I'm making the biggest pitch of my life, and you're the best I know."

The following Monday rolled around too quickly, and I wasn't prepared. I'd spent the wee hours of the previous morning and into the late afternoon putting my campaign together to win Chase back. I'd barely slept five hours in the last two days. My mind wouldn't shut down long enough to let me rest. I kept picturing the hurt in his eyes and hearing the anguish in his cry—things I never wanted to experience again.

I arrived at the office long before anyone else so I could begin working on my special project. I wanted to use our specialized software and equipment to make this campaign myself rather than go to an office supply store and trust a stranger. I was just pulling the final pieces off the printer and got so caught up in their beauty I didn't hear anyone come into the room.

"What are you doing in here?" Ben asked from behind me. "Since when do you do your own printing?" He came to stand beside me and saw the photo on top of the stack. "Ah, when it's personal and precious."

"I fucked up," I found myself saying. "I might have ruined the best thing that has ever happened to me."

"Nah, I doubt that," Ben refuted. "He's crazy in love with you, Gray. I'm sure you'll work it out."

"I hope so," I said softly. I wouldn't allow myself to imagine any other outcome. Ben patted me on the back and left me alone in the print room. The rest of the staff would be reporting soon, so I headed back to my office as stealthily as I could. I wanted to see Chase more than I wanted to breathe, but I was terrified of seeing the finality of our goodbye in his eyes.

I made flight and hotel reservations myself instead of involving Rosie. She and Chase seemed tight, and I couldn't risk her tipping him off. Preston called my extension when he arrived, and we went over my plans one last time.

I packed up my "Take Me Back" campaign materials into my briefcase and waited until I knew Chase would be meeting with Preston before leaving the safety of my office. I stopped by Rosie's desk and told her I'd be working from home and could be reached by email or by phone. She looked surprised but said she'd transfer only the most urgent calls to my cell.

I wasted no time leaving the building, although I would've loved to be a fly on the wall in Preston's office. I hoped he was selling this scheme really well. I didn't want Chase to suspect his trip to LA was bogus and part of my plan to get him back. I had to go big to prove to him how serious I was about us.

I had one stop to make before I had to go home and pack for my flight to LA. Chase wouldn't be flying out until the next day, but I needed to arrive early to get everything set in motion. I was going to need help to pull this off, and Chase was worth swallowing my pride.

I pulled my car into the parking lot of the animal shelter my stepfather, Jeff, told me about when I called him earlier. As a veterinarian, he provided a lot of pro bono services to the area shelters. I walked into the building and was hit with the strong smell of disinfectant.

"Hi, are you Grayson?" asked a perky, twentysomething brunette. The animal shelter wasn't open on Mondays, but Jeff had made a call so I could have a private appointment.

"I am, and you must be Wendy." I shook her outstretched hand.

"Yes, sir. Are you ready to find your new best friend?"

"Definitely," I replied. "Jeff explained that I had to leave town for a few days, right? I have someone coming over to give him or her water and food. Will that be okay? I don't want to traumatize the poor cat by leaving it alone right away."

Wendy laughed charmingly. "Cats are the perfect animal to be left alone at home. They are very independent creatures and don't require the attention a dog needs. In fact, your new forever friend will use the quiet to adapt to their new surroundings. You do plan on using a litter box, right?"

"Definitely."

"Everything should work out fine. Okay, here are the cats we have for adoption," she held her hand up and gestured to two rows of cages.

"There's so many," I said shocked.

"Well, there are lots of irresponsible people." She patted me on the back. "Take your time to see which cat you connect with. I'll go up front to give you some privacy. When you find him or her, just give me a holler, and I'll open the cage for you."

"Thanks," I said, feeling a little overwhelmed.

I took my time checking out each cage and found it very hard to pick. They were all so cute and had such different personalities. It was even harder choosing a cat for someone else. I thought about Chase's personality, and it helped me rule a lot of them out, even though I wanted to save them all. What about the cat's age? Should I get him a kitten? These thoughts rolled around in my mind until I reached the very last set of cages on the right.

All the cats so far were friendly and approached the cage. Some put their paws up playfully, some rolled around on their backs, and some played with their toys. But not the shabby-looking orange tomcat in the very last cage. He sat in the back of his cage and assessed me coolly. He had long orange hair, eyes the same color as his fur, and an ear that was missing a small chunk. The cat had really been through it, and you could see it in his jaded eyes. He looked as if he'd been playing the "pick me" game for too long and was tired of getting his hopes up. He'd built his defenses just like Chase. The tag on his cage said his name was Oliver, and he was a three-year-old tabby cat. He was the most beautiful thing I'd ever seen besides Chase.

"Hi, Oliver." I didn't bother going to find Wendy because I was afraid Oliver would think I was rejecting him like the other idiots. Fuck, the cat had me wrapped around his paws, and I didn't even own him yet. "We'll fix that right away, won't we?" I unlocked the cage and slid my hand inside. Oliver sniffed it, then rubbed the side of his face against my palm. He walked to the edge of the cage, and I lifted him out and held him against my chest. "You ready to blow this joint, buddy?" He began to purr loudly and rubbed his head against my chin, which I took as a yes.

Oliver and I made our way down the aisle, and I swear he puffed his chest out in pride as we walked past the other cages.

"We're ready, Wendy," I said when I reached the front of the building. Wendy had wheeled her chair over to a filing cabinet so her back was to me. She jumped and spun around when she heard my voice. "I didn't mean to scare you." She looked at the cat I held in my arms and a huge grin broke out on her face.

"Oh my god! You're adopting Oliver?" I smiled at her in return and nodded. "I'm so excited. That sweetheart has been here since he was a kitten. He looked like an orange, flea-ridden, drowned rat. He's been passed up at every adoption event we've had over the past three years."

"They were fucking idiots," I told her. Oliver purred even louder.

"I'm so happy for you both."

Wendy helped me load Oliver into a crate so I could complete his paperwork. Once done, she helped me pack my new cat supplies, including his portable potty and kitty litter, into my trunk. I placed Oliver's cat crate in the backseat and strapped the seatbelt around it. I heard Wendy giggling behind me.

"He's going from rags to riches, right?" she asked.

"Damn straight." I gave her a hug to thank her for her help and took my boy to his new house. Fuck, it was going to be hard to leave him. I needed to find someone to come over and cat sit, but who? I had a sudden epiphany and pulled up his contact info on my phone at the next red light. Once I hit dial, the call transferred to the Bluetooth in my car.

"Hello," Xavier said on the second ring.

"Are you allergic to cats?"

CHAPTER
Thirty-Four

Chase

I DRAGGED MYSELF INTO WORK THE FOLLOWING MONDAY, EVEN THOUGH it was the absolute last place I wanted to be. After suffering through nearly two sleepless nights, I felt like a goddamned zombie and looked like one too. The looks people cast in my direction were fucking hilarious, though.

I hid out in the art room and tried hard not to think about Gray in his office. Damn, I couldn't get him off my mind. I had tried jogging until I nearly collapsed, I had tried losing myself in my art, but nothing and no one could distract me from thinking about him.

I wasn't sure I could give him another chance. He had the power to destroy me. If I was this fucked up after dating him for a little over a month, what would happen if he broke my heart after six months, a year, or five? No, I didn't think I could handle it. It had been my experience that the men I fell in love with found it extremely easy to walk away from me.

As soon as I'd convince myself we were over, I'd remember the sincerity in his eyes when he'd told me he loved me. I'd recall every minute of every date we'd gone on. I'd relive every damn kiss, touch, or sound he made while we made love. It had always been making love for us, even when we were animalistic. It was never fucking between us, not even in the beginning. There was always something deeper binding us together. *Fated hearts.* Did I really want to go the rest of my life without experiencing him again? I just didn't know.

I fired up my computer, prepared to lose myself in my work. I was willing to hide out there all day to avoid running into Gray. I was feeling too vulnerable, and I didn't trust myself around him. I was midway through a program when Preston called and asked me to come to his office. My anxiety ratcheted up about twenty notches as I made my way there. He had sounded friendly on the phone, but that didn't mean anything. *God, please don't let him ask me about Grayson.* I walked past my old desk and knocked on Preston's door.

"Come in."

I attempted to paint a happy smile on my face, but I could tell by Preston's grimace that I had failed miserably. "You wanted to see me?"

"Uh, yes," he said after a brief hesitation as if he had lost his train of thought. "Have a seat." He gestured for me to sit down. "I hate to spring this on you last minute, but we really need you to fly out to LA and meet with Mitchell Heston and his team."

"Me?"

"Yes, you." Preston sat up straight in his chair and looked more serious than I'd ever seen him. "Heston and his people are having second thoughts about the campaign, and we need you to see what can be done."

"Me?" I sounded like a broken record.

Preston's lips twitched briefly. "Yes, you. Look, Heston connected with you. We trust you to meet with him to see if we can meet his demands with minimum changes to production and cost on our end."

"I appreciate your faith in my ability, but I'm out of my depth here. Landing this contract is…"

Preston nodded. "Huge."

"Yes, and I don't want to screw it up."

"You won't." Preston smiled but it did little to assure me. "I'm not asking you to make Heston promises you can't keep. Listen to his concerns and tell him you'll bring them back to the team. If he wants concessions, tell him you're not authorized to give them but someone with authority will be in contact immediately."

I blew out a shaky breath. "Yeah, I can do that."

"Perfect," Preston said, rubbing his hands together. I saw in his eyes that he wanted to say something else, but he didn't. My respect and appreciation for him grew even more. "I'll email you the itinerary in a little bit. I had to make the arrangements before Rosie arrived this morning."

"Okay. I won't let you down," I told him, hoping I was right.

"I know you won't, Chase."

I shuffled back to the art department and was surprised to see a beautiful pot of red tulips on my desk. I knew instinctively who they were from because giving up wasn't in Gray's nature.

I picked up the envelope that was tucked inside the planter and slowly opened it, knowing his words would make me cry, but I was powerless to stop myself from reading them. I pulled the note out of the envelope, expelled a deep breath, and began to read.

Chase,

When a person gives you red tulips it is a declaration of their love. It also means they are asking you to believe them.

I love you so much, and I will spend every day proving it to you if you'll just give me the chance.

Love always,

Gray

Damn him! I worked really hard to fight back my tears, but they still slid down my face. My heart was telling me to get over my hurt pride and call him, but my brain urged caution.

I couldn't let his kind gesture go without acknowledgment, though. I sent him a text to thank him for the flowers and to say I needed more time.

Gray replied instantly. He told me that he meant every word and that he'd be waiting patiently for me.

I set the flowers on the corner of my desk, put my phone away, and got to work on completing my project since I'd be out of town for a few days. Uncertainty about my trip crept into my brain and temporarily distracted me from moping over Gray.

I boarded the plane to LAX bright and early the next morning, feeling better than I had in days. It wasn't that I'd come to a decision about my future with Gray, but I'd had ten hours of sleep snuggled up with George the monkey and woke with a peaceful mind. The first thing I saw were the beautiful red tulips sitting on my bedside table. My chest tightened as I recalled Gray's note. I decided then and there that Gray and I would sit down and talk things out when I got back from LA. It wasn't fair to either one of us to drag this out. I either had to set my fears aside and give him a chance or walk away.

The flight to LA wasn't as fun without Gray. I spent the entire time thinking about our first flight together. That led me to remember every moment of our time together in LA, where we had truly discovered each other. I teared up on several occasions but was able to stop the flow before I embarrassed myself.

It was seventy-five and sunny when the plane touched down in California. I selfishly hoped the meetings didn't prevent me from taking time to soak up the sunshine and enjoy the water.

I was surprised to learn I'd been given the same suite I had shared with Gray. It was just me, so I offered to take a smaller room, but the clerk kindly assured me it wasn't necessary. She thought I was being thoughtful, but in truth I wasn't sure I could stay in that room without losing my mind.

With great trepidation, I opened the door to the suite. Memories of our time together rushed at me so hard it nearly brought me to my knees. I saw us so clearly and heard the echoes of Gray's voice and his laughter as I walked through the suite. It was truly a bittersweet moment. I missed him so fucking much. I knew I could have it all again if I wasn't so damn scared.

I wheeled my suitcase into the room he'd used and where I'd spent the night in his arms for the first time. I unpacked my clothes and tried not to spend too much time staring at the bed. I put my toiletries in the bathroom and caught myself staring at the shower in the mirror. I bit my lip to keep it from trembling.

"This is fucking stupid," I said to myself in the mirror. "You're fucking miserable without him. He loves you, and you know it. Quit using excuses to push him away so he can't hurt you sometime down the road, Chase. Not everyone leaves." I let my pep talk sink in and immediately felt lighter. I smiled at my reflection, knowing I was making the right decision.

I pulled my phone out of my pocket to call him but stopped myself. This was something I needed to do in person when I got home. A phone call or text wouldn't be right. Besides, I would want to be held and kissed by him afterward. I pictured the look in his eyes when he made love to me and knew it would be ten times more intense after our separation. I started to get hard, which wouldn't do if I was going to meet with Mitchell Heston soon. I sure as hell didn't want to give him the wrong idea. I splashed some cold water on my face to cool myself off.

Ninety minutes later, I sat in Mitchell Heston's waiting room. I had been too nervous to eat, and my blood sugar was getting low. His personal assistant cast a glance in my direction every once in a while, and I couldn't quite decipher the look in her eyes. Amusement? Sympathy? Whatever it was, it was awkward.

"Mr. Heston will see you now," she said fifteen minutes later.

I stood, squared my shoulders, and let myself into his office. "Good afternoon, Mr. Heston," I said, extending my hand toward him.

"Mr. Heston? What happened to calling me Mitch like I asked you?"

"This is a business meeting, sir. I think it would be more appropriate for me to refer to you as Mr. Heston." I looked around his office and gestured with my free hand. "Where's your marketing team? I was under the impression they had some concerns about the tone of our campaign."

"It's just the two of us," he said.

Something felt off, and I was immediately suspicious. "Why am I really here?" I crossed my arms over my chest and stared him down across his desk.

"Have a seat," he told me. He looked at his watch, and I wondered if I was keeping him from someone or someplace. "My team does have some concerns about the tone of the campaign, and I'd like to address them with you."

"Okay," I dropped into the seat he indicated. "What concerns?"

"Well, for one thing they seem to think the tone of the ads is too starchy. They said it will discourage younger generations from wanting to stay at Heston's."

I leaned forward in my seat, and I'm sure I was making the "huh" face. "Too starchy? The younger generation can't afford to stay at Heston's, sir. You're not operating a forty-five-dollar-a-night hotel chain."

"Mitch."

"Mr. Heston," I said, not willing to budge.

He cocked his head in consideration. He glanced at his watch yet again, and it was starting to annoy me. He'd insisted on this meeting, and now he couldn't give me the time of day. "You have a valid point, Chase."

"Okay. What other concerns were there?"

"Oh, nothing that bothered me much. I thought they were being petty." He waived his hand in irritation. "Some gripe about font size and color. Is it that big of a damn deal?"

"Well, it can be," I replied. "Do you have the specific pieces they were referring to? I can take a look and make sure the lettering matches the concept."

"I don't have them on me right now." He glanced at his watch once more, and I couldn't hold back any longer.

"Am I keeping you from something?"

"I was waiting for the precise moment to give you something, although I don't know why I agreed to help him," he mumbled as he pulled something out of his desk. "I should be taking advantage of his stupidity and trying to win you for myself." Mr. Heston slid an envelope across his desk to me. My name was scrawled on the outside, and I immediately recognized Gray's handwriting.

"Thanks, Mitch," I said as I opened the envelope.

"Now I'm Mitch," he said, throwing his hands in the air.

I smiled when I pulled the card out of the envelope. The front of the card was a picture of Gray's house with crime scene tape forming a big X across the front door. I opened the card and read the words he wrote to me.

Scene of the Crime:

Where you stole my heart, Chase. I was yours from the moment our eyes met. I know I told you I'd be patient, but I can't sit idle when it's something this important. I'm going to fight for you.

By now, you probably realize I sent you all the way to LA under false pretenses. I wanted to remind you of where the magic began for us, but it truly started the night you crossed my threshold for the first time, regardless of the circumstances.

I love you, Chase, and I'm going to prove it. I hope you're up for a little fun. Mr. Heston was kind enough to give you the first clue to help kick off your journey, although he'd rather keep you for himself.

Your next clue can be found at a restaurant by the sea. We sat there and enjoyed seafood and each other's company. They'll be expecting you for lunch. Wear something comfortable.

Gray

I looked up to see Mitch watching me closely. "I don't know what he did to upset you, but he's gone to a lot of trouble to prove his love to you. I hope I find that kind of devotion someday." His eyes had a faraway look in them, and his voice held a hint of sadness. There was more to Mitchell Heston than met the eye.

"Thank you so much for helping him, although he didn't need to go to such extreme measures."

"He's a go big or go home kind of guy. Good luck."

I shook his hand and quickly left his office. I needed to change clothes and get to Alexander's. My heart thumped wildly in my chest with the hope that he'd join me for lunch. Surely he was in LA too if he was sending me to places to gather clues. Those clues had to lead to a surprise. *Please let the surprise be Gray*.

I changed into my casual clothes and headed down the street on foot. I searched the inside of the restaurant for my favorite face as soon as I walked through the door. I was disappointed but not terribly surprised when I didn't see him there.

"Chase, right?" The hostess approached me with a warm smile on her face. "I have a special table set up for you right over here." I followed behind her as she led me to the same table where Gray and I had sat during our visit. "Your waiter will be right out. Enjoy your meal."

"Thank you." I looked out at the ocean while I waited. I didn't bother looking at the menu because I was going to order the same meal I had the last time.

"Hi, I'm Robby," the waiter said. "Do you know what you'd like to eat?"

I ordered my lunch but chose a soda over alcohol. I figured I'd need a clear head for the afternoon and evening ahead of me. The food was every bit as delicious as I remembered. I must have been hungrier than I thought because I nearly licked the plate clean.

"Is there anything else I can get for you? Dessert?" Robby asked.

"Nope. I'm stuffed. It was incredible. Thank you." I reached for my wallet, but Robby stopped me.

"It's already been taken care of, tip and all." Robby handed me a familiar-looking envelope. "I'm so glad I got to be a part of your special day. Enjoy!" Robby clapped me on the shoulder and left me alone so I could open my card from Gray.

This one had a selfie he'd snapped of us on our very first date at the bowling alley. I remembered the pose very well because he'd pulled me close to him and I could feel his body heat through my clothes. Gray's smile was a little wider than mine, but he'd just won our match and a kiss.

You Bowled Me Over:
I may have won the bowling match, but we both won that night when our

lips met for the first time. Walking away from you that night was the hardest thing I'd ever done, but I'd made you a promise, and I wasn't going to let you down.

I ended up letting you down anyway, and I'm so very sorry. I won't lie and say I'll never screw up again because we both know I'll get in trouble. I will never lie to you, and I will never, ever make you feel like less than my entire world.

Your next clue is at the place where I made one of your teenage dreams come true. We climbed on board as the sun set. You thought it was one of the most beautiful things you'd ever seen, but I couldn't stop looking at you.

I love you.

Gray

I grinned like an idiot the entire time I walked to the amusement park. I tried paying for my entrance ticket but was told it had already been paid for. Was he watching me as I accepted my clues? I looked for him in the crowd as I walked to the Ferris wheel, but I never caught sight of him, even though I felt him near.

"You have to ride the wheel first," the attendant said with a smile when I approached with my hand out. I rode the wheel and enjoyed the ocean breeze blowing through my hair. I looked down at all the bustling activity and couldn't help but wonder what Gray had up his sleeve next. "Here you go," the attendant said once I climbed off.

"Thank you," I said as I accepted the envelope.

I stepped off to the side so I could read the card without getting trampled. Damn, it must've been spring break because the place was packed with kids and adults. I opened the envelope and pulled out the card. The front of this card was a picture of me holding George right after Gray had won him for me. I was grinning from ear to ear with both my arms wrapped around him.

Monkeying Around:

Do you have any idea how jealous I was of George? He got to sleep with you all night while I slept by myself across the hall. I hated sleeping separately from you that night and every night I've slept alone since.

268

Holding you feels like every dream come true. There are so many things I want to experience with you, and I hope you feel the same way.

Your next clue waits for you at George's jungle.

Love,

Gray

I wanted to run to the game booth where Gray had won George for me. I hoped like hell I didn't have to win my card by throwing the baseballs. I had a strong arm and good aim, but I wasn't sure I could knock down all the milk bottles like Gray had.

"Hi," I said to the game attendant. "I'm Chase."

"Did you want to play?" I squinted my eyes in confusion and thought about the words of the clue again. This was George's jungle. "Just kidding, Chase. Here you go."

"Thanks." I accepted the envelope and walked away so I could read it in private. I opened it and eagerly pulled out the card. My breath caught in my throat when I saw the smiling picture of us posing beneath the cherry blossoms.

Love Beneath the Cherry Trees:

Chase,

This was the happiest day of my life. You gave me your heart, and I refuse to give it back. It's mine! I gave my heart to you that day, and I don't want it back.

I know the last few days have been difficult for you, and I wanted to give you a special treat to help you relax. I know you're probably tired of trekking from clue to clue, but I hope this makes it worth your while. Here's your clue.

In the heart of the hotel, you'll find a place that is fit for a prince and where tranquility reigns.

XOXO,

Gray

I turned and walked straight back to the hotel, my heart beating happily in my chest. He was talking about the Tranquility Room, which was well known for its spa amenities. I had hoped he'd be there to get a couples massage and was disappointed when I arrived and was shown to a room by myself.

The spa was definitely tranquil as well as decadent. Soothing music was piped through hidden speakers, and the air was beautifully perfumed with a scent I couldn't quite place. It was lavender with a touch of something else. Gray treated me to a full body massage, hot rock treatment, and a facial. I was so relaxed when I was done I had to check my pulse to make sure I was still alive.

"I think this is for you." Jennifer, the spa manager, held out an envelope for me when I returned to the front desk.

"Thank you for everything. I've never felt so relaxed in my life."

"You're very welcome. I'm so happy you enjoyed it. Enjoy the rest of your night."

"I will."

I opened my latest envelope and gasped when I saw the selfie on the front of the card. It was a picture he'd snapped of us while cuddling in bed. Gray was spooned up behind me and the two of us smiled sleepily at the camera.

My Prince:

Do you see that look of happiness in my eyes? It was the first time I woke up with you in my arms, right here in this hotel. I hope you look at all the pictures and see the honest, pure love I have for you in my heart. I hope you enjoyed your day, Chase. It doesn't have to be over, though.

True love waits for you in a room by the sea with a candlelit dinner for two on the balcony.

Hope you'll join me.

Yours truly,

Gray

My behavior wasn't that of a typical Heston's guest. I didn't casually stroll to the bank of elevators. I ran. I tapped my foot impatiently while I waited for a free one. The fidgeting continued until I stood outside the suite door. Our suite door. A sense of calm came over me because I knew Gray was inside.

I inserted the card into the slot and opened the door. I walked inside to find candles glowing on just about every surface. Then I saw Gray standing on the balcony, watching the sun sink into the Pacific Ocean.

"Excuse me, sir. Can you point me in the direction of my true love?"

CHAPTER
Thirty-Five

Gray

I SPUN AROUND AT THE SOUND OF HIS VOICE. I HAD BEEN SO LOST IN MY thoughts I hadn't heard him walk onto the balcony. My heart pounded wildly in my chest at having him near me again. The beautiful smile Chase wore put my nerves at ease. I was pretty sure we would work everything out, but there was a tiny annoying doubt in my brain that said I'd blown it with him.

Chase came to a stop ten feet in front of me. We stood staring into each other's eyes for several long moments before either of us moved. I took a step forward at the same time he moved toward me, and we met in the middle.

I wound my arms tightly around him and swore I'd never let him go. "I'm right here." Our lips met in a languid kiss that demonstrated just how much we missed each other. "I love you so damn much, Chase. Thank you for giving me another chance," I said when we broke our kiss to suck in some air. I rested my forehead against his and soaked in the fact that he was back in my arms again.

"Gray, I had no choice but to give us another chance. There hasn't been any laughter or light in my life since you walked out of my apartment Saturday night. Until you, I'd never had those things, and now I need them to survive."

"I've been doing the exact same thing. I used to work a seventy-hour work week to avoid reality. There was always a deadline to meet or a client to sign that came before my personal life. I made myself out to be a martyr so my brother could spend time with his wife and I could avoid going to an unhappy home. Then I met you, and I could see what Preston meant when he said there was so much more to life than work."

Chase cupped my face in his hands. "Don't let me push you away when I get scared. That's what this was, Gray. You scare the hell out of me, and I panicked. Yes, you were a tad misleading when you said you'd told Devon about us, but I can see how that happened. I just got my feelings hurt on Saturday when I thought you were ashamed of me. I didn't really consider that you didn't want Devon to know our business. I shouldn't have…"

"Shh." I covered his mouth with mine to stop him. I kissed him tenderly for several long moments. "Don't apologize for how you felt, Chase. I was in the wrong, and we both know it. We'll figure out better ways to communicate. I'll learn what triggers your insecurities and avoid hurting you, you'll hold me accountable for my stupidity, and we'll live happily ever after."

"Speaking of happy endings," Chase said in a low voice. He ran his hands up and down my chest. "I had a wicked fantasy about you while I was getting that massage."

"Oh yeah? If you tell me about your fantasy, I'll make it a reality."

Chase smiled wickedly and ran his hands beneath my T-shirt. "I fantasized that at some point you came in and replaced the masseuse. I knew you were in the room before you even touched me because our bodies are so in tune with one another. You massaged me in all the places she didn't."

"God, that sounds so hot. Why the fuck didn't I think of that?" I looked into his eyes and saw the same want and need I was feeling. "Did I roll you over onto your back and blow you or give you a hand job?"

"Mmm, neither." His luminous eyes glowed with desire for me. "You climbed on top of that table and made love to me. I kept my legs closed and you straddled the outside of my legs so it made me tighter around your cock. It drove you wild." That was a position we'd never tried before, and I refused to think about where he'd learned it. "I saw it in a porn scene," he said, reading my mind. "I was slick from the massage oil, and you slid up and down my body, driving us both out of our minds."

I grabbed his hand and pulled him into the bedroom. I picked up the phone beside the table and asked them to delay dinner an hour. Chase pulled his clothes off while I made the call and laid his gorgeous body on the bed. He lay just like he would if he were getting a massage, but he had to turn his head to the side since there wasn't a hole cut out for his face. I whipped my clothes off and looked for something I could use as massage oil.

"Check the inside zipper pocket of my suitcase," he told me. "I bet some of Gram's gifts from our first trip are still in there. I forgot I put stuff in that pocket."

Sure enough, I found a few lotions, and one of them was a flavored oil. I poured a drop on my finger and rubbed it between my thumb and first two fingers to make sure it was the right consistency. It was fucking perfect and smelled like vanilla and honeysuckle. I eagerly climbed onto the bed and straddled Chase's thighs.

I poured a generous amount of oil in a line down the center of his sexy back. I watched the muscles twitch with excitement. I started at the top of his back and worked my way down to his perfect ass. I dribbled some oil down his crack and worked him open slowly before coating my dick.

My breath got stuck in my throat when I eased inside him. It felt incredible, and I could tell by Chase's moans that he was enjoying the tightness of his ass around my cock just as much. I placed my hands on his waist and made love to him slowly for several long minutes before I lay down on top of him. I laced our fingers together above his head and proceeded to love him just like I had in his fantasy.

"Thank you for the most incredible day," Chase told me as we ate our dinner by candlelight on the balcony dressed in matching hotel robes. What was the point of getting dressed when we knew we'd end up naked again very soon? "I want you to know I won't expect you to go to such extremes every time you act like an idiot."

"Good to know," I said with a smile. "Fucking Heston was a hard sell. I thought I was going to have to give him our first-born child. Damn prick," I grumbled. Chase froze, his fork in midair with his mouth hanging open. "What?"

"You said *our first-born child*."

"I did, didn't I? Well, he's not getting him or her. What he really wants is you, and he's not getting you either. He needs to find his own soul mate and forget about mine." Chase still hadn't moved. "Are you freaked out because I mentioned our future children?"

"A little. I mean, we've only known each other a short while, and..."

"Chase, someday I'm going to ask you to move in with me. We're going to be amazing cat dads to Oliver. Someday I'm going to get down on one knee and ask you to marry me and build an amazing life with me, which will include the kids we both said we want. Someday is not today, so you can stop freaking out."

"Oliver?" Chase lowered his fork to his plate.

"He's the best part of your surprise." I jumped up and got the last envelope and handed it to him. I dropped a quick kiss on his cheek before sitting back down. "Open it." Inside was just a picture of Oliver because I hadn't had time to make a card with him on it. "I hope you love him as much as I do. I know he doesn't look perfect with the chunk missing from his ear, but he's incredible." I started to babble when Chase sat staring at the picture without saying a single word. I told him all about Oliver's traumatic beginnings and how everyone passed him by. I even banged on the table in outrage over our cat's rejections.

"That's because he was meant to be our cat," Chase said. He raised his head, and I saw happy tears brimming in his eyes. "He's absolutely perfect. Thank you so much."

"He's smart too. I set up his litter box, and he went straight to it. He strutted through my house with his tail up in the air, swishing from side to side, like he owned the place." Chase smiled broadly at my kitty talk.

Chase broke into laughter. "You're so fucking cute talking about your amazing cat, who happens to be the Einstein of felines."

"Your cat," I corrected. "I adopted him for you."

"I'm not sure I can have pets at my apartment."

"Damn, I should have asked Ava before I adopted him. I'm sorry." A thought occurred to me, and I grinned wickedly. "Actually, I'm not sorry at all because Oliver will help convince you to move in with us." He got that freaked-out look in his eyes again. "Someday."

Two months later...

"Oliver, have you seen where Daddy put his keys?" Chase asked. Oliver just sat there swishing his tail from side to side for a few seconds before he looked over at the entertainment center. Chase followed his line of sight and saw his keys sitting on top. "Fucking genius cat," he said under his breath.

It only took a month for Oliver and me to convince Chase to move in with us. I bribed him with mind-blowing orgasms, and Oliver charmed him with his keen intelligence and ornery personality. Regardless of his reasons, we were living together, and I'd never been so happy. I just had to wait until the time was right to drop to my knee and ask him that all-important question.

"Thanks, buddy," Chase said. He stopped to scratch Oliver's ears. "Daddy can't be late to Ava's wedding. I'm the Man of Honor for crying out loud." Oliver tilted his head and soaked up the attention. "Ready?" Chase asked.

"Ready to show you off," I answered and appraised him. The sight of Chase in a tuxedo pushed all my buttons, and I couldn't wait to get him back home and undress him so I could push *his* button.

We got to the church in plenty of time and went our separate ways.

Chase gave me a lingering kiss before he left to find the bridal party. I went inside the chapel and took a seat on the bride's side. I sat in the peaceful silence and dreamed about my wedding day with Chase. I pictured how he'd look standing across from me, our hands joined as the minister asked us to repeat our vows in front of family and friends. I could so clearly see the look in Chase's eyes as he committed his life to me for as long as we both shall live.

"Hi, honey," Gram said as she and Lennie sat down next to me. "Daydreaming?"

"I'm going to make him mine, Gram."

"He's already yours, Grayson." She reached over and took my hand in hers. "You are everything I wanted for him and more. You know just when to push and when to back off. All I know is how to push." She patted our joined hands with her free hand. "Thank you for being his Mr. Wright."

Gram kept hold of my hand as we watched Ava and Brandon join their lives together. Chase looked beautiful standing beside Ava at the altar. I saw him tear up several times during the ceremony. Our eyes connected at one point, and I saw the raw emotion there. Was he picturing us in front of the altar too?

"He's almost there," Gram whispered in my ear.

The reception hall was beautifully decorated in Ava's colors. I was so happy I got to join Chase at the wedding party table because I was still feeling raw from my earlier emotions. He reached beneath the table and held my hand, and the simple touch calmed me.

"Is Brandon nervous about his dance?" I whispered in Chase's ear.

"A little, but these guys have it down pat."

I was looking forward to seeing the groom's dance, but I mostly wanted to spin my guy around the floor, especially during a slow song. My arms were made to hold him, and I used any excuse to wrap him up tight.

"How long do we have to stay? You look edible in that tuxedo. I've been a really good boy for the past few hours, but we both know that won't hold much longer." We smiled at each other, both thinking about how we'd broken every one of his office rules. If my office walls could talk, they'd tell all about the jacking, sucking, and occasional fucking that had taken place after hours.

"Behave." His voice gave a warning, but his eyes encouraged me to find a quiet room with a door that locked.

The DJ called the bride and groom to the floor for their first dance. We all rose to our feet to gather around the dance floor so we could watch and take pictures of the beautiful couple. I saw Xavier standing off to the side and steered Chase over to stand beside him. Chase placed his hand on Xavier's shoulder when we approached, and he jumped in surprise.

"I didn't mean to scare you," Chase told him and wrapped an arm around him. "Is everything okay?"

Chase was asking about more than his friend being startled just then. Lately, Xavier had been acting strangely. He had seemed distracted and even distant, which worried us a lot. He never told any of us what exactly had gone down between him and his former band manager. Xavier erected a wall anytime one of us tried to talk to him about it.

"I'm fine," he said, waving off the concern. "Pay no attention to me. This is Ava's big day."

"They look beautiful, don't they?" Chase asked us. I heard the wistfulness in his voice.

"Stunning," I agreed, but I was looking at Chase and not the couple on the dance floor. Chase turned and looked at me, and I forgot anyone else existed. Soon I'd make him mine.

"Jesus," Xavier said, bumping his shoulder into mine. "I thought you guys would have gotten past this phase by now. You two are so sappy it's sickening."

We ignored him and kept smiling at each other until the DJ announced the groom had a surprise for his bride. One of the groomsmen carried a chair out onto the floor so Ava could have a seat and enjoy the show. She smiled widely as she looked at her husband, trying to figure out what he was up to. The men got into position on the dance floor and Brandon gave the DJ a thumbs up.

A minute later, "Treasure" by Bruno Mars began to play and Brandon and his groomsmen began to dance with Brandon lip syncing the words to the song. They were perfectly in sync, and it was amazing to watch. Ava loved it and even raised her arms above her head and danced along in her chair. I stood behind Chase and pulled him back so he leaned against me.

"You did good, babe," I said into his ear. "Brandon just threw down the gauntlet for the rest of us hopeful grooms, though." Chase didn't stiffen at the mention of marriage, but his heart raced under my hand. I knew he still wasn't ready. "Someday," I whispered into his ear.

Epilogue

Chase

Five months later…

"**B**ABE, WAS THAT CRUZ ON THE PHONE?" GRAY ASKED AS HE jogged down the steps. "Will he be coming home for Christmas?"

I slipped my phone inside my jeans pocket and continued to hang stockings on our fireplace mantle. We'd spent all afternoon wrestling the perfect tree into position in front of the two corner windows in the living room. I was so excited to decorate our first tree together, but the call from Xavier set me back a little. He'd gone back to California not long after Ava's wedding, and he had sounded more and more miserable every time we talked.

"Yes, that was Xavier, and he's not sure when he'll make it back home. I'm so fucking worried about him. I know, I know. He's a grown man who's capable of making his own decisions, but…" I realized Gray hadn't said anything, so I turned and looked at him. He was staring at me just like he had the first time I'd stood in this very same spot. "What?"

"You're just as beautiful as I pictured."

I cocked my head to the side and looked at him funny for a minute until I remembered the vision he'd had of me hanging stockings on his fireplace. I turned to face him straight on, rubbing my suddenly sweaty hands on my jeans. I had a question I wanted to ask him and a ring that had been burning a hole in my pocket.

He walked to me and laced his fingers with mine. "I have a question to ask you." His voice was thick with emotion.

"I have a question to ask you too." I narrowed my eyes in suspicion.

"This sounds like that afternoon under the cherry tree," Gray said and smiled broadly. "You don't suppose…"

"How do you suggest we handle this? Count to three like we did then?" I laughed at the memory.

"One… Two… Three…" We both paused. "Marry me."

The End

Want to be the first to know about my book releases and have access to extra content? You can sign up for my newsletter here:
http://eepurl.com/dlhPYj

My favorite place to hang out and chat with my readers is my Facebook group. Would you like to be a member of Aimee's Dye Hards?
We'd love to have you! Go here:
www.facebook.com/groups/AimeesDyeHards

Other Books by
AIMEE NICOLE WALKER

Curl Up and Dye Mysteries
Dyeing to be Loved
Something to Dye For
Dyed and Gone to Heaven
I Do, or Dye Trying
A Dye Hard Holiday
Ride or Dye

Road to Blissville Series
Unscripted Love
Someone to Call My Own
Nobody's Prince Charming
This Time Around
Smoke in the Mirror
Inside Out
Prescription for Love

Welcome to Blissville Collection (Both M/M Blissville series)
Volume One
Volume Two

The Lady is Mine Series
The Lady is a Thief
The Lady Stole My Heart

Queen City Rogue Series
Broken Halos
Wicked Games
Beautiful Trauma

Zero Hour Series
Ground Zero
Devil's Hour
Zero Divergence

Sinister in Savannah Series
Ride the Lightning
Mr. Perfect
Pretty Poison

Savannah Standalone Books
Invisible Strings

Standalone Novels
Second Wind

Coauthored with Nicholas Bella

Undisputed
Circle of Darkness (Genesis Circle, Book 1)
Circle of Trust (Genesis Circle, Book 2)

Acknowledgments

First, I need to thank my husband and children for their constant support and encouragement. It's not easy living with a writer who often disappears into a fictional world for long periods of time. They do so many things to help me so that I can realize my dream. I love you guys more than words can ever express.

I have to give a huge shoutout to Susie Selva for tackling this project with so much gusto and passion. If not for her tough love and cheerleading, Chase and Gray probably would've stayed in the vault. Thank you so much, Susie! New to my editing team is Lori Parks, who is an outstanding proofreader.

I've been so fortunate to work with Stacey Blake of Champagne Book Designs since virtually the dawn of my career. In fact, Chasing Mr. Wright was the first book she formatted for me, so it only seemed right that I tapped her to work on the covers for the second editions. Stacey is a brilliant artist, and I'm always so thrilled to show off her pretties.

And I'm sending so much love to the fans who've waited for the Fated Hearts gang to return.

xoxoxo

About
AIMEE NICOLE WALKER

Ever since she was a little girl, Aimee Nicole Walker entertained herself with stories that popped into her head. Now she gets paid to tell those stories to other people. She wears many titles—wife, mom, and animal lover are just a few of them. Her absolute favorite title is champion of the happily ever after. Love inspires everything she does, music keeps her sane, and coffee is the magic elixir that fuels her day.

She'd love to hear from you.

Want to connect? All her links are in one nifty location. Click here:
linktr.ee/AimeeNicoleWalker